MW01128365

KILTS AT THE
RENAISSANCE FAIRE

DRUIDS BIDDING 2

JANE STAIN

WWW.JANESTAIN.COM

Kilts at the Renaissance Faire
Druids Bidding 2

In Kindle form as Renfaire Druids

Also in three volumes:
Renaissance Faire
Renaissance Festival
Renaissance Man

Originally serialized in 18 episodes

I'm writing more sweet highlander time travel romances.
Sign up for new book alerts at
www.janestain.com

ALSO BY JANE STAIN

Druid Magic (Tavish, Seumas, and Tomas)

Celtic Druids (Time of the Celts-Picts-Druids)

Druid Dagger (Leif, Taran, Luag)

Meehall

Ciaran

Baltair

As Cherise Kelley:

Dog Aliens (a cuddly dog story with a happy ending)

High School Substitute Teacher's Guide

1. KILTS

E mily loved the Renaissance Faire. Where else could she see a Shakespearean play performed authentically, with men playing the female parts? Minstrels strolling about with mandolins, asking a kiss for a song?

Where else could she see men in kilts?

And with her freckled skin, she felt like she fit in here, more so than at any other hangout she'd been to. She ran from booth to booth, getting a juggling lesson here, trying to walk a tightrope there—

"Emily, look at these dresses."

Her tiny brown best friend Evangeline was in graduate school too, majoring in elementary education, while she herself was preparing to lead a high school drama department.

Emily joined Vange in a booth made of dyed burlap walls. "They're beautiful, Vange."

A faire employee wearing one of these outfits came up to them. "They are not dresses, milady, but bodices and chemises with two skirts to wear with them, one over the other and tucked up out of the dirt. This is the clothing of our peasant women, milady."

Emily looked around uncertainly for a fitting room. "Could we try a few on?"

The costumed lady nodded enthusiastically. "Certies. Do come stand over here in the corner. I shall hold up this blanket, and the two of you can change behind it."

The faire person said this rather loudly, and a small crowd gathered outside the booth. In particular, Emily noticed this one muscular guy with a dog tattooed on his arm.

Still, the outfits were lovely, and Emily loved the idea of wearing one the rest of the day so that she fit in at the faire. It reminded her of her own drama student days, back in high school.

She looked at Vange.

Her friend winked.

So they turned their backs to the blanket and put the outfits on. They heard several cat calls from their audience, but they could see in a small mirror in the corner that the blanket stayed put the whole time.

The two of them admired each other in the outfits, which didn't show any leg at all, but a whole lot more cleavage than either of them was used to. The faire person had insisted that they lace their bodices up tightly.

Vange gave her a huge grin. "OK, we'll take these."

After they paid, Emily and Vange stowed their T-shirts under their voluminous skirts in the waistbands of their shorts, and the blanket went down.

With smug smiles on their faces at how authentic they now looked compared to the rest of the fairgoers, the two of them turned around to face their audience.

Only, instead of sunburned tourists in shorts, Emily and Evangeline faced a whole clump of whooping Scots highlanders in kilts.

ॐ

EMILY STARED AT THE HIGHLANDERS. In addition to their thick woolen great kilts, they all wore two-handed longswords and heavy boots of cowhide. They had on homespun linen shirts similar to the chemise she now wore, but their sleeves were wide at the wrist and their shirts laced up on their chests. Most of them had long hair and beards.

They all wore big smiles.

Her eye kept drifting to one Scot in particular who stood next to their leader. He stood out, but she couldn't put her finger on how. He was gorgeous, of course, but they all were.

Their leader shouted out with a big grin, "Wull ye dance with us, lasses?"

Sensing herself blush, Emily felt rooted to the cloth floor of the booth. She glanced over and saw that her normally outgoing friend Vange wasn't doing any better.

And then the man her eye was drawn to spoke, and she knew why he stood out. The leader was trying, but this one had a perfect Scots accent. He must be from there.

"Och, Ian. Let us show the lasses we ken how tae hae a good time, eh lad?"

Ian raised his eyebrows and then grinned. "Well enough, Dall."

Emily sighed with relief and was giddy when Dall spoke again.

"Faire lasses, we pray ye please accompany us at oor clan dance, which does begin soon."

Another quick glance at Vange revealed that her friend very much wanted to dance with these sexy bare-legged men. Emily did, too. She grabbed Vange by the elbow and steered her to Ian, while Emily placed herself next to Dall.

The authentic Scotsman held out his elbow for Emily's hand, the way men did in old movies when they walked with women.

For some reason, this made Emily shy. What in the world

was wrong with her? It was just his arm. But her stomach fluttered when she stepped closer and took it.

The band of Scots lined up two by two and paraded through the dirt streets of the fake English village that had been constructed for the Renaissance faire, out in a fallow field.

Dall held his arm out for her the whole way, and she was glad, as she often had to steady herself. He paused when there were holes in the road so that she took notice and watched her footing.

He made small talk, so that she didn't feel awkward walking with him. "Dae ye see the giant there, lass?"

Emily followed his gaze over the heads of the people in the street until she saw the giant. It was about 15 feet tall, held up by four English peasants who walked under it and followed by a few dozen more. They were singing, but too far away for Emily to hear.

She turned back to Dall. "Oh yeah. Why are they parading a giant puppet around?"

He wrinkled his brow as if everyone knew. "'Tis the Green Man."

She gave him a questioning look.

"Och, dinna ye ken the Green Man, then?"

She shook her head no.

"He does bring the springtime—in the minds o' the farmers."

"Oh. OK, that makes sense, I guess."

But even with his small talk, Emily felt nervous the whole time, as if this encounter were significant, somehow.

As they walked, more and more Scots joined the parade, until there were more than a hundred, about equal parts men, women, and children.

Whenever someone joined them nearby, Dall introduced

her. "This is Emily," he'd say, and then he would tell her their names.

All of which she promptly forgot, she was so distracted by the faire. OK, and by this gorgeous man at her side. Heck, the faire itself was distracting, wonderfully so. Everywhere she looked, something was going on.

Brightly costumed dancers held ribbons attached to the top of a huge pole in the ground. As they danced around it, their ribbons formed a braided pattern that coated the pole.

People dressed in black with skeletons painted on them danced around with hourglasses.

There were even knights in armor riding horses in the distance.

Her ears caught a new tune every dozen feet they walked: mandolins, wooden flutes, deep resonant drums, a bunch of sea dogs singing about Bengal Bay...

A good many of the people she saw were dressed in costumes. Some of these were authentically historical—peasants, mongers, nobles, foreigners—but many people wore fanciful costumes—wizards, elves, fairy princesses, Amazon women warriors in furs and little else...

The parade of Scots paused when they came to one of several large outdoor theaters set up all over the faire. It had a large wooden stage that she thought could fit a whole orchestra. Straw bales had been lined up in rows for seating, and hundreds of fairgoers already sat there, eating turkey legs and drinking beer out of large paper cups printed to look like metal tankards.

But Dall didn't make any motion to help Emily sit down on one of the straw bales.

And the Scots were parading right up onto the stage. The musicians were in the front, and now they played as they marched up the steps, bagpipes and drums mostly. The bagpipes were loud.

Before Emily could get used to just how loud the bagpipes were, the whole parade was moving again. Up the stairs to the stage.

Dall was smiling and waving at the fairgoers on their straw bales, and they were waving back.

The next time he glanced her way, she spoke to him. "Where shall I sit to watch your clan dance?"

The way he looked at her then left nothing to the imagination, though he did nothing rude. It was more ... yearning. Inviting. Questioning? "Och, nay, lass. Ye will na be sitting. I intend tae hae ye as my partner."

Why couldn't she look him in the eye? "Your ... partner?" And why did her voice have to squeak?

In that moment, she realized something. Dall was infinitely more confident in himself than the college guys she was used to, more confident even than her professors, and that was saying something.

He gave her a warm smile. "My partner for the dancing, lass."

"Oh."

He helped her up the steps onto the stage, and the two of them followed the procession until they were facing the audience and clapping with the rest of the clan while three young women held their skirts up out in front of them and jumped up and down to the beat of the bagpipes and drums.

In her element on stage, Emily clapped and smiled at the audience while she talked to Dall out of the side of her mouth. "I don't know how to dance like that." She gestured at the three women. "I've seen River Dance a dozen times, but that doesn't mean I know how. And I'm still wearing sneakers."

But he pulled her forward into a dance set of four couples. "Dinna fash. We will na be dancing in that style. 'Twill be easy, if ye follow my lead."

They all bowed to each other, and then the music started, and along with it a dance much like the square dancing Emily had done in fourth grade—only to bagpipes instead of banjos.

Once she relaxed, she enjoyed it.

No one called the moves, but Dall was right. All she had to do was pay attention and let him guide her. There was no skipping involved, thank goodness, and her underskirt was long enough that it hid her sneakers. Most of the time.

When Evangeline and Ian appeared opposite herself and Dall in their next dance set, Emily realized she had forgotten all about her friend.

She smiled at Vange in apology.

Vange gave her a knowing look in reply.

Emily rolled her eyes at that.

But whenever the two friends locked elbows for a turn, Vange whispered something different in Emily's ear:

"Go for it."

"He's delicious."

"If you don't want him, then scoot over."

The first two comments just made Emily laugh at her friend, but the third one made her seriously consider. She looked over at Dall, who was swinging by Ian's elbow.

He smiled at her the way a cat smiles when it is warm and fed and content at home in winter, in front of a roaring fireplace.

She couldn't help smiling back at him the same way.

"I thought so." Vange was laughing now.

WHEN THE SCOTTISH dance show was over and the audience was applauding thunderously, the highland woman nearest to Emily grabbed her hand and pulled her forward into the line of female performers, who all curtseyed. What happened next explained why she had done this. The women backed up and dropped hands to let the men through.

The kilted men all went out to the front of the stage, formed a line, put their arms around each other—and did a can-can dance to the drums.

Ba boom, kick

Ba boom, kick

Ba boom, kick

Ba boom, kick

Emily knew the can-can wasn't a 'period' dance for this faire, but the audience loved it. Too bad she was behind the guys and couldn't see better, but because there were only amused faces in the audience, Emily figured the performers were not authentically (un)dressed under their kilts.

She looked over to see Vange's reaction.

Her friend was whistling at all the hot guys through her forefinger and her thumb.

Their eyes met, and they gave each other huge silly grins.

This was the most fun they had ever had at renfair, and this was their third summer break here together. There were ten more weekends of this faire, and Emily had a feeling she wanted to come back this year. Maybe all ten weekends.

That feeling grew more intense.

Dall was once again at her side, holding his arm out to help her go down the steps off the stage. He made no move to let go of her once they were down, either.

Ian came over with Vange on his arm, and two more couples followed. One of the women had a container that reminded Emily of a bota bag, and she used it to fill metal tankards for them all to drink from.

Emily took a huge gulp when she got hers.

The woman who handed her the tankard dropped her fake Scots accent and whispered to Emily, "It's just water."

The next woman chimed in, "Yeah, we don't really drink

alcohol during the day out here at faire. It's liable to give you heat stroke, especially with all this heavy wool clothing we have to wear."

Emily could see the sense in that, but she was a little disillusioned. All the faire people seemed to be happily drunk all the time. Still, she downed her water and asked for more.

The woman refilled her tankard twice before she stopped thirsting, and then she handed Emily and Vange what looked like cloth bags. "Here, put these muffin caps on, to keep the sun off your heads."

Looking around, Emily now noticed that all the faire people had hats on, and most of them wore muffin caps like these. The color went OK with her dress, so she put it on and helped Vange put hers on. Unlike the faire woman, though, Emily let her hair hang out from under the muffin cap, figuring she would look better that way.

Vange did the same, winking.

Putting his arm firmly around Vange's shoulders, Ian addressed Vange, Emily, and Dall, and incidentally the other two couples. "We're going to see Short Shakespeare. Come with us."

Emily had turned to ask Dall if he wanted to go when she saw him bowing to her with his hand out for hers. It was over-the-top dramatic, but also sweet.

Feeling her face spread into a silly grin, she made a big show of swooning with her forearm on her forehead before she took his hand, thankful again that her drama training got her through her usual shyness when it came to action, if not speaking.

She put her hand in his offered one, and they fell in walking behind Ian and Vange.

Holding hands seemed much more intimate with Dall than it ever had before.

He readjusted their hands every so often so that their palms rubbed against each other.

This sent chills up her arm, even in the late May heat.

Once again, Emily was vaguely aware of the faire atmosphere as the eight of them walked: mongers yelling "Hot cross buns." while throwing buns across the street to each other, women trying to wash their clothes on the rocks of a little stream but being heckled by ... pilgrims, people throwing rotten tomatoes at and saying funny curses at a Spaniard.

But as before, the faire was just background for the thrills going through her at the way Dall was holding her hand and how he hadn't wanted to part since they met. She was even more thrilled by the attention Dall paid her.

Had the two of them really just met an hour before?

As if they were old friends, he met her eye and shared everything with her. They laughed together when a peasant woman dragged her drunken husband through the faire by his nose—theatrically, of course. Emily could see she was really dragging him by the arm which held her hand on his nose.

Dall continued to make small talk, too. "Ye did wull in choosing yer clothes, ye and the other lass."

"Thank you. It's nice of you to say so."

"'Tis true, lass. Ye chose the authentic booth, and that means nae ye can gae where'er I gae."

They smiled at each other intensely for a giddy moment.

But then he added something in a hurry. "Where'er I gae at the faire, ye ken."

Slightly puzzled by that addition but overly conscious that this gorgeous man was trying hard to put her at ease while she was letting him take all the burden of carrying the conversation, she scolded herself. she needed to wake up and show her personality, or he was going to get bored.

But all she could think of to say was something really

nerdy. "Is Short Shakespeare one of those acting companies that do 'Romeo and Juliet' in twenty minutes, and then in fast forward, and then backwards?"

Oddly, Dall looked to Ian to answer her question. It was opening day, but she would have sworn this wasn't his first faire.

Ian got so excited that he forgot to use his Scottish accent and threw both his arms up in the air. "Yeah, and they're really good."

Making one of her goofy faces, Vange teased Ian about dropping his accent. She mimicked him, throwing her own arms up. "Oh, really?"

Everyone laughed.

Ian threw his arm back around Vange, and they all continued walking through the imitation English village, being solicited both by fake mongers and by people trying to get them to shop at all the booths that lined the street.

"Delicious and un-nutritious. Try the Queen's buns."

"We bet you five pounds you cannot climb this rope ladder."

"Chocolate. Iced. Cream."

One costumed group was more serious. There were a few dozen of them, all in raw homespun linen robes with garlands of flowers on top of their heads like hats, both men and women. Their area was a clump of standing stones visible off in the distance. They were all chanting, holding hands, and moving around the stones in a circle.

Emily wondered if the stones were real or just Styrofoam. It was hard to tell, this far away.

"Who are they?"

Dall answered without asking anyone, "Those are druids."

Emily watched the druids circle around the stones until one of the building facades blocked her view. Just before it did, she noticed the guy with the dog tattoo watching her from the archery range, and then the facade blocked him, too.

§🐚

EMILY, Vange, and the Scots arrived at another outdoor theater with a few minutes to spare before Short Shakespeare took the stage. The theater was half full, with about a hundred fairgoers already seated.

Ian found four straw bales together and waved them all over.

Emily had never liked sitting on scratchy straw, but she discovered that with two long skirts on, it wasn't a problem.

Moving differently than they all did—with controlled grace, Emily supposed she would say—Dall sat down next to her. He was close enough that she could feel the heat of him, but not quite touching her. The closest they came to touching was at their thighs, and this made hers burn for his to touch it, even through two skirts.

"Oof." Vange shouted, wriggling around. "It's not easy to sit down in a tightly laced bodice."

Everyone laughed.

From the straw bale in front of them, a few fairgoers in shorts turned around and looked at Vange curiously.

Emily felt sorry for them. Imagining the straw bothered their bare skin something awful, she reached up under her skirts into the waistband of her shorts and pulled out her long Outlander T-shirt.

"Here," she said to them, "you can sit on this."

The woman smiled at her gratefully and put the shirt under her and her friend.

Meanwhile, one of the Scots women leaned over to Vange and said without an accent and just loudly enough that Emily could hear too, "You should try driving in a corset."

"Oh, I know," said one of the other Scots women, "I don't lace it up till I get here."

Emily's curiosity got the better of her, making her speak up, which she generally left to Vange.

"I thought all you faire people lived here while the faire was on?"

The Scots woman closest to Emily answered in that same soft voice that only their group could hear.

"Some of us stay here all week. Dall does..."

For some strange reason, they all looked at him then, and he smiled at them all in turn.

The woman went on.

"...but most of us only stay over Friday and Saturday night, because we have jobs that won't let us take off six weeks for faire, not to mention four weeks before that for rehearsals."

"But isn't faire a job for you?"

What the woman was saying contradicted how Emily had always thought the faire worked. She was eager to find out everything she had been wondering about, now that she had insiders to ask.

All the faire people laughed except Dall.

The first woman answered Emily. "No. Legally, the faire is a college of performing arts. We don't pay to 'take classes' here, but no, most of us don't get paid. Only those with advanced skill get paid, like the bagpipers and those who teach us about how life was in the 1500s."

Again, all of their eyes went to Dall.

It was weird. He was obviously one of the professors at this 'college of performing arts'. Why didn't they just say so?

The Short Shakespeare show interrupted her thoughts.

It was the best production of *Romeo and Juliet* Emily had ever seen, including the video of the one with her own performance as the nurse, in high school. Truth be told, watching that video whenever her parents trotted it out for guests these days embarrassed her now, it was so bad. She had taken her role way too seriously and forgotten to have fun with it, so it wasn't fun to watch.

Conditioned by her training to watch plays with a critical eye in order to see what she might use when she ran her own drama department, Emily analyzed this production—even as she laughed her head off and enjoyed it.

Even as she yearned for Dall's touch and was conscious of his every move on the straw bale next to her, she looked for just what the people on stage were doing to make this rendition of the play about the 'star-crossed lovers' so good.

Aha.

One.

These actors didn't take Shakespeare seriously, not at all.

They didn't see him as some godlike figure whose precious work had survived four hundred years and must be revered.

No, they concentrated on fun, injecting plenty of action and silliness.

Two.

They had cut all but the most necessary lines, making the play move much faster.

This made sense, because society was much faster now, with movies from even a decade ago seeming to move at too slow a pace.

What lines remained, they delivered in a cartoonlike way.

It was hilarious.

All the female parts were played by men, of course, as the people of the 1500s simply would not allow a woman to make a fool of herself on stage.

And all of the actors hammed it up and made a joke out of the whole thing.

Especially the guy playing Juliet. He made Emily see the play in a whole new light.

Far from being the touching love story everyone in

modern times made of it, this was making fun of Romeo. It made fun of him for switching so quickly from being in love with Rosalyn to being after Juliet.

Romeo is being too stupid to live. I never noticed that before.

While she stood with the whole audience and clapped through three quick standing ovations, Emily wondered which way the audiences of Shakespeare's time took Romeo and Juliet: as a serious tragedy the way she'd thought of it in high school, or as a comical farce the way these actors saw it now.

Common sense told her that some saw it one way and some the other.

And then the butterflies started up again in her stomach, when she noticed Dall smiling that unusual smile and once again offering her his arm.

She took it, and smiled back at him.

He escorted her away behind Ian and Vange, with the other two Scots couples behind them.

Only this time, they went over the stage and through the curtains.

§❦

"WHERE ARE WE GOING?" Emily asked Dall as they passed through a burlap curtain back into the sunshine.

"As ye might hae gathered from what Siobhan telt ye, we dinna get much pay. Sae we dinna buy the food they sell in the booths, the turkey legs and such. Ev'n sae, I thought ye might like tae take the midday meal with us."

Released from the man's charm when he stopped speaking, Emily looked around, blinking. There was a whole different faire back here behind the burlap curtain.

She realized now that the fake English village was shaped like a donut, and that they had walked into the hidden center.

Entirely surrounded by burlap curtains and thus invisible from the faire proper, the backstage area was a four-acre camp with no order to the layout.

The place was a maze of tents, trailers, vans, and half a dozen RVs. There were even mobile toilets and showers.

Vange rushed up. "Yes. Of course we want to eat lunch with you, right Em?"

When she looked over at him in a daze, Emily shared another smile with Dall. "Right."

"Verra wull," he said to Vange, and then he turned to Ian. "We wull meet ye at the picnic benches."

Ian nodded and wandered off, but Emily grinned when she heard him whisper to Dall, "Picnic *tables*." Dall was doing well with his English, but he clearly spoke it as a second language. And Scottish was clearly his first language. That, he spoke beautifully.

And then Dall's smiling eyes were on Emily again. "Take my hand, lass. I would na want tae lose ye on the way."

Sharing a goofy smile with Vange, she did as he suggested.

He led them through the maze to a white canvas cabin tent.

Emily thought she just might be able to find it again, and she wondered if he wanted her to. He was difficult to read, so nice and friendly on the one hand and so unassuming on the other. It was confusing. Most guys would have asked for her number by now. Hoping he'd take a hint, she got her phone out.

"So this is your tent?" Vange asked him.

"I hae the use o' it, aye."

He had the flaps open now, and they went in. Gesturing for them to sit on some of the inflatable chairs, he moved to the cooler, poured soda into tankards from a 2-liter bottle, and got out three oranges and three plastic containers with sandwiches in them.

Wondering who had made the sandwiches, Emily did her best not to look at the pair of sleeping bags zipped together in the corner, where Dall must spend his nights. She looked for his jeans and sneakers, thinking his choice of brand might tell her more about him, but she didn't see any. She didn't see much of a personal nature in the tent at all.

And no electronics whatsoever.

Was he some sort of renfaire purist? Or worse, was he one of those losers who still lived with his parents and didn't have a job? Disgusting.

Soon, the three of them had made their way to the picnic tables and all eight of them were settled with inexpensive food, either homemade or bought at the supermarket the night before.

Everyone but Dall was checking their cell phones for messages and returning texts.

Siobhan passed a huge bag of potato chips around. All the guys dug into them greedily and were throwing them into each other's mouths. The women each took a few, looking at each other worriedly about the extra calories.

Dozens of other faire people were back here for lunch, too, including a bunch of preteens who all came in together and appeared to be waiting for a grown-up to bring them food.

One girl said, "I do hope Mistress Maple brings us sustenance soon."

Another cut her off, saying, "The beer's in the pickup." He said it with a Southern accent, which to Emily's ear was about as far from Elizabethan English as could be.

The girl said, "Huh?"

A third kid turned to her and explained.

"He's telling you to just talk normal. That's a saying we use to remind each other that we don't need our faire accents backstage."

It was midday, but some of the faire people were just waking up.

One of these was part of the Scots clan. Emily could tell because he arrived at the picnic tables with a plaid that matched theirs, bunched up in his arms. His shirt was so long that she couldn't tell if he was bare under it or not, and she didn't want to know.

One of the highlanders at their table noticed her looking.

"Hey Emily, know what Scotsmen wear under their kilts?"

Blushing, Emily shook her head no, feigning ignorance.

The guy had a huge grin on his face when he delivered his punchline:

"McNuggets."

He laughed at his own joke.

Several of the other guys slapped his hand.

Emily rolled her eyes and looked back at the Scot who had just woken up. After he put his food down, she watched, mesmerized, while the man donned his great kilt.

First, he spread out a large tarp on the ground nearby.

Next, he spread out his plaid on the tarp. When he saw her watching, he joked, "Here it is, the whole nine yards."

Emily then saw that the 16th century great kilt was indeed just nine yards of thick wool plaid, with nary a stitch sewn into it.

Siobhan noticed her watching, too, and came over to comment.

"The stitched thinner dress kilts of modern times are a product of Queen Victoria's reign, three hundred years later than we portray here."

Once the nine yards of woolen plaid were spread out on the tarp, the Scot lay down on one end and rolled to the other end, pleating at his waist as he went, and then grabbed it and stood up, belting the pleats to keep the great kilt on him.

Siobhan tapped Emily's arm. "We call that 'rolling a burri-to,'" she said with a smile.

"Hah. Really?"

"Yep. You should see it earlier in the morning when they're all rolling up like that. It's quite fun."

"Ha. I would LOVE to see that."

"Me too," said Vange, giving Siobhan a nudge.

Siobhan smiled and nodded.

All three women grinned at each other.

Vange turned to Dall. "So you're from Scotland, huh." It wasn't a question.

"Aye, lass. That I am." Dall took a bite of his sandwich.

Emily knew Vange wouldn't just leave it at that, and sure enough, Vange went on. "What brings you here to America?"

Emily was curious about this as well, so she looked at Dall with interest.

He had a pained look on his face, and he appeared to have stopped breathing.

Emily hoped he wasn't choking. Sure, she had seen a video about the Heimlich maneuver in the first-aid class they made her take, but that didn't mean she knew how. Searching on her phone for her textbook with that video, she started to stand up behind Dall.

"Are you OK?" she asked him.

Dall held out a hand. "Stay yer hand, lass. All is wull with me."

Whew. He couldn't be choking if he was talking, right? She was pretty sure of that.

But he still had that pained look on his face, and everyone else was pointedly talking about other things and not noticing.

Just to be on the safe side, Emily pulled up her textbook and re-watched that video on the Heimlich maneuver.

Her mind was trying to figure Dall out, now that his

charm was temporarily unengaged. Of course Dall still spoke with a Scots accent backstage, being from Scotland and all. But while the others had dropped the 16th century speech patterns back here, he hadn't. No one told Dall the beer was in the pickup. They let him stay in character backstage. He moved differently than they all did—as if he were expecting to be attacked every second. He was one of their professors, yet until they came on stage, he hadn't known who Short Shakespeare were. And he was broke to the point he had to offer them sandwiches someone else had made for him. Last but not least, he didn't appear to have a phone. Who under 50 these days didn't have a phone?

It couldn't all be explained by his being a professor at this college of performing arts. Something so unlikely occurred to her that at first she dismissed it. Emily had read all eight huge tomes of Diana Gabaldon's *Outlander* series, but that was just a story. People didn't really time travel. Right?

§

DALL WAS GUZZLING the rest of his soda.

Siobhan turned to Emily. "The guys have a sword demonstration next. Want to come watch?"

"Of course," she said eagerly.

Consistent with his old-fashioned speech patterns and manners, Dall again held out his arm for her.

Emily couldn't help herself. She had meant to ask him why he was the only one not dropping the act backstage, why he didn't have a phone, how come he didn't have a job that paid real money, did he ever plan to, and so much else.

But Dall was being so sweet and charming, and his eyes smiled at her with such interest, that she just didn't care right now. Later would be soon enough to ask him what was up.

Her common sense told her that if she was this smitten with Dall now, she would only care less later.

She ignored it.

The butterflies started up in her stomach again the moment she touched him, and despite his disarming small talk, they didn't let up until he deposited her in a large gazebo next to a small arena where a dozen costumed men were swinging swords around.

The audience sat on grandstands around the perimeter of the arena.

Emily and Vange and Siobhan all had chairs next to each other in the gazebo, and twenty other costumed women were inside with them, most dressed as English nobility.

The two-handed longswords that the clan called claymores were huge. Emily didn't think she could hold one up for long, let alone swing it around. She was interested in things like that because of her drama teaching aspirations.

To test her theory, Emily stood and beckoned to Dall.

When he left the rest of the highlanders out in the arena and came over to her, smiling, all the Scots made hooting noises.

Emily understood. The clan were teasing Dall for being so attentive to her. She blushed.

"'Tis sorry I am for their commentary, lass. They mean no harm. I can tell them to stop, if you like."

"Will they listen to you?"

"There is a wee chance they will."

"Only a wee chance, eh?"

"It is not so bad, aye?"

"I suppose it isn't."

They stood there smiling at each other for a moment.

"Well enough. Was there something you wanted to see me about then, lass?"

"Oh, I almost forgot I wanted to try to lift your sword, if I could?"

"Very well. I had best prepare to catch it, though. They have given it quite a shine, and the dirt would spoil that."

He stepped up quite close to her and held the sword out in front of him as if he were serving it on a tray.

"Use both hands, lass, and heft your best."

She did.

She put both of her hands on the handle and heaved with all her might.

She was in decent shape. She took PE in college even though she didn't have to. But sports had not prepared her for this.

His sword was longer than her legs, so its five pounds felt like much more when she held it up. She managed to raise it up and hold it there for a few seconds, but then she was grateful to be lowering it back into his grasp.

Behind him, one of the men called out, "Dall. Art thou in this demonstration or not?"

He looked at her with a twinkle in his eye. "Shall I go, lass, or were you not done with me?"

Emily laughed. "Go, go." She made shooing gestures with her hands.

Laughing and pretending to dodge her hands, he ran back to the men.

When Emily got back to her chair, Vange held up her hand. Emily slapped it. The two of them nudged each other, and then Siobhan was nudging Emily's other side.

Dall owned the sword demonstration.

If the other contenders had been cats, then he would have been a lion. He led the others through their moves, but all eyes were on him.

Afterward, a young man in an English noble costume approached Dall at a swagger.

"Uh oh," Emily said to herself.

Siobhan and Vange squeezed her hands, but all of their eyes were glued on the scene unfolding before them.

Dall greeted the young English noble, "Hello, lad."

"Lad? Thou wilt respect thy betters, man."

Without taking her eyes off Dall, Emily asked Siobhan, "Is this part of the show?"

Siobhan kept her eyes on Dall as she answered, "This is the improvised portion of the show."

Having hefted Dall's sword, Emily knew it was real, not just a prop. It could hurt. She said to Siobhan, "I hope the ground rules include not hurting each other."

Meanwhile, out in the arena, Dall stood calmly.

The lad continued to swagger toward him.

Dall's right hand held his two-handed sword as one might hold a shovel parallel to the ground. "Respect is earnit, lad, nay demandit."

The youth was anything but calm. He shook as he stormed up to within ten feet of Dall with his sword up between them. "I do demand thy respect. Thou wilt bow to me as is my due as a noble, and thy superior."

Dall hadn't moved. "Nay Englishman is the superior o' any Scot. I will na bow, lad."

"Errrgghh." The youth ran at Dall, holding up his one-handed sword like he was about to serve in tennis.

In one fluid movement, Dall swung his claymore like a baseball bat into the one-handed sword. He battered it out of the youth's hand by brute force.

The audience cheered.

The next thing Emily knew, the youth was on the ground amid a cloud of dust, and Dall was picking up the smaller sword.

"What happened?" Emily asked no one in particular.

Siobhan said, "Dall knocked that kid's sword right out of his hand, and the kid fell over trying to hold onto it."

Some other English nobles helped the kid get up and leave, shaking slightly.

The audience applauded.

Two other Scots fought next. Their duel was much longer than Dall's short run-in with the young English noble.

Emily could tell the two of them had practiced stage fighting together. She had learned some of the same techniques. Their claymores never quite touched the other person, but they reacted as if they had. She knew Dall would prevail in a real fight, but this one was more entertaining, with them twirling and their kilts flying up. Emily grinned to see the neon yellow swimming shorts they all wore underneath. No wonder the audience had laughed when the highlanders did the can-can.

And that reminded her she was going to ask Dall about his ever-present 16th century speech patterns and his second-nature swordsmanship.

Either he had traveled forward in time, or he was a re-enactment enthusiast who had made this his life.

The latter was worrisome, but the former was hopelessly attractive.

HOWEVER, Emily was interested in Dall more than in his puzzling situation. So interested.

As if it could curtail her wanton attraction to the man, her common sense brought up the fact she had only known him five hours.

Telling it she was at the faire, time for fun, she jumped up, grabbing Vange as she rose and pulling her out of the gazebo to greet the kilted men. Watching them approach made her mouth water.

Pumped up from their swordplay, Ian, Dall, and the rest of the highlanders all but strutted over. Most of them smiled at the audience. Some even waved.

One was smiling at Emily.

Filled with sudden inspiration, Emily picked two of the wildflowers growing nearby and gave one to Vange. When her friend looked at her funny, Emily held the flower out in front of her.

Dall strode up just then, smiling that smile she imagined was just for her. "Hae ye a favor for me, lass?"

"Yes, and if you'll hold still, I'll put it on you."

He walked up as close as he had been when he held the sword out for her to play with. She could see his chest rising and falling with the heavy breaths he was taking from his exertion, running about supervising the other men's sword bouts.

Trembling slightly, but also thrilling every time they touched, Emily wove the stem of the flower through Dall's shirt lacings, very aware of his breath mingling with hers while he stood there. She had been this close to a few men before, but she hadn't ever felt so intimately connected that she was aware of their mere breathing.

Five hours, her common sense reminded her.

Shut up, she told it. Out loud, she said, "There, now you're mine ... for the day. I've marked you." She forced herself to smile and look away from her handiwork with the flower, up into his eyes.

Thank God, they were twinkling. "I was already that, lass. Wull ye be mine as wull, for the day?"

Emily melted inside, even after he paused as she had and added 'for the day'. What should she say, 'I thought you'd never ask'? No, that was too cliché. Maybe just 'Yes'? Was that interesting enough? She must have stood there enjoying that for too long like the shy fool she often was around guys, though.

"Answer him." Vange nudged Emily and walked away.

Dall took both her hands, then leaned back and swung her from side to side with a hypnotic motion, gazing in to her eyes. "'Tis ainly fair, Emily. If I'm tae be yers, then ye should be mine ... for the day."

"I was already that," Emily said, lost in his eyes and lulled by the gentle swinging of his hands.

His smile took over his face, and he swung her all the way around.

"Ahem." That was Ian.

"Uh ..." That was Siobhan.

Dall stopped gently, let go of her hands, and nodded to them before he turned back to Emily and asked, "The clan does hae a break in the schedule now, lass. What shall we dae?"

That was a loaded question, but with the way Ian and Siobhan were standing with crossed arms, she came up with something harmless. "Could you teach me a little of how to swordfight? I don't think I can handle a claymore, but a shortsword maybe, or even just a dagger might do. I feel a little defenseless in this environment."

"Ooh, me too." That was Vange.

Emily thoroughly enjoyed the next hour.

Dall coaxed Ian into giving them each a historically authentic-looking dudgeon dagger. They might as well have been short swords, they were so big. "Ye lasses ought tae keep yer daggers hidden till ye hae need for them." As Dall said this, he pantomimed it for them, complete with lifting his imaginary skirts so he could unsheathe his imaginary dagger.

Looking over at Vange, Emily could tell her friend found this every bit as funny as she did. She did her best to keep a straight face. "Could you show us again? I'm not sure I get how you did that."

Dall obliged, but right at the end, he lunged forward and skewered her with his imaginary dagger.

Most of the audience had left when the men stopped the sword show, but a few dozen had stayed to watch the women get fighting lessons. They laughed louder at Dall's pantomime than the women did.

Dall then showed the ladies how to parry sword attacks with their daggers, explaining that besides sneak attacks, the wielder of a dagger killed by stepping within an attacker's reach and counter attacking under the arm, which was generally unprotected, even when an attacker wore leather armor.

He and Ian demonstrated a bunch of these different scenarios, and then Dall let Emily and Vange try acting them out in slow motion on him.

Unlike during the sword show, now the audience participated, calling out humorous suggestions, all in favor of the women.

"Kill him."

"Cut his arm off."

"Don't let him get away with that."

Stage fighting had been a required part of Emily's high-school drama major. However, because all the sword fights in the historical plays they had put on were between men, she had never previously had the opportunity to perform stage fighting in front of an audience.

Now she knew she loved stage fighting.

Really loved it.

Melodramatically feeding off the audience's silly suggestions, Emily hammed up all the fake stabbing:

Creeping up on Ian from behind, stepping into his reach, and stabbing him under the arm.

Pulling out her dagger to stab him when he crept up on her.

Even more fun was parrying Dall's sword attacks. For the show aspect of this training exercise, Dall came at her just slowly enough that she could move into position to block him every time.

But stage fighting is fundamentally different from self-defense.

After that hour performing in front of the audience, Ian left on an errand and Dall took Emily and Vange backstage for some more practical instruction with their daggers. The moves were all the same, but this time he told them not to move slowly. Of course, he had them stabbing straw bales instead of people, commenting as they did so.

"That is the way o' it."

"Yer thrust must be strong and sure the first time, lass."

"Yer advantage is the element o' surprise, aye? 'Tis na likely ye wull get a second chance."

Emily had stabbed the straw bale a hundred times before she realized she was tired and her arm would be sore the next day.

Vange met her eyes, and the two of them slumped to the ground.

Vange said, "Thank you Dall, for the daggers and the lessons. Can we do something easier now? We're tired."

"Easy, eh?" Dall smiled at them. "Verra wull. Hear them singing at the stage on the other side o' this burlap wall?"

Emily and Vange listened.

"Yeah."

"Uh huh."

Dall explained, "If ye can be quiet, then we can sneak..." He paused as if to think of a word.

"We're not going to ruin their singing show with stage fighting, Dall," said Emily.

Dall laughed. "Ha ha ha. I roused yer temper, eh?"

"Oh. Was that a Scottish he-man warrior joke?" Emily smiled a small hopeful smile at him.

"Aye, lass, it was."

Emily put her hand over Dall's.

He turned his hand over so they were holding hands.

Emily could feel herself glowing with happiness, but in the back of her mind, she worried. Would this warm and wonderful connection she felt with him only be for the day? Would she ever see him again? He still hadn't asked for a way to contact her.

Dall had finished laughing at her seriousness surrounding his joke. "I was gaun'ae say, lass, we could sneak intae the audience and sit on the ground in front, sae as not tae disturb the singing. 'Twould set us up with good seats for the last performance o' Short Shakespeare today. I think ye lasses like those lads, aye?"

They did.

Even more than watching the performers on stage, Emily liked sitting on the ground next to Dall with his arm around her. They were both wearing so much fabric around the lower halves of their bodies that she didn't even notice how hard the ground was. Well, probably his arm around her had something to do with that, too.

When the singing show was over, some of the faire goers got up and left, poor souls, not realizing that a much better show was soon to start there.

Dall, Emily, and Vange moved a little so they could lean back on the first row of straw bales. Now they were quite comfortable. Even better, Ian, Siobhan, and a bunch more of the clan joined them. There wasn't much room on the ground, but the bales behind them were still good for sitting.

Ian sat next to Vange.

Emily passed her phone to Siobhan, whispered, "Gimmie

your number," and watched, fascinated, as Siobhan got her
own phone out of a small pouch that dangled from her belt.

What a perfect spot for a phone while wearing these voluminous skirts. Emily hadn't even noticed the pouch dangling
there. Smiling, she put her own number into Siobhan's phone.

Relieved that she had a way to get in touch with Dall,
Emily relaxed and enjoyed Short Shakespeare's show. And his
arm around her.

❧

AFTER THE NOW-EXPECTED three ovations for Short Shakespeare, Dall once again held out his arm for Emily.

"We hae clan meeting now, and 'tis mandatory that we
attend. Ye lasses may find it a wee bit o' a bore, but I would
be honored tae hae ye by my side for it."

"I pledged myself to you for the day, and I meant it,"
Emily said, hoping he saw the twinkle she was trying to put in
her eye.

Dall put his own twinkle on.

"Well enough then, off we gae, lass."

Emily walked as slowly as she could, reveling in the feel of
her hand on his arm. The appreciative looks other women
gave him as they passed by didn't hurt, either.

Dall was right about the clan meeting. To most people, it
would be boring, because nothing much happened. But Emily
—who loved historical re-enactment because of the sense of a
different time period, not just for the sword fights— loved it.

The clan meeting took place in a roped-off area surrounded
by walkways where the audience was constantly passing by. It
was decorated to resemble the inside of a 16th century castle,
with heavy wooden furnishings and rugs covering the ground.

Emily and Dall and their friends sat in the center, where

they could be seen but not heard while the meeting went on around the perimeter, with the people who were speaking close to the audience.

She and Vange were the only ones dressed English. They stuck out a bit, but everyone seemed to want them there, so it was OK.

The center was less fancy than the perimeter, so they sat on benches around a table—remarkably similar to their lunchtime setting, except now they drank water out of pewter goblets.

Dall sat so close once again that Emily could feel the heat radiating off him, but not quite touching. Except when he leaned close and his lips brushed her ear when he whispered to her. Which was often.

"Guthrie kens a bit tae much aboot the crime at hand, aye?"

"Mark the way he does grin while he tells it."

"Camden be not grinning, though. Mayhap we should hae the story from his side."

Emily loved how clever he was. She thought he should be the clan chief and arbitrate these silly disputes. He'd be good at that.

She also loved the soft tone of his voice and the feel of his breath in her ear.

Even more, he was being so irreverent that each of his utterances gave her an excuse to jab his side with her elbow or tap his impressive bicep with the back of her hand—to touch him, which gave her a little thrill each time.

Her thrills didn't go unnoticed.

Each time she elbowed or tapped Dall, Vange tapped Emily's leg lightly with her toe from across the table and gave her a big know-it-all grin.

All in all, Emily found it difficult to keep up with what

was supposed to be going on at the clan meeting, but Dall's whispers actually helped.

"All this keening ower a dead cow?"

"Hoo. They should hae settled the matter with swords. 'Twould na hae taken nearly sae lang."

"Padruig has the right o' it. Cattle should na be allowed tae wander off."

Emily had learned and promptly forgotten twenty more Gaelic names before she asked Siobhan about them.

"Are you all of Scottish descent, then? Because you have the right names."

Siobhan smiled. "No, these are just our faire names. My real name is Hailey."

"Oh." Covertly under the table, Emily added (Hailey) to Siobhan's contact in her phone, and then she turned to her favorite whisperer.

"Is Dall your given name?"

"Aye, lass, but then I truly hail from Scotland, sae..."

"So do you know Gaelic, Dall?"

"Aye, o' course, lass. I am the clan's Gaelic teacher."

Emily felt sure she would get Dall to admit something about coming here from the past now, because Gaelic was all but dead. The English had seen to that.

"Well—"

But Siobhan interrupted.

"What Dall means is he is a professor here at the college of performing arts—for the Scots, no less—so of course he has studied Gaelic. That's one of the many reasons they hired him, right Dall?"

"Aye." He looked down, which killed the conversation.

Emily couldn't let it go, though. The day would be over in a few more hours, and Dall hadn't spoken of seeing her again.

It seemed Siobhan wouldn't be as much help as Emily had

assumed. Why had she interrupted? Would she even answer if Emily called or texted?

Emily's curiosity demanded to know as much as it could uncover about the mysterious and alluring man.

Her heart agreed.

Her common sense told her to relax and just enjoy the few hours she had left with Dall.

Shut up, she told it.

"What else have you studied, besides Gaelic?"

Dall took a moment to think this time before he answered. "English, French, Norwegian, Swedish, and a little Dutch."

Emily felt her jaw dropping. Only the nobility could read and write back then, let alone study other languages. A thousand more questions formed in her mind, but before she could ask even one, a smattering of applause broke out in the streets.

Everyone around her stood.

Dall extended his arm to her, and with quite a clamor, all two hundred of them quickly exited the roped-off clan meeting area.

EMILY WAS DYING to ask Dall to stay in touch, and at the same time she didn't dare for fear of shortening what little time she had with him. Clinging to his arm as if it were a life preserver and she couldn't swim, Emily tried her best not to cry as the entire clan paraded down the street. The sun was getting low in the sky, and the air was going chill. None of the stages had anything going on anymore.

No one tried to get her to buy their wares. Most of the fairgoers were crowded around the ale stands now, or busy shopping for souvenirs at the now crowded booths. The streets were empty of play and singing and laughter.

Emily figured that those actors who earlier had been in the streets pretending to sell hot cross buns and playing small tricks on the tourists were likely all backstage now, winding down from their day together.

She wanted to ask Dall to take her back there, as a way to sort of sneak in and be part of that, a faire insider. And she would have if she weren't certain that Siobhan would tell Dall no, grab him, and pull him away from her forever.

Very soon, Emily would be in Vange's car, speeding away from the faire until next year. So she clung to Dall's arm, miserable in her head even while her heart soared at being near him.

Emily's mood soon brightened, though.

Out in the street with Vange, Ian, and Siobhan nearby, Dall took both of Emily's hands and twinkled his eyes at her.

"Emily, I had great pleasure in oor day togither. I dinna want it tae end. Would ye and yer best lass like tae come back for the run o' the faire?"

Finally.

She had the urge to hug the man, but...

She willed him to make a way to come see her, once he knew her plight.

"Oh Dall, we would love to, but we spent all our extra money for the whole month getting into the faire today and buying these costumes."

Unexpectedly this made him smile. "'Tis good that ye did, lass."

"Huh?" Too late, Emily remembered not to scrunch her forehead up. Her mother always said that would give her wrinkles.

Dall calmed her a bit by squeezing her hands. "Yer

costumes—and meeting us—mean ye can come back for free, as faire people on the gate list."

"Really?" This was everything Emily had dared to hope for. Not only would she keep seeing Dall, but she and Vange would be faire insiders. They would find out if all the rumors of wild night shows and late night parties were true. And she would have more chances to find out where Dall really came from. But she had to admit, the best part was she could keep seeing Dall...

Afraid to get her hopes up and have them dashed away, Emily looked at Ian and Siobhan's faces to see if they thought this was possible.

They seemed to agree that it was.

They were nodding and smiling at her and Vange.

"Aye, lass," Dall said with his hands warm and real in hers. "Yer costumes are English, sae ye canna be part o' the clan, but Ian has found ye other places, if ye want?" His face was hopeful and showed such ... longing for her.

Emily looked at Vange for her reaction.

But her friend was already nodding. "What will we be doing?"

Dall looked to Emily for her answer.

She nodded an emphatic yes.

"Let us hae Ian show ye," Dall said, raising the burlap wall to create a gateway to the backstage area.

2. HIGHLANDER

I an took them to a booth that sold handmade boots. Some of them were ordinary brown, but most were multicolored pictures made of leather: Celtic patterns, birds, animals, trees, flowers...

A sign said "Custom orders welcome."

Emily looked at the prices.

Yikes.

The least expensive pair—plain brown leather shoes— were $200. The fancy decorated boots that went up to the knee were $1,000.

Vange slowly turned in the middle of the booth, taking it all in.

"Wow, someone is a master cobbler."

"Five generations of someones, actually," said a smiling grey-haired man.

"These are the two lovely ladies I told you about, Simon," said Ian.

"Well met, lovely ladies."

Vange Laughed.

"This is Emily, and I'm Evangeline. We both love your booth. Ian says you can get us on some sort of gate list where we can get into the renaissance faire for free. What type of help do you want in exchange?"

Simon gazed at their new English peasant costumes and then looked pointedly at Vange's sneakers, and then over at Emily's.

"Ian is a good friend," he said. "I'll gate-list you both just as a favor to him. But I offer you each your choice of a pair of boots—and gas money—if you'll hawk for me just two hours a day for the run of the faire, which is the next ten weekends."

"What's 'hawk for me' mean?" Emily said.

"Deal." Vange shouted at the same time, without even finding out what that meant.

Sometimes Emily worried that her friend's second-graders were going to walk all over her, once the two of them were done with graduate school.

Simon pointed to a man and woman out in the faire street.

The woman was proudly displaying her colorful leather boots for passersby, and the man was calling attention to her. Both of them were directing people into the booth.

"That looks like something I could do," Emily said, studying the woman's sales technique and remembering a play where she'd been a shoe salesperson. She had spent every weekend for a month at Macy's, observing the shoe sales-people there and learning their mannerisms and techniques.

"Can you spare the ladies for the rest of today Ian, so I can get their gate-listing squared away and show them the ropes—and so they can pick out which boots they want?"

"I suppose so," Ian said, looking at Dall.

Dall turned to Emily, and they shared a smile.

Taking in the magnificent sight of her kilted admirer, Emily kind of forgot where she was for a minute.

Dall said, "Is that agreeable tae ye, lass?"

Oh, right, working at the boot booth.

Looking around, Emily noticed that Ian wore boots from this booth. She vaguely thought Siobhan and all the other Scots at the faire might, too.

But Dall didn't.

Trying her hardest not to get lost again in the vision of manliness in front of her, Emily took a good look at Dall's boots.

They were plain brown leather, of course, but they looked warmer and sturdier than Ian's. Unlike any others she saw here, Dall's boots were stained by rain and snow. The souls were thicker than on the boots at the booth, and the buttons were made of some type of shell rather than metal. And they had subtle dagger sheaths built into them, which he wasn't using at the time, but which Emily could see might be very useful indeed when concealed by her two long skirts.

She smiled at Dall to let him know he would have his answer soon.

He smiled back.

She was pretty sure his smile said that he realized she was going to negotiate—and that he was impressed. But that could have been her imagination.

Emily was forcing herself to negotiate. It was a skill she would need when she ran her own high school drama department. Well, she had other reasons, too. For one, she was broke.

"Simon?"

"Yes, Emily?"

"I want my boots made the same way as Dall's."

Simon came over and studied Dall's boots.

"Would you mind taking one off, Dall?"

Dall was looking at her with realization in his eyes. He wasn't panicking, though, and that was a good sign. Maybe he would take her into his confidence and she could confirm what she thought was going on here: that he had time traveled from the Scotland of the 1500s. She tried to put reassurance in her own eyes as she gazed back at him. That seemed to work. He gave her his comfortable smile again before turning to answer Simon.

"I dinna mind," he said, unbuttoning his boot and handing it to the cobbler with a friendly smile before he turned back to Emily and included her in his smile.

Simon took Dall's boot over to his workbench and made various measurements. Emily noticed he was taking notes with a pad and pencil that he kept hidden behind the workbench because they weren't 'period' for this faire—'not period' was drama slang for an anachronism.

When he brought Dall back his boot, Simon held it reverently. He also held a colorful pair of shoes under his arm.

"I won't be able to have your custom boots ready tomorrow, Emily, but I will by Friday. They won't be typical of my work, though, so I'd like for you to wear these shoes when you hawk for me." He handed Dall back his boot and handed the shoes to Emily.

Ian put his hand on Dall's shoulder, and Dall turned to him, still buttoning his boot.

"We have ring-out today."

Dall turned to Simon to say something.

Simon had his hand up.

"Leave the ladies with me. I'll get them passes in time."

Dall stretched out his sword hand to Simon, but instead of shaking hands, he grasped Simon's forearm and waited for the cobbler to do the same before they shook.

Emily had a brief moment of panic, as if Dall were leaving to his own time right now and she would never see him again. What was this about getting passes, and in time for what?

But before he left, Dall turned to Emily. "Will ye take the evening meal with me, lass?"

"Yes." She tried to make her smile one of joy and not one of relief.

Dall took her hands and squeezed them again, then gently swung her back and forth as the two of them stared into each other's eyes.

Emily tried to use her stare to communicate just how much she enjoyed Dall's company. She thought his stare was saying the same about her.

Ian spoke in a sotto voice meant only for their group and not for the audience walking by in the street.

"I hope you'll stay for dinner too, Evangeline."

"You betcha," Vange told him with a rascally wink.

"OK," Ian said to both women, "we have to go help close the faire. Go with Simon and get your passes, and we'll meet you back here in about an hour. Dinner will be more sandwiches from Dall's cooler, just so you know."

Emily squeezed Dall's hands again before she let them go.

&.

SIMON'S PICK of shoes fit Emily perfectly and matched her costume. They were cute, too, with pointy curled toes like elf shoes, and the soft leather was more comfortable than sneakers.

Simon told her, "Wear them while you work here and then keep them, with my compliments. And like I said, I'll have your boots ready for you on Friday."

Emily started to say, "Two pair is too much—"

But Simon cut her off.

"No, a deal's a deal. I offered you boots of your choice, and I must say, you made a wise choice. I just need to shop for the shell buttons, or I could make your boots tonight. It's nothing to worry about."

He looked inside a small pouch. He must have had a time piece hidden in there, because he got antsy.

"Except we really do need to get over to the gate and put you on the list before they close. Evangeline, you can pick your boots out when we get back, OK?"

Vange nodded yes.

"Emily, you can stow your sneakers inside this bench seat." He opened it and waited while she stowed them. "Tom, you've got the booth."

"I've got the booth, Simon," said a younger man who looked like Simon.

The three of them all but ran to the front gate. It was where Emily and Vange had entered the faire seven and a half hours before. Good thing it wasn't far. The area near the front gate was crowded with merchants selling souvenirs out of handcarts and customers clamoring to buy them.

The inside of the gate booth was almost like the driver licensing office, including the line. Two dozen people were already there, trying to get passes at the last minute. When the three of them came in, the faire administrator called out:

"OK Chuck. Block the door. These three are the last ones for today."

"Whew," Simon said, giving Emily a nervous smile.

She smiled back, trying her best to give the impression she understood why he felt so relieved.

The faire administrator took the women's pictures and looked at their IDs, Simon signed something, and then Emily and Evangeline both had gate passes for the duration of the faire. This, Emily understood: she was coming back all ten weekends of faire for free.

"Let's get back to the booth where we have good seats, ladies. You won't want to miss the Scots' ring-out, trust me."

Simon introduced Emily and Evangeline to everyone at his booth, most of whom were part of his family. They had brought out lawn chairs from backstage and were all seated facing the street, leaving empty chairs for the three of them. Emily became aware of the bagpipes while Simon was reminding them they could stow things inside the wooden bench seat, where she had already stowed her sneakers.

"Let's take our seats, ladies. The show is almost here."

Shrugging at each other, Emily and Vange sat down.

Just in time, too, because around the corner came all the highlanders, marching in kilts. Oh my, they were a wonderful sight. But it got better. Every twenty feet, the three dozen kilted men would stop, turn to face the audience on the sides of the street, and do their non-period but oh-so-wonderful can-can dance again. The drummers made sure it was lively.

And this time, Vange and Emily were in front of the guys and able to see the show:

Kilts.

Hairy legs.

Big smiles.

Neon yellow swim shorts.

Both women had their phones out in seconds and were taking video.

Before the guys passed them by, Vange pushed Emily up, saying in her ear over the bagpipes, "Go hug him, Em, and I'll get a picture."

Vange got up too, so she could run and get a better angle.

Emily had to time it just right, between can-can dances. When she saw her chance, she ran to Dall, grabbed him, and turned him so she could hug him while Vange got a good picture.

Only, Dall must have misinterpreted her intention. It really seemed like the idea of posing for pictures was foreign to him.

When she grabbed Dall and turned him, Emily expected him to look for the camera, pose for it, and smile. That was what any normal guy would do. It was almost a ritual, here in the 21st century.

Instead, Dall pulled Emily close and kissed her.

During their first kiss, she figured out that the French must have taught the other Europeans how to kiss long before the 1500s. It was a long wet kiss. In the back of her mind, she knew Vange was laughing her head off and taking a dozen pictures of this kiss. On Instagram.

Emily didn't care.

Not even a tiny bit.

Too soon, Dall was being pulled away from Emily by the other highlanders so that they could do their next dance twenty feet down the street.

"I'll be back for you soon, lass." he called out as they dragged him away, smiling.

"I'll be here." she yelled back as she waved at him, smiling.

When the bagpipes were far enough away that you could hear singing—which took a while—the Scots women paraded by, arms around each other and singing a song that Emily realized was meant to let all the customers know it was time to go home:

> *You've drunk your ale.*
> *You've drunk your wine.*
> *Your noses are quite rose-I-ed.*
> *Way, all the way, go all the way home.*
> *It's getting late.*
> *Head for the gate.*
> *The faire it now be close-I-ed.*
> *Way, all the way, go all the way home.*

Last but not least came a line of security guards carrying radios and wearing red sashes. And checking everyone for gate passes. Those who didn't have them were herded toward the front gate. Finally understanding what the big rush to get their passes had been about, Emily and Evangeline proudly showed them with big grins and were allowed to stay.

While they waited for Ian and Dall to come escort them to Dall's tent for dinner, Evangeline picked out her boots.

It didn't surprise Emily at all when her best friend picked the most colorful non-period pair they had—purple leather with red and green and yellow jewel patterns on them. They'd be hidden by her skirts most of the time, and they suited Vange.

ૐ

EMILY GOT anxious again while she waited for Dall and Ian to come back for her and Vange. The sun was setting. The fear had crept into her mind again, fear that Dall would be sent back to his own time and disappear out of her life before she ever saw him again.

As if the fear weren't enough to deal with, her common sense reminded her she had only known this man for eight hours—that he was a stranger and she should guard her heart.

Simon and his family were nice. They gave Emily and Vange gas money ahead of time, showed them around the booth, and told them some tidbits they could share with the customers they directed to it. After Simon arranged their hawking schedule with them, he even invited them to have dinner with him and his family.

"Thank you so much," Emily told him, "but can we do that some other time? Because we're having dinner with Dall and Ian tonight."

"Sure."

"Looking forward to it."

Emily's mind eased a bit when Simon and his family had gone under the burlap wall behind their booth to eat and she sat with Vange in their lawn chairs, giggling over the pictures Vange had taken of her and Dall kissing.

Emily was a bit worried about her parents seeing the pics Vange had posted on her Facebook wall, but maybe that was a good thing. It would tell them the story for her and save her the trouble.

"Ooh hoo hoo. Girl, you were going for it."

"Can you blame me?"

"Nope."

Still huddled over Vange's phone, the two of them high fived.

"Well, glad to see you've become one of us ... both of you."

Emily looked up to see the biker with the dog tattoo smiling at her, surrounded by his gang. They were sexy in their own way, all leather and muscles, so of course Vange made them feel welcome.

"Hi, I'm Vange, and this is Emily."

Stuffing her phone back in her shorts pocket under her long skirts, Vange stood up and pulled Emily up.

Tattoo guy spoke for the group.

"They call me Dog, and this is my crew. We run the archery range."

Vange put on the charm.

"Dog, eh? You look kind of like The Rock."

Dog flexed his bicep with the dog tattoo on it.

"Heh, I get that all the time..."

Now that she had an eye for such things, Emily could see that Dog and his crew's costumes, like hers and Vange's, were period enough for working in a booth, but they weren't good enough for belonging to a stage cast—such as the Scots, the peasants, the nobles, or the mongers.

Nope, Dog and his 'crew' looked like what they were: a motorcycle gang dressed up as 16th century archers. They looked friendly, though.

Dall's voice came from behind her. "Are ye lasses ready tae come sup with us?"

Emily jumped up, but what she saw made her pause a moment.

Ian had a restraining hand on Dall's shoulder and was looking at the bikers.

But Dall's posture was relaxed, his smile amused, his hands far from his claymore.

Emily gave Dog and his crew a brief smile. "It was nice meeting you. I'm sure we'll see you around."

"I'm sure you will," Dog said, smiling back at her a little longer than she was comfortable with. It wasn't a leer, though, just a friendly smile, so she didn't say anything.

Emily made her way over to the arm Dall held out for her and took it happily, reveling in the now-familiar butterflies his touch gave her. But Dog had made her too self-conscious to lose herself in Dall's eyes, which was what she wanted to do. She told herself they would be in a more private setting soon enough, and that she would get her chance.

To her surprise, Dall and Ian took her and Vange under the burlap behind the booth, instead of down the street. Oh yeah. The faire was shaped like a big donut, and the hidden center 'backstage' area was right here. She felt silly for being surprised, but it turned out she wasn't the only one.

Vange laughed. "Ha. I forgot backstage was right here, heh."

Ian was nice about it. "Yeah, while the faire is open, we only come back here through the stages. It keeps up the illusion of the English village, because people are used to seeing actors go behind stages. But after hours we go right through the fake buildings."

Emily started to feel disappointed about the break in the illusion of the fake English village, but then she was distracted. Everyone was rushing straight through the backstage area to crowd onto the straw bales in front of one of the larger stages, which were visible now from the center of the donut, thanks to the burlap being lifted pretty much constantly. She saw why. Going through the backstage area would be much faster than walking all the way around the donut shape of the faire street.

"What's going on over there?"

"That's our dinner show," Ian explained. "Opening Saturday only, everyone does night versions of their day plays. Short Shakespeare is doing their night-show right there. I'm so excited for it. Come on. We'd better grab our food and get over there before we have to stand while we watch it."

The night-show was even funnier than the day version. Romeo and Juliet referenced movies and TV shows, texted each other, played jump rope, and pretty much threw the period out the window—along with any residual reverence for The Bard that the Short Shakespeare acting troupe might have harbored.

Thanks to his being good friends with pretty much everyone, Ian had managed to find the four of them seats on the crowded straw bales up front. Emily liked this for two reasons —and being up close to the action of the play was a distant second reason.

She and Dall were crowded so close to each other, their thighs actually were touching this time, albeit through two long peasant skirts and the thick wool pleats of a great kilt. As always, he was a perfect gentleman, but just that contact alone had all her nerve endings humming. Even better, though, the crowd was so distracted by the performance on the stage that no one noticed the two of them getting lost in each other's eyes whenever they turned to each other in reaction to something funny, which was often.

"Aren't you guys going to eat your sandwiches?" Ian said.

"I get yours if you don't start eating it in the next ten seconds," Vange chimed in.

Well, almost no one noticed, but Emily didn't care. She was having the time of her life. Just by being with her, Dall made her feel amazing: light and a little dizzy, and happy. In the back of her mind, she knew that was just chemistry, but mostly she just enjoyed it.

Emily hadn't noticed Siobhan there before, but when the night-show was over, Ian and Dall's cast-mate approached them, or rather, Hailey did. She had changed into jeans and a T-shirt and wasn't wearing her hat, which Emily figured explained why she hadn't realized the woman was there before. Now that she saw her in street clothes, she figured Siobhan / Hailey was about 30, which was seven years older than her and Vange.

Siobhan was saying, "Emily, Vange, congratulations on getting passes. You know, you don't have to drive all the way home tonight just to drive back again in the morning so you can hawk for Simon. Stay here, with me. I have plenty of room in my trailer. In fact, let's go there now so you can hang up your peasant clothes to air out so they won't itch tomorrow. I have hoodies you can borrow too, because it gets a little chilly out here at night. Dall and Ian can come get you in a little bit. You won't miss any of the night-shows."

Siobhan's offer was too good to pass up gracefully. Emily wanted to stay right here with Dall all night under the stars, lost in each other's eyes until they succumbed to sleep, but she wasn't bold enough to say so.

❧

"THIS ISN'T A TRAILER, it's a mobile home," Vange said when Siobhan took them to it.

Yeah, it is. Wow.

"Heh. Hardly," said Siobhan. "I only have the one bedroom. You and Emily will have to sleep on the couches."

Once the two of them were inside, but before Siobhan came in, Vange elbowed Emily. "OK Em, I know you would rather be in Dall's tent, but you have to admit it's nice not having to go outside to get to the bathroom."

Unable to deny anything her friend had said, Emily just shrugged and nodded.

"You'll stay with me for the run of the faire: at least Saturday nights, and Friday nights, too, if you want to avoid getting up early to drive out here Saturday mornings," Siobhan said as if she were Mary Poppins and the two of them were little kids—complete with little hugs for both of them, one in each arm.

Emily wrinkled her brow at Vange behind Siobhan's back, trying to say, "Who does she think she is, bossing us around?"

Vange gave her that knowing look again.

Emily shrugged again, but she felt like something odd was going on.

Why is Siobhan so intent on us staying with her? We're practically strangers.

Twenty minutes later, their costumes were hung up, they were back in shorts and T-shirts under some of Siobhan's hoodies, the couches were made up for them to sleep on, and they had both called their parents to explain they wouldn't be home that night.

There was a knock on the trailer door.

Siobhan called out, "Come on in, guys."

Ian had changed into jeans and sneakers, but Emily wasn't surprised to see Dall still wearing his great kilt and boots. He did have a matching cloak with him now, though.

Dall was eyeing her bare legs and smiling.

Emily was shy when it came to speaking her mind, but

acting was her specialty, after all. She struck a few leg-model poses for Dall, up on tip-toes with one leg bent.

He turned beet red.

This was fun.

She posed some more.

"Hae a care, lass, or I canna promise tae keep control o' myself," he said with a kind smile.

She had only known him 12 hours now, but Emily's gut told her this highlander was the real deal, a true gentleman. His sexy accent didn't hurt. She kept saying things to him just to get him to talk so she could hear it.

"I can tell that you have good control of yourself. It's one of the things I admire about you."

What? How had she allowed herself to say *that*?

"Och, nae I must needs tell ye what I admire, lass." He took both of her hands. "Ye think tae play a part. Howsoever, you are the most genuine lass I hae e'er met. I ken what ye are thinking by the look in yer eyes. Indeed, yer eyes tell me more than anyone else's words e'er said."

Emily's eyes teared up, his speech was so moving.

He dried them with his thumbs and looked at her with such admiration, she had to draw several deep breaths before she had enough of that control she so admired in him.

Siobhan helped. "You kids better get going if you want to catch the rest of the night-shows. They're tonight only." She kind of shoved them out of her trailer, and Emily was grateful.

Ian and Vange stayed with her and Dall the whole evening, but Emily only had eyes for Dall. It seemed he only had eyes for her, too. She didn't get hung up on what she had done to deserve him or why he picked her out of all the much finer-looking women at the faire. She tried to stay 100% in the moment and to relish each and every second. She figured she would have plenty of time to second guess herself about it later, when she was alone in her room at her parents' house. He was here with her right now, and she was going to be all here with him.

She walked from night-show to night-show on Dall's arm.

Each time they arrived at their straw bale, he spread out his cloak for her to sit on so her legs wouldn't get scratched up. He was still wearing his cloak, for the warmth.

So this meant she sat next to him with their thighs pressed together.

Every time they laughed, they looked at each other and laughed together.

It was the best Saturday night ever.

VANGE AND EMILY figured Siobhan had saved them ten dollars per weekend in gas money. The next morning, they tried to give that to her as a hostess gift, but she refused it.

"I tell you what, though," Siobhan said, "I *will* take that money toward serving you hot breakfasts here in the trailer instead of you always eating cold sandwiches from Dall's cooler."

They were about to refuse.

She added, "And Dall and Ian are welcome to eat breakfast with us here, of course. Let's start now." When the two of them smiled, she whipped out her phone. To Emily's disappointment, she called Ian. Of course Dall really didn't have a phone, though, just like he didn't have jeans or sneakers, his own tent—or any money.

Hoping and praying Dall was just a time traveler and not a deadbeat, Emily checked the charge on her own phone. Almost dead.

Siobhan saw her checking it. "I was just getting to how you can keep your phones charged up the second day of each weekend. Here's a solar charger for each of you. I filled them from a wall outlet at home Friday, so they should be ready to go, but put them in the sun whenever you can. Your phone draws on them faster than the sun fills them up, so always keep the charger as full of sunlight as you can, and only plug your phone in when it's charging."

Emily took the shiny plastic thing and stared. It was the same size as her phone and looked multicolored when she wiggled it under the dining room light. She'd had no idea such a thing existed. This would give her access to all the files she stored on her phone no matter where in the world—or where in time—she went. She would always be able to access the complete works of Shakespeare. And her first-aid textbook. And... She looked up, meaning to give a vigorous thank you, but Siobhan was halfway into the bathroom.

"Get dressed, ladies," their hostess called out.

After they donned their costumes, Vange and Emily helped Siobhan prepare Denver omelets, Coffee, hash browns, and freshly squeezed orange juice. When the guys arrived, they all sat down together. While she was helping dish up plates, Dall took the seat closest to Emily and sat there smiling at her. She sat down next to him. The guys ate three times as much as the women and made satisfied grunting noises.

They all helped Siobhan clean up, and she made it clear they were to come here every faire morning for breakfast, then helped the guys walk Vange and Emily to Simon's booth. It was now a given that Emily held Dall's arm while they walked.

It was new when Dall lifted Emily's hand to his lips and kissed it.

She wasn't sure, but she thought she actually swooned at that.

Still holding her hand, he was saying, "We'll come for you

in two hours, when it be time for the clan dance. I've made you my partner now, lass, and I do not wish to do the dances with you not by my side."

She was thinking yeah, and after that I'm going to get you alone awhile so I can ask you a few questions.

Out loud, Emily just said, "I'll be looking forward to it."

She and Vange were stowing their sneakers, T-shirts, and phones in the covered bench and hiding the solar chargers in the sun when they heard a parade coming. Sadly, there were no bagpipes this time.

Emily looked up. This time, it was the English peasants parading. Now she could hear them singing:

> *Awake, awake,*
> *The day doth break.*
> *Good craftsmen, open your stalls.*
> *Alight, alight,*
> *Shake off the night.*
> *The faire is open to all.*

As the peasants approached, Emily got a good look at their costumes. She saw several things about theirs that she wouldn't be able to change about hers: leather bodices looked really cool, it was best to use drastically different fabric for each piece, and of course, the older and more weather-beaten it was, the more period a peasant costume looked.

But she did notice a few things she planned to implement. They all wore old leather belts which passed through and thus held pouches of various shapes and sizes—almost like Batman's belt. Their belts also held objects that dangled from leather cords: wooden spoons and bowls, sheathed eating knives, small musical instruments, and profession markers such as spindles and wooden washboards. Also, all the women hid their hair, either inside muffin caps or inside

snoods under their hats. Emily made note of this, just
in case.

"Those who don't have five years to allow their clothing to
become weather-beaten soak it in an infusion of black tea for
that period look."

Emily jumped and let out a little squeal. "Eek."

The voice had been right in her ear, and she hadn't seen
the speaker coming. She saw now that it belonged to a sun-
darkened older man wearing one of the druids' homespun
linen robes, with a flower garland on his head like a hat.

"Sorry dear, I didn't mean to startle you, just to avoid
embarrassing you by allowing anyone to overhear my advice.
I'm Aiden." He held out his hand.

Haltingly, she took it. "I'm Emily, and your advice wasn't
embarrassing. Thank you for it. I think it will help." She
looked back at the peasants, who were now parading by,
singing and beating drums and playing wooden flutes.

Right in her ear, Aiden hissed, "I'm certain the black tea
will help, but here's my advice: you won't get much time alone
with him. We cannot allow it. But learn as much about him
and his home life as you can."

When Emily turned to confront him about his advice, the
man was gone.

&

EMILY WAS ALL AFLUTTER AS usual with her hand on Dall's
arm as they paraded to the stage where the Scots danced.
Knowing what to expect didn't diminish that at all. She
smiled at the plan she had for finding out about Dall.

Just like the day before, they paraded up onto the stage,
smiling at their audience of hundreds and clapping to the
bagpipe music while three women did that skipping dance.
Once more, Dall took her hand and pulled her into set dance

after set dance that reminded her of square dancing in fourth grade PE class.

But instead of whispering with Vange whenever the two of them turned, Emily whispered a question to Dall whenever the dance brought the two of them together.

It was the perfect opportunity.

No one can overhear anything over bagpipes.

Dall smiled and treated it as the game it was—and the next time the dance brought them together, he answered each question.

"So who do you live with, over there in Scotland?"

"I live with my clan, o' course."

The set circled.

"Who all is in your clan?"

Dall's eyebrows scrunched up.

Their corners turned them.

"Who shares your hearth?"

"Och, lass. Dae ye ask if I am marrit?"

Their opposites stepped up to greet them.

"Yes."

"Ye wrong me. I would na carry on with ye, if my wife yet lived."

They turned by palms with their corners.

"I'm so sorry to bring up your loss. Forgive me."

"Nay, there be nowt tae forgive. 'Tis glad I am, that ye asked."

They admired each other while their corners turned them by elbows.
Clap clap.

"Well, then you'll forgive me for asking how she died?"

"Aye, she died giving birth tae oor second son, two years ago."

Their opposites turned them by palms.

"Who's watching your sons while you're away?"

"The clan cares for them, o' course, and for their sister. Does na a clan care for all children?"

He finished escorting her around. They all bowed, and he led her to the next dance set.

"No. In my t ... in America, most couples live alone with their children. They visit their relatives, but only the lucky ones have relatives who babysit."

"Aw, 'tis sad I am tae hear that."

They bowed to their new set.

"What's the name of your clan?"

"MacGregor."

Smiling at each other, they arched their arms for all to go under. They didn't get a moment to whisper during this set, which consisted entirely of arching and going under. The next dance set was better.

"So you have three children. How old are you?"

"I hae twenty and five years, lass. How is it ye hae twenty and three years and are na yet marrit?"

Their corners turned them.

"How do you know I'm twenty three?" At the look he gave her, she added, "Here in ... America, only half of us get married anymore, and if we do, we wait until we're 30."

"Och, sae auld? How dae ye manage tae hae children?"

Their opposites did a dance step she didn't know, and Emily had to concentrate for a moment, mirroring her opposite's moves.

"Women take fertility pills if they have trouble having children."

"This ... country is sae verra different tae mine."

The only time Dall and Emily had any privacy to talk was while they were on stage being displayed. After the Scot clan's stage dance, they went to see Short Shakespeare, and after that, backstage for lunch, and then to the sword demonstration, and then Dall and Ian gave Emily and Vange dagger lessons. Another Short Shakespeare show, and then the women hawked a second hour for Simon.

Ian and Dall hung out nearby, watching the women display Simon's work on their feet and direct the passersby into Simon's booth.

Emily was distracted by Dall the whole time, but at least every time she looked at him, he was smiling at her.

Vange was her usual exuberant self. When they heard the ring-out parade coming, she ran over to Ian. "Bye, Simon. See you next week."

"Bye, ladies. Thanks very much for your help. I'll have your custom boots ready Friday night, Emily?"

Emily looked at Vange since they shared the car and it was a two-hour drive.

Vange gave her a thumbs up and a big grin.

Emily turned to her first ever employer.

"Yep, I'll be here Friday for them, Simon."

How I wish I could just stay here all week.

But Emily's parents expected her home each Sunday night for a late dinner, and for dinner every weeknight during her university's four-month summer break.

And Emily didn't want yet another argument about how they were paying for college, so the least she could do was spend time with them while she was home for the summer. The last time she had argued for more independence, they had said they might just quit paying for school.

It wasn't fair.

It's just one more semester, and then I'll get that job they want me to get so bad and be able to do what I please.

Dall seemed to understand it was time for her to leave. Giving her their special smile, he pulled her in for an embrace.

Fireworks went off in her head, and the world disappeared.

In her ear, he whispered, "Sae I wull see ye Friday, aye?"

All tingly from feeling his breath in her ear, she whispered in his, "Yes, and I will try to call you during the week."

He kissed her then for the second time. It was another long wet kiss, but while their first kiss had been an insistent hello, this one was a sweet goodbye.

THE TIME before Friday crawled by.

As Emily had suspected, her parents had seen Vange's Facebook posts with the pictures of her and Dall kissing.

Her dad teased her about it as soon as she walked in the door.

"So who's the hottie, Emily?"

Her mom joined in.

"I'm not so surprised you got a job at that faire now. So who is this guy? He's really handsome. Does he have a name? What does he do?"

"His name is Dall ... and he's from Scotland" was all she could think to say.

Big mistake.

"Oh. Does he still live there?"

"Yes."

"Honey, you really shouldn't get too attached to him, then. It will only break your heart when he goes back home."

"We just want the best for you."

Yeah, those conversations weren't any fun, and they had one every day.

At least I distracted them from asking again what Dall does. I think they would put their foot down about me working at the faire if they knew that was the only job he had. Little do they know.

Each evening, Emily suffered through dinner with her parents and some of their friends. It was a small town, so for example they were good friends with their family doctor and his wife. Emily had known him all her life. At least he no longer made comments about how much she'd grown.

During the days her parents were at work, so Emily was free to hang out with people her own age for a change. But out of all those who were in town, Vange was the only one who understood Emily and liked the same things she did, such as the renaissance faire.

It had been that way since fourth grade. When her parents were at work from 8 to 5, Vange was Emily's only company.

She spent as little time alone missing Dall as she could.

Instead, she and Vange practiced with their daggers by setting up a dummy made of rags and taking turns stabbing it. When they were too tired to practice daggers, they tea-dyed their peasant clothes, scrounged their parents' attics for old leather belts, and made several pouches each out of some old leather purses Emily's grandmother had used in the 1960s.

After Emily tested an old all-natural bota bag to make sure it didn't leak, she was happy to add the water-carrier to her ensemble, along with an old pewter beer stein, minus the lid. She hoped it would pass as a tankard.

The best thing Emily found in the attic was a reversible hooded wool cloak. One side was green, the other brown. It was moth-eaten, but that made her shout for joy because it revealed the waterproof oilcloth between the layers. She silently thanked her hippie grandma.

She wanted to tell her best friend about Dall being a time traveler—and that she hoped to go back to his time with him, probably at the end of faire in nine more weeks.

But Emily's memory of the druid Aiden stopped her. She could tell the man was powerful, could sense it. And she had a feeling he would be the one who decided if she went with Dall or not. She didn't think he would approve of Vange knowing, and although Vange wouldn't tell anyone, her knowledge would show in her behavior.

Emily tried Monday night to call Dall, through Siobhan.

But the woman was adept at not allowing Dall to get on the phone—without saying that was what she was doing.

When she called on Tuesday night, Emily got voicemail. Three times. Rather than leave more than one message and sound desperate, she stopped calling. She got Siobhan's message, loud and clear.

"THANK YOU SO MUCH, Simon. They're perfect." Emily twisted and turned every which way to admire her new custom boots on her under Simon's flashlight. She had wanted to come earlier, but her parents had insisted she have dinner with them and a few of their friends before she left for another whole weekend away.

"I took a few liberties with their construction," Simon was saying. "They have steel plates inside the soles and steel toes inside their uppers, so even if you step on a rusty nail, your feet should be well-protected. Also, they are weather-proofed. It won't last more than a season, but your feet should stay dry."

Emily hugged Simon, she was so grateful.

"Also," he said, "I saw the devices you ladies were using to charge your phones last weekend. I had a friend disguise a few as brooches so you can wear them all day, instead of leaving them here. I see you've acquired a cloak, Emily, so that's perfect. Here, let me show you."

The tin-encased solar panel did look like a brooch, albeit a large one, but for connecting Emily's cloak to her so that her hands were free, it was actually perfect. It also looked like it might afford the solar charger some protection if it were dropped, always a plus. It protected her phone, too, where it slipped into a groove behind the charger, connecting to it with a cord.

With a smile, Simon handed each of them a spare phone cord. They each stowed them in one of their new pouches. Vange had three and Emily had five, plus the stein and the bota bag.

Emily was starting to worry that something had happened to Dall when all of a sudden he and Ian emerged through the burlap right next to Simon's booth, along with Siobhan and a dozen more Scots. By now it was almost bedtime, but all the Scots were in good spirits, like someone had just given them a pep talk.

"Sorry I was na here tae welcome ye, lass." Dall's strong arms were around her and they were kissing again. This time, it was a happy kiss. They both left their eyes open and eye-smiled the whole time. Emily felt the way she remembered a rollercoaster making her feel, the moment she topped a hill and started to descend.

"Ooh." Emily was dimly aware of Siobhan saying to Vange, "Look at you, all complete now with your boots, belt, and pouches."

Complete was a good word for it, because Vange wasn't even trying to look historically accurate.

That thought ruined the kissing mood, as Siobhan no doubt had intended for it to. Sure enough, the woman set upon Emily next.

"You too, Emily. When you reach up like that, I can see how much your new boots look like Dall's. Simon outdid himself this time. They are the spit and image."

Emily pulled away to acknowledge the compliment.

Dall didn't let her completely separate from him. He firmly held onto her hand.

"Thanks, Siobhan," Emily said. "It looks like you all just came out of a clan meeting."

Siobhan smiled sincerely at Emily. "Yes, we meet at the picnic tables backstage. Please join us next Friday. Just walk on up. Everyone knows you're welcome."

"Thank you. I'm sure we'll be there." Emily smiled just as sincerely at Siobhan and then turned to Dall to ask if he wanted to take a walk with her before bed.

But of course, that was not to be.

Siobhan grabbed Emily's other hand and Vange's hand, saying, "Party's in my trailer, guys." While everyone followed her to her trailer, she said to Emily and Vange, "You girls are welcome to my room if you need to crash before everyone leaves. You have to be back here at opening, and I don't have anything until the stage dance."

The party was fun. Someone had made real mead, and they all tasted it. That stuff was good.

Someone else had real home-stilled whiskey. That stuff was nasty, but Emily was glad for the experience of tasting it. Others had brought various store-bought spirits. Some had even brought snacks.

Siobhan's trailer was quite jam packed full of people. More sat on the floor than on the furniture. They sang songs to go with their drinking: some period, but most just popular songs of the past few decades. Once in a while, someone would stand and say something like, "OK, this is to the tune of 'Waiting on the World to Change'." Everyone would hum the tune, and the person would sing words they made up to it. Usually, the words were funny.

Through all of this, Emily and Dall snuggled together on the couch, with people pressed in on both sides of them and against their legs.

Other couples were making out heavily, even getting up to leave and go be alone in their tents.

But the first time Dall and Emily tried even kissing, Siobhan stopped the singing and led everyone in that hooting noise again. It worked as it was no doubt designed to. Dall and Emily didn't wish to continue with an obvious audience, so they stopped kissing and just kept on cuddling.

The cuddling was heaven, anyway. Emily had no real complaints. She wished this evening could go on forever, actually. She fell asleep cuddled next to Dall on the couch. He was long gone when she woke up, but he and Ian came back for breakfast and walked her and Vange to Simon's.

THIS WENT on for eight more weekends. Every Friday was a lot like this first one, except she and Vange joined in on the clan meeting first.

Late Saturday nights were much the same. After they all

enjoyed the night-shows, they stayed up late partying in Siobhan's trailer.

Other couples were practically having sex on the straw bales at night, and they could be heard doing so in their tents.

But Siobhan and the clan only allowed Emily and Dall to kiss hello and goodbye. If they kissed any other time, they got the hooting noise.

Dall always held his arm out for Emily when they walked, though, and they cuddled on the couch for hours and hours.

As it had been that first Sunday, the only time Emily and Dall got enough privacy to have a serious conversation was twenty minutes each weekend day, while they were dancing on stage in front of five hundred people. These conversations were personal at first, only gradually and slowly insinuating their way into the metaphysical question of time travel.

"So you never answered my question. How do you know I'm 23?"

"I asked yer best lass."

Elbow turn with corner

"Oh no. What else did she say?"

"Ainly that ye hae ne'er marrit, and ye dinna hae any children."

Elbow turn with opposite

"Wow, you don't waste any time asking unimportant questions."

"This life is but a dream, lass, and we wake from it all too soon. 'Tis a waste tae spend oor precious time on frivolous things."

Bow to corner

"Yes, time is of the essence, wouldn't you say?"

"Ye ken it is, lass."

VANGE'S PARENTS invited her to their insurance agency for an open house the Friday before the last weekend of faire. They invited Emily, too, but she could tell they wanted their daughter to themselves, so Emily stayed home alone. She tried to distract herself by playing games on her phone.

The new app appeared then. Just popped up out of nowhere, covering her game.

"Siobhan, what are you up to?"

Emily poked around. It was a huge app that took up almost half of Emily's free memory on a new top of the line phone that she got for her birthday just recently.

Oh, the app was named Time Management.

"OK, maybe I want this app."

Siobhan was the only other person who had handled Emily's phone.

Emily hadn't surfed the net or opened any emails or downloaded anything onto this phone, so she reasoned Siobhan must have installed the app. She was mad at Siobhan for keeping Dall from talking to her alone, but she didn't delete the app.

Emily understood why Siobhan was doing that. Time travel was a huge deal. People would be pushing and shoving to go along, if everyone knew about it.

The military would take over to use time travel as some sort of weapon if they found out, and everyone would end up running from The Terminator.

So yeah, Emily was kind of glad the druids—and she realized here that Siobhan must be one of the druids—were all hush-hush about the time traveler Emily had fallen for.

Still, it was frustrating.

Hoping for some answers, Emily opened the app.

A bunch of buttons appeared, but they were all greyed out. The map showed her current location, with a large glowing dot in the direction of the faire. A message in the middle of the screen read:

-Hello Emily. You are in your home time and home location.

Well, that was stating the obvious. Not much help. Based on a hunch, and asking what she really wanted to know at the moment, she typed in:

What is needed to travel?

-Clearance is needed for Emily to travel.

Who can give clearance?

-See the person who gave you the Time Management app.

She was back to square one. Except ... the fact that she had the app on her phone reassured Emily. When Dall went back to his own time—soon—she would be going with him. And they were able to bring her back here to her own time.

And then it hit her.

She would be going back 500 years in time.

No emergency room.

No Walmart.

No industrial revolution.

Emily called her parents' best friends.

"Doctor Anderson's office, this is Stacy."

"Hi Stacy. It's Emily, George and Sandra's daughter?"

"Hi Emily. So you're in town for the summer, eh? How are your parents?"

"They're fine."

"What can we do for you?"

"I'm only home for a few more days. I'll be traveling this weekend to ... the third world. Can I get some antibiotic pills to take with me?"

"Sure. Come on in."

When Emily got back from her doctor's office, antibiotic pills in hand, she rummaged through her parents' cupboards, stuffing things into the pouches on her faire costume belt. She packed a big tube of antibiotic ointment and a huge bottle of iodine tablets, some anti-diarrhea pills, anti-vomiting pills, anti-fungal cream, and aspirin. Then she also grabbed her Diva cup, some moisturizer, and a small magnifying glass. And changes of wool socks and cotton underwear. At first she grabbed some toilet paper, but on second thought she packed six small cakes of handmade soap and a linen dishtowel her aunt had given them for Christmas.

For good measure, she threw in a cloth bag of handmade hard candies, too, wrapped in wax paper. That gave her the idea to pack several unused sheets of wax paper—both for her own use and to trade with other women. From her study of literature, she knew paper was very rare and expensive in this time, but that it did exist. She didn't bother crumpling the wax paper up, knowing that just walking around with it in a pouch would do that for her.

Gathering up her costume and packing her pajamas and street clothes in an overnight bag for the weekend gave Emily the idea to include several sewing needles in her gear. She stuck them all through a small piece of leather that she doubled over so that the points didn't stick out. She figured the women of the time would trade her almost anything for such fine sewing needles. She added some safety pins, since they were small and safe to carry.

Again from her literature studies, Emily knew that if she tried to trade in gold or jewels while dressed as a peasant, then she would be accused of thievery—and considered guilty till proven innocent. Likewise, she knew it was pointless to buy a fancy costume at the faire and try to pass herself off as nobility. For one thing, all the nobles of Europe knew each other well, being cousins and all. No matter how well she studied up on an obscure noble from faraway Spain, for example, a local noble was sure to spot her fakery and have her drawn and quartered.

And anyway, a noble lady would have attendants. Emily was sure she and Dall would be traveling alone.

She already had her first-aid textbook on her phone, along with the complete works of Shakespeare. She browsed through the free ebook section about Scotland and chose a history book, a survival guide, a recipe book, and an herbal. She had downloaded an elementary engineering book and another three dozen free reference books when her parents got home.

AND THEN AT dinner Thursday night came the hard part.

Thank God her parents hadn't invited anyone over. She needed them to know she and Dall were getting serious, or they wouldn't be ready for what she hoped might happen. She couldn't tell them the whole truth. It was too ... supernatural. They would freak. But she told them the gist of it.

"Mom, Dad, Dall's going home to visit his family this weekend, and he just invited me to come meet them."

For all they know, we talk on the phone constantly while they're at work. I wish.

Emily could tell her mom meant to say she couldn't go. She got ready to say that too bad, she was going anyway.

They won't stop paying for school just because I take a trip to Scotland. They might threaten, but they won't actually do it. I know them too well.

But her dad put a hand on his wife's arm and spoke for them.

"I can see that you're set on going, Emily, so we won't forbid you to go."

Emily blinked at him, not quite believing what she was hearing.

"I know you often think we're out to spoil your fun and that we forbid things just to do that."

"No I don't."

"Heh. You do though. It's written all over your face. The fact is, you're an adult, Emily."

She raised her eyebrows at her dad.

"I never thought I'd hear you say so."

"Well, you are. We have some sway over you because we're paying for grad school and we paid for college, but very soon you'll be done with that and out in the real world making adult decisions. So I think you should practice that a bit now. And, I think it shows maturity in your Dall, that he's asked you to come meet his family. I hope we get to meet him next."

❧

THE SCOTS CLAN meeting and Friday evening party were full-blown revelries this final weekend. They danced to modern music on Siobhan's iPod—both outside her trailer and in, thanks to a networked set of speakers. The liquor flowed even more freely than usual.

Emily and Dall couldn't get away alone, and they couldn't hear each other whisper over all the noise. They held each other close and slow danced the whole time, even though all the songs were fast.

Siobhan surprised Emily Saturday morning. Handing Ian two covered plates and a Thermos, she said, "Please take Vange over to the picnic tables and eat your breakfast. I need to talk to Dall and Emily."

Vange looked at Emily uncertainly, but Emily gave her a big grin, so she and Ian left.

"I saw that you found the app yesterday, Emily. I'm going to save you and Dall a lot of angst and just lay everything out on the table. Then, I'm going into the next room so you can give him your decision in private and say your goodbyes, if that's what you decide."

Dall smiled at Emily reassuringly. "Lass, whatever ye decide wull na change the strong feelings I hae for ye, and if nowt else, we can still see each other at the faire each year."

Emily smiled back at him. "Of course I'm—"

But Siobhan gently put a hand over Emily's mouth. "I've discussed this with Dall at length. He wants you with him, Emily, but he is concerned about your safety—"

Again Emily tried to speak. "I've seen you fight, and you're more than capable of—"

But Siobhan talked over her. "It's a valid concern. By now, you have surmised that Dall is returning to his own place and time—which is Glen Strae, Scotland in 1540. The MacGregor clan is tough, but there is danger, Emily."

Emily spoke to Dall, not to Siobhan. "I'm coming with you. I want to meet your family. I want to get to know you better."

And I want to see the highlands as they were in 1540, before the modern world came along and spoiled them. Would any Outlander fan turn down this opportunity? She'd be nuts to. I did the girl-scout thing. I'm prepared. Bring it on.

Dall brightened. "I want ye with me, lass. Ye make me verra happy, saying ye want the same."

Siobhan was brisk now. "If you're sure, then get everything you want to take along, take out your phone, and open the app."

Over her tea-stained English peasant costume, Emily strapped on her belt with the pouches and wrapped her cloak around her. She made sure her dagger was sheathed in her boot and put on her muffin cap, hiding her hair. Finally, she got out her phone and opened Siobhan's app.

"OK, but I have stuff in my pouches that I was hoping Simon and his friends could disguise first."

Siobhan shoo'd Emily's hands toward her pouches. "I took care of that while you slept. Have a look."

Emily took her time and examined the faire crafters' work. Her pills—including the oral antibiotics—had been crushed into powder and placed in several tiny earthenware jars, each one protected by a soft leather pouch that was branded with a symbol which identified the medicine's use. Each pouch also contained a tiny metal dosage spoon. The ointments—antibiotic and antifungal, as well as moisturizer —had been squeezed into the intestine of some animal, perhaps a sheep, and tied off at both ends like sausages, the opening end with a bow. These too were branded with pictures that let her know which was which.

Her magnifying glass and Diva cup were wrapped in wax paper and put in with the similarly wrapped hard candies. Each sheet of wax paper had been crumpled over and over so that it looked to have been used a dozen times. Each sewing needle and safety pin had its own tiny leather sheath.

Emily took Dall's hand with her left and in her right held her phone so that it looked like she was admiring her reflection in the back of her brooch.

Dall squeezed her hand. She squeezed back.

Siobhan put her hands behind her back and paced. "You and Dall are programmed to come back two months from now, on July 19. See the countdown in the top corner of the app?"

Emily nodded yes.

Siobhan turned and paced the other way. "In order to come back, you must return to the same spot where you arrived in his time and push the green button. If something happens to your phone, you can still come back by contacting the druids of that time and explaining the situation ... but it would be better if you protected your phone. Understand?"

"Yes."

"See that red button, Emily?"

"Yeah."

"When you're ready, push it."

Just before everything went all swirly and the world felt like it was closing in on her, Emily heard the trailer door open and felt several people bump into her. She also noticed that Siobhan had texted her:

"Your job is to make sure Dall comes back."

3. SCOTLAND

Emily blinked, but the darkness remained. The brightest light in the huge windowless room was coming from her phone, which she still held in front of her as if she were admiring her reflection in the back of her brooch. She quickly lowered her phone under her cloak, hiding the light coming from it. The screen had shown her current location and time, which were Loch Awe Scotland, May 20, 1540.

She heard the distant muffled voices of many people upstairs, and their footsteps caused the wooden floor above her to creak and whine. All around her, she heard a dozen men groaning and getting up, complaining about the cold stone floor. Hopefully, if anyone had seen the light from her phone shining on her face they would tell themselves it had been a reflection of the candle behind her.

Dall dropped her hand and made gestures that included her and the people she could hear behind her, who had now finished getting up. He was saying something incomprehensible but very Scottish-sounding to someone she hadn't seen until now.

When her eyes were finally adjusted to the darkness, she

took a good look. Dall was talking to a druid. She recognized the white linen robe and the crown of flowers.

"What are you saying?" Emily asked Dall.

"Hello, English people," Dall said to her now in English with a formal smile, including in his glance the others around her. "Welcome tae Kilchurn Castle."

"Very funny, Dall. And wow, I didn't know we were coming to a castle. I thought we would arrive in your glen." Her smiling delight slowly dissolved as she watched him. He smiled politely—and even a little interestedly, which gave her some relief from her growing horror—but there was no sign that he recognized her, let alone shared in her delight.

Startling Emily, the Druid spoke.

"Aye, welcome tae Kilchurn Castle, English people. I am Eamann. In the Gaelic language o' the highlanders, Dall MacGregor was asking me why I brought him doon here tae meet ye. He asks if his business with ye is urgent, because he was on his way tae sit doon tae the morning meal with his clan. Dall, these people hae ainly just arrived, and ainly they can tell us their purpose here."

Dall and the druid now looked at Emily for an answer. She turned around to see who the other people were, and why they were so quiet.

Dog and his crew of biker-archers stood there blinking at her, and sort of panting. They looked like they might go into shock. They were definitely in no shape to speak up.

At least they had their semi-period bows and arrows with them. They had each packed some sort of gear, too, though who knew if she should be glad about that. They probably had cigarettes, and lighters, and any number of other things they couldn't be seen with here...

The druid cleared his throat.

In one last attempt to wake Dall up and make him remember her, Emily looked deep into his eyes.

The druid cleared his throat again.

"Yes, our purpose here is," Emily said, turning again to look at Dog and his crew, "that we are an English troupe of actors."

Dall and Eamann looked shocked. Emily was puzzled for a moment, but then she recovered.

"The men are actors, that is. Of course I am not an actor. I am their ... director." Emily smiled.

Dall and Eamann gave her blank stares.

"Yes. I am their ... coach."

Eamann looked at Dall, who shrugged.

"Teacher?" Emily tried, getting frustrated.

Dall and Eamann nodded and smiled at her and each other.

"Yes. I am their teacher. I will make them great in the art of drama if it's the last thing I do, by golly." By now, Emily's smile was plastered on and kind of idiotic looking.

Smiling kindly at Emily and yet piercing her eyes with a very pointed stare, Eamann said, "We believe ye are their teacher. Most folk will na. Ye ken that a lass traveling with many lads looks loose, Mistress ...?"

Emily felt her cheeks turn bright red. "Mistress Emily, and it isn't that way at all."

Eamann put his hand out in a halting motion. "I ken it is na. Perhaps ye can be my apprentice—"

"But I really do need to teach them, if they're going to put on a play."

Eamann exaggerated the piercing stare he was giving Emily.

Oh. That gave her a better excuse for being here. She finally relaxed.

Eamann turned to Dall. "After ye hae broken yer fast, wull ye see aboot having them perform a play here in say, two weeks' time?" He looked to Emily with a question in his eyes.

"Yes, two weeks is enough time to get them ready," she said, looking the biker-archers over and making plans in her head.

Eamann nodded at her and continued addressing Dall. "See tae lodgings for oor guests."

Dall turned to them. "Wull met, Emily and company. Certies, oor clan chieftain wull be glad tae provide accommodation."

Emily despaired until she saw Dall turn his eyes toward her a second before he disappeared up the stairs. She was sure he was interested in her—interested again rather than still, but interested, nonetheless.

Dall had only been gone a moment when there was a commotion upstairs and a man called down Eamann's name along with something incomprehensible in a tone that could only mean someone needed help urgently.

Emily raced up the stairs after Eamann.

ﳑ

LAUGHING, all the children took turns imitating Alasdair spitting out the meat and Emily squeezing Alasdair from behind. They reveled in telling everyone who ran into the room to see what all the fuss was. The dining hall got more and more crowded.

Emily couldn't understand the children's Gaelic words, but they were easy to guess when coupled with the action.

"Pfftooh." And it went all the way over there."

"She grabbed him from behind like this, and squeezed him all at once, and pop. Out it went."

Emily had stowed her phone/solar brooch combo in one of her pouches while she charged up the stairs. She was standing around with the other adults laughing at the chil-

dren's antics when Dall approached her. Alasdair was
with him.

"Alasdair, allow me tae introduce ye tae Emily, the lovely
lass who did save ye from yer choking fit. And Emily, please
ken this is Alasdair, the chief o' Clan MacGregor, constables
of Kilchurn Castle."

Feeling a bit of hope that Dall might remember her after
all, or at least come around again to the level of affection they
had shared in her own time, Emily smiled.

Alasdair looked about forty. "I thank ye, lass, for the wee
bit o' help. Would ye join us at table?"

Emily might have been imagining it, but she thought he
was looking at Dall with a bit of speculation about her.

"Thank you, but I already breakfasted," Emily said,
thinking of the eggs and bacon she and Dall had eaten
together in Siobhan's trailer backstage less than an hour
before. "The actors downstairs might like some food,
though," she added as an afterthought.

Before addressing Emily again, Alasdair said something in
Gaelic to a young man, who ran toward the kitchen. Then he
smiled back at Emily. "'Tis odd for a lass tae arrive with a
troupe o' actors, but 'tis glad I am ye did!"

They all laughed.

"Which one o' them is yer husband?"

"Alas, I'm not married," Emily said with a bit of a sigh
while glancing at Dall, who didn't seem to notice.

Alasdair did. "Sorry tae hear it. Ye are English. What
brings ye sae far from home, then?"

Emily answered as truthfully as she dared. "I wanted to
see the Highlands, to travel a bit before I settled down to
grown-up life." There. That was as much of the truth as she
could give him. She couldn't very well tell him most of the
reason she had come was to follow Dall and meet his family

because she was falling in love with him in another time period.

"Ah, a bit o' the wanderer in ye, aye?" Alasdair said with a smile that included Dall in a way that said non-verbally, 'isn't that adorable?'

Emily about fainted when Dall nodded yes. Her hope was growing. He didn't seem to be able to take his eyes off her. Maybe everything would be OK.

"Well now," Alasdair went on, "we wull accommodate ye and yer actors." Here, he exchanged nods with the same young man who was now running plates of food down the stairs, and then he said to Emily, "Ye can stay in with the one other unmarried lass, Annis. I wull hae them set yer place at the table next tae Dall here. He tells me ye are the actors' teacher?"

To his credit, Dall put a hand on Alasdair's shoulder at this point, and to Emily, this appeared to indicate Dall would not change his story. Holding her breath, she let her smile shine at Dall.

He unaffectedly returned it. Things were going to be OK.

She needed to answer Alasdair's question. She turned to the chief, and he looked amused. She was happy to let him think this was all new to her and Dall.

Forcing herself to keep looking at Alasdair, Emily said, "Yes, we will need to practice the play in your setting before they are ready to perform."

Alasdair nodded once decisively. "Oot in the courtyard is the ainly place we hae that is large enough. I will hae the word spread far and wide. Annis."

A slender girl about 15 years old came over.

Alasdair smiled at the girl and held her hands. "Lovely Annis. Emily here needs tae share yer room for the next moon or sae. She saved my life, sae be good tae her, aye?"

Annis smiled at him and said something in Gaelic.

"English, please, for oor guest."

"Och, aye, Uncle."

"There's a good lass." He smiled at Annis one last time. "Emily, let Annis show ye tae her room. Ye wull fund yer actors in the courtyard. Dall and I wull see ye at mealtimes."

Emily tried not to trip on her way out, staring at Dall for as long as she could, and smiling because he was staring back. When she could no longer see Dall, she finally turned to her new roommate.

"Say, Annis?"

"Aye?"

"Where do we lasses relieve ourselves? I know the men probably pee on the outer wall of the castle."

Annis showed Emily to an empty room with a hole in the floor and then to her sleeping room—and then promptly left —probably to go tell the other women about Emily's theory on where the men whizzed.

Emily used the hole in the floor—right after she closed the door, whipped out her phone, and took pictures of it. Vange was not going to believe this.

And then she went to Annis's small stone room. It had a tiny third-story wind opening that looked down into the courtyard, two cots, and a large wooden cabinet. She took advantage of the privacy—first to wash her hands with soap and her damp dish towel, and second to look at her phone screen again before she shut it down to conserve the battery, mounted it with the solar charger, and used the 'brooch' the two formed to pin her cloak at her throat. She thanked her hippie grandma again for leaving the cloak in the attic at her parents' house. The shutters were drawn, and there was no glass in the wind opening, of course, so the room was a bit chilly on this Scottish May morning, let alone the courtyard.

Yes, just as Emily thought, there was a second line to the

last-minute text Siobhan had sent. Her breath caught in her throat when she read it:

Beware: If you join with him, then you will be stuck there.

KILCHURN CASTLE COURTYARD was an awesome place for putting on a play. It resembled the models of William Shakespeare's Globe Theatre that Emily and her classmates had built out of Popsicle sticks, based on old etchings. The second and third-story rooms like Annis's were reached by an outdoor system of wooden walkways that would serve remarkably well as seating.

Emily had no illusions about why they were rehearsing inside the castle walls rather than out on the hillside: they were much safer from raiders inside the protection of these walls. Still, smiling a huge smile as she gazed up at those wooden walkways, Emily saw theater balconies. She wondered if maybe the Globe Theatre would be modeled after castle courtyards such as this one. It was weird to think The Globe hadn't yet been built, but Shakespeare wouldn't be born for another twenty-six years…

Her biker-archers snapped her out of her daydreams.

They didn't realize everyone in the whole castle could see them here. Or they didn't yet care. Two had tried to light cigarettes and three had tried to look at their phones. It had been tempting to watch and see their reactions when they realized there were no cell towers in 1540, but so not worth being burned as witches if the people of this time saw the anachronisms.

Emily had to find a solution to this right away.

Using gestures in case English was not widely understood among Clan MacGregor, she asked a passerby if anyone in the castle had an extra pipe. In trade, she gave him a handful of her candies wrapped in the wax paper—making sure not to give him her magnifying glass or her Diva cup. He came back a few minutes later with not only a pipe, but a leather bag of tobacco, and the smokers were happy.

Most frustrating of all, the gang loved the idea of putting on a play with so much sword-fighting in it, but no one wanted to be Juliet.

"But I don't want to play a girl."

"Fine, then don't," Dog said. "Someone has to though, because Emily's right: women in this time don't go on stage. Didn't you see any of Short Shakespeare's shows?"

"I'll do it."

Everyone looked around, unsure who had spoken.

"Over here," said the smallest biker archer there, with a tentative hand raised.

Dog turned to him. "Mike, I can't even imagine you up on stage you're always so quiet. Are you sure you want to do this?"

Mike stood up, faced the rest of them, held out his hands dramatically, and started reciting Juliet's lines like a pro, in a loud falsetto voice:

> *O Romeo, Romeo. Wherefore art thou Romeo?*
> *Deny thy father and refuse thy name.*
> *Or, if thou wilt not, be but sworn my love,*
> *And I'll no longer be a Capulet.*

Everyone clapped and cheered—not only them in the courtyard, but people stopped on the wooden walkways and leaned out of wind openings to clap and cheer.

Like a born showman, Mike bowed to the cheers. He even kissed his hands and blew kisses to the people who had stopped on the wooden walkways. Some of them laughed and caught the kisses.

Emily stood there clapping and cheering right along with everyone else. "Well, we have our Juliet." she announced to everyone. That got more cheers. She waited until the audience sensed the preview was over and went back to their business, and then she said more quietly, "Way to go, Mike." She shook his hand, then turned to the others. "I'm guessing no one wants to play the nurse, either?"

None of her biker-archers met her eye, not even Dog, who generally was staring at her whenever she looked.

"Very well. Mike, can you handle playing all the female parts against yourself?" Emily suspected that Mike had been a star in high-school drama, but from her teacher-training classes, she knew better than to bring that up in front of his fellow gang members.

Mike outdid himself. Not so loud this time so as not to attract an audience, he gave them the scene with not only Juliet and the nurse, but also Juliet's mother, and he played all three parts.

With a huge grin and a ridiculous bat of his eyes, Mike recited the nurse's lines in a gravelly falsetto that was so different from his Juliet voice, Emily would have thought it came from a different actor if she hadn't been able to see Mike:

> *Now, by my maidenhead at twelve years old,*
> *I bid her. What, lamb. What, ladybird.*
> *Where is this girl?*

Mike returned to his Juliet voice and added a skipping movement, which was both sweet and hilarious at the same time:

> *How now, who calls?*

Saying only the best and most necessary lines like Short Shakespeare had, Mike then gave them a very serious, 'prim and proper' Lady Capulet in his own tenor voice:

> *Think of marriage now, Juliet.*
> *The valiant Paris seeks you for his love.*

"What happens next?" said one of the biker-archers.

All the rest of them were mesmerized by Mike's performance, too. Emily went up and shook Mike's hand again, then held it up as if he had won a prize fight. "Give it up for Mike, you guys." The biker-archers all clapped and cheered. Several patted Mike on the back.

Emily gave them as long as it took, knowing that applause would be all the payment Mike got—and that his performance would make or break the show.

She took advantage of this opportunity to talk with Dog in private.

"Dog, why did you guys follow us here? And don't tell me you didn't know what would happen when you ran in and touched us."

Dog smiled at her with mischief in his eye. "We knew you two were coming back to old Scotland. We figured it out. We just thought it would be fun to come along, and so far, it is."

All Emily could do was sigh and shake her head, so that was what she did.

Glad she had thought to bring much more water-purifying iodine than she would need for herself, she also used this opportunity to ask a passerby where the actors might get water to drink.

Laughing, the kilted man took her to the castle's front gate.

Emily laughed, too. Careful as always to tell only the truth lest a lie tangle her in its web, she explained, "We arrived in the dark. I had no idea this castle sat on the bank of a huge lake. I take it this is fresh water and not seawater, Mister _?"

He nodded, still laughing a little. "Ewan."

"I guess you know I'm Emily. Will you show me the best place to draw water, Ewan?"

He sobered a little. "Aye, but 'twould be best if yer men came along, lass. The MacGregors and the Campbells hae many enemies, sae we bring up as much water as we can, whene'er we gae doon."

Idly wondering who the Campbells were, Emily went and got the actors. Ewan got several buckets, and they all went down to the lake. Their guide pronounced it 'loch'. While they were out on the castle's large grassy peninsula, Emily saw cattle grazing.

Once they were back inside, Ewan showed them where to dump the water into a cistern, and he explained that was where they got water after dark and when the castle was under siege. When he said 'siege', Emily pictured the castle courtyard full of cattle, imagining a hundred or so would fit.

Her bota bag was already full of good water from home, but she had noted the men all had tankards, but nothing to fill them from. She whispered about this to Dog, and he promised to spread the word: don't drink the water unless either you draw it yourself from the loch or Emily has treated it with her iodine powder.

After thanking Ewan, Emily took the area of the courtyard that Mike had used as a stage.

"Next, we cast the sword-fighting parts," she announced.

Of course, everyone wanted one of those parts. The bikers argued among themselves about who was the best fighter, even resorting to pushing and shoving before Emily put her thumb and forefinger in her mouth and whistled.

"Fwee."

They all stopped and turned to her.

"Thank you for turning to the whistle. So long as you always do that, I think we'll be able to get this play ready in two weeks," Emily said, reminding them they didn't have all summer to squabble—and feeling just a little amused at how juvenile these big muscular men were. How about that: she was gaining actual hands-on teaching experience in the most unlikely of places. She would be ahead of her classmates when their practicum started this fall. Too bad she'd never get credit for it.

Seeming to get the message, the guys relaxed a bit.

Emily looked them over, hoping to find at least two swords among them. Thankfully, she did. Pointing to those two guys, she said, "You and you, come on up and give us a mock sword fight."

When they did, she saw just how much work she had cut out for herself.

Helping them memorize their lines was going to be the easy part.

FEELING like something between a teacher and a prissy kid sister, Emily took the guys down to the loch again just before lunch—to draw a bucket of water for hand washing. She noticed that none of the locals were washing before the meal. She also knew that infectious diseases were the main cause of adult deaths in this time period.

As soon as she took her place next to Dall on the bench at the long crowded lunch table, he said softly to her, "I did na truly believe ye were their teacher until I saw ye with the actors this morning, lass." His eyes were amused, yet impressed and respectful.

"I do not lie," she declared to him heatedly, yet just as softly as he had spoken. She cringed a bit after she said it.

Her declarations of honesty often got her ostracized. But rather than regretting her impulse as she usually did, she was glad she had said it.

"I believe ye."

And there it was. He was smiling at her. She smiled back at him, and the contentment on his face appeared to deepen. She was getting lost in his eyes... Their smile had become so familiar to her over the past six weeks that she almost forgot where they were right then, almost forgot that so far as Dall knew at the moment, the two of them had only just met five hours before.

But unlike at the faire—just the night before to Emily— the two of them weren't cuddling while they sat. They were close enough that she could feel the heat from his body, but they were back to not touching, which was almost unbearable to her. They weren't whispering secrets into each other's ears, nor smiling when their eyes met over private jokes.

Feeling someone else's eyes on her, Emily looked around until she realized Eamann was at the table too, giving her that hard knowing stare as if to say, "Heed Siobhan's warning. We're serious about that." She quickly glanced away, resolving not to look at the man again until July 19 came and it was time for her and Dall to go back.

Someone came to fill Emily's tankard, and she was relieved to see it fill with beer rather than water. Few germs could survive in alcohol, so she didn't have to worry about treating it under the table. She held up her beer. When everyone else held theirs up, Emily caught Dog's eye, said, "To your health." and took a long drink.

"Aye, to your health," said everyone else. Many also crossed themselves before they started eating.

Dog nodded and drank, and so did the other actors. Thankfully, where this beer was strong on taste, it was weak in its alcohol content. Otherwise, Emily imagined the bikers would have been useless all afternoon, and they needed every possible minute of rehearsal over the next two weeks.

"Wull ye pass the butter, lass?"

Startled out of her reverie, Emily looked over at the amused face of the woman who had spoken.

"Of course."

Emily was reaching for the butter when Dall's hand collided with hers. It was just a brief touch, and then he let her be the one to pick up the butter, but as usual when they touched, imaginary sparks flew between them. Just being there, he made her feel even more alive than she had in the courtyard, teaching her actors how to stage fight.

Inevitably, their touch made her eyes meet Dall's. His eyes searched hers, looking for the depths of her being. She tried her best to tell him with her own eyes that they had already done this part, they were already past the flirting stage and into the cuddling stage. She knew she was being silly to try, but she did anyway.

All that happened in just a second, and then Emily passed the butter to the woman sitting on her other side.

"Here you go." She smiled at the woman in what she hoped was a friendly way.

The woman winked at her.

Emily gave the woman a nervous toothy grin in response.

The woman elbowed Emily.

Looking around the table, Emily saw that all the women and most of the older men knew what was going on between her and Dall. They all gave her knowing looks and friendly smiles. At least they approved. She did not want to be on the bad side of these tough real highlanders. Even the old women looked like they could take her in a fight.

Relieved, she saw that the meal was cooked: a stew of some sort. It tasted good: beef, cabbage, carrots, onions...

But Dall was making conversation with her. "What wull the play be aboot then, lass?"

This question roused the interest of everyone at the table —including, Emily noted with amusement, the actors. She put on her teacher hat and did her best to keep them interested.

"Romeo and Juliet is a story from Italy. It's about two families who are at war with each other. A boy from one family and a girl from the other family get married in secret, which just causes more fighting."

General nods of understanding followed.

"Aye, that it would."

"Nay son o' mine wull gae skulking off tae marry."

"Especially na tae a Menzies."

"Aye."

They were all pounding on the table.

Dall touched Emily's arm to get her attention, and she almost didn't hear him, she was so busy being buzzed by the contact.

He said, "It does sound like a good story, lass, but why dae the two young ones marry in secret? Why dinna they tell anyone?"

This was one of Emily's favorite questions in all of literature, so she warmed to it.

"Ah, I'm glad you asked that. The reason is that they are selfish and immature little brats, these children Romeo and Juliet. Their families are wealthy, you see, so the children wish to make a show of pleasing their parents, but to still be together—and Juliet's father has promised her to his friend Paris."

"Wull," said Dall, looking Emily in the eye, "this Romeo then should stand up tae his Juliet's father. Should tell him plain that he and Juliet wull be marrit. Make their oon way, and forget aboot her father's wealth."

"Aye," said the man across from Emily.

"That be the right of it," said Alasdair, and everyone nodded.

"Yes, that is what Romeo should do," said Emily, "only remember, the play is about how he and his bride Juliet are selfish and immature. Instead of making a home for them, Romeo marries and has the pleasure of Juliet's bed in secret, thinking to avoid the work of providing for his bride, letting her instead remain in her parents' home."

"Och. Tis na wonder ye call the lad a boy and na a man." Dall slammed his hand on the table. "A man provides for his wife," he said with his eyes searching Emily's.

She did her best to open them up for him and let him see how much she really did understand and want to be part of that way of his thinking. They sat there once again lost in each other's gaze for a moment.

The discussion had intrigued everyone, though, and for the most part they were supportive and even started offering to help make the production a success.

"It sounds verra good."

"Indeed, it does."

"Hae ye need o' any props, lass? I hae a robe that wull dae wull for the Italian father."

"Aye, I ken the one."

"We hae a few more o' those one-handed swords they use in Italy, as wull."

"I hae a dress for the Italian daughter." This older woman looked askance at Mike and grinned, thrilled when she received a grin from him in response.

Everyone had been watching rehearsal, Emily realized.

"I hope this play does na give the young ones bad ideas," said the older woman.

"It won't."

"How can ye be sae certain?"

"Both the little brats die in the end."

"Och, aye, that wull dae."

THE FIRST PART of the afternoon went much as the morning had. Emily cast all the parts of the play and ran the actors through their lines over and over. Good thing she had seen all 21 of Short Shakespeare's performances. Fortunately, most of the guys had seen a good many of those performances, too.

When she found out Mike knew all the lines as well as she did, Emily had Mike take turns with her, feeding the actors their lines. That helped save her voice.

Rehearsal stopped often for a water run to the loch. Emily took advantage of the relative privacy to wash and to change underwear. Long skirts were starting to make more and more sense to her. They were like a traveling private bathroom.

She was so glad she had two skirts that she traded one of her sheets of wax paper for a second blouse. The woman was so impressed with the wax paper that she gave Emily her very best blouse for it, a lovely one with flowers and vines embroidered round the neckline.

When they came to the sword-fighting parts of the play, Emily had difficulty. She knew stage fighting and some real sword-fighting techniques, and the bikers were knife fighters. But when it came to period weapons, they only knew archery. The two actors who wore swords only wore them to look cool.

So it was a big relief when Dall showed up with a small barrel full of practice swords, even some one-handed Italian ones.

Well, it was always a relief to see Dall. Who was she kidding?

"Could ye use a hand teaching the actors how tae handle

swords, lass?" He looked ... sheepish.

She was sure the men would rather learn sword techniques from a man than from her. That was why she was so
eager to see Dall in action. Yep, that was a good excuse.

"Could I ever."

He looked at her uncertainly.

Right, she knew better than to use modern slang. She
would need to really watch herself. "Yes. Thank you for the
help." She gave Dall her most sincere smile—and resisted the
urge to bat her eyelashes at him. He wouldn't get that joke.
"Uh ..." Facing everyone now, Emily fought her training a bit.
In teacher school they had always said OK to get things
going, and OK was way too modern.

"Well enough," she tried.

There, that did it. Everyone looked at her. She was glad
she hadn't had to whistle in front of Dall. That was just too
unattractive.

Now that she had their attention, she went on with her
instruction. "In the first fight, two Capulet servants insult
two Montague servants until there is a general brawl. Dog, I
am going to leave the brawl up to you. You and your crew
know how those go."

Dog smiled and put everyone through the moves of a
brawl, and they were more than convincing. This was going to
be good.

Emily went on. "Romeo's cousin Benvolio tries to stop the
brawl, but Juliet's cousin Tybalt starts a swordfight with him."
While she spoke, she pointed to the actors playing those
parts, and they took the stage in front of the brawlers. "This
one needs to be really active." She looked to Dall.

"Wull then lass, let us show ye an active fight, sae that ye
mayhap can choose the parts that best fit yer play, aye?" Dall
smiled.

Emily nodded eagerly. "That would be awesome."

Awesome was OK to say, right? Apparently so.

Dall called another kilted highlander over. "Hendry." The two of them each picked out a one-handed Italian practice sword—and then they were at it. They swung high and low, twirled around making their kilts fly, banged each other's swords, and even slashed each other's shirts a bit, yelling and huffing and chests heaving...

Everyone sat dumbfounded and watched the sword show.

After Dall and Hendry finished swooshing all over the courtyard for ten minutes, everyone broke out in cheers and applause, just like after Mike recited those first lines.

The biker playing Benvolio said, "I think you guys should just play the sword-fighting parts."

The one who was Tybalt said, "Yeah, really."

They both looked impressed, but cast down in spirit.

Before Emily could reassure them, Dall did it for her. "I wull na hear o' it. Ye insult my abilities as a fight leader. I wull hae ye doing these moves by the end o' two weeks—on stage, if na on the battlefield."

They ran through the whole play twice then, having Dall and Hendry stage all the sword-fights. When the two high-landers left to put the barrel of practice swords indoors, Emily and the actors washed up again before supper.

While they were down at the loch, they saw a boat approaching and rushed up to warn the castle. It turned out to be someone important named Colin Campbell in the boat, with twenty other kilted highlanders.

When he came in, Campbell made a show of clasping forearms with Alasdair and generally being everyone's friend, but there was a hard look in his eyes that worried Emily.

He did draw all the attention at the supper table in much the way Emily had at lunch. This was fine with her.

It meant she and Dall could have a casual conversation without everyone listening in. They were careful to look away from each other now and then, to avoid being teased for the crazy amount of attention they were giving each other, having only just met 10 hours before.

Dall started it. "I heard ye tell Alasdair ye came tae Scotland tae see the Highlands."

"Yes, and it is beautiful in the way I had heard—and much more. Loch Awe is aptly named. I am in awe." She smiled about the loch with her mouth, but she smiled admiration at Dall with her eyes.

"Are ye? I dinna suppose ye hae lochs down there in *England*, after all." The way he said England made it a question, and his eyes held many more questions.

Very conscious of Eamann listening nearby, Emily tried her best to answer Dall's questions with her own eyes.

Everyone stayed at the supper table into the evening, singing songs about battles and lovers old long before. Dall and Emily's eyes continued their discussion about awe, but all their words were about Scotland.

Much later, Emily and Annis went up to their third-story room. After they had bade each other to have a good night, Emily took her belt with all its pouches and her 'brooch' under the covers for safe keeping.

Emily ducked her head under the covers as well once she heard Annis's breath go into sleep mode—and turned on her phone, glad she always kept it silenced. She found the Scottish history book she had downloaded, and searched in it for 'Colin Campbell'.

Oh no.

1547: Kilchurn Castle was administratively taken from the MacGregors—constables since about 1400 because of their relation to medieval lord Donnchadh Beag—by the servant of the servitor of **Colin Campbell (Cailean Liath)**.

1550: **Colin Campbell** became the 6th Campbell chief and gradually took over all the MacGregor lands with the administrative help of the earl of Argyll. Ironically, Campbell was aided by the MacGregors in this, who served as his infantry and intermarried with the Campbells.

1569-70: **Colin Campbell** himself beheaded the MacGregor clan chief Gregor Roy (Griogair Ruadh) under false accusations and gave Glen Strae to his own son instead of to the rightful heir: the son of Gregor Roy and Marion Campbell. The clan's response was to reclaim their cattle by force—and they were deemed outlaws.

1604: As a direct result of outlawry alleged by **Colin Campbell**, King James VI made using the MacGregor name a hanging offense—and he made mating with a MacGregor a tar-and-feathering offense for a woman. The clan dispersed, though many were sold into slavery in the colonies, where they kept the MacGregor name and multiplied, sometimes as McGregor.

&

EMILY HADN'T SLEPT MUCH the night before, tossing and turning with worry over how to warn Alasdair not to trust Colin Campbell. But when she went down to breakfast, he wasn't there. Hardly any of the castle men were, just Eamann, Campbell, and a few of those Campbell had brought with him.

Her actors had remained, and they spent the meal loudly boasting about all they had learned of sword-fighting the day before. Campbell hid it well from them, but Emily could tell by the hard look in his eyes that he thought the actors were useless and ridiculous.

"It is away they are, set tae keeping Colin's borders for him" said a soft voice in Emily's ear.

Emily turned to the young woman. "Please tell me your name. I don't want to keep thinking of you as 'the butter lady'." She noticed that the man usually seated on the other side of the woman was gone.

"Mairi." The woman smiled. "Glad I am tae meet ye."

Emily looked up and listened to the actors boasting for a bit before she addressed the woman again. "Is it so obvious, my attraction to Dall?"

Mairi's smile was joyous. "Aye, lass, tae those o' us who ken love." She looked over toward Eamann and Campbell. "Which does ne include everyone."

The two women watched Campbell hold court for a while. People jumped when he said boo.

"How long will the men be away?" Emily tried not to pout.

Mairi was matter-of-fact, like most military wives whose husbands are deployed. "Mayhap as long as a week, but most times ainly three or four days."

Emily asked Mairi for a tour of the castle, especially including which rooms had arrow openings to the outside. She also asked Dog to teach her how to shoot, and she practiced while the men loitered over their meals each day. They all kept up their rehearsal schedule for the next five days.

At first, the men grumbled that they needed Dall and Hendry to keep them doing the sword-fighting parts correctly. Even though she missed Dall too, Emily soon saw to it the actors had confidence in her. With her background in stage-fighting, she really was the better teacher for this, now that the fight choreography was done. The actors needed to make their fight look convincing without it being dangerous, and she knew how to accomplish exactly that.

Late each night under the covers, Emily read up on the history of the MacGregors and the Campbells. The more she read, the more intrigued she became—and the more worried and sad. She also tinkered around with the Time Management app, peeking into menus and reading screens that popped up here and there. It looked like it could be programed to take her—and anyone touching her—just about anywhere on Earth during any time, but she didn't dare mess with its current settings. She wanted to see Vange and her parents at least one more time, and she was afraid of getting lost in time.

During their extended meal periods, Dog worked with Emily on her archery and arrow-making. He and the others also practiced shooting at birds when they flew overhead. They even got one and used its feathers to make more arrows. They were able to collect most of the arrows they shot, but some landed in the loch and were lost.

On their sixth day at the castle, Emily found out all the Scots women knew how to shoot arrows.

Really well.

She and the actors were getting water from the loch when Ewan ran up. "Get back inside the castle." He was running full tilt, and there was terror in his face, which she figured must be for her sake, or else he would have been running to safety, not to warn her.

Emily didn't have to be told twice. She and the actors left the buckets lying there. As they ran, they saw cattle being herded the same direction, and they ran inside the courtyard alongside the cows.

"Up here." Mairi called from the stairway facing the road.

Armed with their bows and equipped with their quivers, the actors and Emily ran up the stairs after Mairi. She led them into the largest third-story room: the one above the front gate spanned that whole wall, with many tall narrow wind openings, facing the road. Most of these windows were already filled with women of the castle, all with bows and arrows. Emily saw that these tall narrow windows were perfect for shooting, giving the archer cover from incoming arrows while letting her arrows through.

Dog took one of the windows and directed his men to fill the rest of the open ones.

Emily asked Mairi, "Should the rest of us go around to the back of the castle, to fend off the siege from there?"

"Och, nay. This wull na be a siege, Emily. 'Twill be a slaughter." Mairi still was matter-of-fact.

Emily didn't have long to worry about that matter-of-fact tone. Almost immediately, the castle women started shooting their arrows.

Emily wasn't at a window, so she yelled, "What are they shooting at?"

From the bottom of Dog's window, Mike answered her. "A bunch of other highlanders who are chasing the MacGregors and the Campbells."

Eerily, all the castle women started made that familiar hooting noise.

Emily could hear it from other front-facing windows, too, all up and down this wall of the castle. She also heard men groaning as the arrows hit them. Dog and the other actors in windows had started to shoot, too.

And then men's voices joined in with the women's, making the Scots cheer even more eerie.

"What's going on?" Emily cried out.

Mike said, "Dall and them turned around to face the ones chasing them, who are being shot as they run now."

Emily couldn't stand not knowing what was happening. She copied Mike and crouched down to peek out the bottom of Mairi's window.

Mairi was right. It was a slaughter.

THAT NIGHT WAS quiet and somber, with the dead being prepared for shipment to their clan burial grounds and the wounded being moved inside the castle and set up for tending until they either died or were well enough to go home.

Emily's sense of responsibility and leadership bade her help. She stopped wounds from bleeding with pressure or a tourniquet, washed wounds with alcohol, and applied her antibiotic ointment. Seeing just two of the castle women stitching wounds, she dug in her pouch for the needles and freely offered one to every woman there, explaining she herself was terrible with needles, but she had a supply back home.

Explaining she had heard a rumor this prevents the fever, she showed the women a trick she had learned of singeing the needle in the flame of a torch before stitching. Hearing it this way, as a superstition rather than a charm, they were receptive. She was glad.

After the men's wounds were stitched, she bandaged them up and made the men as comfortable as she could. She prepared makeshift cots with the cleanest linens available. She washed linens and bandages. It was all that she—or apparently anyone here—knew how to do. She was at this all night and into the morning, and then she slept all the next day and night.

Not normally a praying person though nominally a Christian, Emily thanked God that Dall had not been hurt. She felt guilty for being relieved about this, because Mairi's husband had suffered a sword wound, and so had Hendry.

But the castle men were all in high spirits at having won the fight, especially after Colin and the other Campbells left on Emily's ninth morning at the castle. They were 'in their cups' before they started eating the noon meal.

Alasdair wasn't among the drunk, and when Emily came downstairs, he approached her. "So Emily, how is the play coming along?"

"Oh. Well, I thought we would forget about the play, now that we have all these wounded to take care of."

"Nonsense, lass. The men need tae celebrate that they still live. There canna be any better time for a play. 'Twill be on in five days' time. I hae already sent oot for the audience, and they are coming." He escorted Emily to her seat beside Dall and left her there with a smile.

Dall tried to be matter-of-fact, but his eyes were smiling at her. "Wull ye hae a run through the stage directions with me?"

Dog butted in, a bit drunkenly. "She has been running us through the stage directions without you for the past week, and doing a mighty fine job."

Dall looked pleased that the actors supported their teacher. "Mayhap she can show me a move or two. Eat up, everyone, and let us get oot there."

Emily looked around the table, and sure enough, the actors were eating up in a hurry so they could get out there and see the show Dall had promised.

"Thank you," she said for Dall's ears only. "A few minutes ago, we all thought the play had been cancelled. Now you have raised their spirits for it again."

For everyone's ears, Dall said, "Lass, ye should dae less talking and more eating, if ye want the strength tae run all the fight scenes with me oot there."

Emily smiled at Dall and kept quiet for the next few minutes, stuffing her face full of food and chewing as fast as she could.

He offered advice on her eating. "Ye hae a bit on yer upper lip there, lass. Nay, on t' ither side. Aye, ye got it."

Once all the actors were done eating and had been herded out into the courtyard, Emily and Mike ran them through the whole play for the fiftieth time. The actors knew most of their lines and their movements—except for the fight scenes, which were the showpieces of the play.

Dall was right. While Emily had them moving through the fights safely, the men needed a refresher on how the fights were meant to look.

As usual, they had brought down the barrel of one-handed practice swords. Emily chose one and moved into Benvolio's position for the first fight.

"Now, lass, I wull gae a bit slowly with ye." Dall raised his sword to block her attack.

They were off into the choreographed fight, and they did it just the way Dall and Hendry had the week before, full speed ahead. Their swords made satisfying clacking noises whenever they hit, and they both made the convincing grunting noises of exertion while they tramped all over the courtyard.

Whenever Dall and Emily had one of those moments where their swords were caught in each other and their eyes met, she tried to stare into him the fact that they had been in these positions before when he sparred with her in front of the audience at the faire.

He met her stares face on and didn't look away, and while a certain understanding was developing between them, it was developing again and not anew, for no hint of memory came into his glance. And in this time period, speaking about it before she was sure of it was terrifying.

Clap clap clap.

They turned to see Alasdair standing there in the court-yard, applauding them.

Dall took Emily's hand and turned her toward Alasdair, and they both smiled and bowed. Dall hadn't let her hand go. His hand was telegraphing warmth and security and ... affection up through hers, right into her heart. Or was that just her imagination?

❧

FOR THE NEXT FOUR DAYS, they ran the play four times a day. Dall was there every moment, which made it a little difficult for Emily to concentrate, but it also made her happy. He wanted to spend his time with her. She had less and less to do, because the actors were almost ready to perform without her feeding them their lines.

Two weeks was the shortest rehearsal period she had ever heard of for any show, but presumably, a traveling acting troupe would already have a show ready. And then, Alasdair had seen the spark between her and Dall and for some reason had wanted to fan it.

And their spark had been fanned.

Dall took every opportunity to hold Emily's hand: helping her up the one step into the dining hall, catching her attention at the table, and swinging her around to bow after each time they demonstrated a fight scene. Emily didn't think the actors needed the sword-fighting demonstrations anymore, but they sure were ... stimulating.

And here they were, the day before the performance. Emily and Dall and the actors were in the courtyard doing as many dress rehearsals as they could fit into the day. Audience members were arriving from every direction—all of them Campbells or MacGregors. Most of the injured had either died or gone home, but the few who remained had been moved to cots in the kitchen to make rooms available for the multitude of guests.

Every time someone arrived, Dall's face got eager and he looked toward the front gate ... only to look disappointed and turn back to the actors on the stage.

Finally, when this happened in the middle of a fight scene and it was obvious that Dall wasn't even paying attention, Alasdair stepped in.

"They canna be here, Dall."

Dall's face got angry for a moment as he faced his chief, and then he calmed it. "Why did ye na tell me sooner? Is something amiss?"

"Nothing is amiss. Some hae tae remain behind tae hold the lands, and someone must lead them. He is the best I hae up there."

By now, the two of them were clasping forearms, and Alasdair was looking straight into Dall's eyes without flinching.

Dall spoke so softly that Emily knew she wasn't meant to hear it.

"Then I wish tae take her tae them."

Alasdair nodded once.

IT SEEMED funny to Emily that everyone watched the dress rehearsals and then stayed for the show right afterward, but it was nice. It gave the play a casual feeling that soothed the actors' stage fright, as did the absence of a curtain.

The only real challenges now were the costume changes, especially for Mike. They had streamlined Mike's costumes. He stayed in the same dress—borrowed from Mairi's mother—and just moved parts of it around in order to change into each character. For the nurse, he held out the stomach and was corpulent. For Juliet, he held out the bosom and was endowed, and for Juliet's mother, he held the neckline up to his chin and was proper. Mike was hilarious, and he stole every scene he was in.

That was OK, because as Romeo, Dog was all about the fight scenes. Emily thought they rocked. She was proud of her pupils.

It was a good thing she no longer needed to feed the

actors their lines, because Dall sat close beside her in the first balcony—and he grabbed her hand and squeezed it every time the actors did a complicated move with their swords clashing, which was often. But that wasn't the most distracting thing her kilted highlander did. Emily was sure that Dall couldn't access his memories of them whispering to one another on the dance stage at the renaissance faire, but he did the same thing here anyway.

Here they were once again on display. Everyone was seated on dining-hall benches that the actors had carried up onto the balconies. All the audience members could see each other's faces.

Dall took advantage of the attention everyone was paying to the actors down in the courtyard and whispered in Emily's ear during all the most exciting parts of the play. What he whispered got better and better.

"Sae, lass, I dinna suppose ye find my company too disagreeable?"

"Not too terribly disagreeable, no." She smiled at his jest, and she shivered at the feeling of his breath in her ear.

"How dae ye like Scotland?"

"I love what little I've seen of your faire land so far." She lifted her head to visibly gaze up at the snow-peaked mountains she could see over the castle wall.

He took a deep breath. "I ken ye hae tae gae back tae *England*," he said it that funny way again, letting her know he suspected she was from elsewhere, "but dae ye hae tae stay there? What I mean is, would ye like tae come back here, some time?"

She looked deep in his eyes, trying to make him understand. "If I could be part of a great clan and be connected to the right people, then yes, I would like to come back here. I would also like for you to journey with me, to *England*."

He let out his breath and seemed to relax a bit, which

brought their thighs close together on the bench for the first time since she had pushed the button that brought her here.

It would be so easy for her to relax just that little bit so that they were touching ... but that would send him the wrong message. She wasn't prepared to stay here this time, and Siobhan's warning had been crystal clear.

Dall took another deep breath and said a bunch of words all in a rush, not giving her any chance to answer until he had said them all. "Wull ye come on a journey with me, tae meet my family? It will na be a long journey, ainly four and ten days. I thought they would be here for the play, but they canna be. 'Twould be a great opportunity for ye tae see more o' the Highlands, which I ken was the reason ye came up here from *England*."

Unwilling to let him suffer one more second of uncertainty, Emily simply said, "Yes." and waited for Dall to show relief and to smile.

He still looked uncertain.

So she went on. "Yes. I will journey with you. I want to meet your family."

The sword-fight that had covered their whispered conversation ended, so they had to wait for the next one before they could whisper about the details of their journey: when they would leave and where they would go, what provisions they would take, whether they would walk or ride...

In the meantime, Dall's hand found its way into Emily's, and there it remained throughout the rest of Romeo and Juliet.

Emily's joy in his touch was punctuated every now and then by his glance of affection and admiration. She was ecstatic that he wanted her to meet his family. That could only mean he was as serious about her as she was about him, right? But mostly, she just kept thinking that finally she would be alone with the man who meant everything to her.

D all sat on horseback in front of the castle, extending his hand to her. The horse was laden with odd saddlebags, and Dall's claymore was sheathed in the horse's odd saddle, which didn't have any stirrups to help her climb up.

"Come on up, lass."

Squinting the rising sun out of her eyes, Emily grabbed his hand and prepared to hoist herself up.

He pulled her up far enough that she could swing her leg around and climb on.

This was not easy while wearing a tight bodice, two long full skirts, and a cloak, not to mention the extra shirt she had tied around her waist by the sleeves under the two skirts. She was in Heaven, though.

When Emily wrapped her arms around Dall and held herself close to his back, the world disappeared for a moment. She was only aware of hugging him. His warmth. The way he smelled of the outdoors and campfires and lavender soap. The way his muscles were so firm beneath all the yards of plaid wool. How solid and comforting he felt in front of her.

Being so close to Dall made her giddy, as if her body was as light as the clouds floating over Kilchurn Castle.

And then Eamann called out to Emily and ruined the mood, his stern face bright in the direct sunlight. "Remember what I telt ye." He had tried to prevent her from going on this trip, but Alasdair had overruled him. The castle's old healer looked fearful now. Emily could see his mind worrying about what she would tell Dall if she was alone with him. If she dared.

Dall spoke softly over his shoulder while staring at the white-robed druid. "What did the man tell ye, lass?"

"He claims we must be back by mid-July, or something terrible will happen," she said, careful to stay as close to the truth as she dared.

There were many people around who would think she was a witch if they heard talk of time travel, so she couldn't tell him any more than that—not with all of them so close by all the time.

Dall patted her knee, sending fresh shivers down her spine.

Would it really be so terrible, to be stuck here with him?

Dall was talking. "Dinna fash. I wull hae ye back afore ye must leave on the journey back to *England*. I ken ye dinna wish tae abide oor Scottish winter." He laughed, but it was forced.

Before she considered the possible consequences of making such a declaration before leaving on a long journey alone with him, Emily whispered in Dall's ear, "Winter couldn't keep me away from you."

From what she had seen so far, she believed that if she made it back to Kilchurn Castle with Dall by July 19, 1540, then the two of them would return to the US in her time the moment they had left it. Vange and Ian would come back to the trailer with their dirty Tupperware from breakfast to find

Dall and Emily still there after their 'private talk' with Siobhan, and they would all walk to Simon's boot booth together
and enjoy the last weekend of the renaissance faire.

Dall called out in Gaelic to the small crowd outside the
castle. At the same time, he kicked the horse's sides and it
took off running down a pathway to the east, the only direction that wouldn't take them into the fresh waters of
Loch Awe.

Ahead, all Emily saw was the forest and the rising mid-
June sun peeking out between the snow-peaked mountains
and the cloudy sky.

She felt the rhythm of the horse's hooves pounding the
ground and the haphazard sway of the horse as it moved. She
felt the cool highland wind whipping at her cloak and skirts
and tugging at her muffin cap. She drew the hood of her cloak
up over her cap, but she only barely felt those things.

The vast majority of Emily's awareness was taken in by
the feel of the man in front of her, or more exactly, by the
way he made her feel. He felt solid and safe and so, so alive—
bursting with life. He made her feel the same, especially when
she held him close. Finally doing so again after a month of
missing it felt like coming home.

Dall kept running the horse until they had turned left to
cross the sandy shallows of a river, turned left again, and run a
ways more. Emily clung to his back, not minding the ride at
all. In fact, she loved it.

DALL URGED the horse through the woods along the curve of
the mountain on their right. Down at the waters of a smaller
river that came out between this mountain and the next one
to the north, Dall slowed the horse to a stop.

The horse drank.

For the first time ever, after wishing for it for two months, Emily was alone with Dall.

Once he could be heard over the horse's breaths, Dall spoke. "Sae we need tae be back tae the castle by the 19th o' July sae that we can travel tae yer time, eh lass?" He looked over his shoulder at her, and his look was knowing and open ... and amused.

"Dall. Oh Dall, you're here." Emily squeezed him as tight as she could. "Why have you pretended all this time not to know me? It's been so hard. I was so lonely without holding you close like this."

He turned at the waist in the odd saddle and put his hand on her shoulder, then gently tapped her there.

Finally, Emily quit squeezing him and looked up into Dall's eyes.

They were sincere. "Lass, I hae ainly pretended na tae ken from whence ye come. If we did ken one anither afore ye came tae Kilchurn, then I hae na memory o' it, sorry I am tae say." He put a sympathetic hand back on her shoulder.

Emily wiped a tear on her sleeve and nodded that she understood him. She couldn't speak. Her throat was closing, she was so upset. She'd thought she had him back for one brief moment, but she only had him anew.

Having him anew was wonderful all on its own, her common sense told her.

For once, she listened to it. She clung to Dall while she breathed deeply and waited for her choked-up throat to quit aching so she could talk to him some more, tell him what she knew. And that reminded her to check and make sure her phone was switched off.

Seeming to understand Emily's difficulty, Dall started the horse walking through the woods again, this time to the right, north-east once more along this new smaller river.

Emily appreciated the one-sided small talk he made as the horse walked.

"The River Strae wull take us tae my family in the Rannoch. 'Twill take the horse three days, God willing. If the weather does stay dry and we hae na trouble, then we should na hae tae sleep in the heather. The clan has settlements along the way."

Gradually, her throat relaxed enough that she could speak again. "Dall, you came with me when I arrived here in your time four weeks ago. You were there in my time for at least six weeks, and very likely two months. You were teaching your accent and your fighting style and your ways to historical re-enactors of my time, at the renaissance faire."

Sounding almost like the horse when it puffed, Dall blew air out between his lips while patting her knee sympathetically and keeping his eyes on the terrain ahead.

"Pfft. Eamann has been preparing me a year now, tae dae just that, sae I dinna doubt ye. If I had the deciding o' it, I would remember every last second with ye, lass. O' that, ye can hae certainty."

At his sweet declaration, joy swelled in Emily's heart, bigger joy than the disappointment she'd been crying over just moments before. She hugged him with gladness and affection this time, instead of desperation and despair.

And then puzzlement wove its way into Emily's mind, sneaking past the cozy warm fog of just being snuggled up close behind Dall on a horse walking through the highlands.

"Are you doing this for Eamann? I don't trust him." She hadn't even realized this until she said it.

"Nay, and neither dae I trust Eamann, but the druids made a pact with one o' my fore-sires, long ago. Every fourth son must serve them, if he lives tae be five and twenty, and I am my da's fourth son."

Emily couldn't see his face, but his voice got sad as he said this, like he was sure she would reject him then.

She rubbed his shoulders, trying to let him know she was not so easily put off from him. But while she was doing that, curiosity made her ask him a bunch of questions all at once.

"Wow. How long have you known about this, and how did you find out, and what kind of service do you have to do for the druids?"

Dall laughed, a deep heart-felt laugh from the bottom of his lungs.

Emily was glad to hear him laugh, guessing it meant he was done being afraid she wouldn't want to be with him now that she knew he had to serve the druids. They were out of the woods and in a grassy area now, and he urged the horse into a trot. The sun was fully up now but invisible behind thick clouds.

He answered her questions. "Da telt me o' the curse just afore Iona and I marrit. Traveling through time tae dae the druids' bidding is the ainly service asked o' me thus far."

He turned to look at her then. A deep look that searched her soul and yearned for her. If this was his idea of happenstance, then she was all for it.

But he looked serious again. "Aboot why they brought ye here tae my time, lass, the druids. My best guess is it's in order tae hasten me back tae the castle. Ye can dae that better than anyone, ye ken, hasten me."

Emily enjoyed his rapt attention for a moment, and then her curiosity made her keep questioning him.

"Does everyone here know about time travel, then?"

"Nay, and we must na tell them. Ainly my two remaining brothers and their wives and my mother ken. My brothers and I will tell oor children just afore they marry, as oor parents and their parents did. Let us bide here awhile."

He trotted the horse over to the river, stopped,

dismounted, and handed her down. After putting one foot through the reins to secure the horse, he let it go drink and graze.

Neither of them said anything until he got them back on the horse and moving north-east again, along the River Strae through a meadow.

She broke the silence. "So you think they sent me here to make sure you got back to my time on schedule, eh?"

Facing forward to steer the horse, he tapped her knee again. "I canna think o' any other reason, though I am verra glad they did."

He ran the horse awhile then, and Emily was grateful for the excuse to cling to him. The wind whipped their clothes, and the green rocky scenery sped by.

The sun shone out through the clouds when they stopped at the crest of a hill, and Emily saw a vibrant green valley full of cattle, dotted with stone houses and small vegetable gardens.

"This is Glen Strae, lass. My homeland."

As if on cue, the horse took a dump, and they both laughed.

AS THEY RODE BY, ranchers came out to greet them—men in kilts, women in long plaid skirts, and older children dressed much the same as the adults. Dall responded to their greetings. They spoke Gaelic, but from visual cues and the tones of the conversations, Emily imagined she knew what they were saying.

"Hello, Dall. Who is that English woman?"

"Hello. She is Emily, someone I want my family to meet."

"Oho. Emily is a very lucky lady, then. Where did you meet her?"

"At Kilchurn Castle."

"So when will you be wedding?"

"I have not yet asked the lass, but soon, I hope."

"Ha ha. I bet you want it soon. Good journey."

After the first of these exchanges, Dall said to Emily, "Sorry, lass, but we canna stop lang enough for me tae tell them tae speak English for ye."

Holding back her laugh, Emily told him, "No worries. I understand."

The older people who came out to greet Dall asked different questions, and his answers were more somber.

"Hail, Dall, what news?"

"Kester and Lachie passed on last night."

"Oh, so sad. When we heard they were only wounded, we dared hope."

"Aye, but that be the lot of the warrior."

"Aye, that be the way of it. Good journey home."

After a few hours of greeting rancher MacGregors, Dall and Emily and the horse were out of the glen and on their own again. They all took a long drink, and then Dall had them both get off the horse, talking in a manner that made Emily think they had gone out of their way to visit Glen Strae.

"We, ah, wull need tae climb ower the foothills now tae Glen Orchy, where the going wull be easier."

In a familiar gesture, he put his forearm out for Emily to steady herself on as she climbed. He led the horse by a long rein in his other hand, allowing the creature to make its own way up.

Gladly, Emily held his arm, reveling in the tingles his touch gave her even as her vague familiarity with the area from studying Google Maps before she left home allowed her to tease him.

"Shouldn't we have taken Glen Orchy from the beginning?" She gave him a sly grin.

He raised his chin at her in play. "Aye, but I want as many MacGregors as I can possibly manage tae ken yer face and yer name."

Emily felt her face glowing from his declaration. "I'm glad we have this climb. It will give us privacy for a while, and I have so much to tell you."

"Verra good, lass. I dared tae hope ye would."

The climb wasn't too difficult. They followed one creek up to the crest of the foothills and then another creek down into a much larger and much greener valley. Still, it took hours.

Smiling most of the time and hugging him sometimes, Emily told Dall *everything* as they climbed.

She started with how they had met and he had escorted her all over the faire on his arm, much as he was in that moment. How they had become close over those four weekends: dancing staged sets, practicing with swords and daggers, him getting her and Vange jobs at Simon's boot booth ... She proudly showed him her boots then, fashioned like his, and how one held the dagger Dall had convinced Ian to give her. And she demonstrated the dagger techniques Dall had taught her. She told him of the parties in Siobhan's trailer, where the two of them had sat cuddled together for hours.

Her face turned red then.

Dall had stopped climbing to take both of her hands in his, and his face was desperate with longing and loss. "What is it, lass? Hae we children togither?"

"No. No, we haven't ... but Dall, I'm used to kissing you each time we part and each time we meet again. I miss that so much. Can you imagine what it's like to have had that, and now for you to barely know who I am all over again?"

And then he was kissing her for the first time in his

current memory. An insistent hello kiss, long and wet, with an embrace to go with it. Warm enough to silence the cold highland wind as it blew furiously over the rocky crest of the foothills under the grey clouds.

The horse stomped.

Dall was still embracing her. "I would dae this with ye all day, lass, but up here near the crags, we feel the cauld, and we are expecting tae eat with folk along the way ... and I want ye tae meet my family, sae we hae a journey ahead o' us yet."

The horse stomped again as if in agreement, and they both laughed.

Dall caressed her face. "And 'tis na right, that we dae this too lang afore we wed. I wull dae right by ye, lass. I ken 'tis early yet, but I hope ye wull think on wedding me."

At first, Emily smiled big and squeezed Dall tight.

He squeezed her back, picked her up, and swung her around.

After he set her down and their eyes were smiling at each other, her lips started to say that of course she would marry him—today, if he was ready.

But then she remembered.

Her smile dissolved into a worried grimace.

He started to let her go, hurt showing on his face.

She grabbed him and held him close, and then let him loose enough that she could show him the sincerity in her eyes and reassure him that she wished things were otherwise.

"Dall, the druids put a curse on me, too."

She took out her phone to show him Siobhan's text warning, but when she switched her phone on, she gasped.

"WHAT IS WRONG, LASS?"

"Nothing's wrong. Things are inexplicably right. My phone is fully charged."

Emily held her phone out in front of Dall, pointing at the charge indicator.

But of course he had never seen anything electronic and was understandably fascinated. He sat down on a nearby rock and held out his hands the way one would to be passed a baby. "May I look closer, lass?"

Reminded just how fragile and irreplaceable it was in this time, Emily sat down next to Dall and passed her phone to him just as carefully. "It was only halfway charged when we left the castle this morning. And now, see? The charge indicator is full." She pointed again.

They sat there, intent on her phone, for quite some time, letting the horse graze. Every once in a while, they drank from her bota bag and each of them ate one of her candies.

While she showed him how the phone worked, she explained electricity, satellites, computers, the Internet, ebooks, text messages, and finally apps, leading to the story of how Siobhan had put the Time Management app on this phone, how that app had brought the two of them here to his time and country, and how she dared not fiddle with the settings because she wanted to go home on July 19 and arrive the very moment they had left.

"Now lass, what caused ye such alarm?"

"I forgot to wear this brooch to charge the phone. It was going dead." She set it up.

"Come, lass. The candy was good, and I thank ye, but we wull be wanting a hot meal. We can ride. The way doon this side is easy."

He was already standing up, and after getting on the horse, he held out his hand for her.

Sliding up close to Dall let loose the warm waves of thrills in her body again, and that made her remember why she had taken her phone out to begin with.

They had been riding a few minutes before she got up the courage to tell him. "Dall."

"Aye?"

"The Campbells are only using you MacGregors for your fighting prowess. In six years, when you have taken for the Campbells all the land they want, they will start to betray you. Over the next fifty years, they will intermarry with your chief line. Then they will behead your chief and his sons, taking all your lands and cattle for their own."

"I dinna doubt ye, Drusilla." He squeezed her knee, and she knew he was teasing her with that name. "Howsoever, here we come intae Campbell lands, ye ken?" He nodded toward the huge green valley that now opened up below them. The part she could see was ten times the size of Glen Strae and just as full of cattle, and the mountains cut off her view to the north and south. It was dotted with stone houses, as well. A much larger river ran through.

Not getting his point, Emily pressed hers. "Dall, we need to tell Alasdair. We should turn around now and go back to Kilchurn Castle and tell him all I know so that he can avoid the Campbells' betrayal."

Dall stopped the horse and turned in the odd saddle to look Emily in the eye. "Och nay, Drusilla. My clan derives its power from oor honor. We gave oor oath tae the Campbells. I hae faith that if ye read on further in yer history book, ye wull find that oor honor reclaims the MacGregor name."

Touched by Dall's deep sense of honor, Emily nodded, thinking she was going to have to look up Drusilla while she was at it.

He gently caressed her cheek with the hand not holding the reins, bringing her face up again to meet his eyes. "We are entering now into Glen Orchy, Campbell lands, and ye dinna want a one o' them tae hear talk o' betrayal, aye?"

"Aye."

A new admiration for Dall grew in her that moment. She admired his leadership. As a leader herself, she recognized it.

Riding through Glen Orchy was similar to riding through Glen Strae. The Campbells spoke Gaelic too, of course, as they ran out to greet the travelers. Riding through Campbell lands was different, though. Just as Emily had feared, Dall was not an insider here. Even though many MacGregors and Campbells were related through intermarriage, the MacGregor plaid was mostly red and the Campbell plaid mostly blue. Each person had to pick a side.

The Campbells treated Dall more as an ally than like family. As before, from their tone and actions and mention of names—along with her knowledge of what he'd been up to the past two weeks—Emily thought she knew what they were saying.

"What news, MacGregor?"

"Colin the Grey (Cailean Liath) was at Kilchurn Castle for a week. He came by boat and left by boat a few days ago."

"Did he look well?"

"Aye, he looked well, and he passed the time pleasantly, even though some Menzies followed us back there. They were fought off. No Campbells died."

"How goes the effort at the Menzies border?"

"The border holds, and we have pushed it away a wee bit."

At long last, one of the more hospitable Campbells invited Dall and Emily in for some soup and ale.

Dall grabbed his claymore from the saddle and sheathed it on his back before they went inside one of the hundreds of two-story stone houses dotting Glen Orchy.

In gratitude, Emily gave the family one of the empty wax

paper wrappers from the candies she and Dall had eaten
earlier.

Aghast at such a lavish gift, the family pressed on them to
accept a small keg, a bag of apples, and a pouch of jerky for
the road. Eyeing the horse, they added a bag of oats.

After tying these provisions to the odd saddle, Dall
climbed on and handed Emily up.

THEY RODE on through Glen Orchy at a walk for the rest of
the day, snacking on their provisions as needed, though
taking it easy on the beer. With Dall busy answering ranchers'
questions and giving them the news, Emily didn't get much
chance to speak with him. She took the opportunity to
appear as if staring at her reflection in the back of her
brooch, which she held tightly in her right hand and rested
against Dall's back while she clamped herself firmly to him
with her left hand.

She looked up Drusilla: first in the dictionary, and then in
the general history book she had downloaded. She ended up
learning all about the Roman rulers. She smiled at the
thought that Dall found her beautiful, but worried whether
he meant she would be inconstant.

They didn't exit inhabited Campbell lands until after the
sun went down, and then they got off the horse and walked
on farther over hill and dale by the moonlight.

Dall spoke softly. "I am verra sorry tae hae ye oot walking
in the dangerous night air, lass. I had na planned on stopping
sae lang and learning sae much from yer stories aboot
England."

Daring to hope they would indeed sleep alone out in the
heather that night, Emily slapped his shoulder with the back
of her hand. "You have much more to learn, Germanicus."

Smiling yet still walking, he turned his head to sparkle his eyes at her. "Oho. Sae I am loved by the people, am I?"

Emily held Dall's gaze and locked her eyes on his. "At least by one of the people."

Still walking and leading the horse, he took her hand and led her, too. "Lass, ye should na say such things tae a man who is na yer husband. The man might get ideas, and ye deserve tae be wedded afore he gets those ideas." He looked at her then with that hope in his eyes.

She let her own hope shine through, but she kept her face reserved. At least she tried to. It was difficult to hold back from him.

He turned to watch where he was going again. "And we need tae decide first what tae dae aboot the curse the druids put on ye. We shall arrive in aboot an hour's time at a MacGregor place, and there ye wull spend the night in assured safety."

For a few minutes, Emily relaxed, forgot about everything else, and just let his talk of marriage and his firm hand on hers stir up her emotions. And then, as they walked, she took off her brooch again, opened the book on Scottish history, and read the entire part about the MacGregors aloud to him.

"Ye see, lass?" he said proudly. "Oor honor wull redeem the MacGregor name."

"But it will take two hundred years."

"Well enough." He held his head up high and walked with that confounding confidence that both attracted her and provoked her.

They walked on in silence awhile, and then Emily's curiosity got the better of her again. "Dall?"

"Aye?"

"Why do you call me Drusilla? Do you think I would be so unfaithful?"

"Och, nay, lass. I am ainly impressed with how ye involve

yerself in politics, far more than most lasses, and the name
Drusilla sounds sae serious. It does suit ye. And she was beautiful, aye?"

Though his steady hand kept her walking, Emily was
stunned. She involved herself in politics? And then she realized that telling Alasdair about Colin's planned betrayal
would be politicking. She hadn't thought of politics that way
before: as simply telling a leader what was going on so that
they could be prepared. It left her thoughtful for quite
a while.

Dall snapped her out of it. "Here we are, lass, a place tae
lay oor heads for the night."

These remote MacGregors took their like-kilted kin and
his companion into their tiny cabin without asking questions.
Emily wasn't used to walking so much. She was asleep as soon
as her head hit their goose-down pillow. She awoke to the
wonderful scents of stew warming and fresh bread baking. Dall
spoke in Gaelic with their hosts over the morning meal, and
then they were getting on the rested horse and off on their way.

The horse walked them northeast through the highlands
while the two of them cuddled together on its back and
charged the phone. They alternated riding up the hills and
walking down, to give the horse a rest.

Much of the time, Emily read to Dall from the future
history of England and Scotland, but he didn't allow her to
ignore the scenery. And splendid it was, especially whenever
they came into a new valley with a loch at the bottom. The
June sky was blue with big puffy clouds, the hills were green,
and the water was clear and clean.

The second night of their trip, they slept in the humble
outpost home of an Orson MacGregor and his family.

"Emily, this is my cousin Orson. He kens tae much aboot
me, sae I will na hae ye speak alone with him."

They all laughed.

With a smile, Orson beckoned them inside, where his wife was already putting the supper on the table. "We will na need tae speak alone for me tae tell yer lass aboot the time ye let all o' Dand's coneys out o' the pen. Heh heh. Yer behind was sore a fortnight."

Emily couldn't believe her ears, and her face must have shown it.

Orson socked Dall's shoulder. "Aye, yer bonnie lad, king o' correctness, was a might intae the mischief in his youth. I wull wager ye ne'er guessed."

The two of them went on to tell story after story, through dinner and well into the night.

Emily was once again asleep as soon as her head hit the pillow, and she dreamed of a bonnie young lad who sneaked extra pie when his mother wasn't looking, tied all his cows together so they couldn't wander far while he fished, and slid down the icy hill on his father's new saddle without permission.

They arose early the next morning, to get a jump on their journey. Before they left, Emily gave Orson's wife one of her sheets of wax paper and showed her how to use it to keep food fresh.

And then Dall was climbing up onto the horse in his kilt, and Emily was watching him, fascinated as usual by his strong and graceful movements. He handed her up behind him, and then they waved goodbye to Dall's cousin, calling out that they would be back this way in a week.

Emily was reading to Dall from her Western Civilization textbook about Mary Queen of Scots and Queen Elizabeth I when the Time Management app opened itself. The countdown now said 30 days until July 19, and the display had changed color from blue to purple. There was also a map showing her current location with a line stretching out to Kilchurn Castle. Her first thought was how handy. But...

"Dall. This map must be magic, because the Global Positioning Satellites won't be launched until the 1970s." Carefully, she showed him.

He didn't look surprised. "We wull ken the druids possess magic, aye?"

"But if the app knows where we are, then so do the druids." She turned her phone off and put it in her boot, trying to get some privacy. Yet she still whispered in his ear, just in case. "They might even be able to hear what we're saying."

So that started their whispered conversations. His breath in her ear stirred her, and the sound of his voice so close made her head swim.

"Wed with me. I want ye for my own, lass. I canna bear the thought o' another man with ye." As if to illustrate his point, his hand grabbed her thigh and held on as if their lives depended on it.

She gasped. His hold thrilled her and weakened her resolve not to 'join' with him until she had brought him back to her time. Before she got stuck in 1540 and just never came home again, Emily wanted to introduce Dall to her parents and make them know she was happy, but that she wouldn't be able to stay in touch because they would be ... living someplace far away from any cell towers. Yeah. That was the truth, too, as much of it as she could tell them.

Immediately, Dall let go of her thigh and reached up to gently pull her ear to his mouth again. "I beg ye, forgive me, Emily. I lost control o' myself a moment. Till ye tell me ye are ready tae be stuck in one time and wed with me, I wull restrain myself. Dae ye forgive me?"

She hugged his back tight and whispered in his ear, "Dall, I cannot bear the thought of you with another woman, either.

I promise that one day, I will be ready to join with you—and remain in one time. I forgive your loss of control. Do you promise to be mine only and to wait for me to be ready?"

He stopped the horse and turned in the saddle to embrace her. "I dae."

They kissed quite a bit before he got the horse moving again.

❧

EMILY COULD TELL they were nearing a settlement. Cattle dotted the green hillsides beneath the cloudy highland sky. She took a deep breath and let it out slowly when Dall told her the settlement they were nearing was his family's. He dismounted and helped her down, then kept her hand in his. She found his gentle hand squeeze reassuring. They walked on together hand in hand, and around the next bend, there it was.

The settlement reminded Emily of the model of a feudal town she and her classmates had made with shoeboxes in social studies class in sixth grade. Dall's family had built themselves a large grand house at the craggy top of a green rise on the mountainside. Sprawled out on the hill below it were two dozen more houses. These were cabins, really. All the structures were built of a much lighter color of wood than Emily was used to, and they looked almost like more crags in the green rise. The effect was quite pretty.

"Da!"

"Da!"

A boy and girl about six and four ran down the hill and put their arms around Dall's waist.

Dall met Emily's eyes and smiled.

She smiled back at him.

And then he dropped her hand, scooped an arm around

each of his children, and swung them around as if they were on a carnival ride. They screamed, but in delight, not in fear. When he was quite spin dizzy, he pretended to fall down with them, and when they landed on the soft green grass, he tickled them until they were so giggly, Emily started giggling, too.

"Och," Dall said to his kids, "I did miss ye. Here, meet my friend Emily." He turned them around to face her. "Emily, this strong young man is Peadar, and this lovely young lass is Peigi."

Keeping one arm each around their Da's waist, the children scrunched up their little foreheads and studied Emily as if she were in a cage at the zoo. The boy looked just like his dad, whereas the girl must have favored her mother. They looked healthy and happy. He wore trousers rather than a kilt —which Emily figured was best for playing. But the girl was dressed like a miniature highland woman in a plaid skirt and bodice with a shift underneath.

Emily knelt down so that she was face to face with the children and smiled. "Hello. Oh. I have treats for you." She was digging in one of her pouches for two pieces of hard candy when she realized what she had better add. "If it's all right with your father?"

While she looked to Dall for his permission, she let the reality of Dall being a father sink in. Sure, she had known before that he had kids. But having his flesh and blood right here, standing in front of her with red cheeks and curious eyes and loving devotion for their da? That was still a bit of a shock. All the people her age that she knew were college students, and none were parents. Well, worse still, their own parents still called them kids.

Dall smiled and nodded that it was OK for his kids to have candy. "Best unwrap it for them. And keep the dear wee bits o' waxed paper, lass."

When Emily handed the children the small bits of hard candy, they looked to their Da with puzzled expressions.

Saying a bunch of words that Emily didn't understand, Dall pretended to put one of the candies in his mouth and roll it around on his tongue.

When the small boy and girl copied him and put the candy in their mouths, their eyes lit up with great surprise. They smiled while they rolled the candy around in their mouths.

Dall smiled back at them and nodded. All the while they enjoyed the candy, their da spoke to them. It was in Gaelic, but Emily guessed what he was saying. "It is good, aye lass? Aye laddie? Resist the urge tae bite, and 'twill last a while. I did try it myself na sae lang syne. Emily gave some tae me, as wull. She's a nice lass. I hope ye wull be good friends with her."

As Dall talked, he beckoned Emily over to him and took her hand once more in his.

She took it gladly.

With his other arm, Dall held both Peadar and Peigi, and so the four of them stood as a family, watching an older Scots woman who could only be Dall's mother walk at a stately pace down the hill in her long plaid skirt, with a toddler on her hip.

Dall reached for the tiny boy when she got close, and the father spun this child around, too, though instead of pretending to fall, he tossed his youngest son in the air to make him giggle. And then, holding the toddler in one arm, he pulled Emily close with the other arm and beckoned the children and his mother close to him, so that they were all in a group hug.

As they walked up the hill that way to Dall's family's house, the lower neighbors came out to greet him.

"'Tis wull ye hae come haime, Dall."

"In all ways, 'tis good tae see ye hae made the journey once more."

Dall greeted each one in turn by name, so that it took a while to walk up the small hill.

Once they were up in the relative privacy of the hilltop, Dall's brothers and their wives came over to meet Emily. At first, they looked at her foreign clothing and eyed her with suspicion as Dall made introductions. Once they had all gathered round, though, Dall explained how Emily had saved Alasdair from choking on his breakfast.

Just like that, Emily was treated to knowing smiles about the way Dall was holding her, as well as teasing remarks about how they would sleep in separate beds until a priest could be rounded up to their tiny kirk.

Dall and Emily looked at each other sorrowfully for a moment at those remarks, but then Dall's mother invited them in for a hot meal, and they soon got lost in pleasant conversation.

And they spent the week that way.

Mostly, they played with Dall's children. Domhnall, his two-year-old son, was allowed to run loose on the bottom floor of the house, and of course he got into everything. Emily took her share of turns picking him up and untangling him from yarn or prying his hands off the dog's tail, and she grew fond of the little fellow.

But their visit was also about having Emily get to know Dall's mother and his brothers and their wives and all of Dall's nieces and nephews. The other people who lived in the settlement pretty much left Dall's family alone at the top of their hill.

Always the settlement kept a watch. Feeling uneasy about that, Emily asked the other women about it one night while they were washing up the dishes after supper, using two basins they had filled with water hauled up from the creek earlier that day.

"The watch is so on guard," Emily said casually, looking out the wind opening in the family's large kitchen. "Who do you expect to come attack?"

She turned to look at Dall's sisters-in-law for their answer, curious.

The two Scots women continued washing, rinsing, and drying dishes.

The taller one cast a stoic look at Emily. "Why, the Menzies Clan, lass," she said as if it was something Emily should have known.

Not any more enlightened than she had been before, Emily tried again. "But, why are the Menzies Clan your enemies?"

Still with stoic looks on their faces—not unfriendly, just serious and resigned to their lot in life—the two women put their dishes down and stopped to glare at Emily. The taller one put her hand on her hip, and the other cocked her head sideways, as if they thought Emily knew the answer and just needed to think about it.

"Sorry, I'm not from around here," Emily tried by way of explanation, gesturing at her English clothing. "I really don't know why the Menzies Clan and the MacGregor Clan are at war, and I really would like to understand." She looked them in the eye in what she hoped was a sincere and beseeching way.

The taller one nodded then, and picked up her towel once more to dry another cup and set it on the board that had been fastened to the wall. "This land used tae be Clan Menzies territory," she said to the dish boards as she dried another cup and put it away. "Ower the past ten years, we hae taken it for the Campbells."

"Oh." Emily held out her hands. "Can I help?"

The taller woman handed her the dishtowel.

Quietly helping them dry the rest of the dishes, Emily wished she could make all the highlanders see that the English were the enemy, that the highland clans needed to unite against the English and quit killing each other off. However, she knew that effort was doomed to only cause more heartbreak when it failed. And, they thought she was English. They intimidated her, these tough stoic women. She really didn't dare try and tell them what to do.

She held out hope that she and Dall could save these few people who were closest to him, and whose names weren't in the history books.

Most of the time, Emily could almost pretend she was on her uncle's farm back home. Aside from the watch and all the men in kilts and their Gaelic speech and the women's long skirts and the weapons mounted on the inside walls of the house, this was just country life. During daylight hours, everyone worked some. Emily gardened and canned with the women. They used pottery, much like the small medicine containers in her pouches. With the men, Dall herded cattle and went hunting.

In the evenings they had wonderful family dinners, and afterward, they sang—much like in Siobhan's trailer at the faire.

Dall's children took to Emily. Once they got over her being a stranger, they invited her to play with them and their cousins. The boys pretended to be cattle raiders, mostly, imitating what they heard the grown-ups discussing. But when they would deign to play in a big group along with the girls, Emily learned their versions of tag, and hide and seek, and king of the hill, and capture the flag. The girls cheerfully let Emily teach them jump-rope and hopscotch. She grinned while they copied her favorite jump-rope chant and wondered if they would bring it forward in time so that she could learn 'Miss Mary Mack' five hundred years from then.

It was a lovely week that Emily planned to treasure for the rest of her life.

But she was aware that in the background, Dall and his oldest brother talked politics, and that it was mostly about the brother being Alasdair's right-hand man in this region. Emily was starting to realize that meant Dall's family couldn't just pick up and leave because his new woman said the sky was going to fall in seven to twenty-nine years. Not even if they believed her.

EMILY LOVED DALL'S FAMILY, and she could tell they were growing to love her. But she and Dall had to leave them soon, not knowing when they would be back, or if.

First shoving Emily's phone into one of her boots so that anyone listening through it—with the power turned off— hopefully wouldn't hear, Dall and Emily took frequent walks. As they walked together, Dall showed her the majesty of the highlands: craggy hillsides, deep green valleys, and panoramic views from the tops of the crags.

But whenever the two of them left on one of these walks with an arm around each other, they were teased.

"Dinna catch yer deaths o' cold, oot there bare in the wind."

"'Tis warm in the kirk, I hear."

"Aye, best spend a bit o' time in there first."

The two of them stayed within sight of the watch on their walks, but they strayed far out of hearing range. Sooner or later, their conversations always sounded something like this:

Emily would suggest, "Let's take them all with us, back to

my time. They can all manage body contact just before I push the button."

Dall would counter, "Eamann would ne'er allow that, lass. He would ken oor plan as soon as he saw them all coming."

"We could have them hide in the trees, and then sneak them into the castle after dark," she'd say.

"Ye mean tae hae them leave here and ne'er come back?"

"Yes. They would be far safer in my time."

"Och, my brothers would ne'er agree tae leave their places here in Alasdair's service. And their wives would ne'er agree tae gae withoot them, nor tae let their bairns gae alone."

She would all but beg him, "Let's take your mother and your children with us, then. She can watch after them while we need to be away."

He would smile at her sadly. "My mither canna live on her own, lass, withoot my brothers tae bring her meat. And see here: Peadar, Peigi, and Domhnall are better off with the rest o' the clan tae guide them, and happier with their cousins tae keep them company."

He was right, so Emily stopped arguing. Until the next walk, when her peacemaking nature urged her to bring it up again. Finally, there was a walk when she didn't bring it up at all.

Dall noticed. "Nay maire scheming, Drusilla?" He pulled her into an embrace, all the while looking into her eyes playfully, seeming to dare her to scheme some more.

"I just feel so bad about you being separated from your children, Dall." There was no playfulness in her at all. She felt wretched … guilty.

He gently put his arm around her head and tugged it close to his own, where he spoke in her ear softly. "I would be going away from them tae serve the druids' pleasure even if ye were na with me, lass. Ye canna take the blame."

Her own joy at just being with Dall took over then,

spreading itself through her like a shot of whiskey and making her relax and smile at the man she now knew she loved. And wanted to marry. She tried to tell him just how much with her eyes, and then with her kiss.

The evening before she and Dall were to leave for Kilchurn Castle, Dall waited until all the children had gone to bed. Braving the dangerous night air, he took Emily and his mother and his two brothers and their wives for a walk around the top of their hill. Once they were out of earshot from the cabin, Dall and his mother, Beitris, did most of the talking.

Dall started. "Perhaps ye hae guessed this already, but it was in the service o' the druids that I met Emily. She is from the future, and we gae there together soon."

Beitris tenderly took her son's face in her hands. "We ken, Dall."

Dall looked over at Emily with his brows wrinkled.

"Ne'er fear," said Beitris. "'Twas ainly from kenning the secret of the druids' curse."

Dall sighed. "They hae cursed Emily, as wull. We canna marry here, or she wull be stuck in this time, away from her kin."

Emily grabbed him. "That isn't decided yet."

The watch sounded the alarm.

DALL GRABBED EMILY'S HAND, made a run for the cabin, and ushered her inside.

The other women were already in there, grabbing the bows and quivers off the racks on the walls and setting themselves up at the small windows, to defend the house. Everyone's children woke up, and Dall handed them all down through the floor of the house into the root cellar. They went without whining or complaining or fussing. Emily went down there with them, more to keep herself company than to comfort them.

Tough as nails, the children seemed more curious than afraid. All twelve of them whispered in Gaelic to each other, no doubt sharing their theories on why the alarm had been sounded. Not even little Domhnall was afraid. He kept banging on the wall and saying something in Gaelic that Emily was sure meant 'out'. Peadar and Peigi hushed their little brother without having to be told.

The noise above the floorboards overhead died down quickly, but when no one came to tell the women all was well, Emily worried. The children began to fidget, and she started a game of funny faces with them. It worked so well to distract them that she had to remind them to be quiet and not laugh out loud. She put on a brave face for them, but she worried.

Finally, she heard Dall's voice overhead and breathed easier, though his words puzzled her until she heard a dozen sets of footsteps following him.

The root cellar door opened, and Dall handed Emily up through the floor into the house.

Peadar started to follow Emily up.

Dall put a hand on his son's head.

Peadar backed down into the root cellar once more, looking curiously rather than fearfully at the dozen English archers who had followed his da into the house.

Emily looked at them, too. She thought Dog and his crew looked guilty, more than afraid, especially Mike, who tried to smile at Emily but didn't quite manage it.

"Eamann sent us," said Dog. "He told us we would be stuck here unless you returned to the castle in time, Dall." He looked at Emily. "He was adamant that Dall be back, but he didn't mention you at all."

"Ye were na following us when we made oor way here,"

Dall said to Dog. "I would hae kennned if ye were. Ye ainly arrived this evening. How did ye find us?"

"Eamann did something to my ... device." Dog looked anxiously at Emily.

She looked around at the faces of Dall's brothers and their wives and his mother, and then met Dall's eyes.

Dall closed the root cellar door and said softly, "Ye can speak freely in front o' my adult kin in this room, but let us spare the children all this, for a time yet."

Dog nodded. Taking out his phone and placing it on the kitchen table, he said in an equally soft voice while everyone gathered around, "See this dot here? It shows me where you are." He was talking to Dall, but he showed the phone first to Emily and then to everyone else.

Emily stared at Dog's phone. "How did Eamann install that app in this day and age? And how did he even know how?"

Dog shook his head. "We don't know." He looked around at his crew, and they shook their heads, too.

"We didn't see," Mike said to Emily.

Dog nodded. "That old druid just asked for my phone and went in the other room. He was only there for a minute. When he came back, he showed me how to use this app like he was a salesman at Best Buy or something. It was weird."

Emily held out her hand.

Dog gave her his phone.

She noted that his screen showed the same map with a line to Kilchurn Castle. It had the countdown, too. And yes, she showed up on it—or rather her phone did—as a big glowing dot. But this was not the Time Management app that she had on her own phone. Dog's app didn't have settings, and most importantly, it didn't have the button she had pressed to bring herself and Dall here.

Afraid to ask, but needing to know, Emily said, "Does it let you listen in on my conversations?"

Dog pursed his lips and looked down at the floor.

"I knew it." Emily turned to Dall to see his reaction.

Dall's face was thoughtful. "Could ye always hear us, or ainly betimes?"

Emily was impressed with Dall anew. He had only just learned about electricity, and he was already speculating about the microphone only working when powered up, even though some weird druidic magic was obviously involved.

"We could hear you most of the time," said Dog, still looking at the floor. "And if I could hear, then I bet Eamann could hear, too."

***

Early the next morning, Dall hugged his children and his mother goodbye and clasped forearms with his brothers.

His mother smiled extra warmly at him, and kept smiling really big at Emily.

"Safe journey," his family called out in Gaelic as he mounted the horse and handed her up behind him.

Emily was surprised to see Dog and his crew already mounted, each on his own horse, all with leather packs on their backs. She made a mental note never again to underestimate the resources at the druids' disposal, nor to count on escaping their clutches—if only for a week—through the element of surprise. This made her check to make sure her phone was securely fastened to her cloak inside its brooch, along with the charger she hadn't needed to use these two weeks she'd been in close proximity to Dall.

The countdown had said ten days. Plenty of time.

They were half a day's ride away from the settlement when they heard Clan Menzies' battle drums behind them, getting closer.

5. CASTLE

D o you think we lost them?" Emily's voice was nearly breathless as their horses ran. She and Dall were mounted together in the lead, with Dog and his crew following. They still had a ways to go before they got to the shelter of Orson's cabin. They had left the Menzies clan drumbeats behind a while ago.

Abruptly, Dall turned and ran their horse into a shallow side canyon, along a small creek. "Nay, they follow us yet. They wull na stop until they catch us or they are dead."

"Where are we going?" Emily knew she should keep quiet and let Dall worry about their safety, but she couldn't help asking.

He didn't need to answer, though. Even to Emily's inexperienced eyes, it was obvious that Dall was setting up to ambush their pursuers. Ambush was their only option, really.

The small canyon narrowed. Dall must have been headed for it on purpose. Just after a rock formation made it almost unbearably narrow—room for only one horse and rider—the canyon widened up again.

Dall stopped, dismounted, and led the horse up the hill to the right, into some trees. "Up here, lads. Dae hurry."

Dog and Mike and the rest of the crew rode up and stopped noisily, their horses stamping and snorting. They dismounted and tied their horses to the trees.

Dall pointed out the best places for them to climb up and shoot from. "Ower there. Up that way, the two o' ye. On top, ye. The rest, up that way."

The archers scrambled up the rock formation. In moments, they were positioned.

Dall dismounted, helped her down, and held her close a moment. "Stay hidden behind the horses, lass. If it does look bad for us, then ride on. When the canyon opens back up intae a glen, bear left along the river." He kissed her then, fiercely, before he drew his sword and ran down the hill to hide behind the rocks that served as a narrow gate to this part of the canyon.

Emily wished she could offer to help with their defense, but she knew she would only slow the men down. Instead, she huddled behind the horses, fighting the panic that threatened to take her over.

And then the archers were shooting. And their targets were screaming.

The first sky-blue kilted rider got as far as the rock gate, and Dall cut him down in seconds. The Menzies man already had two arrows in him. Emily cringed when the man's horse neighed and reared, battering the air above Dall with its front hooves. But Dall ducked in time. The next Menzies rider rode right into it, though. Between Dall and the Menzies horse, the bodies were stacking up down there.

Huddled down among the horses with her back against the rock wall, Emily couldn't take her eyes or any of her attention off the action surrounding Dall. Mostly, she feared he would be injured, or worse.

But also, he was just so amazing to watch. His sword swung, he leapt with his kilt flying, he ducked, he swung around the horse. If Dall's life hadn't been in danger, this fight would have been a better show than Cirque du Soleil.

"Got ya." A sky-blue kilted man appeared in front of Emily with his hands reaching out to grab her. He spoke in Gaelic, but she understood him perfectly. Mostly because of the leer on his face.

Over the Menzies man's shoulder, Emily saw that Dall saw him, too.

It was tempting to stay put and let him come save her, but if Dall broke away from his fight at the gate to come help her, then the attackers would be at his back.

Looking for whatever cover there was, Emily edged to her right along the rock wall, behind one of the horses. While the man couldn't see, she reached down to her boot and pulled out the dagger.

Again he spoke in Gaelic. "Think ye can hide from me, dae ye?"

She feigned ignorance and kept easing around the horse, readying her stab as she had in the drills.

"Ha. I wull hae ye now."

Their entire exchange took only seconds, not long enough to cause Dall to expose his back to their enemies.

Before Emily could think about what she was doing, she stabbed her attacker under his right arm with the dagger, just as she had practiced on the straw bales.

The man loosened his grip on her.

Emily got away from him, grabbed one of the far horses, and ran down the canyon with it until she found a fallen tree to climb up on so that she could mount. Unpracticed as she was, getting up onto the horse by herself took Emily an uncomfortably long amount of time. She kept trying and failing, and she vowed to take riding lessons once she got back home. Once on horseback, she could see over all the brush back up the canyon.

The sky-blue kilted man leaned against a tree, holding his wound with his other hand and huffing for breath. He was the only one back here. He must have climbed over the rock wall.

Hoping no more men did that, she sat there on horseback watching him, planning to turn the horse and gallop away if he moved to follow her, but hoping he didn't, because she had only ever ridden rental horses that followed each other in a pack, and only a handful of times.

But she didn't need to worry about the Menzies man for long.

Dall called out to the archers, "Behind ye, lads."

The man's sky-blue kilt acted as a target. He was full of arrows in seconds, pinned to the tree he'd been leaning on for support.

Emily was glad she was far off down the canyon. Afraid as she'd been of the man, and glad as she was he could no longer come after her, she didn't want to see his dead face. Back here, she could pretend it was all fake, a movie or something. She didn't want to get close enough to make his death real.

As quickly as it had started, the battle was over.

Dall called down the canyon to Emily, "Bide there, lass. We gae tae make certain they are all dead." He started to walk through the rock gate. Away from her. Out of her sight.

"No." she called back to Dall down the canyon. It echoed all around, making an eerie sound. "No, no, no, no, no..."

Dall stopped and turned toward Emily again, halfway through the rock gate. "Are ye hurt, lass?" He started running to her.

Dog and his crew were climbing down the rocks. She watched them gather what arrows they could off the bodies that lay still on this side of the barrier and then mount their horses to come join her.

Emily's common sense told her she was being childish. She didn't listen.

Maybe she had grown up a little, but she couldn't bear for Dall to leave her sight right now, and she also couldn't bear to go back up the canyon to him and see the carnage. So she stayed right where she was and let Dall come to her. She let him think she was injured and bleeding, rather than just afraid.

Dall was in the saddle behind her almost as soon as he got there, looking her over for wounds. To her surprise, he found one, a slice on the top of her left forearm, through what she knew as her 'tennis muscle'. It hadn't even hurt until she saw it. Too shocked to move, she watched it bleed for a second, and then everyone fell silent, and Dall gently put his hand over her mouth.

She turned to look at Dall.

He had his hand over his own mouth, and a question in his eyes.

She gently brushed his hand aside and hushed her own mouth, nodding to show that she understood: for some reason, Dall didn't want the druids to hear them talking about Emily's injury, through her phone.

He pointed to her brooch and then to her boot.

She tucked it away, but she put her finger over her mouth and pointed to her injury and made sure everyone nodded that they understood.

Dall said out loud, "Let us ride for a bit, tae make certain we are safe afore we stop tae decide what we wull dae."

Mike rode up then and whispered something in Dall's ear.

After hesitating, looking at Emily, and then nodding to Mike, Dall whispered in Emily's ear so softly she could barely hear it, "I hae given the lad a minute tae clean and bandage yer wound tae stop the bleeding. He says he wull stitch it later."

Even as Dall spoke, Mike gently took hold of Emily's arm and poured iodine-treated water through her wound.

Rather than relaxing, though, Emily could feel Dall stiffen in the saddle behind her. She could picture him scanning up at the rocks all around them, looking for intruders. She fought a giggle. Her arm didn't hurt yet, and she was content to sit there quietly and let everyone take care of her.

A second surprise was that Mike had his own soap. He lathered it in his hands, rinsed, made more lather, and used the lather to clean her wound. It stung like nothing she had ever felt, and she gasped over and over, fighting the scream that tried to form.

A third surprise was Mike's own tube of antibiotic ointment, which of course wasn't disguised like hers was. He dressed her wound and then bandaged it with part of someone's clean shirt they had dug out of their leather backpack and ripped. Just for her.

Once the bandage was on and she wasn't watching her life's blood drain away, Emily snapped out of her daze. Having Dall behind her on the horse was a brand new and comforting experience.

Now, *he* was the one hugging *her*. It almost let her ignore the ache that formed in her arm.

A fourth surprise was when the guy who had played the apothecary in their play wordlessly handed Emily the dagger she had left in the Menzies man's underarm. He had cleaned it.

"Thanks," Emily told him just as quietly, re-sheathing the dagger in her boot.

Dall was talking to everyone, though. "Lads, let us ride as far from here as we can in one gae."

They all kicked their horses and took off down the canyon.

Emily was glad to leave the dead and dying behind.

꙳

WHEN THEY SAW the first of Orson's cattle grazing about the green hills, Dall slowed the horse to a walk and all the men followed his lead. From her week of highlands experience, Emily knew Dall had slowed so as not to spook the livestock. But the cattle lowed anyhow, and by that means of warning, red-kilted Orson MacGregor was in his open front door, alerted to their arrival by the time the riders got to the house.

"Cousin Dall. Are ye growing lads oot in the fields now? How came ye upon such a large company?"

"Cousin Orson. I hae traveled the waurld, dinna ye ken?" Dall gave Emily a squeeze and then jumped down from behind her and greeted his cousin with a hug and several manly slaps on the back, which made both of their red plaid kilts sway.

There was general hubbub over the next several minutes while all the archers dismounted and Dall helped Emily down with a smile and an embrace and Orson's children took the horses to the barn and Orson's wife in her long plaid skirt shooed all of the adults into the house and bade them sit around her huge kitchen table. Bows, quivers, and Dall's claymore were stacked in the weapon racks on the walls, tankards were filled with beer, and plates of bread and cheese were plunked down.

For the first few hours of the traveling party's merry time at Cousin Orson's, the crew whittled new arrows while they told Orson how they had turned the tables on their Menzies pursuers that morning. If Emily hadn't been there and seen the fighting for herself, they would have given her the impression that their battle had been a marvelous and even a glorious thing, rather than the terror she had known it to be.

"There were at least FIFTY of them, all on horses."

"Dall got us to this sweet spot where we picked them off with arrows from on top of some rocks."

Dall cut in then and gave his cousin the Gaelic name of the place.

Orson made a noise of recognition and sat back to hear the rest of their tale.

Dall explained to Emily much later that Orson would get word to the Menzies of the location of their kin's bodies, so that they could be taken to the Menzies burial grounds.

But right then, the bikers continued bragging about their second real battle.

"I shot fifteen of them."

"I got ten."

"Twelve."

"Nine for me."

"They were all bottled up there at that narrow gap in the rocks with nowhere to go. It was like shooting fish in a barrel."

There weren't quite enough chairs, so Mike was sitting on a crate by Emily's left side in the corner of the kitchen, quietly stitching her wound together while Dall sat on her right, caressing her back through her thick bodice and letting her squeeze his other arm with her right hand. Emily was biting down on the rolled-up remains of the shirt Mike had torn to make bandages for her, but she was breathing heavy through both nose and mouth, visibly in pain all the time Mike was stitching and bandaging and measuring out doses from her pouches for her—of Ibuprofen and Tylenol and oral antibiotics.

"Sorry," Mike said to her quietly, "but I don't think there's any ice."

Wondering what would happen if she took her phone out of her boot, brought up the Time Management app, and pushed the time travel button right now, Emily managed a weak smile for Mike at his joke. "Thanks for all you've done, Mike. I mean it." She had counted twenty stitches.

Dall held forearms with Mike for a moment, in silent thanks for his help.

The gesture made Emily smile a little bigger, for some reason.

The guys went on and on about the battle, as if it were a football game. And then the conversation came around to Emily's small part in the fray.

"They were all so full of arrows, they looked like voodoo dolls."

"Of course Dall got twelve with that crazy big sword of his."

"Yeah, but even Emily stuck one."

Everyone turned to look at her then, and seeing her stitched-up wound and her unamused face, they quieted a little. But they still talked of the battle.

"Yeah, all of us men except Dall were hiding up there on the rocks, shooting from far away."

"The one woman in our group is the only one who is going to have battle—"

Mike put a hand over that one's mouth and concluded for him without revealing Emily's injury to the druids.

"You're a tough one, Emily."

"Yeah, no one should me messing with you once this gets around."

And then someone handed her a tankard of beer laced with whiskey.

She sipped it, and once she was halfway through that, the pain had subsided and she was having fun again on this epic adventure.

Orson's children were the only ones not drinking. They were up in a loft most of the time, only coming down to go out to the privy to relieve themselves, and when dinner was announced.

Dinner. Emily thought she remembered dinner being

good, but she couldn't remember what it had been, really, only that she had lost count of her tankards of beer and whiskey.

And then she was laughing, because Mike was up on top of the empty kitchen table, doing Juliet and the nurse and Lady Capulet in much more daring female voices than he had used at the castle. He sure was funny. She looked around and everyone thought so. It was good to hear them all laughing and having fun.

And then Dog and the others took turns in the kitchen, showing off their staged sword fights with pots and pans round and round the stove with much yelling and groaning and other exaggerated theatrics.

The children peeked down from the loft to watch, and the whole play went by, acted in various parts of the house around the kitchen table, wherever there was room.

But the room was spinning, and she was so sleepy. Dall was giving her the usual goodnight kiss, and then someone who reminded Emily of her mother walked her through a door, undressed her, and put her to bed.

She drifted off to the sound of men singing.

EMILY'S full bladder woke her. She had a warm fuzzy moment when she thought she was in her bed at her parents' house. She meant to go start the coffee maker, guzzle all the orange juice in the fridge, and then take a shower. Until she opened her eyes. It took a few seconds for her to realize she was in Orson and his wife's bedroom. It took one more second for her to remember why they had given her their bed and slept elsewhere.

Her wound ached, but it was healing with no signs of infection, thanks to the antibiotics. That thought served as a reminder to find her pouch belt and measure out another dose of everything and wash it all down with the water someone had left on the night table for her, next to a candle.

Light poured in through the wind opening, so Emily didn't need the candle. Her full bladder urged her to get out to the privy, though, and soon. She dressed as quickly as she could—which wasn't too fast given she had to put on two skirts, a bodice, a muffin cap, and boots, not to mention she didn't dare go anywhere without her belt and her brooch. She threw on her cloak and tied the extra shift around her waist under her skirts too, figuring she might as well keep all of her belongings with her.

As soon as she opened the kitchen door, the snoring sounds assailed her. She was barely able to tiptoe across the kitchen/dining area to get to the front door, the wooden floor was so full of snoring men.

Dall was one of them. He lay curled up in just his shift, using his kilt as a blanket and his pack as a pillow. Even sleeping, he simultaneously made her want to stare at him and cuddle him. She would have done both, but nature was calling her rather loudly now.

She was on her tiptoes in the middle of that floor-full of snoring men when she heard the dog barking outside. It sounded distant, here in the warm kitchen with all the snoring bodies. It didn't wake any of them. She tiptoed through them slowly in the dim light from the small wind openings, being careful not to step on anyone's fingers.

At first, the sounds Emily heard when she finally unbarred and opened the front door didn't make any sense to her. She heard the dog barking, of course, but also horses running. A lot of horses. All these noises came from the far side of the white-wood barn, which stood against the green mountain across the green and colorful flower garden.

And then she saw them all, her people's horses. They were

all tied together, and one sky-blue kilted man was riding the lead horse, away.

Faced with a difficult decision, Emily did what any 21st century woman would. She ran to the privy and relieved herself first.

"WAKE UP! WAKE UP! WAKE UP!" She rattled the pots and pans for good measure and dramatic effect. "He's taking the horses. A Menzies man is taking our horses."

That got them all on their feet with varying degrees of quickness.

Orson came down the ladder from the loft, telling the children in Gaelic to stay up there with their mother.

Dall was up and out the front door in three seconds on his flat bare feet, which made Emily feel bad for pausing to relieve herself. She realized that Dall might have caught the guy if she hadn't been so slow to realize what was going on... but it was over now. They had to deal with the situation they had, not the one they wished they had. Emily kept quiet about her guilt.

"Should we run after them?" Dog asked when Dall came back inside.

Dall stepped over to Emily and made a show of hiding their usual good-morning kiss behind his hat. "Nay, we canna catch them on foot, and I dinna wish tae try riding the cattle that fast." With his arm around Emily, Dall smiled at Orson then, a thin ghost of a smile.

Orson smiled back.

Emily thought the two of them must have been loads of fun as children.

Dall became serious, talking to the whole group. "We hae a long journey by foot, ye ken. We can make it in nine days, but..." He stepped up to Orson and put his hand on his cousin's shoulder. "I will na be staying tae help ye castrate the bull-calves. Perhaps next year, aye?"

Orson smiled big at his cousin, and they clasped forearms.

Dall turned to her and the bikers. "We can break oor fast, but then we had best be on oor way."

They said their goodbyes over bannocks and hot herb tea. Orson had several dozen head of cattle, so he had plenty of dried jerky, with which the travelers stuffed their leather bags and packs. A few more water skins like Emily's bota bag were added to their water-carrying capacity. A few old cloaks were gifted to the men who didn't have one to sleep in.

When they were all ready to go, Orson spoke up again. "Wull ye take the direct way through the glens, cousin?"

"Nay," said Dall. "We wull climb up intae the crags, where nay horse can follow. I will na allow the Menzies tae use oor ain horses tae pursue us. Let them come on foot."

IT WAS a decent temperature in the valleys in July, but up on the highland mountaintops Emily was glad she had her cloak, and she hoped the two guys who hadn't brought cloaks were asking blessings on Orson for giving them some. The view, however, was glorious: green valleys with deep blue lochs at their bottoms and green mountains with cream-colored crags near their tops, crowned with white billowing clouds.

With his sword sheathed on his back, Dall was in the front where he could lend her his arm over the difficult parts —which he did often, to Emily's delight. Almost as often, their eyes met when she took his arm, and they smiled at each other. It wasn't nearly so fun as riding on the horse together, but it was nice.

All the archers followed the two of them, with Dog guarding their backs. The guys managed to talk almost the entire time. Emily mostly huffed to get enough oxygen in the thin air.

Dog was saying, "This isn't really mountain-climbing by modern standards. That requires pitons and rope."

The other guys commented.

"No, but it's a good workout anyway."

"Yeah, I'm pretty pumped up."

"Hey, gimmie a puff of the pipe."

"You empty one of your own cigs for it. This one's mine."

"OK OK, I see how it is."

Emily heard his lighter then, and a moment later she smelled cigarette smoke nearby.

"What?" he said. "No one's going to see us up here except Dall, and he's cool."

Huffing almost as much as Emily, and giving her a weary smile, Mike spoke up. "It's brutally physical up here, if you ask me. Like climbing stairs, first up and then down, over and over again, and we've been climbing for hours. I don't know how you can smoke, too."

Emily gave Mike a grateful smile, then turned to Dog. "Just don't leave anything from the future on the ground. Pack out what you pack in."

Emily huffed a bunch more, telling herself it was just to make up for the breaths she hadn't taken while she was talking. She knew she wouldn't have been able to climb like this at all at the beginning of her adventure.

Now, after walking the stairs and hauling water from the loch at the castle for forty days and trudging over hill and dale with Dall for twenty days, she could hike almost as fast as the men wanted to go. If she huffed for breath.

Dall squeezed her hand.

She looked up at him.

He spoke softly so only she could hear. "Dae ye need rest, lass? Can ye make it tae the top o' the rise first?" He looked up to a point about ten more flights of stairs up.

Trying really hard not to wrinkle her forehead with the

worry she felt—because she didn't want to look ugly in front of Dall—Emily spoke just as softly. "Do we have time to rest? We have to be at Kilchurn Castle in eight and a half days."

Dall sounded concerned when he whispered back to her. "We wull make the time tae rest, lass, if it means ye wull na be ill."

"What if I do get … ill?"

"Then I wull carry ye."

She let him take away her worry, and she made it to the top of the rise.

Dall then spoke for everyone to hear. "Well enough, let us stop now tae look oot upon the lochs and the moors while we slake oor thirst."

Emily collapsed on some soft grass. Once she caught her breath and drank her fill and took doses of her medication, she got a bright idea. She spoke to everyone, but she looked at Dall. "Guys? If the druids can hear us anyway, maybe we should ask them to send us some horses."

Displaying the leadership that Emily admired once more, Dall looked at everyone, apparently for their opinions.

Most of them shrugged.

Dog looked eager. "Yeah, they probably know right where we are, and they are the ones who want Dall back, so I don't see why we shouldn't ask for their help."

Dall made a show of keeping quiet and pointing to Emily's brooch and then holding out his hand.

Nodding her understanding that he wanted to be the one to speak to the druids, she unpinned the brooch and carefully handed it to him.

Dall switched the phone on and watched the screen while it powered up.

Emily thought he looked almost like a modern man while he did that—a buff and rugged modern man in a kilt, anyway. She felt herself smiling a goofy smile as she gazed at him. She saw that Dall brought up the Time Management app, and she nodded, thinking that was the most direct point of contact for the druids, absent texting Siobhan.

And then Dall spoke right into the phone. "We ken ye are listening, Eamann. The Menzies hae taken oor horses. Send us maire. Ye ken where we are and the way we gae. Hae horses tae us by this time tomorrow. We wull check this map for yer answer this evening, and if ye hae na replied, then again in the morning. See that ye send enough sae all o' us can ride togither. I will na leave any behind."

Admiring Dall, Emily took her phone back and powered it down to put once more in her boot. "Do you have family we can stay with tonight?"

Looking down at the expanse of crags and valleys and lochs in the direction they were headed, Dall addressed them all. "Nay, na that we can get tae this day withoot horses. We wull sleep oot in the heather this night. We wull set watches and be wary."

﹩

THEY KEPT ON HIKING, with Dall's arm always holding Emily up toward the end, she was so tired. She wasn't complaining. At dusk, the bikers started to point out semi-sheltered places where they might all stop for the night.

"That overhang looks promising."

"We could camp out under this big tree."

"This little canyon is protected from the wind."

Each time, Dall would glance over where they pointed and then reject it without much examination. "Och lads, we can dae better than that."

Finally, Emily voiced her suspicion. "You have a certain place in mind Dall, don't you?"

"Aye, lass. That I dae."

The guys loved to talk, though, so they started speculating on the type of place they would find up here in the windy crags.

"Probably the old home of someone who liked the view but was too stupid to realize there wasn't any water."

"Ha. Maybe they raised eagles. Seems like they'd be happy up here."

"Maybe it's a beacon, like up on those hills in Lord of the Rings."

"Oh man, I hope so. A fire would be nice right now."

"Ha ha. You would be the one to light a fire and bring the bad guys right to us."

"Oh yeah, that's why we're way up here, isn't it, to stay away from those bad guys."

They stumbled around in the near dark for a few minutes, and then one by one, they started using their phones as flashlights—except for two guys who had worn out their batteries playing some dumb game or other. Emily tried to recharge their phones with her touch while holding Dall's hand, as she had with Dog's phone, but nope, that didn't work.

"I guess it only worked with Dog's phone because of that druid app Eamann installed, like Siobhan did with my phone." She handed the guy's phone back to him.

Taking Emily with him as if they were dancing, Dall turned and faced the group.

They all shined their phones on him.

Looking like he was on stage in a dark theater, he said, "We are nigh upon the spot where I was planning on stopping for the night, lads and lass."

This picked up their spirits some, and they hurried a little.

Around the next bend in the mountain crags, there it was. Emily could tell by the guys' excited 'oohs' and 'ahs' that they all knew it as soon as they saw it: a stone structure built up so that a ledge in the crag formed its roof.

Mike and Dog ran on ahead to check it out. They came back all smiles.

Dog said, "There's enough room for all of us to lie down inside, just barely."

Mike said, "I thought it was a house, but it's a church. There's the cutest little altar inside." He gestured something smaller than a pillow.

Dall was looking around at the surrounding hills as if he still expected the injured Menzies men to be following them. "Was there aught on the altar?"

Dog and Mike looked at him with puzzled expressions.

Dall tried again. "Ye hae the right o' it. This is a kirk for the heathers. Any fresh offering inside wull be a clue tae warn us someone bides near."

Dog let out his breath. "Oh. No, there's just a bunch of dried offering remains—flowers, and bones from a pigeon or something."

Breathing easier but still looking everywhere at once, Dall led everyone inside the small stone church that was built away from the prevailing wind. He and a few of the other guys crossed themselves upon entering, and they put some of their jerky on the altar for an offering.

As soon as they had finished paying their respects and thanking their sovereign for the shelter, it started pouring rain outside.

"I wull take first watch," said Dall. He closed the door and stood with his back to it. "Can I see yer phone, lass? It be time tae see if Eamann answered me."

Emily dug her phone out of her boot, powered it up, and handed it to him.

"Och, nay word yet."

Emily powered it down and put it back in her boot.

She thought setting a watch was a bit excessive. The kirk didn't have any windows people could attack through. The walls and roof were rock. And surely the rain would make anyone following the party duck under a tree or something until it stopped. Still, she was so sleepy, she only thought about it for a minute.

And then all her thoughts went blank while she and Dall shared a tender goodnight kiss. "Rest easy, lass. Hae a pleasant night's sleep."

"Wake the men up if you hear anything, Dall. Don't go out there alone."

He squeezed her hand, and then she lay down on top of her cloak near him on the dirt floor of the kirk and fell fast asleep.

EMILY WOKE in the middle of the night, needing to go outside. Dall lay asleep next to her, curled up on top of his kilt. Dog stood at the door, holding Dall's claymore. He waited for her to get up, and then he opened the door, headed outside in front of her, and closed the door again behind them.

Pointing to a cleft in the crag, Dog whispered, "That's where we've been going, so that if the mad Menzies men come, they can't sneak up on us."

Giggling a bit at Dog's nickname for their attackers, Emily was headed over to the cleft to do her business when Dog grabbed her.

He put his hand over her mouth, saying, "Shhh."

Emily struggled. She had been starting to think of Dog as a friend. She stomped on his toe as hard as she could.

"Why'd you do that?" he whispered.

She couldn't answer with his hand over her mouth, so she

pulled her lips back and bit his hand instead, thinking if the worst happened, then at least she could empty her bladder all over him.

And then Dog said something that didn't make any sense. "I hear you over there."

Finally realizing that Dog was protecting her from the mad Menzies men and not trying to have his way with her after all, Emily relaxed and let him put her behind him against the wall of the kirk, where she squatted and relieved herself under cover of darkness—and her two long skirts.

Dog said, "You better be gone when we come out with our bows in a few seconds." Still facing the cleft in the crag, Dog gently shoved Emily toward the door into the kirk.

Once she was inside, she let out a breath she hadn't realized she was holding and she stood there trembling.

Having more wits about him, Dog said in a normal voice once he was inside, "Get up. They have followed us here and they are outside."

Dall jumped up and wrapped his kilt about him in one fluid motion that took all of five seconds.

For some reason, the ease with which Dall did it by comparison to backstage at the faire made her see this was reality and not some game—even better than had being in a position where she'd had to stab that one Menzies man.

Meanwhile, half the men had gotten up and gathered their bows. Dog had handed Dall's claymore back to him.

Dall led most of the men outside, gesturing to the remaining three to stay inside and guard Emily.

They finished getting their bows ready and their clothes back into day mode, and then they stood around facing the door with arrows cocked.

Emily felt a little guilty for falling apart and needing to be looked after, but mostly she just felt grateful that the men were looking after her. She let herself step over into the corner, behind the door.

To the light of someone's phone, she and the remaining three guys just stood there watching each other listen for sounds outside. She was glad one of them was Mike, and at the same time she chided herself for not learning the rest of their names. She knew their character names from the play, but not their real names. She highly doubted these two wanted to be called Tybalt and Mercutio all the time.

She was thinking about how disrespectful that was when they finally heard fighting outside: archers whooping and their targets groaning, mostly.

With a big grin on his face, Tybalt started to go outside to get in on the action, but Mike grabbed his arm, pointing to Emily. The guy deflated, but then he gave Emily a small smile. She smiled back the same small way, as if to say, "Yeah, it's probably more fun out there, but they might come in here, and I really would not be able to handle that, so thanks."

They waited there watching each other's faces for alarm for what seemed like a long time.

But then Tybalt showed them his phone. "It's been fifteen minutes. Do you think we should—"

And right then, the door opened.

Scared out of her wits by the sound of the opening door, Emily cowered in the corner with her arms over her face.

"Och, Drusilla. None o' means ye harm."

At the sound of Dall's voice, Emily was so relieved that she sank to the floor and started crying, but she reached out to Dall and grabbed whatever she could find of him, trying to tell him she was glad he was all right. Her hand settled around his calf muscle.

It seemed to work, and even better, Dall sat next to her and put his arms around her until the sobbing subsided and she felt like herself again. And then he still held her close.

❦

WITH THEM ALL gathered inside the early morning darkness of the stone heather kirk, Dog was telling everyone who had remained inside what happened.

"Four that we wounded back there at the canyon followed us all the way up here."

Tybalt said, "Dang. Did you shoot 'em all?"

Dog shook his head no. "No, but we got 'em all. Dall got the ones hiding too good for us to shoot."

Tybalt shined his phone right on Dall's face. "Why do the MacGregors and those Menzies hate each other so much? Is it a family feud?"

Done with her crying and feeling safe and secure again in Dall's arms, Emily tried her budding teacher voice on Tybalt. "Please get that light out of his face. That's rude."

To her surprise, it worked. Tybalt lowered the phone right away and said, "Sorry."

Dall gave her an appreciative squeeze. "We dinna hate the Menzies. We fight tae hold the land. With land, we hae meat aplenty and raise our children withoot want. The Menzies strive tae hae the land once maire."

Mike spoke up. "And how long has this clan war been going on?"

"For as long as anyone remembers," Dall said.

"That's intense," said Mike in a hushed tone.

"Dude," Tybalt said to Dall, "you've been fighting like this all your life?"

"Aye, lad," said Dall.

"No wonder you're so good with that sword."

They were all quiet for a moment.

"See if Eamann wrote tae us?" Dall asked Emily.

"It isn't morning yet," she said.

"But it is. In a few moments, the light wull come through the cracks in these walls."

Emily got her phone out of her boot and powered it up while Dall watched over her shoulder. The Time Management app came up all by itself. There was a new red dot on the map. Using two fingers to zoom in on the map, Emily revealed that under the new red dot was the word 'horses'.

"Och," said Dall. "They mean for us tae enter Clan MacIntyre lands."

"Is that another enemy of the MacGregors?" Mike asked Dall.

"Na enemies, but dinna mistake. We rival all but the Campbells. And we ainly dinna rival the Campbells because we hae sworn fealty."

"Will the MacIntyres let us go down there and get the horses, Dall?" Emily asked it loudly enough for all to hear, yet softly, as he still cuddled her, with both of them seated on the floor in their corner behind the kirk door.

The sunrise entered the kirk through chinks in the stone wall at that precise moment, illuminating all the bikers' faces as they looked to see what he'd say.

"'Tis na ainly getting the horses," said Dall. "If we gae doon their side o' the mountain, then we wull be in MacIntyre lands for the duration o' oor journey. Nay family tae stay the night with, nor any allies." He looked at Emily then, and hugged her tighter. "And if the horses ae na there…"

She gave him a nervous laugh. "I get it," she said. "I'm the weakest link in this chain. If not for my difficulty climbing, you would choose to stay in these mountains and walk back to Campbell territory."

"Nay, lass. Thanks be tae ye, I see an opportunity." He smiled at her.

She gave Dall her practiced quizzical look, with her eyebrow raised just so.

He smiled again, and her heart melted even more. "We have numbers enough against all but an organized attack, sae the MacIntyres wull let us get the horses. And with the exception o' one lone MacGregor guide," he put his hands on his own chest, "we appear English."

She smiled back and got lost in his eyes for a few moments, and then she remembered what they were talking about. "But how is that an opportunity?"

"'Tae strengthen what ties the MacGregors hae with the MacIntyres. Both hae Clan Donald overlords, and both need tae see, with clear eyes, the Campbells taking that ower."

"Oh." She thought of more fun things. "So, what's our story? Shall we be a traveling troupe of actors?"

Dall suppressed a grin. "Nay, lass. That story wore thin at the castle and ainly worked because ye saved Alasdair from his choking fit. And ainly just. Nay, we tell the MacIntyres the truth, but nay all o' the truth, ye ken?"

Everyone nodded.

"Yeah, that's the best thing."

"Yep, that would be easier."

"Then we won't contradict each other."

Mike beat Emily to the applicable Shakespeare quote. "Oh what a tangled web we weave when we practice to deceive."

The way down off the craggy mountains into the green forests and glens was easier than the way up had been, but Dall still held his arm out for Emily, and she still held on to it. Every time they saw a bird take flight or animals running from a water hole or anything else at all remarkable, their eyes would meet and they would enjoy it together.

Just before they entered MacIntyre lands, Dall whispered in Emily's ear so softly she could barely hear, "Lass, hae ye aught tae cover yer wound? I dinna want *them* tae ken."

"Why not?" she whispered back.

"If what I suspect is true, then it will cause them tae separate us."

"What do you suspect?"

"I dare na say." He looked at her brooch.

So Emily went behind a bush and put on the long sleeved Scottish shift with the embroidered neckline, resolving to insist that he scrawl his next secret in the dirt.

THEY CAME to a river that twisted and turned down a steep canyon, and they kept seeing it all the way down into a lush forest, where they were able to use the river as a guide through the woods. The forest was dim even in the daylight, but peaceful.

"Should we go scout ahead?" Tybalt was talking to Dall, but he had already moved on ahead of the group, and he was peering off as far into the distance as he could, between the trees.

"Nay, stay togither," Dall said softly. "Dinna make sae many sounds. We are like tae see MacIntyres any moment."

Tybalt spun around on his heel and fell in behind Dall and Emily.

They all walked as quietly as they could, and didn't talk. It was hardly quiet, though. Twigs broke under their feet. Birds called to each other from the tops of the trees. The river babbled over rocks.

One moment things were tranquil. The next, they heard thundering hoofbeats.

Emily froze, unsure where the sound was coming from or what she could do to get out of the way.

Dall grabbed her uninjured arm and pulled her uphill away from the river. "This way," he hissed to the bikers.

They snapped out of their own frozen indecision and

followed Dall up the hill between the trees just in time. A dozen deer charged through the forest along the river, right through the spot where they had stood moments before. Emily gasped at how beautifully they ran, how gracefully they jumped over fallen trees.

A few of the men gasped, too, but she didn't think it was because of beauty. Sure enough, the guys were readying their bows, but they were too late. The deer disappeared as fast as they had come.

And then the reason appeared, for the running of the deer: a dozen men in green kilts with bows out and claymores swinging at their sides or riding on their backs.

"Harness yer bows," Dall said to the bikers. His voice was calm.

For a moment, Emily could feel how ready his body was for whatever action might come, but then Dall made himself even more ready by gently moving her behind him and stepping forward unhindered by her. Out of the corners of her eyes, she saw Dog and his crew putting their arrows back in their quivers and slinging their bows back over their shoulders for carrying. But she kept watching the MacIntyres. They walked with purpose, keeping their bows raised.

Dall called out something in Gaelic, and one of the MacIntyres answered. Bit by bit, Emily could tell how the conversation was going, even though she only understood a few words.

"Hail, MacIntyres." Dall said as if he were greeting old friends. But he wasn't waving.

"Hail, MacGregor. Are ye leading English hunting parties now?"

"Ainly when the pay is good." Dall relaxed a bit, but he was still on alert.

The green-kilted men laughed, but they didn't lower their bows all the way. "Ye canna hae oor deer."

"Nay tae fash, we are na here tae catch yer fine deer, just oor ain horses."

More laughter erupted. "Lost yer horses, hae ye? Best tae keep a lead on them, aye?"

They spoke as if they were old friends sitting around a campfire, but the property owners kept their bows trained on the trespassers the entire time. Slowly but surely, the MacIntyres walked up within sword range, and only then did they make their move. Their leader stood by Dall's side. The others spread out until all the strangers were within sword reach.

Their leader said something to the effect of, "We will keep you company during your search for your horses."

Nodding, Dall reached his arm back for Emily.

She gladly took it, as much to show these not-quite-hostiles she was under his protection as for the joy that touching Dall always brought to her.

They all walked on along the noisy river, the MacIntyres talking amongst themselves in Gaelic. Emily intuited that Dall was keeping quiet so he could hear them. It couldn't be easy for him, because she and the rest of the 21st century travelers were comparatively loud when they walked. She winced whenever one of her feet dragged over the uneven ground, making a scraping sound loud enough to obscure a few of the standoffish highlanders' words.

An hour later, they arrived at a settlement similar to the one Dall's brother headed.

A Gaelic argument broke out between Dall and their leader. Terrified, Emily could tell it was about her, but not much else. She clung to Dall's arm and shrank into him, trying to disappear. For the second time, she wondered what would happen if she pushed the time travel button on her phone right here and now. Unfortunately, it was in her boot and she didn't dare let go of Dall long enough to fish it out.

In the end, Dall coaxed her into the main house with him, whispering, "All is wull. Please be silent, though, Drusilla."

Emily nodded yes for him, wondering about Mike and the others. Looking over her shoulder, she saw them all seated on the ground in a circle with the deer hunters standing over them, casually talking amongst themselves. Supposing they would be all right, she swallowed the lump in her throat and let Dall guide her into the house.

The two of them were shown into an office, and the door shut behind them.

"Wull, if it is na Dall MacGregor, then my eyes are tae auld tae be trusted." The grey-haired green-kilted man behind the desk spoke in English, presumably for Emily's benefit. He was looking at her curiously.

Dall inclined his head. "Well met, Ian MacIntyre. This is Emily ..."

"Emily Shaw," she said, habitually reaching out to shake the man's hand.

He took it and instead raised it to his lips, simultaneously meeting Dall's eyes. "Ye keep charming company, Dall MacGregor."

Emily took her hand back and stepped close in to Dall once more.

He told the man, "She wull be my wife once I hae met her kin."

"Congratulations. Now, I understand ye are the owners o' the horses I hae been asked tae hold."

ALTHOUGH THERE WERE plenty of horses, Emily chose to ride with Dall for the sheer pleasure of it, let alone her contemptible horsemanship. They slept in the heather two more nights, but although they were jumpy from their confrontations with the Menzies, there were no incidents.

They all teared up when they finally turned the last corner on 14 July 1540 and saw Kilchurn Castle over the waters of Loch Awe. The crude four-story building was a safe haven in a wild and dangerous land.

It was then Emily knew she hadn't appreciated just how safe the castle was, and just how dangerous the outside was. She thought this was why the druids insisted that Dall be inside the castle when he time-traveled, and why they had gone to the trouble of bringing her here to make sure he made it back in time to leave from there.

The party all looked at each other and smiled, and then they were all urging their tired horses into a gallop along the shores of Loch Awe. Their joy at riding into the safety of the castle was dampened when someone wearing a Campbell kilt greeted them at the front gate. This meant that Colin was in residence, and in charge.

As soon as their party of fourteen had finished clearing the gate, someone called out a command and all the men mustered in courtyard, mostly red MacGregor kilts swaying.

"See ye in Eamann's healing lair in five days," Dall whispered before he handed her down off the horse, squeezed her hand, and ran out to take his place with Colin's militia.

A Campbell gestured for the archers to come out.

With a worried look at Emily, Dog gestured for his crew to follow.

A young MacGregor took Emily's horse, and then she stood there alone, without the slightest idea what to do or where to go.

A gentle hand rested on her shoulder.

When she turned to see Mairi there, she started to talk.

The older woman put a hand over her own mouth.

Emily nodded.

Mairi gestured for her to follow, and took Emily into the huge kitchen, where she recognized several women she had given needles and the woman who had given her the embroidered shift she was wearing.

All of these women waved to Emily and smiled.

She waved and smiled back. Then she turned to Mairi. "Is it safe to talk now?"

Mairi nodded yes. "Sae lang as ye are na loud." She looked significantly out into the courtyard through a small wind opening.

Seeing that all the other women were working, and wanting very much to show her appreciation for being brought into this haven out of harm's way, Emily said, "How can I help?"

They set her to work cutting up onions and turnips.

Presuming these would be cooked, Emily didn't worry about washing her hands first. But she had mentioned wanting to talk, and she noticed that all the women kept looking at her expectantly.

"The actors and I are supposed to leave soon," she said, "back to ... England, and Dall has agreed go with us." She paused to wipe a tear away.

Mairi gave her a warm smile. "But that is wonderful."

Emily nodded yes. "It is, isn't it?" She smiled in spite of herself. "But now Colin's sending them away—"

"Aw," Mairi put her arm around Emily and held her close. "He wull come back, and e'en if he is injured, I dinna doubt he wull gae with ye. We all see the way Dall looks at ye, lass."

Word was the militia would leave in the morning.

After supper, when the men had started their drinking

songs, Eamann stuck his head out of his doorway and called them down into what Emily thought of as his dungeon.

Emily gave Dall a bewildered look.

Dall shrugged at her and looked to Alasdair for permission to answer Eamann's summons.

In turn, Alasdair looked to Colin, who was busy talking and didn't even acknowledge him. So Alasdair nodded to Dall.

The biker-archer-actors all got up and followed Dall and Emily down to Eamann.

Emily guessed what was up. "You're sending us home now, aren't you."

Eamann nodded. "Aye, sae gae up one at a time and get any belongings ye left." He pointed at the floorboards over his head.

Each actor came back down with the leather backpack, bow, and quiver full of arrows he had left somewhere up top.

Emily always brought everything with her into every room, she was so paranoid of losing any of it. She turned to Dall. "Dae ye need tae get anything?"

"Nay, lass. I always hae what I need upon me." He held up his sword. He had not been wearing it at the table, but he must have lain it near at hand. He sheathed it at his side.

Emily was curious what Dall had in his sporran and in the various pouches on his own belt, but she didn't want to ask him in front of Eamann.

Dall moved in to kiss Emily, but at the last moment— while Eamann dealt with someone who had followed one of the bikers into his lair—Dall instead whispered in Emily's ear, "When it all goes swirly, hand yer phone tae me." He looked for her response.

She nodded yes to Dall, but wanted to ask him why. She kept watching Eamann for her chance, but she didn't get one, so she asked about the other thing that was bugging her.

"Eamann," she waited for him to look at her and then went on, "won't it mess things up if we time-travel now, instead of waiting until the 19th?"

Eamann didn't answer. He just stood there and tilted his head sideways at Emily.

"Oh yeah. You can just travel us forward to July 19th, huh."

Looking smug, Eamann waited for everyone to gather, and then he asked Dall, "Are ye ready?"

Emily looked into Dall's eyes.

He looked at her phone and tickled her hand.

She gave the smallest nod she could.

"Aye, ready we are." Dall told the druid healer.

E mily was so excited. Siobhan was explaining that tomorrow after faire, she and Dall would be time traveling back to his highlands home in 1540 Scotland.

Dall opened his mouth to speak.

But Siobhan gave him a dirty look, almost like she was a teacher and Dall was a troublemaking student.

Oddly, it worked. Dall obeyed Siobhan.

Emily squeezed Dall's hand gently, trying to get him to calm down. They could whisper to each other at the staged dance set later, so why was he trying so hard to talk to her now?

Looking at both of them, Siobhan said, "As you can imagine, time travel is a big secret. That's why I sent Vange and Ian out to the picnic tables with their breakfast. You can't tell Vange about this, Emily. Not a word. Ian knows enough to be able to tell if she knows, but ... You know what? Both of you, don't discuss time travel with anyone besides me. Do you understand?"

Emily nodded yes vigorously. "Oh, I totally understand

why time travel needs to be kept secret. I've seen all of the Terminator movies."

Siobhan turned her eyes to Dall and stared at him significantly.

Dall sort of bowed to Siobhan. "I dae understand, and I wull obey." How weird.

"Good," Siobhan said, giving Dall another stern stare. "Let's eat our breakfast before it gets cold." She gestured to her little kitchen table.

They all sat down to bacon and eggs and toast with lots of hot coffee.

Dall sat a little closer to Emily than usual at the table and put his arm around her, too. She wasn't complaining. His touch always invigorated her, and the more they touched, the more alive she felt.

Still, it was yet another way Dall was acting strange. It alarmed Emily a little. It brought back the feeling she'd had that first day of faire, when she wondered if she would ever see him again. But that was a silly thought. They were going to time travel together tomorrow. Not only would she see him, but hopefully she would also meet his family. She dared to hope this meant he was as serious about her as she was about him.

He was caressing her back through her thick bodice, but Siobhan got up to walk Emily to Simon's boot booth, so Emily and Dall got up too, and off they went.

Vange was already at the booth when they arrived. "What took you so long? I thought maybe Siobhan had killed you and was burying your bodies."

Emily was trying to push away from Dall to sock Vange in the arm. It felt like she hadn't seen her friend in months.

But Dall pulled Emily back and kissed her so eagerly and tenderly and desperately that by degrees Emily forgot missing Vange, wanting to sock Vange, and even that Vange was talking to her. After fighting it for only a few seconds, Emily relaxed into Dall's kiss and gave as good as she got.

"Ahem." Siobhan interrupted them.

Dall released Emily ten times more reluctantly than he usually did after walking her to Simon's booth. She wasn't all that keen on him going off with Siobhan right now, either. But he would be back in two hours to escort her to the dance set like he always did, so she didn't understand why he was so clingy.

"My love for ye does stretch through the ages," Dall said instead of goodbye as Siobhan led him away. He turned his head to watch Emily until he and Siobhan rounded a corner and went out of sight.

Two inexplicable things occurred to Emily as she recovered from that awesome kiss and watched Siobhan walk Dall away. One, she was wearing an amazingly authentic embroidered Scottish shift. Two, her left forearm itched as if it had been deeply wounded a week ago and was healing.

"Earth to Emily."

Emily came back down to reality with Vange's hand waving before her eyes. "Sorry." She turned and smiled at her best friend.

"It's OK." Vange grinned at her. "You guys are getting serious, huh." It wasn't a question.

"Yeah, he's asked me overseas to meet his parents."

"Squee." Vange smiled even bigger. "So you're going to Scotland. When? How? Both you and Dall are broke, last I heard."

"I'm not really sure how, to tell you the truth, but we leave tomorrow after faire."

"Wow. Wow."

They just grinned at each other for a moment, and then Vange said, "Maybe his parents are flying you over there." She looked happy for Emily. "That's so great."

"Morning, ladies." Dog posed in the street in front of them with his biceps flexed as big as a honeydew melon. His crew stood behind him like back-up singers.

"Ooh, Now it is." Vange sauntered over and felt his muscle, dutifully pulling up her skirts to show off Simon's colorful boots while she did so.

In turn, Dog called attention to her boots, and they both pointed passersby to the boot booth.

The two of them made a show of this every morning during Emily and Vange's shift at hawking the boots. Simon loved it. He had invited Vange, Emily, and Dog to hawk for him at this faire again next year.

Figuring she'd better call her parents, since she was going to Scotland the next day, Emily went under the burlap wall to the small enclosed backstage area where Simon and his family had their meals. That was when she noticed she didn't have her phone. She searched all of her pouches, but she didn't find it.

"Looking for this?" said a small voice Emily didn't recognize.

She looked up to see her brooch in the hands of a little girl about ten years old, who wasn't in costume.

"Yes." Emily held out her hand.

The girl put her finger over her lips and gestured for Emily to follow her into a trailer.

Figuring she had little choice, Emily followed. There was no one else inside the motorhome, at least not where she could see them.

The little girl handed over Emily's brooch.

Emily looked for her phone inside, but it wasn't there. "Do you know where my phone is?"

The girl handed her a different phone. "Dall says they can hear you on your phone, whatever that means. He wants you to text him on this one as soon as you can find a private place, because he usually can't talk. He says you'll know what that means."

Emily took the new phone, wondering how Dall had managed to get it. "But I'll see him soon, so why do I need to text him?"

The little girl shrugged. "That's all he told me to tell you. He gave me a twenty." She smiled. "You better go now, though. My grandma and grandpa will be back soon."

"OK. Uh, thanks." Emily showed herself out.

Thinking perhaps she shouldn't call her parents just yet, she went to the ladies' room and checked out her new phone. It didn't fit in her brooch. It was one of those cheap pre-loaded flip phones you could get at the supermarket. It was only good for texting and calling, no apps. Maybe he'd bought it here at faire, but where had he gotten the money?

Shrugging, Emily checked the contacts and was not surprised to find that they matched the contacts on her old phone. She was relieved to see a contact for Dall, and that it was not her old phone number.

In fact, there was a text from Dall. "Take yer medicine for yer wound, lass, in the red vial inside yer main pouch. Keep the wound hidden. Dinna tell any faire people we are in touch. Hide that phone. They are taking me tae the next faire site. Apply in costume next Saturday. Yer dagger should fetch enough tae get ye there all summer. 'Tis an antique." He gave the name of a county park in the next state.

Emily texted Dall back: "Are you safe? What's going on?" She waited five minutes for an answer, but none came.

While she was waiting in the privacy of the ladies' room, she examined her wound. It looked nasty, but someone had sewn it up. Antibiotics against infection were needed, then.

She measured out a dose and noticed that about half of it was missing. She swallowed the medicine.

€

"WHAT'S WRONG?" Vange asked Emily when she came out from the backstage area.

Emily gave her best friend their look. It meant she wanted to discuss something in private. That would have to do, because they didn't have a look for 'Someone has kidnapped my boyfriend and anyone within earshot might be in on it.'

Vange nodded discreetly, and then she looked around for a spot they could go to.

Emily grabbed Vange's arm and said loudly enough for Simon and his family to hear, "I don't feel good." She added some panting, to sell the idea that she was going to throw up. "Vange, take me home, please, right now."

"OK, we'll just go to Siobhan's trailer and get our stuff. Simon—"

"Vange, just take me straight to your car, please. I really don't feel good." Emily grabbed hold of Vange as if she was so sick that she needed her friend's support to walk, yet she was the one dragging Vange away from everyone.

Once they were far enough away to whisper without people at the booth hearing, Emily dared a quick, "I want out of here. Now. Forget about our stuff."

"OK." Vange whispered back.

Emily continued her sick act all the way to Vange's car, and Vange played along. They got in and closed the doors.

And then Vange turned to Emily with excitement on her face. "So spill. I'm dying to hear what's so secret we had to come all the way out to the car."

"We're not out of here yet. Please go. I'll explain once we're on the highway, I promise."

"Wow, you really want to leave before the faire's over?"

Emily just looked at her friend and allowed the panic to show in her face.

"OK. OK." Vange started up the car and drove the obligatory five miles per hour over the dirt field that served as the faire's customer parking lot.

Emily decided now would be a good time to be on the phone with her parents. "Let me borrow your phone."

Still driving, Vange nodded at the brooch pinned to Emily's bodice. "Where's yours?"

"That's part of the 'Once we're on the highway' story."

Emily got Vange's phone and pushed a contact.

Her mother answered. "Vange? Is everything alright?"

"Hi Mom, it's me, Emily. Dall got ... called away on business, so our trip to Scotland got cancelled."

Emily felt Vange's hand grab her upper arm, luckily not the injured arm. She turned her head and nodded yes at her friend's disbelieving face.

Her mom sounded relieved, though, which made sense, seeing she hadn't wanted Emily to go to Scotland. "Oh, that's too bad, Honey."

Emily took a deep breath to vent her frustration. "Yeah, and without him here, I'm really not into the faire, so Vange and I are on our way home, after we run an errand. Remind me to tell you about it later. You'll be impressed with Dall's ... business sense, I think. And, um, he'll be working at another faire starting next weekend, and he's invited us to come apply to be part of that faire, too."

Now Vange was dancing in her seat, and Emily was glad her friend liked the idea. That was one worry off her mind.

Her mom sounded skeptical. "Well, maybe your father

and I should come along when you apply at this new faire, so we get a chance to meet Dall."

"Actually, I think that's a good idea." Emily kept her mom chatting on the phone with her while Vange drove up to the parking lot gate where the faire people took your ten bucks for parking on top of your fifty bucks for getting in. She looked around, realizing that, if instructed to do so by the druids, they could keep you from getting out of the fenced field, at least with your car. Miles from anything.

"Leaving so soon?" said the smiling parking-lot attendant.

"Yeah," said Vange, "my friend doesn't feel good."

Emily waited what seemed like forever for the attendant to respond, but then finally he just waved them through.

VANGE PULLED onto the highway and opened it up to 70. "So are you OK really? And what the heck happened back there? Where's your phone, and what errand do we have to run?"

Emily turned on the radio, pushed buttons until one of their favorite songs came on, and cranked it up. She sang along with attitude until Vange joined in and finished the song with her.

"Yeah, I'm really OK. I was just faking sick to get us out of there."

Vange laughed. "What about our stuff?"

"Who cares about our PJs and shampoo. Like I told my mom, Dall had to go to the next faire site and help get it started, and I'm not into being around here without him. He has my phone. I *loaned* it to him." She smiled.

"Hahahahaha. Did it work?"

"Yep. I have to get it back, right?"

"Right. So are we really going to work at the next faire?"

"Yep. It finishes just before classes start. And this time

we're going to make them pay us real money. Don't get me wrong, I love the boots Simon gave us, but I heard some of the hawkers at other booths talking. Vange, we can get fifty bucks an hour."

"No way."

"Yep, and that isn't all. Our errand is selling these daggers."

"But—"

"We can buy new ones at this next faire."

"I know, but Ian gave us these."

"And these two daggers will sell for enough gas to get us all the way out there and back for all eight weekends, plus a cheap motel if we act fast and reserve ahead."

"Oh, that sounds so good."

"I know. Staying with Siobhan again is out of the question. Way too creepy."

Vange held up her hand.

Emily slapped it.

᭡

RIDING in the back seat of her parents' SUV with Vange the next Friday all the way out to the new faire site reminded Emily of when they were kids on summer vacations. Just for fun, they sang some old favorite songs.

Her parents sang, too. Whoa, they were way more excited about this weekend than expected. They needed to take more vacations.

It was after dark once they had inquired of the park rangers where the faire would be and made it to the hotel her parents had booked with the deposit Emily had given them. She couldn't wait till she had a job and could get her own credit card. Asking them to book the hotel room had been embarrassing.

"Mom. This hotel is way nicer than Vange and I can afford. And we're paying our own way. I insist."

Her parents exchanged a look and then smiled their 'I'm so proud of you' smile.

"Normally, it would be," said her mom, "but do you remember Jake and Nancy, our friends who moved away your junior year in high school?"

"The guy who could talk through his nose?"

Her mom laughed. "Yeah, him. Well, Nancy's cousin is the manager here."

Emily and Vange looked at the place with new eyes, and they gave her mother huge smiles while her dad opened the hatch so the bellboy could load all of their luggage onto a cart.

Emily's mom went on. "Now don't get too excited. Your room isn't free, but we got you the corporate rate, so it's not much more than you would pay at one of those cheap motels, and so much safer. You'll pay about the same anyway, because Dad and I are paying for this first weekend. We insist."

Emily hugged her dad and then she walked arm-in-arm with her mom all through check-in and meeting the manager and touring the pool and Jacuzzi area on the roof.

Emily and Vange were to share a modest room that was reserved for eight weekends. It was near the stairs on the level just below the pool, so people in the elevator wouldn't have to see them in their wet swimsuits—which the hotel provided for those who had forgotten to pack one.

They all had a great night's sleep and a hearty breakfast in the lobby restaurant.

While they were eating, Mr. Simmons the manager came by and gifted the young women with a hotel parking pass and meal tickets, after complimenting them on their costumes. They all thanked him profusely, picked up the boxed lunches he'd had the kitchen prepare for them, and then piled into the SUV and headed to the new faire site.

IT DIDN'T LOOK like the faire yet. For one thing, this time it was in a meadow surrounded by forest instead of in a wheat field. But the main thing was that the village was still being assembled, along with the stages and all the burlap walls that would eventually hide the customer parking lot outside the circle as well as the backstage area inside the donut hole.

Emily and Vange touched up their hair and makeup in the car before getting in the boothie version of the two long lines to register as faire workers.

Emily was glad she and her friend had forgotten about period authenticity and opted to be as attractive as possible while still wearing their costumes, because most of the other hopeful workers in the boothie line had done so as well. Emily's wound was safely hidden under her sleeve.

Emily hadn't had much opportunity to ask what to expect. Dall hadn't texted with her nearly as much as she would have liked, but she understood he could only spend so much time in the men's room and that was likely the only privacy the poor man got.

They had mostly texted:

"Miss you."

"Can't wait."

When Emily finally saw Dall after exactly a week of being apart, he was up on the main stage getting ready for the opening meeting.

Emily waved, but it appeared he couldn't see her. He was squinting, and the sun was right on his face. She pointed him out to her mom, who agreed he was very handsome, especially since he was the only one up there in a kilt.

All of the students in this 'college of performing arts' were in the audience along with the booth owners. About twenty 'professors' were on stage.

They explained that each student needed to pass ten workshops over the two weekends of rehearsal in order to get a gate pass. They handed out workshop schedules. They said the booth owners were free to watch any class they liked and to hire any worker they liked.

And then each professor introduced him or herself and described his or her workshop.

During the introductions, Emily checked off the workshops she wanted to take. 'Basic faire accent' and 'costuming' were already checked off for her because she was still considered new. She also checked 'Scottish dancing' and 'songs of the period'.

Most importantly, Dall was the head of the six-person 'stage fighting' instruction team. His students had to take sixteen hours of instruction in just two weekends, practice on the weekdays between rehearsal weekends, and pass a test the second day to even remain in the class. But it counted as six of the ten required workshops. And there was limited space.

Emily ran over to Dall the instant the meeting was dismissed, holding out her program card for him to sign so she would get a spot in his class.

Dall ignored her program card, ran out to meet her, picked her up, swung her around, put her down, and locked lips with her for five full minutes before the crowd pressing around them with catcalls brought the two of them to their senses.

Her dad's voice did that even better, saying, "Hello, Dall. I'm Emily's father, and this is her mother."

Emily was proud of her dad. He didn't miss a beat when Dall clasped his forearm instead of his hand.

"Yep," Emily smiled at her parents. "This is Dall." She

turned to him. "And these are my parents, George and Sandra Shaw."

Still clasping her father's forearm, Dall said, "It is good, at long last, to meet Emily's kin in person. I am not so comfortable on the phone, you ken."

He smiled at her parents and they smiled back.

Wait, you talked to them on the phone? About what? Why didn't you talk to me?

But much to Emily's delight, Dall kept his left arm firmly around her waist the entire time he signed students up for his class and walked them over to his instruction area, which she recognized as the arena. The gazebo where all the faire people sat and watched was almost done being put back together.

Emily was vaguely aware of her parents sitting inside a weapons booth nearby and chatting with the owner, but her attention was all for Dall.

DALL SMILED and held out a one-handed Italian sword for her while beckoning her off her straw bale and out into the arena with him.

"Emily lass. Come help me show everyone a roving stage swordfight such as between Romeo and Tybalt."

Emily jumped up and ran out to Dall. She was ecstatic to be stage fighting so soon.

But how does he know I won't make a fool of myself? I mean, I won't, but...

He handed her the Italian sword and saluted her with his. She saluted back.

And then they were in action, going through several cuts, parries, dodges, and a disarm. It was fun. It was helping people learn.

It was drama.

It felt so right.

At the same time, it seemed to Emily that she was the only one who wondered how on Earth Dall had guessed she knew stage fighting so well. Sure, he had taught her how to use a dagger and they had sort of performed together at the last faire, but they hadn't done anything near this complex. Yet he had casually called her up to do it without even discussing it beforehand.

So risky.

Ian and Siobhan stood outside the arena chatting with tea-dye Aiden—whom Emily had learned at the morning meeting was the director of the entire faire.

This felt almost like a secret audition for Emily. No, it felt exactly like a secret audition.

But for what?

Emily glanced over where her parents were sitting. Could the weapons booth owner have set this all up to get hawkers for his booth? It didn't seem likely.

Oh well.

This was the most fun she'd ever had.

And curiously, I'm not even getting tired.

Aware that Dall was watching—along with everyone else —Emily did two more demonstrations: daggers with Ian and a cat fight with Siobhan. Ian was no problem, but Emily was afraid of Siobhan. Especially when she had to privately reveal her two-week-old wound to the woman and ask that she please avoid aggravating it.

But Siobhan just nodded and said, "Of course," in a very businesslike way.

And then the two of them went out into the arena and started to perform. After the usual insults to give them reason to fight, the two women faced each other with their chests heaving in false outrage.

Emily ran toward Siobhan and grabbed her hair, pausing as if for effect while she shouted more insults.

Siobhan used the pause correctly. She grabbed Emily's wrists to secure the two of them firmly together without really pulling her hair out. And then Siobhan began to move as if Emily were shaking her.

Emily went with the new move, changing the rhythm of her insults to match, as if she really were shaking Siobhan.

Siobhan used the cover of this apparent shake to make it look like she kicked Emily, but she really only tapped where she supposedly kicked and then kicked near her.

Right on cue, Emily yelled, "Ouch." She turned their fight into a comedy by grabbing the kicked leg and hopping up and down on the other leg.

It worked nicely. Everyone laughed.

Emily took Siobhan's hand and led her into a bow, and everyone clapped.

"Good job," Siobhan told her with a pat on the back and an odd smile.

Confused, Emily did her best to smile back before she sat back down on her straw bale.

Emily was certain this was a secret audition after all the demonstrations and the group instruction time. Dall divided the class by experience levels and gave each level to one of his assistants. He had her stay with him and help give the beginners the one-on-one attention they needed. She had even more fun while teaching stage fighting than she had demonstrating it.

And again, Aiden, Ian, Siobhan, and the weapons booth owner and other important-looking people stood off watching her. They kept their eyes on her and said things to each other. And now they nodded a lot.

When stage-fighting class was over for the day, Emily left Dall's side for a few minutes so he could discuss with his assistants who might make the cut and who might get the bad news the next day, after the test. Dall had already invited her and Vange and her parents to have lunch with him afterward. She wasn't surprised to see Aiden's group join Dall and his assistants after she left.

🐾

EMILY WENT over to the weapons booth where her parents were once again talking with the owner, Murray. Vange had joined them, and she did a funny impersonation of Emily clinging to Dall's side. Emily laughed in spite of herself and then hugged her friend.

Murray was saying, "Oh no, some of us do this year-round."

"You have faire in the winter?" said Emily's dad.

"Nope, we do April through September in the US, and then we go down under and put on fairs in Australia from October through March."

Emily's mom asked him, "Isn't that terribly expensive for you, taking so many people all the way to Australia?"

Murray got a faraway look in his eyes for a brief moment, and then he recovered himself. "We don't take everyone, only about forty people: the richest booth owners, the directors, and the professors. Most of the people you see here today are locals who we train during these rehearsal weekends. We get regulars who come back year after year, so it works out."

Emily's dad said, "Yeah, you appear to be doing well for yourself. Is that your truck they're unloading your weapons from?"

Murray smiled huge. "Yep, and let me show you pictures of my RVs. I have three here in the US and three in Australia."

"Excuse me," said Emily's mom, leaving to walk over toward Dall.

Emily looked. Dall's meeting didn't appear to be over yet.

"Mom." she started to try and stop her mom from interrupting, but Vange held her back. When Emily looked at Vange, her eyes were smiling and she shook her head fast.

"What?"

Vange said, "I bet your mom can get them to let Dall come out with us tonight."

Emily gasped. "That would rock."

They both watched her mom talk to the ruling group of faire people, who were stubborn at first, but whom she wore down and apparently impressed.

In the end, they all nodded yes.

Emily felt Dall's arm sliding around her waist. She turned to smile at him, and they were kissing again, a tender kiss this time. It made her heart soar. It made her forget her parents were there.

Until her mom said, "Where should we eat our boxed lunches? Watching you all exercise made me really hungry."

※

OVER BOXED lunches at the picnic tables, Dall convinced Emily to switch out of 'songs of the period' and into 'beginning jousting'.

Emily said, "But jousting is a stupid event to have at a renaissance faire. It isn't period."

"Och, lass, if we ainly portrayed what was period, nay one would hae any fun at all, ye ken?" He looked at her as if she would know, as if she had been to his time.

She did her best to convey her confusion in her eyes.

Dall kind of shook himself, and then he nodded. "Aye,

wull jousting gives one practice on horse, and that is verra period." He gave her a look that said, "I rest my case."

"But I hate horseback riding," Emily said.

"Ooh. Not me," said Vange, "and I signed up already. You should take it with me, Em. It's going to be fun."

While everyone's attention was on Vange, Dall hugged Emily close and stealthily whispered in her ear, "You *need* to be able to ride a horse, lass. Just take it easy on the wounded arm."

So that was settled.

Emily and Vange learned how to get on and off horses by themselves and how to ride a bit while Dall and her parents watched. Every time Emily looked over, they were all talking, and they seemed really into their conversation. It made her feel a little left out.

At a brief meeting that closed rehearsals for the day, Emily found out Ian would accompany Dall to their hotel that evening.

It figures.

But at least Dall would be with her.

And then her dad put the third seat down and Dall was climbing into an automobile for the first time. Guessing that he was probably nervous but too manly and oath-bound to let on, Emily pretended to be in her faire character for his benefit.

"Oh. It be one of the new horseless carriages. I hear they give much more comfortable rides than horse-drawn carriages."

Ian played along. "Yes. I hear they have shrunken musicians and singers hidden inside, and they serenade you while you ride."

Even Vange joined in. "And it's a much faster ride. They go seventy miles per hour. I never would have believed it unless I saw it for myself."

Dall sat next to Emily in the back. He started to cuddle up to her as he would on the sofa in Siobhan's trailer, but she helped him with his seatbelt. That kept them far enough apart that they couldn't kiss, darn it. He jumped a little when the engine started, and then he squeezed her hand.

Emily squeezed back in a way she hoped was reassuring.

Likely realizing they were too spread out in the car for conversation, Emily's mom turned on the radio to some oldies station.

"Wow," Emily whispered to Dall, "are we finally getting a chance to talk in private?"

But Vange turned in her seat and grinned at her. "Did you get your phone back yet, Em?"

So much for that idea.

୧ⓐ

MOM CHATTED at them while they walked down the hall and took the elevator up to the tenth floor and walked to their rooms. She and her husband seemed oblivious to Dall's rapt fascination with the modern accoutrements of their hotel, let alone its size and the general extent of civilization present in her time period.

Vange kept giggling about it. Thankfully, she seemed to think Dall was acting.

Ian played off Dall in order to add to that impression.

Amid stares at their costumes and appreciative looks from other women at Dall and Ian's kilts, it was decided they would first change for dinner, and an hour after that, for a swim and a soak in the Jacuzzi.

"You men can change in the swim lounge," said Mrs. Shaw. "Emily, why don't you and Vange show them where it is."

Ian spoke up. "That's OK, Mrs. Shaw. We didn't bring any change of clothes, so we'll just wait out here in the hallway.

We'll have to go to dinner as we are, if it's alright with you and Mr. Shaw."

"We'll eat poolside then. Emily, you and Vange show the guys where the hotel swimsuits and terrycloth robes and towels are, and where they can shower and change, and then we'll meet them up there in an hour." Her mom smiled at everyone and waited for her orders to be obeyed.

Ian and Vange were along, so it wasn't as fun as it might have been, showing Dall the swimsuits and imagining him wearing one. But the view from up there was spectacular in the daylight, right into the trees of the forest.

And then Dall was kissing Emily goodbye before they would be apart for just an hour. As usual, she melted into his kiss and let the world disappear.

"Come on, Emily. Hahahaha." Vange pulled Emily away, and they went down to their room and took turns showering and changing into their own hotel swimsuits and terry-cloth robes. All the while, Emily imagined Dall marveling at all the modern conveniences, and wishing she were the one showing them to him, instead of Ian.

What are we going to eat by the side of the pool, anyway?

When they all emerged from the stairwell in their swimsuits and robes, an umbrella table was set for six and two waiters stood by, just like in a movie.

It scared Emily a little, honestly.

Why are they going to all this trouble? It isn't even my birthday.

And then Dall came out of the men's locker room, freshly showered and wearing only swim trunks, and she forgot about everything else and drank him in with her eyes. Only gradually was she aware that his eyes were feasting on her in her hotel bikini.

She felt herself grinning at the idea that she was the first woman he'd ever seen in one.

He threw his arm around her and walked her to the table,

where he pulled out her chair and then scooted it in for her after she sat down.

"This is our treat," her dad said once everyone was seated and they all had menus, "so get whatever you want. Mr. Simmons says steaks are their specialty."

"Ooh, that sounds good," said her mom, "with a baked potato."

Knowing Dall had no idea how any of this worked, Emily was proud of how he sat back, watched, and learned without revealing how mystified he was. They all ordered steaks with various accompaniments, and then the conversation started.

"So is Mr. Simmons your kin, then?" Dall asked her dad with a smile.

Her dad smiled back. "Not family, no, but part of the circle of friends Sandra and I have accumulated over the years. Emily has known them all since she was a baby, so they are much like family."

"If not kin, they are clan." Dall nodded and offered this as a toast.

Everyone toasted.

"Clan."

Dall said, "It is good to have clan about, watching over you." He caressed Emily's back while he said it.

They all spent the meal and the obligatory hour afterward in pleasant conversation about family and clan and how much support they got from both, and then they all went for a swim in the pool and enjoyed the warm July evening. Well, Emily kept her robe on to hide her wound and just sat on the edge with her feet in the water.

And then Emily's mother pulled Dall over to Emily's edge of the pool and said to them, "Why don't the two of you go into the Jacuzzi alone for a while. I'm sure you have things you would like to say in private."

Emily met Vange's eyes, and her friend gave her a goofy grin and a thumbs up.

With a small portion of her mind, Emily marveled at the way her mom kept Ian occupied with games in the pool and gave him no good excuse to interrupt her and Dall. But the vast majority of her mind was dancing with anticipation at what Dall would say to her now that he finally had the chance.

≈

EMILY RESTED her wounded arm outside the Jacuzzi on the side away from everyone. It was fun watching Dall get into the hot bubbling water, and then they both sighed as they eased back against the jets and let the hot water massage away their sore muscles.

And then Dall spoke so forthrightly, Emily actually pinched herself to make sure it wasn't a dream.

"Lass, I have much to tell you, but I will start with this. I want you to be my wife. I have already asked your father for your hand, and he has already consented." Dall's gaze was sincere, and as he spoke, he moved away from his jet to embrace her there in the water.

This was when Emily pinched herself on the leg under the water. It hurt.

"Oh Dall, I want to marry you too. I have since I first saw you, and that desire has only grown every minute since then—"

Dall was kissing her then, and if she hadn't been so aware of her wounded arm needing to rest outside the hot water, she thought she might have crawled into his lap and let things get out of hand.

But her wound reminded her of all the questions she had for him.

Also, that old sense of the imminent loss of him came back and nagged at her, saying this might be her only chance to ask him. That he might disappear forever at any moment. And that gave her even more questions to ask.

He spoke first though, holding up his hand to ask that she listen.

"Och, I must tell you so much first, Drusilla. Do not prevent me, or I do have the fear we will not ever be married."

"Did you just call me Drusilla?"

Emily edged away from him slightly so that she could see his face, but they remained in an embrace in the hot waters of the Jacuzzi.

"Aye, and I have before, many times, but you do not remember it, lass..."

He went on to tell her a fairy tale of how she had traveled back in time with him.

How he hadn't remembered being here in her time, just as she didn't now remember being in his time.

How she had impressed and intrigued him by teaching Dog and his crew to wield swords...

How much his kin already loved her, including his children.

How something she had said there had inspired him to bring back a bunch of antique weapons, which he had sold to Murray for a pile of money.

He talked for a good twenty minutes, and without the mysterious knife wound on her arm, Emily knew she wouldn't have believed him.

But Dall showed her a birthmark that resembled standing stones around his ankle, and he reiterated the disturbing part in what he'd told her.

"Aye, so we are both cursed by the druids. I must travel in time to serve them, and you... they threaten that once you marry me, you will be stuck in whichever time that happens."

She clung to him then, fiercely. It was all she could do. She felt so helpless in the face of that double curse.

"I will that we marry here in your time, lass. It is safer here for you and for our children, when they come."

She just clung to him and nodded, her head still spinning with the enormity of the situation.

He stroked her hair and went on.

"Whenever I do go back to my time, I return the next moment. It will be as if I had never gone. So you will not be without me. Until I die."

"But I want to go with you."

Emily knew she was whining, and she became so frustrated that tears fell off her face into the hot water around them.

"And I do want you with me, lass, you ken? However, the fates be against you going again. For one, you will not be safe there. For two, you will not remember being there once you come home. For three, you will be heartbrokenly stuck there, if we should slip and marry there in God's way."

Emily opened her mouth to protest, but he kissed her quiet. She fought his kiss as long as she could, and then she gave in and enjoyed it even longer. And then a thought occurred to her.

"So, if I won't be going back to your time, then why did you insist I needed to learn how to ride a horse?"

Dall took in a deep breath and let it out, and then he took both of her hands in his and looked her firmly in the eye.

"I was a fool to say that, but... Do not trust in this, lass, but I do have a feeling it was not the truth, what they told you about being stuck in whatever time period we do marry. Why would you be stuck? I do not know this to be true. I just... feel it to be true. I do suspect that if we were to marry, you would be able to time travel with me—until you were with child. Do not count on it when you make your decision, howsoever."

He looked at her with deep concern in his eyes.

Emily was confused.

"What decision?"

"Och, lass. Your decision to marry me or no."

Emily laughed.

Dall's brow wrinkled, and he started to look concerned about her sanity.

"Don't look at me like that," she said, still laughing. "I've already decided to marry you. We're just working out the details."

※

DALL'S EYES turned warm and tender, and then he nodded with seriousness, as if they were just negotiating a business deal. But his eyes sparkled mischievously at her.

"Well then, do let us work out the details, lass. That does seem a goodly idea..."

They smiled their contented cat smile at each other and enjoyed a moment of pure pre-marital bliss.

But he hesitated, and Emily could tell he was thinking. Slowly, his face turned serious again.

"Emily, there is very little we can change about my living arrangements—"

"I won't mind living in your tent with you."

She moved in and embraced him again in the hot water, wondering if his thoughts were drifting the same way as hers, getting impatient to be *married* already.

To her disappointment, Dall pulled back just a bit so they were eye to eye again.

"I do not mean the tent, lass. When we are married, we can get a better accommodation—"

"Really."

"Aye."

They shared a smile about that, and Emily pictured their married life.

But for some odd reason, Dall seemed set on talking her out of marrying him. He went on with his downer message.

"However, what I mean to tell you lass, is that while I'm in this time period, I work the faires for them—"

"And I will, too. I know they were auditioning me today, Dall. It was rather obvious. It was more fun than I've ever had in my life, Dall. I feel like I won the lottery, getting you and the faire."

He smiled at her.

"Och, lass, it is I who would talk of winning..."

They spent another while kissing and hugging, and then Dall broke away and looked serious again. This time, he gave a little speech, and he didn't let her interrupt.

"Do not make a decision without thinking it through, Drusilla, I beg of you. We have only one more faire in your lands after this one, and then we will be in faraway Australia for six months. As Mrs. MacGregor, I would have you come with me to Australia. You wouldn't have to work the faires if you didn't want to, lass, but you might be bored if you didn't. Some of the locations are very remote. However, it is all very remote from your kin and your friends and the course you had your life on, lass. Your teaching."

His body language finally indicated that his speech was over.

Remembering what Dall had told her about the way her eyes told him more than her words, Emily fixed her eyes on his now and willed her feelings to shine through them.

"Dall, demonstrating and teaching the art and practice of

stage fighting with you today... That was even better than the course I had my life on."

Emily felt her cheeks aching, she was smiling so big. Staring into Dall's eyes was yet again better than teaching stage fighting, but only by a little bit.

Dall grabbed her then and brought her into a fierce embrace, still being careful of her wound.

"Your da said the same as you, lass, when I did talk it over with the man again this day. It is settled then. We will marry tomorrow."

Emily enjoyed his embrace and reveled in the idea of being his wife, and then she started thinking about all that went into planning a wedding.

"Tomorrow." she said to him, not quite believing it was possible.

"Aye, lass, and it is soon we should be telling Ian and your da and mum. I did give them the money already, hoping your answer would be yes, but they have many arrangements to make."

Emily opened her mouth to say more.

But Dall kissed her again.

"Your da tells me the lasses now have what is called an engagement before they marry. I say that is rubbish. I shall have trouble waiting until the morrow."

§.

THE REST of the evening before Emily's wedding passed by in a blur. She and Dall told her parents and Vange and Ian they were getting married.

None of them were surprised, which made Emily mad at first, and then it kind of tickled her.

Dall gave Emily a big kiss goodnight up on the roof of the

hotel right at sunset while Ian and Vange and her parents all
made phone calls.

Ian and Dall's kilts and leine shirts were delivered to them
freshly laundered by the hotel, and the men were taken back
to the faire site by a hotel shuttle.

And then Siobhan arrived on the roof of the hotel—with
a big smile on her face and two big garment bags in her arms.

"If you're going to be a MacGregor," she said to Emily,
"then you had better dress the part."

Everyone 'ooh'ed and 'ah'ed over the period clothing
Siobhan had brought for Emily.

There were two red plaid wool skirts—each of which
coordinated with Dall's kilt in a different way, two fancy
embroidered shifts similar to the one Emily must have
acquired during her forgotten time travel, two pairs of full
and billowy bloomers, two different hats, a plaid bodice that
had optional long sleeves which tied onto it, and a leather
belt with built-in sheaths for sword and dagger and built-in
pouches for all her belongings.

It was all handmade and new, with no signs of wear.

"Well," said Emily's mom with a big grin as she sat holding
hands with her husband, "Go try it on and model it for us."

"Come on," said Vange, helping Siobhan scoop it all up to
carry into the women's locker room.

Siobhan started to leave once she had put everything
down.

"Oh, stay," Emily said, grabbing the woman and hugging
her. "Thank you so much for the Scots clothes. It can't have
been easy coming up with all that in just a week."

"Easier than you think," Siobhan whispered into Emily's
ear so that Vange wouldn't hear.

Emily giggled a little.

"What's so funny?" asked Vange with a big smile as she
hung the clothes up.

"I'm so happy." Emily yelled, going to Vange and hugging her, too. "Dall and I are getting married."

Vange laughed too then, and Siobhan showed Emily how to tuck her skirt up into her sword belt for the best look while leaving her legs free to move about the way she would need to while stage fighting.

When it all looked just so, they went out to show Emily's parents.

"You look beautiful, Emily," said her dad.

"I really like those colors on you," said her mom. "That red brings out the rosiness in your cheeks just perfectly."

"OK," said Siobhan, "Let's go hang it up in your room so it's all ready for you to put on in the morning."

They all stayed up for another hour talking about who all was coming to witness Emily's wedding the next day and how long everyone had known this was happening and how on Earth Emily was going to get through a day of rehearsal first.

Until Vange and Emily were alone in their room, they all talked about everything except the fact that Emily would be leaving for Australia in a few months, for half the year.

"I'll miss you, Vange."

"You don't have my permission to miss me. We can email. Go be happy with your hottie, have lots of babies, and post me pics of them on Facebook, silly."

Emily laughed.

"Good night."

"Night."

EMILY SPENT the morning in a state of disbelief. She show-ered, lovingly put on her new Scottish clothes, and let Vange do her hair in a loose French braid with some flowers that had mysteriously arrived with a knock at their hotel room door.

The flowers had come with a note that said it was fine for a maiden to go hatless on her wedding day. It wasn't signed, but Emily was sure Siobhan had sent it. After all, Siobhan was the one who had given Emily and Vange the hats and explained that women of the period had to hide their hair.

Mr. Simmons clapped when Emily got off the elevator.

"You look stunning, my dear, just stunning." He gestured for her to twirl.

She obliged him.

"Congratulations on your wedding day. I wish your parents had told me the real reason for your visit earlier. You could have had the wedding suite. But no matter. Call us when you are ready, and we will send our limo to pick you up. You will have the penthouse suite tonight, with my compliments. It's almost as nice as the wedding suite." He handed her his card, which had his phone number underlined.

Stunned past knowing what to say, Emily glanced at her mom and fell back on the manners she had taught her. "Thank you so much." she said to Mr. Simmons with a smile and a shake of his hand.

"You're very welcome. My cousin Nancy says you're a lovely girl. I corrected her. You're a lovely young woman, a credit to your parents," he turned to them, "who Nancy is very fond of and says hello to, by the way."

"See you at dinner." the Shaws called out to him as they all rushed out to the SUV to go to the faire site.

Vange joked in the back seat all the way there, but Emily was only half paying attention. Every once in a while she would catch Vange's eye and Vange would grin and nod at her, as if to say, "Yes. You're really marrying Dall today. Enjoy it."

Emily's dad drove up to one of the reserved parking spaces.

Dall was waiting for her there. Looking even more handsome than usual somehow, he held out his arm. When she took it, he lowered it and put it around her waist as he had the day before, and then he squeezed her. And then he picked her up and swung her around, laughing and smiling and twinkling his eyes at her. And then they kissed for a long time.

Dall stayed by Emily's side the whole day, almost as if he was afraid she would disappear suddenly if he lost sight of her.

She knew the feeling. She still couldn't believe this was their wedding day.

It both dragged and flew by.

Emily had been switched from the 'Basic Faire Accent' workshop into the 'Scottish Faire Accent' one, which was on her wedding day. Dall went to it with her and amusedly went through all the exercises meant to teach them how to sound like Scots from his time period.

"I'll teach you Gaelic during the weeks between the faire weekends," he whispered in her ear, and he winked when she met his eye.

The two of them took a more stately approach to their stage fighting workshop that day, in order to preserve the cleanliness of their wedding clothes. Instead of doing demonstrations, they asked the students to spar. Dall said they needed to see who would be staying in the workshop anyway, and this was as good a test as any.

Finally, all the workshops and the closing meeting of the day were over, and Dall was escorting Emily to their wedding site.

❧

EMILY DIDN'T KNOW how her parents had managed it in just

a week, but all of her relatives were there, as well as many of her parents' friends. Her clan, as Dall called it.

The wedding site was the gazebo by the fighting arena. It had been completed the night before, and someone had been busy during the closing meeting that day, festooning it with ribbons and flowers. It was beautiful. Everyone was seated inside it, and a priest was waiting up front.

Glancing over to the backstage area, Emily saw that the picnic benches had been covered in white tablecloths, and uniformed waiters and waitresses were putting out china and silverware and glasses. There was a wedding cake and a champagne fountain and even a raised parquet dance floor.

A bagpiper played as Dall and Emily walked to the priest, and everyone smiled at Emily. Some of the women had tears in their eyes.

The ceremony was short.

The priest explained about marriage being a solemn and holy sacrament. He asked if Dall had a token he wanted to give his bride.

"Aye, I do. It was my mother's wedding ring, and now I give it to you, lass, with joy in my heart."

Emily had a strange vision when Dall put his mother's ring on her finger. She saw the woman's face in front of her, and she was sure it was a memory. She smiled big at Dall, bursting to tell him.

But she couldn't until they were alone, which she was looking forward to for all kinds of reasons...

The priest had them sign the marriage license right then and there, and Emily's parents signed as witnesses.

And then, the priest had them speak their vows.

Dall said his "I do" first.

And then it was Emily's turn. She was so ready for this to be over and to get to the hotel, and ...

But as soon as Emily said, "I do," all her memories came

flooding back.

She remembered.

She remembered all the details of time-traveling with Dall. And she remembered how lonely she had felt when she first arrived in his time and Dall didn't remember her.

Emily looked into Dall's eyes and willed him to understand that she knew. She knew she had met his family and where they lived and how he spent his days in his own time. She remembered playing with Peadar and Peigi and little Domhnall.

"I now pronounce you man and wife. You may kiss your bride," the priest said.

And Dall did.

And Emily kissed him with everything she had, with all the pent-up longing she had stored, in both their times. With all the love and tenderness she felt for him. With the sympathy she had for the loneliness he must have suffered this past week while she hadn't remembered how much closer they had grown in his time.

"I remember." she whispered in Dall's ear when at last their first kiss as man and wife ended. "I remember everything."

While the two of them walked to the reception area arm in arm, Dall handed Emily her phone. It was vibrating.

Mystified, Emily looked at the screen.

The phone was fully charged. But she had her memories back now, and after that kiss, this didn't surprise her.

But the Time management app icon was blinking, so she touched it. The app opened up, and Emily gasped. None of the buttons were locked anymore. It looked as though she could travel to any time and any place she chose.

Looking over her shoulder, Dall closed Emily's hand over her phone, and he helped her stow it in one of her new pouches.

"Later, Drusilla. We shall speak about it later. And now, let us enjoy our wedding supper."

THEY ENJOYED a nice dinner with their wedding guests. Ian toasted the groom and the bride. They cut the cake and fed each other and posed for pictures. They taught Emily's family and friends how to do a few Scottish dances. The guests all gave the new couple envelopes, which Emily stuffed into one of her pouches, explaining there was an ATM at their hotel.

Siobhan led everyone over to a brand new mobile home in the backstage area and gave Dall and Emily each a key. Theirs was much like Siobhan's, but big enough for a family.

Dall carried Emily inside while everyone cheered.

And then everyone crowded inside to check it out. It was fully furnished, complete with bedding and all the kitchen items they would need.

Emily was wondering how the two of them were ever going to get out of there when Vange helped her out.

"OK." Vange said to Emily, and then in her teacher voice that everyone could hear, she said, "Time to call the limo that whisks you off to your hotel so we can't shivaree you all night."

Everyone laughed.

Emily made a show of calling the limo on her old phone so that Vange could see she had it back.

Vange laughed, and they slapped hands.

Absentmindedly, Emily put her phone in her pouch and forgot it was there.

While Emily was hugging her parents in thanks outside, Murray the weapons boothie came over with a nice bottle of Scotch whiskey and a handful of glasses, which he passed out to Dall, Emily, her parents, Vange, Siobhan, and Ian, who were all standing there.

"I suppose you're wondering why I've gathered you all together here," he said with a smile once everyone had their drink. "Well, Emily needs a job at the faire—and sure, she'll be teaching workshops with Dall. But I offer you both paying jobs."

Ian and Murray and Siobhan all laughed at that. Emily looked at Dall, and he seemed interested. Her parents looked puzzled.

Siobhan elbowed Murray, and he looked at Emily's parents and sobered up. "Oh, don't get me wrong. The faire is very good to its ... professors. As a married couple now, Dall and Emily will live in a trailer rather than a tent, and all their needs will be provided, for them and their children." He smiled at Emily's parents.

They gave him puzzled smiles.

Murray looked at Dall then. "But it's nice to have spending money, you know? To be able to have a car and see the town now and then, get out a little."

Fortunately, just then the limousine came.

Dall and Emily rushed inside and waved at everyone until the doors and windows were all closed and they were on their way, alone.

Emily turned to Dall.

"What was Murray saying all that for? He knows about our antiques business."

"But very few other people can know, lass. They must think our money comes from some explainable source."

"Ah, yes. Ha. The druids think they have us under control, but we sure showed them. I'm almost as excited to continue the antiques business as I am to get you into that penthouse suite at the hotel."

Emily's phone buzzed.

7. CLANS

Siobhan ran out from between the trees with a big smile on her face and her arms held out for a hug. "Welcome home, Mrs. MacGregor."

It took Emily a moment to realize the druid was talking to her. That she, Emily, was now Mrs. MacGregor. When she finally did catch on, Emily felt a huge smile crack all over her face.

"Morning, Siobhan."

Dall only released half of Emily so that the two women could hug. He fiercely kept her in a half embrace as he might if he was afraid she would disappear if he let go of her. He picked up the two heaviest suitcases with one arm, still clinging to her with the other.

Enjoying that immensely, Emily managed to pick up the next heaviest bag with her one free arm, leaving Siobhan to get the last three items, which she did cheerfully and easily.

They all made their way past the front gate of the faire, around the half-constructed fake English village street, and under the burlap wall into the center of the donut-shaped faire site, the backstage area.

Siobhan put Emily's bags down at the door of the large travel trailer the druids were letting the newlyweds use.

"You remembered to keep your keys handy, right?" she asked them with a teasing grin on her face. "You have an hour to unpack, Emily, and then we have a staff meeting at the picnic tables. Oh, and make a list of any groceries you want and bring it to the meeting." Siobhan smiled and ran off.

Even though he had carried Emily inside the day before, just after their wedding, Dall scooped Emily into his arms now and did so again. Once they were inside, he kissed her soundly and reached out the door to drag her bags in.

"Do you really need an hour to unpack?"

Emily giggled in his arms.

"Probably, but I can unpack later."

They found the time to list the groceries they wanted, but just barely.

"Leave your phone in the trailer, lass," Dall said after he spent all of thirty seconds repleating the nine yards of homespun plaid wool that made up his great kilt and had belted it back on.

Emily stopped trying to stuff her phone in the pocket of a different pair of shorts and looked at her new husband. She made a face that was meant to say, "Why on Earth would I leave my phone here?"

To Emily's surprise, Dall opened his sporran and got out a tiny spiral notebook and a ball-point pen. She didn't have much time to wonder where he'd gotten them. He opened up the notebook and wrote:

"I do not think the druids know that all of the buttons on your Time Management app came unlocked after we said our 'I do's, lass."

Emily reached out her hand for the pen, and when Dall gave it to her, she wrote in the tiny notebook:

"Surely they knew that would happen? I think they didn't

want us wandering away from your time without seeing them again first, and that was why they told me I would be stuck in your time if we got married there."

Dall held out his hand for the pen and then wrote:

"I am the only professor who has married while in the service of this particular set of fair directors, you ken? I do not think they know."

Emily shrugged and put her phone on the nightstand before she ran into his half embrace and walked out to the picnic tables arm in arm with her husband.

EMILY AND DALL were the last ones to arrive at the staff meeting. Siobhan and Ian smiled at them and gestured to two seats they had saved together. Emily looked around and tried to guess which other professors were time travelers like Dall. She suspected that the jousting professor was, Lews, as well as the woman who taught the costuming workshop and had to approve everyone's period clothing, Marion. She very much wanted to speak to them and hoped she would get a chance, until she noticed that Lews was scowling at her. What was that about?

Tea Dye Aiden was the only one standing, and he started talking as soon as she and Dall sat down.

"Welcome, Mrs. MacGregor, as our first new staff person in two years, and our first new staff person ever by way of marriage."

Everyone except Lews clapped and smiled at her. Lews just sat there scowling.

Trying her best to ignore him, Emily smiled back at everyone else and took a bow as best she could while sitting down. She felt Dall doing the same, beside her. When she looked at Dall, he gave her a know-it-all look that she found infuriating and endearing at the same time. She poked him in the ribs. It hurt her finger.

Aiden continued.

"This meeting has been called to discuss how best to introduce you as the new Mrs. MacGregor back in Dall's own time, Emily. I expect that Dall has told you everything that transpired while you were there..."

Emily didn't hear the end of that sentence. She was reeling over hearing him discuss time travel right there out in the open like this. But Siobhan's elbow nudged Emily back into the moment.

Aiden was still talking.

"So you see, we'll need to send you back about two weeks after you left, and without Dog and the rest of those bikers, this time. You would have been married a week, in that case, most of it traveling back up to Kilchurn Castle from England..."

Emily thought he knew everything for a moment, when he said England with just the same emphasis that she and Dall had while they were in the highlands. But then she remembered how the druids could eavesdrop on her by way of the Time Management app on her phone. She would have to be very careful, she realized all over again now, wishing there were some way she could negate that ability of theirs.

But Aiden hadn't paused in what he was saying.

"...so we will send you back a week after your wedding. You'll go a week from right now, next Monday morning. And your only mission will be to announce your marriage to everyone there." He smiled as if that would be as easy as making a few phone calls.

Emily knew darn well it would be dangerous, as was everything in the 1500s. She smiled too, though. She couldn't wait to time travel again. She squeezed Dall's hand, and he squeezed back. And then she had a thought.

"I guess I'll have to wear my English period clothing when I go back," she said to Dall sadly. She already loved her MacGregor plaid outfits.

Dall surprised her, though, speaking loudly enough for the whole meeting to hear.

"Nay, lass. My mother did give you the plaid clothing you wore yesterday." He smiled at her in a goofy way. "She has the full awareness of this clothing, and she would be sorely disappointed if you did not wear it, lass."

Emily gave her husband a baffled look.

He smiled at her smugly.

"I smuggled it back to Kilchurn Castle inside Dog's pack, lass. Inside Mike's as well. All of the men volunteered space for your new Scots clothing. 'Tis a shame they don't remember." He cowed a bit at a stern look from Aiden. "A needed shame, I ken. However, it was a bit expensive to get it back from them."

Now Emily was sorry she hadn't unpacked. She suddenly needed to know for sure that all her Scottish clothes were indeed packed in her luggage.

"May I be excused?" she asked Aiden, lovingly running her finger over Dall's mother's ring, now on her wedding finger.

Aiden looked at her kindly.

"You may, but remember, you must not discuss time travel with anyone who is not at this meeting, understand? No phone discussion, either."

"Yes..." Emily fumbled with how to address the man. "Sir."

Aiden nodded and went on to discuss some other business.

Dall pulled Emily by her hand so that she was looking at him.

"Are you right in your heart, lass?"

Wanting to reassure her husband that he hadn't married a ninny, Emily smiled back at him.

"Right as rain."

And then Emily got up and almost ran back to their trailer, where she unpacked and took a deep breath of relief at finding everything was indeed there. She held the plaid skirts and embroidered shifts and the tailored bodice that fit perfectly up to her nose and breathed in deeply, imagining herself inside her mother-in-law's house up on the highlands hill in what recently had been Menzies lands. She looked at the woman's ring on her finger and felt the hug she'd been given on first meeting her, and she sighed with how much love was there.

EMILY'S LUGGAGE also contained all her favorite summer clothes, her toiletries, and a care package from her aunt with a note:

"Your mom noticed that you ate all my candies and used all my handmade soap, Emily. Here is more. Give me mailing addresses for you, and I'll send you some for every wedding anniversary, birthday, and Christmas."

After carefully locking the door and checking to make sure all the windows were securely fastened (the air conditioner was on) and the curtains closed, Emily stayed in the trailer by herself and used her phone to check her email and update her Facebook status to married. She included that picture Vange had taken of her and Dall's first kiss. That seemed like yesterday, in a way, but then so much had happened since then. She got lost in the memories while she answered comments from old friends who were congratulating her and saying what a hottie she had caught.

She was so wrapped up in that, she didn't notice Dall had come home until he plopped down onto the bed next to her.

"Ooh. You scared me." Emily giggled, and they spent a while being newlyweds.

Emily came up for air first.

"So, anything I should know from the rest of the staff meeting?"

Dall squeezed her.

"Och no, lass. You did well to leave when you did. It was all very dull after that. So are you ready for your first lesson in the Gaelic?"

She nodded yes, and they spent all five of the weekdays between workshop weekends getting her as versed in Gaelic as possible before their next trip to the 16th century. Dall wasn't a bad teacher, and she was a willing and eager student, so it was a pleasant experience for them both. They didn't have a computer or a TV, though, which might have made it a bit easier.

For the most part, the two of them stayed in their trailer alone without interruptions. This was their honeymoon after all, such as it was. But they did have some visitors, and they did get out a bit.

Murray came to Dall and Emily's trailer Tuesday morning.

"Have you two lovebirds thought about my invitation to hawk for my weapons booth?"

Dall came up behind Emily and put his arms around her.

She looked for Dall's opinion on his face.

He answered Murray for them.

"Nay, we have been a wee bit busy."

They all laughed.

"Will you come inside, Murray?" Dall said, "And we can have a talk about it."

Once they had the burly man settled on their new cloth couch with a glass of water, he pitched his offer to them again.

"Yes, the druids supply you with a home and food and

health insurance—everything you need, but there will be additional things that you want: evenings away, to rent a car and go visit friends and family, to keep your data plan so you can keep in touch on Facebook... Your independence. I know you received wedding gifts, but they won't last forever. You need some money coming in. Come work for me."

Murray was offering a good deal, and the MacGregors accepted.

The two of them would do an extra demonstration with all the various weapons Murray sold right up next to his booth in the arena each fair day. They would stay afterward to answer questions from the audience. They would make $400 a week in spending money for one hour's work each per weekend day. They scheduled it first thing after fair opening ceremonies, during the time Emily used to hawk for Simon.

Dall and Emily went for a jog each evening, leaving her phone in the trailer. It was their only chance to talk candidly. Even if they ditched her phone outside somewhere, who knew how many bugs the druids had planted inside the trailer? On these jogs, Emily explained modern life to Dall, including debit cards. They agreed to deposit most of their money in Emily's bank account.

Emily called the DMV and her bank and everyone else she had business with and arranged for them to mail forms to add Dall as her husband and to change to her married name. They all agreed to use the hotel as the MacGregors' temporary mailing address, and her parents' address as their permanent mailing address.

She checked her messages every morning while Dall was in the shower. There were always texts from her mom, which were mostly teasing but also a little worried. Emily did her best to sound cheerful in her responses, even though she herself was a little worried about being under the druids' complete control.

Ian delivered groceries Thursday morning.

Dall clasped Ian's forearm.

"You ken this is easier than making me sandwiches, aye?"

Ian laughed.

"Yeah, I suppose it is."

Emily gave Ian what she hoped was a warm smile. He seemed like someone they should have as an ally.

"Will you sit down and stay awhile?"

"Sorry," Ian said. "Normally I would, but I have more groceries to deliver."

"It is all right, man," Dall said, clasping forearms with Ian once more.

Ian seemed to enjoy this attention from Dall, because he said more when he hadn't appeared to plan on it.

"You and Emily should come out into the arena in the mornings and spar with us, if you can drag yourselves out of bed." He smirked at them. "We start at sunrise, before it gets so hot out."

Dall looked at Emily to see if she wanted to accept Ian's invitation.

Emily nodded yes eagerly. That was a really good idea, and she was grateful to Ian for thinking of her, too.

So Dall accepted for them.

"We will see you at sunrise tomorrow."

THEY SET Emily's phone as an alarm and were up when it was still dark the next morning. Emily put on sneakers, shorts, and a T-shirt while Dall belted on his kilt and claymore and buttoned up his boots.

When they got to the arena, it was only just getting light, but a dozen other staff members were already out there. Half of them sat in the gazebo drinking coffee, eating donuts, and chatting animatedly, including Siobhan and Tea Dye Aiden. The other half were inside the arena, sword sparring in pairs. Since they weren't in period clothing, they wore white padded fencing jackets, and they were all using one-handed swords, mostly rapiers. Of those sparring, the only names Emily knew were Murray's, Ian's ... and Lews's.

Emily briefly noted that Murray knew how to use his weapons and made a mental note to explore that more later. Right now, her attention was on Lews.

She knew it was rude to stare at the man, but she was unable to help herself. Judging by the way he was dressed and his comparative mastery of his weapon, Lews was definitely a time traveler. However, he was from England rather than Scotland. That made sense. Most of the faire was about English history. Emily didn't dare say anything about it, though. Not with all these people around. Despite what had happened at the staff meeting earlier that week, she and Dall had not been released from their promise not to discuss time travel with anyone but Siobhan.

And something told Emily not to trust Ian quite that far.

So as Dall walked her into the gazebo and found the two of them seats next to Siobhan, Emily just watched Lews spar with Ian and did her best not to stare. She tried to smile at Siobhan's witticisms and to generally be friendly—while everyone out in the arena tried their best to disarm each other.

After a time, someone sounded a bell and yelled out.

"Time. Take five and then change partners."

All the combatants came into the gazebo and grabbed bottles of water from a cooler.

Ian came up to them, smiling.

"Glad you made it. The jackets and practice swords are over here. Now's the time to get geared up so you can make the next bout."

Dall helped Emily into a padded fencing jacket, and she did the same for him. She chose her practice rapier, and then they wandered out into the arena with the rest of the people who wanted to spar. Ian and Dall partnered up right away.

And then Lews was in front of Emily, giving her what looked like an attempt to smirk. But he was a bad actor.

Emily could tell it was really a scowl.

Lews spoke to her low enough that only she could hear.

"Do come and show me why thou deservest to be on staff here." And then he put on a better act and a sweet vocal tone, saying loudly enough for everyone to hear, "Emily. Pray, join me." He added a sickly sweet smile.

A glance at Dall showed Emily that he was occupied. She glanced at Aiden and Siobhan.

They were half paying attention.

No one had overheard what Lews said.

For once, Emily wished she had her phone on her. Then at least the druid on spy duty would know Lews had it in for her.

"Actually," Emily said, backing toward the gazebo, "I think I'll sit this one out." Keeping her eyes on Lews, she managed to take two steps.

And then Lews was lunging at her. A real lunge, meant to do harm.

Shocked but not surprised, Emily raised her hilt up just in time with her blade down, catching the tip of the other sword in the middle of her blade and deflecting it away from her. The actor in her knew she should turn from him now and run, make it obvious to their audience that she was not play-ing. However, the survivor in her would not allow her to take her eyes off her attacker's blade.

His sword tip went up above her head and was coming down with all his strength.

This was the move she dreaded most. She raised her blade

up to block his blade's descent, but she feared that gravity and his manly strength combined would overwhelm her—and her head would get bashed in.

And then his blade whooshed to the side, and Emily heard him grunt as he hit the dirt.

"Dall." Siobhan called out. "What did you do that for?"

Whirling to look for Dall, Emily jumped when she found him right next to her.

"Are you hurt, lass?" Dall said, looking her all over.

Still kind of shocked, Emily just shook her head.

"We will be seeing you later." Dall called out to everyone in general as he put his arm around Emily and walked her back to their trailer.

Once inside, they took off the fencing jackets and put them outside along with her practice rapier.

"Dall. He—"

Dall pointed at her phone, saying "I know, lass, I know."

They stayed in the rest of the day.

❦

AFTER DINNER, Siobhan came knocking on their trailer door.

"Come to the Scots guild meeting, you two."

With her spirits up again after a whole day of Gaelic lessons, Emily tried to be funny. She called out to Siobhan through the trailer door.

"Go away. We don't want any."

Apparently unamused, Siobhan used her own key and opened their door.

"It's not a choice, you guys. Guild meetings are part of Dall's ... job. Now straighten yourselves up and come meet this location's Scots guild members. Emily, you might want to wear your Scots clothes. They would make a great first impression."

Emily wasn't surprised that Siobhan had a key, only saddened that she had used it instead of playing along with Emily's joke. Good to know, though. This confirmed that Siobhan wasn't really her friend. No, the druid woman was something between a boss and a jailer.

Still, Emily had walked into this jail of her own free will, and on balance, she was happy. For now.

Anyway, the local aspiring actors and dancers and sword fighters who would be their fellow guild members at the renaissance festival in this location weren't part of the druids' scheme. No sense in making a scene by being dragged to the guild meeting kicking and screaming.

There were potential friends among these locals.

Emily didn't want them to think she was high maintenance.

And Emily agreed that she should wear her Scots clothing. For one thing, the way the two of them matched clearly marked her as Dall's—and Dall as hers. For another, she was new at being a Scot, and she could use all the practice she could get.

Emily was dressed in her plaid and ready to go in five minutes. She actually smiled on the way over to the picnic tables where the Scots' guild meetings always were. Dall's mother's loving attention to her new clothes made Emily feel good.

"Vange." Emily separated from Dall to run over and hug her friend. "I don't know why I didn't realize you would be here. Yay."

Evangeline's brown face smiled as she reached up and hugged Emily back.

"Of course I'm here. It's tradition, isn't it? And look at you. All decked out in the Scots garb. You know what? I'm going to have to join the Scots, too. Something tells me that's the only way I will get any time with you." Vange was in jeans and a T-shirt at the moment.

Emily noticed Ian standing there next to Vange.

"Can she join, Ian? It's not too late, is it?"

"I'm sure we can squeeze her in somehow," Ian said with a grin at Vange. "But the Scottish fair accent workshop was last weekend, and what will you do about a Scottish costume, Vange?"

Siobhan opened her mouth to say something.

But Emily didn't want Vange beholden to the druid. She hugged her best friend. "I have two Scottish skirts and three Scottish leine shirts, and I can only wear one at a time. We have a week to shorten one of the skirts for her before the festival starts." She looked at Ian. "Surely her English bodice would work along with the Scottish skirt and leine?"

But tiny Vange held her hands up as if she could block the sounds of everyone's voices with them.

"I was thinking I would just buy my own Scottish outfit, Emily, with the money I'm going to save by staying in one of your spare rooms instead of blowing so much on a hotel room."

Emily felt her face fall at that.

Siobhan and Ian were talking to some other people.

So while they were distracted, Emily whispered in Vange's ear.

"You didn't cancel the reservation, did you?"

Vange looked puzzled.

"No, not yet, but—"

Emily sighed deeply. And then she whispered some more.

"Oh, good. Please don't. I've been looking forward to time away from here."

"But the money—"

Emily was so worked up, she gave up on whispering.

"You know what? I want that room so bad that I'll pay for

it by myself, all seven weeks. You can crash here in our trailer, and we'll go stay at the hotel."

Emily got out her keys and took the trailer one off and handed it to Vange.

Vange gave Emily a sly smile and handed over her share of the hotel meal tickets—and her car keys.

"It's parked by the front gate. The parking pass is in the glove box. Oh. But my stuff's in it. So I'll have to walk you guys out there after the guild meeting."

Emily nudged her friend's shoulder.

"Yeah, we'll need to stop by the trailer and pack a bag. Help yourself to whatever's in the fridge."

The guild meeting went OK.

Emily made a point of bringing Dall and Vange over to sit with some of the new people who hadn't been in Dall's sword-fighting class, just to meet as many of the locals as possible. She promptly forgot their names, but they seemed nice enough. They were so eager for the festival to start, it kind of made Emily excited about renfest again.

And good thing.

After they were dismissed, several of the women fussed over Emily's Scots clothing.

"Wow. Look at this embroidery."

"Oh my gosh. How long did this take you, Emily?"

"Dall's Scottish mother made my ... costume. She made me two, even, and all by hand. Isn't her work wonderful?"

All the women came over to ooh and ah over it, and those who were still making their own costumes took careful notes.

Emily was amused to see the men surreptitiously doing pretty much the same with Dall's great kilt.

And then Siobhan handed Dall a tarp.

"Take the men over there and show them how your kilt looks on the floor, and how you put it on. You did wear your shorts underneath, right?"

Emily thought her husband looked just a tad annoyed at that last bit, but she was proud of him for hiding it well.

All he said was:

"Aye."

LATER THAT NIGHT at the hotel registration desk, Mr. Simmons said he was happy to let Dall and Emily use his hotel as their temporary mailing address. He even gave Emily his personal email address and said that if she gave him the location of their next faire site, he would see if he knew any of the hotel managers nearby from conferences he'd attended.

Emily scoffed a little, thinking that was above and beyond what was reasonable.

"Oh that's OK. I don't want to be so much trouble."

Mr. Simmons took both Dall and Emily's hands and looked earnestly into their eyes.

"I have kids of my own. They aren't your age yet, but when they are, I would hope my own friend's cousin would look out for them if they moved halfway around the world. It's no trouble. I really want to help make sure you get your mail," he swung her hand up in a playful way, "and to help your parents keep an eye on you, Emily."

They all laughed.

"Thank you again, Mr. Simmons, for everything."

"You're very welcome, Mrs. MacGregor."

It felt odd to be called a misses, but it felt wonderful to be called a MacGregor. Emily could tell her smile was beaming at the hotel manager as she and Dall looked at their mail.

Most of their papers had already arrived, but what still came in would be held for them at the front desk in a special box that Mr. Simmons had set up for them. She and Dall signed all the papers, and Mr. Simmons promised to keep copies for them and to get them into Saturday's outgoing mail.

Emily's driver license and passport name changes would take the longest, but she felt sure the druids would be able to transport her to their next festival site—on the other side of the world in Australia.—without the passport. She also figured her US driver license wouldn't be good or needed over there, anyway.

Well, free transportation was one good thing about being connected to the druids. Besides, Dall didn't even have ID, let alone a passport. She hoped that wouldn't be a problem.

Mr. Simmons' hotel felt like a haven of privacy compared to the huge trailer the druids provided for the newlyweds in exchange for Dall's servitude.

Dall and Emily MacGregor enjoyed what felt like their second honeymoon, after less than a week of marriage. They enjoyed being served a lavish dinner on their food vouchers in the lobby restaurant, and they particularly liked talking in the Jacuzzi. It reminded them of Dall's second proposal.

Besides, even a hotel room could be bugged, but who could bug a Jacuzzi?

Emily smiled amid the bubbles from the Jacuzzi jets.

"Will we go and visit your family again, Dall, once we go back on Monday?"

He gave her a sincere and earnest look and a little hug.

"They are your family too now."

She smiled and caressed his face.

"Thank you. I hope we'll go see them."

Dall gazed at her stoically and used his nickname for her.

"I very much do as well, Drusilla. However, you know that Alasdair and Colin rule what I do there."

Emily felt her face grow serious.

"Somehow, that doesn't seem near so oppressive to me as how the druids rule what you do here. Do you know exactly what your service to the druids entails? Is it spelled out anywhere, like in a contract, or ..."

"Nay so far as I know, lass."

He pulled her close in the steaming water, and that just had to be enough comfort, it seemed.

In the morning, Emily donned her Scots attire once more.

Dall donned his kilt in less than 30 seconds as he always did, and Emily enjoyed watching as she always did. He made it look as easy as pulling on a pair of pants, compared with their guild mates who made a production of it rolling around on a tarp.

Emily knew he had exaggerated and extremely slowed down his demonstration the night before, in front of their new local Scots guild mates.

They drove to the fair site, parked the car, and walked arm-in-arm to the opening meeting of rehearsals. Vange called out to Emily from where she was sitting on the straw bales with Ian and a bunch of people in jeans whom Emily recognized from the Scots guild meeting the night before.

"Is my wife's best lass in our guild then, Ian?" Dall asked matter-of-factly.

"Why yes, I do believe she is," Ian said with a wry smile and a tug on Vange's hand, which he was holding.

Vange chortled. "It's not what you know; it's who you know."

Everyone laughed.

"Love your new Scots clothes, Vange." Emily cooed.

Vange nodded to an older woman sitting behind her and then stood up and slowly turned around, showing off her new plaid skirt and bodice and her new drawstring-sleeved chemise. "It used to be Audrey's. Turns out she's been doing faire for thirty years. I didn't believe her when she told me she had something my size, but she showed up with this an hour ago, and now it's mine."

"Yay." Emily said, taking Vange's hands and jumping up and down with her in excitement. "Now we're guild mates." They grinned at each other like kids for another moment.

And then everyone sat down again and got quiet for the meeting. After it was over, Ian and Dall stalled at getting up and moving on to workshops, and then Emily got a pleasant surprise.

Tea Dye Aiden and his entourage of co-directors came over, and Aiden himself said to Emily, "As you are now Mrs. MacGregor, you are considered staff. This means you must attend staff meetings and do various ... duties." He looked at her significantly.

Emily nodded. Yes, she had already been shown that, hadn't she.

Aiden smiled. "It also means you will automatically receive a gate pass and you are exempt from the compulsion to attend workshops, though I'm pleased you have agreed to help Dall teach his workshops. That should continue, so long as you are not with child."

Emily was a little embarrassed to have a relative stranger discussing her possible imminent pregnancy, but she had a feeling it would only get worse if she let on that it bothered her. All she did was sort of nod her head at him in agreement and hope he went away. The man gave her the creeps, a little.

But it was time to go help Dall teach stage fighting, and Emily loved that. She hugged Vange goodbye saying, "See you at lunch." and she let Dall walk her arm-in-arm as he always did now, since they wed.

Emily managed to avoid Lews all weekend. That night was Saturday night, but it was still workshops, not faire proper. Dall and Emily enjoyed the privacy of the hotel once more. Sunday morning, their whole guild attended the Scottish dancing workshop together. Ian and Vange were partners once more. They seemed to always be together, which made

Emily smile until she remembered that Ian—and Dall and she herself—would be with the faire in Australia half of every year, away from Vange.

The two of them came to Dall and Emily's trailer for Sunday dinner and stayed late talking and laughing. It was a good time, and Emily had trouble letting them leave. She was anxious about leaving them the next morning, even though she knew the druids could bring her back the moment after she left.

Monday morning, Aiden supervised Dall and Emily's time travel right inside their own trailer.

Emily made sure first that all her supplies were in her various pouches. She had bought a new period-looking dagger from Murray, and it was now sheathed in her boot. She wore her favorite of her two new skirts, hats, and shifts, with the shift she had traded for tied around her waist under her skirt, for a clean change. She wore an additional new belt minus the sword and dagger sheaths, which would have made her a target for sword attacks back in the 16th century. Women of that time simply did not wear swords, even if they did know how to use them.

Dall wore his usual kilt outfit complete with a claymore sheathed at his side. He looked gorgeous as always from where she stood glued to his other side.

"Alright, Emily," said Aiden. "I sent the destination information to your phone. It should be on the screen now along with your arrival date of August 2, 1540 and your return date of October 2, 1540. Remember: in 1540, your wedding day was July 26."

"It's on the screen." Emily couldn't help being excited at the prospect of her second time-travel adventure.

"Well, whenever you're ready, push the button." Aiden smiled.

⋆

THE WORLD WENT SWIRLY, and then once more, Emily woke up in Eamann's dark healer basement inside Kilchurn Castle. It must have been during preparation for the midday meal, because a lot of bright light filtered in through the wooden floorboards overhead. She could hear a large amount of activity up there, including footfalls immediately above them to indicate a meal was in the making, just like the last time she had arrived here with Dall.

Emily had a moment of panic, remembering how alone she had felt the last time. She didn't normally pray, but she said a quick silent prayer right then and there. "Please God, don't let Dall have forgotten all about me again." Mustering up her courage, she looked at him while she stowed her phone in her boot.

Dall winked at her.

"Thank you, God." Emily said silently while looking up. Some sort of spilt food falling through the noisy ceiling kind of ruined the mood, though.

There was a coarse burlap curtain drawn in front of them. That was new. Gingerly, Emily started to open it.

Out loud and with a huge smile, Dall said in Gaelic, "Well lass, shall we go up and tell everyone your new name?"

There was a profane exclamation from the other side of the curtain, and then Eamann opened it. He was wearing his white druid robe, and there were several bloodstains down the front of it.

Emily gagged. On a wooden table in front of her was a kilted man whose wounded but healing hand was covered in leeches. They were sucking his blood. He was just lying there like this was normal. Emily had to fight hard not to lose her breakfast on the stone floor.

Eamann had collected himself, and now he covered for

their mysterious arrival in front of the man with the wounded hand. "It is glad I am to see you have both recovered from your traveling sickness. Did you make up the cots?"

Emily looked behind her. Sure enough, there were two made-up cots back there. She nodded.

Dall was bolder. He stood up straight at attention, as if in front of a drill sergeant. "Aye, we did, Eamann."

Eamann appeared to examine the two of them. He opened Dall's mouth and looked inside. When he started to touch Emily's face, she cringed away from him. He rolled his eyes and said in Gaelic for the man on the table to hear, "Very well, on up the stairs you go."

Dall reached out his hand as he hastened to the stairs, and Emily grabbed it. She was willing him to speed them on up and out of the gruesome scene before Eamann changed his mind and started talking to them. Or worse. The castle healer had been jealous over all the fuss about Emily being the one to save Alasdair from his choking fit.

But of course Dall had to stop and clasp healthy forearms with the MacGregor who was being bled by leeches. Of course. The two of them spoke in Gaelic. This time, some of the parts that Emily didn't understand through context, she got by actually knowing some Gaelic words. She didn't feel she could respond coherently in their language yet, but hearing it spoken was helping solidify her learning of it.

"Och Sean, did you give as good as you got, anyway?"

"Aye Dall, the other fellow shall not stand on his legs for at least a fortnight."

"How be Molly and your children?"

"They be fine. Looks like you have a new mouth to feed."

"Aye, but I do not mind at all."

The two men laughed.

When Dall and Emily climbed the steps and emerged into the crowded dining hall, the meal hadn't quite started yet.

What with the raucous talk of the battle with the Menzies a few days previous and all the people coming and going from the kitchen, no one noticed the newlyweds. Dall led Emily along the stone wall around the huge plank dining table until they stood behind Alasdair, who sat alone at its head next to Colin's empty throne-like chair.

Emily was glad not to see Colin, nor any other Campbells. All the plaid in the room was MacGregor plaid, the colors she had on. It wasn't yet regimented into tartan of a specific pattern. That didn't happen until Queen Victoria's day. But the clan had its colors so that members could recognize one another at a distance, especially during raids.

People called out as they noticed the new arrivals. Some smiled at Emily, but others looked uneasy.

"Look, it's Dall."

"Hello, Dall."

"And is that Emily?"

"I think it is. And she's wearing good highlands clothing this time, the dear."

"Hello, Emily."

Emily called out in Gaelic, "Hello." which made everyone smile big and relax a little.

Alasdair plainly heard all this, of course, but he let the greetings crescendo before he turned around and spoke to her and Dall, in Gaelic this time. "So... you sneaked off with the actors in the middle of the night, Dall." His words were harsh, but the grin on his face and the twinkle in his eye reassured Emily it would be OK.

Dall changed his grip on Emily from holding hands to hugging her by the waist. "More importantly, I snuck off with Emily here to her people in England—and made her my wife."

"Oooh."

All the women who were close enough to hear squealed,

and then they flooded the hall with high-pitched shouts to the women who had missed it.

"They're married."

"Dall married Emily."

"Emily's his missus."

Alasdair stood, and when that caused everyone to quiet down, he addressed the men. Judging by the looks on their faces, most of them had still been too busy discussing the battle to even have noticed much but that Dall had returned with that pretty girl, whatever her name was.

Still in Gaelic, Alasdair said, "Dall has returned to us from England." The men cheered. "And he has brought with him his bride." Alasdair picked up his tankard. "Let us drink to Emily here, the newest MacGregor."

Everyone raised their tankards in a toast. "The newest MacGregor."

They all drank heartily, and then everyone got out of their seats and rushed toward the new couple. The men all slapped Dall on the back. Mairi and the other wives all hugged Emily, and she hugged each one back with the one arm that Dall wasn't holding.

After everyone had looked either the bride or the groom in the eye and acknowledged their union, they all sat down. As they ate their meal, they all eagerly told Emily what it meant to join their clan.

"Your children will be descendants of King Alpin through Prince Gregor."

"And we MacGregors are constables of Kilchurn Castle here."

"Aye, your sons will have to fight to gain lands for Cailean Liath's father, but there be honor in that, you ken."

That was the one sad note in the day. Emily knew that when Colin (Cailean Liath) inherited the chiefship of Clan Campbell in 1547, he would not only kick the MacGregors out of this castle, but also Colin would begin an oppression so severe that by 1594 the MacGregors would all end up either sold as slaves in the new world or hiding their clan name for fear of their very lives.

But that was tomorrow's trouble. Emily resolved to enjoy this day. It was one of the best of her life. There wasn't any cake, and they didn't get any presents, but Emily loved this wedding reception nonetheless. All the welcoming and love and acceptance brought tears to her eyes. She smiled her sweetest smile at everyone, trying her best to let them know these were happy tears and that she was very glad to be a MacGregor.

THE NEW COUPLE were given their own small room on the third floor of the castle. In August, it was quite comfortable there at night with a breeze coming through the wind opening, but Emily kind of dreaded the winters there. To amused comments, she hauled a bucket with a bit of water up three flights of scaffolding to use as a chamber pot. She soaked her dishtowel in the clean water first, so that she and Dall could wash. All this in order to avoid having to use the small room with its holes in the floor down at the end of the balcony.

Which reminded Emily of the photos she had taken of that small holed room the last time she had visited Kilchurn Castle. She wasn't surprised to find the pictures missing from her phone. She wouldn't expect the druids to create an elaborate app that could magically transport people in space and time and spy on their conversations—and then for the druids not be able to erase photos through that app.

Dall and Emily enjoyed a relaxing night there before they headed out on horseback, riding double once more on a two-week journey out into the highlands to see Dall's family. It was still fun to cling to Dall's back as he guided the horse, even after a week of marriage.

"It does not get much warmer here, lass. Enjoy the warmth, you ken?"

Emily clung to Dall tighter and hummed in contentment. "Oh, I am."

Dall gave her a rewarding laugh.

They took the same route as last time: north along the River Strae to see the MacGregor cattle lands and most of the clan, and then east over the hills into Glen Orchy, where the Campbells ranched their cattle along the easiest passage north.

This time, whenever people asked Dall for the news, he introduced Emily as his new bride as the first item. Everyone congratulated them, and some gave them small bits of food or a tankard of ale. Dall's cousin Orson and his wife didn't seem at all surprised by the news that Dall and Emily had wed, and Emily suspected they'd known before she had.

At sunset on the third day of their journey, they at last came to the small MacGregor settlement were Dall's oldest brother was in charge and Dall's three children lived in the company of their grandmother, aunts, uncles, and cousins.

"Da. Da." Peadar and Peigi ran out and grabbed Dall as they no doubt always did when he came home to see them between deployments. "You are home again very soon, but we do not mind."

Dall and Emily laughed, and Emily gave each child a candy again.

Dall knelt and gathered his children close to him for hugs. "Peadar, Peigi, I have married Emily. She is now my wife and part of the MacGregor clan, you ken?"

Mouths puckered from the candy inside, they both nodded. Peigi spoke around hers, "Grandma told us that was going to happen," the candy clicked and clacked against her teeth, "just after you left with those odd men who raised the alarm."

"Ah," Dall said, still kneeling and hugging them, "I hope you will welcome Emily. She is part of our family now. Not your mother, but a woman to be obeyed just like your aunts and Grandma."

The children smiled at Emily from their father's arms and nodded yes. Dall stood and put his arm around Emily. Peadar put his arm around Dall, and then Peigi tentatively went to Emily's side. Emily hugged the little girl to her, and the four of them walked up the hill together. This time, Emily understood the greetings that the other MacGregors who lived on the hill gave them in Gaelic.

"It is well you have come home, Dall and Emily."

And then the children's grandma came walking sedately out of the house, leading little Domhnall by the hand. She had a warm smile for Emily, and she stopped and held out her arms.

Tears streaming down her face, Emily rushed to her and spoke to her in Gaelic. She tried her best to be grammatical, but she knew her mother-in-law loved her and would appreciate the gesture even if she messed it up. That gave her the confidence to try. "Thank you so much. For your ring, and for making these clothes for me. Yours were the best wedding gifts I received."

Dall's mom smiled at them and held out her arms.

Emily looked at Dall and he smiled and nodded. And then she rushed into his mother's arms and hugged her as if she were her own mother.

And then his mother took them both by the hand and led them into the house and up the stairs and over into a corner, where she dropped their hands and pulled down a hatch. A freshly built mini staircase came down with the hatch.

Dall hugged his mom and then started up the stairs, reaching back for Emily's hand.

She took it, went up, and gasped. The attic had been made into a love nest for the two of them. Everything was freshly cleaned and dusted. All of the stored items had been moved to the low areas on the sides so that Dall had room to stand up in the middle, just barely. A new bed stood near the middle of the room, and a new lamp stood on a lampstand by the top of the new staircase. There was an actual chamber pot on the floor nearby, and a large chest of drawers stood against the far wall.

Dall's mom followed them up there. "Do you like it?" she said in Gaelic with a smile.

Dall hugged his mom again, and Emily joined in, saying, "It's wonderful. Thank you so much."

"None of the children are allowed up here," his mom said, "though we women will be up to dust and clean. It is a place you can keep secrets safe." She gave Dall a sad but loving look, as if to say, "And I know you have many secrets to keep, Son." And then she went over and opened two of the drawers. "There is a change of clothes in here for each of you, and something separate to sleep in."

They hugged her again.

She stroked both of their hair once, and then she raised her chin and put on a mock serious face. "But you must come down and have supper with the family before bed." Her face cracked and she grinned at them teasingly before she shooed them down the stairs.

❦

AFTER A FAMILY SUPPER complete with more hugs and back slaps and toasts for the newlyweds, and an hour playing with Dall's children, Dall and Emily made their excuses to all their grinning adult relatives and went up to their lovely new attic bedroom.

Emily had her phone with her, of course. She was deathly afraid of misplacing it here in Dall's time. That would mean having to beg Eamann to send her home when the druid sent Dall to do his oath bound duty to the druids. She would almost rather just remain in the 1500s. She had an idea, though, and she wanted to share it with Dall. She tapped on his shoulder.

Dall turned to her, grabbed her, and threw her on the bed. "Impatient are you, lass?" He smiled and fell in next to her.

Emily couldn't help giggling, and anyway this bit of business might help hide what she wanted to try. She got her phone out of her boot and put her finger over her lips while she put on a bit of a show by giggling more and saying, "Ooh. That's the husband I married."

Dall's face turned curious, and he nodded, and then he played along by kissing her noisily.

It felt good. Emily had trouble concentrating on powering her phone up and bringing up the Time Management app. When it did come up, she showed Dall the screen so he could see what she was doing.

Figuring the druids' time travel app was much like a GPS app with the added dimensions of time and transport, Emily wanted to see if she could bookmark their current location. She wanted to be able to come straight here sometimes, rather than always arriving in Eamann's creepy healer hole at Kilchurn Castle. Dall's mom had seemed to be suggesting that, even, by saying this was a place they could keep secrets safe.

There it was, the map with their location indicator, and all of the colored buttons surrounding it. Holding her breath, Emily hovered over one of the buttons to see if it would tell her what it did. Yep. Sure enough, it did, but Emily hastily moved away from that button. She didn't want to edit the map. Who knew what that might do?

After twenty minutes of trial and error and braving some drop down menus, Emily finally found a button that said it would save their current location in memory. After a really long kiss—which Emily wondered if Dall had also given just in case it was their last—Emily pushed that button.

The result was almost a let-down. A little window popped up, saying, "Your current location has been saved as a destination. Please name this destination." Emily looked at Dall, who shrugged, and then she typed in, "Home."

Much later, Emily checked to see if she had any other saved destinations. Yep. Apparently, their trailer had been saved as a destination when they traveled from it. That destination was only named for the date they had left, and she changed it to something she would remember better. She did the same for Siobhan's trailer's old location. She also named the Kilchurn Castle destination that instead of the date it had been named the last time the two of them left from there.

Dall was still watching over her shoulder, but then he held out his hand for a turn playing with the phone. They were certainly not equipped to travel right at this moment, but she trusted Dall.

She smiled at him and handed it over, snuggling up to him to watch what he would do with this dangerous toy.

❦

EMILY WOKE up the next morning still safe in that new bed in the attic of her in-laws' highlands house. She was surprised to realize she was disappointed. Being back here in 1540 was more relaxing than being in her own time. Too relaxing. She was only 23. She would relax when she was old.

She wanted excitement. Adventure. Besides, she was really curious.

"Dall?"

"Mmm?"

"Are you awake?"

"Nay."

Emily hit him with her pillow. "Are you sure?"

Dall caught her pillow when it hit him and used it to pull Emily to him. He grabbed her with his whole body. "Aye."

A long while later, Emily looked at her husband in a way that she hoped told him she had a fun idea. "Let's try..."

And then she remembered the druids could hear them. She debated with herself for a moment. Did it really matter if the druids found out Emily wanted to experiment with the Time Travel app? Now that they were married and Emily was on staff at the fair, there didn't seem to be any big secrets kept from Emily. So why did she feel the need to keep secrets from them?

She didn't know, but something made her point to Dall's sporran, and they used his tiny spiral notebook and ballpoint pen to discuss it.

She wrote, "Let's try traveling with the phone instead of our feet, and while we're at it, let's travel in time, too." She could feel her face cracking, she was smiling so big.

Dall wrote, "I do think we should put our clothes on first, lass." While she giggled about that, he wrote, "And mayhap go down and break our fast."

Smiling at him, she wrote, "I suppose you're right."

So they got dressed and went down to breakfast. And played with Dall's children. And hugged them a lot. And heard Dall's brother tell a tale about the biggest Menzies raid the settlement had ever withstood. And walked down the hill because he said, "Oh, did you not know there was a faire on this week?"

At this real Scottish renaissance fair, they danced real Scottish dances and played rounders and ate all sorts of uh, good Scottish foods such as haggis, which made Emily blanch, much to Dall's amusement. There was no jousting. Nor were there any displays of sword fighting, but Dall walked arm in arm with Emily all over, and they talked with the neighbors while examining the crafters' goods. She traded wax-paper wrapped candies for another dagger, which she sheathed in her other boot when they got home.

And they had another family dinner. And played with Dall's children. With one thing and another, it was late and they were sleepy again. And the faire was on all week, so this happened again and again.

Finally, it was the night before Dall and Emily were supposed to leave on horseback for Kilchurn Castle, by way of Orem's ranch.

Emily said, "We can still try using the app, in the morning."

Dall's face looked puzzled. "But then would it not be time to leave, the next time we came back here?"

"Why would it be time to leave? We saved this destination two weeks ago." Emily felt her brow scrunching up and did her best to relax it so she didn't get wrinkles.

"But then we stayed here, you ken. We cannot come here from the future when we are already here in the present, lass."

Emily tried to think that through. It did make sense, and Dall's logic especially impressed her because he hadn't seen Doctor Who. He must have come up with it all on his own. "Well what good is having a time travel app if we never use it?" She said it out of frustration, and then she realized they had been speaking out loud. She gasped.

"What is it?" Dall's face was all concerned for her now.

Emily looked at her phone and spoke to it. "Well, now

you know that we're thinking of using the app on our own. If you have any advice for us, then make sure we get it soon. We aren't going anywhere until after we sleep, but then all bets are off."

SURE ENOUGH, when Emily checked her phone in the morning, there was a message from whichever druid had been monitoring their conversation.

"I set it up for you to arrive at Kilchurn Castle three days from now," the Druid had texted to them. "It just happened to be convenient this time, but don't count on us always being your travel agency."

Emily covered her mouth to stop giggles from coming out as she showed the message to Dall.

He started to say something.

She shook her head frantically while making writing motions. When she got the pen and paper, she wrote, "Good thing a fussy druid who isn't very bright was on watch last night. They still don't know the settings are unlocked. We'd better make it count when we use it, because they'll probably lock them up quick after that and only allow us to come home so you can work for them."

The two of them beamed at each other, both caught in the daydream of what big adventure they might be going on soon.

Dall brought them back to the here and now. "Well, shall we be going then, lass?"

"Yes, we shall." She checked around to make certain they both had everything they'd arrived with, glad they had said their goodbyes the night before, explaining they would get horses at Orem's and would be leaving on foot before anyone was up. And then she got her phone out and examined the new settings the druid had told them were set. Yes, she saw how their current destination was Kilchurn Castle, three days from today.

And there was a menu where she could change that if she wanted.

"Dall?"

"Hm?"

She showed him the destination place and time, and the menu where it could be changed. She hit the menu button and went through the saved selections: Kilchurn Castle, Home (You are here), Siobhan's Trailer Faire 1, Our Trailer Faire 2, and Custom.

Her finger paused over the Custom menu item, and then she tapped it. A map appeared. She could go anywhere in the world, it seemed... but she hesitated. That also seemed very dangerous.

While she was hesitating, Emily got out the tiny notepad and wrote, "How about if we stay here in this house, but go forward in time?"

"Is that not dangerous?" wrote Dall. "You have said the MacGregors get a hard time of it in future years."

"We can use the history book to make sure and skip over all the years that MacGregors were outlaws."

"Aye, and what if someone is here inside the house when we arrive, lass, inside a bedroom? You ken? Or what if the house is not here at all?"

Emily huffed. She was starting to understand why the druids had originally done this time travel thing out in the middle of a sacred grove of trees, and why they added a circle of standing stones to protect them on arrival once the Romans came into the picture. And why they so carefully controlled it even now, when this magic app had made it more scientific.

8. GAELIC

She held her phone out where they could both see and moved it forward to the 21st Century, and then even further forward to the 22nd Century.

Abruptly, Emily lowered her phone. "As much as I would like to go gallivanting off into the future right now ... I hate to say it, but I'm too chicken to try that, Dall." She knew her brow was scrunched up, but this once she didn't worry about getting wrinkles.

Dall let out a deep sigh, pulled her closer into an embrace, and stroked her hair. "It is a great relief to hear you say so, lass. I would have gone with you into the great unknown, but my heart was heavy over it. Mostly for the sakes of Peadar, Peigi, and Domhnall. They do have the clan, but I would be remiss to deprive them of their father just to suit my fancy."

Emily relaxed into his embrace and breathed easy, enjoying his caresses. "So you need to go back to Kilchurn Castle?"

Dall sighed, but not heavily. It was more a 'back to reality' sigh. "Aye. Warriors such as I who are stationed at the castle stay there three fortnights, you ken, and then we are free to visit home for one fortnight. You and I just spent my one fortnight here. I must go report to Alasdair for my clan duty." He started the two of them swaying together side to side, almost like they were slow dancing. It was soothing.

She went with it and sighed her own 'back to reality' sigh against his chest. "And then we have to go back to the 21st Century faire, right?"

Dall stopped the swaying and raised her chin so that they were looking eye to eye. "Och, lass, is it so bad, having to spend time at the faire? I did think that you loved it." He looked worried. Of course. He had been worried that she was giving up her career as a drama teacher in order to marry a lowly professor at the college of performing arts and travel with the renaissance faire.

"You know what I mean," she said, trying to convey with her eyes that she did not regret marrying him, since her words weren't doing the job. "Your fellow time-traveling professor Lews hates me, and the druids are always up in our business. I like it better here in your time." She put her arms around his neck and started them swaying side to side once more, smiling up at him.

He returned her smile, and it turned into their contented cat smile. "I ken your meaning, aye. But the faire is duty just as much as the castle is duty. My duty to serve the druids." At that, he looked worried again. Worried that she regretted marrying him. As if.

Emily kissed all his worries away, which took not much time at all, and then she grinned at him playfully. "I still want to try traveling to Kilchurn Castle by phone rather than by horse, though."

Dall laughed. "My heart lies easy with that plan, you ken?"

"Are you ready?"

"Aye."

"Here goes." Still holding the phone out where they both could see, Emily used the drop-down menu to get the settings back to the Kilchurn Castle destination bookmark and made sure their arrival time was set for three days from their current time.

She looked to see if Dall agreed the settings were correct. And then she pushed the 'go' button.

§.

THE WORLD WENT SWIRLY, and then Dall and Emily were once again in Eamann the Druid's castle dungeon surgery, in the corner behind that burlap curtain he had recently added.

There were screams coming from the other side of it.

Emily gingerly pulled back the curtain so they could peek into the basement room to find out what was going on.

This time, instead of leech-encrusted Sean, the wooden table held a man who was tied to it. He was struggling. Eamann's back was in the way, so Emily couldn't tell what was going on, but the druid 'healer' was bent over the struggling man, intent on doing something.

"What are you doing?" Emily yelled at Eamann while she rushed so fast to untie the man that she still had her phone in her hand. But she felt Dall grab onto her from behind. Startled, she turned a horrified face to Dall. Why was he stopping her? Couldn't he see that Eamann was torturing someone? Surely he wouldn't stand by and allow that to happen?

Dall embraced Emily gently and caressed her back through her stiff bodice, whispering in her ear, "Drusilla, Gregor there has a bad tooth, and Eamann is doing the man a favor by pulling it. Leave well enough alone."

It was the first time Dall had given her an order without adding an "Aye?" or a "You ken?" onto the end of it. Emily was a bit shocked by that, but her relief at finding out Eamann wasn't torturing poor Gregor won out and she relaxed in Dall's arms. For a moment.

However, then scary old Eamann yelled at them in Gaelic. "Don't just stand there, help me hold him still. Both of you." It was an order directed at Dall, who had been cursed by his order of birth with a duty to serve the druids.

Immediately, Dall let go of Emily and rushed to obey his druidic master, holding Gregor's head while Eamann struggled with some tongs to get a hold on the bad tooth.

After a few seconds, Eamann growled at Emily in Gaelic, "Now, lass. Pin his shoulders down and stop his thrashing."

Emily burst into tears, she was so afraid and upset. It was a gruesome enough sight with just the men involved, and now she was being asked to participate. What's more, she had no idea how to pin a man's shoulders down, and Eamann was just plain scary. "Wwwaaaaa." she wailed like a baby, hating herself for being so weak and useless in a medical crisis, but hating Eamann even more for exposing that about her. Dall was probably the one regretting their new marriage now, and who could blame him?

God bless him, Dall stepped away from his druidic duty long enough to try and comfort his wife. He put his arms around Emily and swayed back and forth in that soothing way, caressing her hair and making shhhh noises with his gorgeous lips.

Frustrating Emily even more, her husband's kindness made her even more emotional. She felt like he would think of her as one of his children, with her blubbering, and now her throat choked up on top of the chest spasms and all the tears. Dredging up memories usually calmed her, so she tried to remember how to explain to Dall in Gaelic the way she felt.

Eamann was really angry now. He threw the tongs and whirled with his hands out to grab her and do God knew what.

At the same time, Emily remembered the Gaelic words

she was looking for in order to say the phrase that had come
to mind from her childhood. "I want a do over."

EMILY BLINKED. She was still choked up and sobbing with
tears streaming down her face. She still clutched her phone,
and now her knuckles were white. Dall was still holding her.
But now they were back in their attic bedroom at his family's
house. A moment ago, they had been in the castle dungeon,
hadn't they? Yes.

Dall chuckled softly, a rich sexy grumbling noise in his
throat. "Look at that, Drusilla. You commanded the wee
phone app, and it obeyed you."

Scarcely believing it was possible, Emily laughed while she
was still crying. "I didn't command it. I whined like a baby."

"I do believe it thinks you did command it, lass." He
started that swaying thing again.

She could feel his kilt swishing into her long plaid skirt. It
was working to relax her. Emily slowly felt her sobs and tears
stop. "Far from commanding, I thought I was being really
childish. I translated a saying we used to use on the playground, 'I want a do over.'"

Dall stopped swaying. And he laughed. "Well, the Gaelic
phrase you said back there, in front of Eamann, translates to
English as 'Take me back again.'"

"Really?"

"Aye."

"What did I say, again?"

They spent a good hour going over the subtle differences
between the ways one could say Gaelic words and then
drilling Emily in how to say 'Take me back again.' exactly the
way she had said it, with the same inflections. By that time,

the rest of the people in the house were awake and the two of them were hungry.

Emily tried to put yearning in her eyes as she looked into Dall's. "It's tempting to just go down to breakfast now."

Dall pulled her close and sighed. "Aye, lass. However, we have given in to that temptation over the past fortnight. I have duties, and I must go do them."

"We could really leave on foot to Orem's and borrow a horse from him like we told the children," Emily said, looking up into his face with her most practiced hopeful expression. She liked that idea more and more. It would give her more time alone with Dall, which she needed right now.

"Och, no lass. Remember what happened the last time we rode to Orem's from here? Now that we have a choice in the matter, no. It is not safe, and I will not risk you with no need. We will use the wee phone app. Adjust the time for half hour later, and the tooth should already be out, you ken?"

Shrugging, Emily did just that, making sure to show him so he could check her settings. When he nodded that they looked right, she pushed the 'go' button and the world went swirly again.

THE CASTLE DUNGEON was quieter this time. Emily hoped that meant the screaming was over. When she'd had a moment to listen, she discovered that things weren't much better, though. Instead of screaming, she and Dall heard the painful groaning of a man whose tooth had just been yanked out of his mouth without the benefit of anesthesia.

And then their situation got even more unpleasant.

Eamann yanked the curtain aside. "Oho. So you thought to come back after all the hard work was done, did you? Well

I have news for you, Emily. You will now be in charge of nursing this man while he suffers."

Emily opened her mouth to refuse such duty. And in truth, she was not suited for it. She had first aid training, but she really hadn't the foggiest idea how to nurse a man back to health. She didn't think she had the patience for it, either.

Eamann cut her off and moved so close to her face, she could smell his horrible breath. "Ha. You may be able to shirk your duty while your husband is here to naysay me, but rest assured that as soon as Colin orders him out on patrol, you will be under my authority—"

In the meantime, Dall kept giving Emily's hand a quick succession of squeezes.

She had no idea what they meant, and they were starting to make her angry with him. She was near tears again at feeling all alone in a nasty situation that would get far worse. Eamann was right. Dall would have to leave the castle to go help the Campbells steal more land from the Menzies. She would be left here defenseless.

Finally, Dall reminded her she could get out of this mess. He whispered the Gaelic phrase she had been studying for the past hour.

"Take me back again." Emily repeated after him in Gaelic, and then she thanked God with all her heart as the world turned swirly.

THIS TIME, when they landed in the love nest Dall's mother had made for them, Emily congratulated herself. At least she wasn't crying. She knew that was mostly because this time, Dall hadn't let go of her. It was a fact that the two of them were strong together. "I guess we'd better go back earlier than any such unpleasant situation, from now on."

Dall nodded yes while still holding her in his arms. "Aye, lass. Will you recognize the signal next time?"

She leaned into his chest and sighed in relief, trying to calm her adrenalin-charged body down. "The signal?"

Perhaps sensing the battle heat in his wife, Dall helped her relax by rubbing her shoulders, which made her moan in an unladylike way, but she didn't care. "Aye," he said, "when I churn your hand like butter, that is the signal to command the wee phone app to take us back." He demonstrated the quick succession of hand squeezes she'd been wondering about back there in the dungeon.

Getting flustered and not wanting him to know, Emily rushed on with the business at hand. "Yeah, now I get that. OK, I'm setting it for ... an hour before we first tried to go there?"

If he noticed how flustered she was, for once he didn't tease her about it. Bless him, Dall nodded in a businesslike manner. "Aye, an hour should be enough time to guarantee that Gregor will not have gotten up the courage to go down to see Eamann yet about his bad tooth."

After she finished the settings but before she pushed the 'go' button, Emily had an encouraging thought. "But it sure is cool how the app obeys Gaelic commands, isn't it."

Dall gave her their contented cat smile.

She gave it back, and they rested in that a moment.

Dall kept holding her, and he started that rocking back and forth motion again.

She kept trying to turn it into slow dancing, but that hadn't been invented yet. He didn't know what she was doing. She was going to have to fix that one day soon.

But he was talking. "I'm going to tell you a secret now, lass. I hope you will not be cross with me, but if you are, please remember we need to stay in my time three more fort-nights, and I am your best protection against the likes of

Eamann, both in my presence and even in my absence, by reputation."

She leaned back in his embrace to smile up at him, and that stopped his rocking. She giggled. "You're threatening me with Eamann if I get mad at you? This must be some secret. It can't be that you haven't a penny to your name. I already know that."

He smiled back and continued looking her in the eye. "Och, that you do. Well now, quick and finished is best with secrets. That morning at your faire when you first noticed me in my kilt, when you and your best lass Vange were buying your English clothing?"

"Yeah?" Emily felt her brow gnarling up, and she fought to smooth it. She really didn't want wrinkles at 23.

He swallowed, which made his Adam's apple bounce up and down noticeably. "Well now, that was not the first time I noticed you, lass."

Emily felt her face crack into a teasing smile. "Oho. Were you and Ian and the guild all following me?" She knew her brows were both arched up all the way, but she wanted the effect they had, wrinkles or no.

Dall's brows answered hers and did the same. It was working. She was affecting him. "Aye, but this is the secret you cannot reveal that you know, lass: even then, you had been to my time once before. You just do not remember." Dall was breathing heavily.

Now she lowered her brows in an accusing way. It was automatic because of her actor training. "I had been here before, in the 16th Century?"

"Aye" He raised his chin, but he swallowed audibly.

She still had the upper hand, but she didn't want to worry him, so she just said softly, "Why didn't you tell me this before?"

"I did not tell you before because I was sworn not to. But

Emily," he took her left hand and caressed his mother's wedding ring on it, "my primary duty now is to you." His brows lowered in a guilty way.

Ooh, that was too much. She felt bad and let up on the browbeating, allowing her love for him show in her eyes. "Why don't I remember?"

He relaxed a little and started caressing her lower back. "I do not know why you do not remember, lass. I reckon because we were not in contact at that time. Our physical contact does seem to be what makes the magic of the wee phone app bend to your command, aye? Mayhap our contact was what conjured up our memories of each other's times, as well."

Emily searched his eyes for the reason behind her being brought to his time before, knowing he probably was unaware and just doing his druid masters' bidding. "Why was I brought here before? What did I do while I was here?"

Dall blushed. He kept his arms around her, though. "A whole passel of women from your renaissance festivals was brought to me, to see which one I ... cared for."

Emily felt her mouth drop open. She heard Dall continue talking, faster and faster as if to get as many words in as he could before she ... she didn't know what.

"And I do care for you, Emily. I did choose you out of two dozen women. That must needs count for something, aye?"

Emily still wasn't sure how she felt about this. She blinked again and again, letting her subconscious mind mull it over. She was a physical person, a kinesthetic learner, and her teacher training classes had helped her understand that most of her thinking was done outside of her awareness.

Dall was still talking. "Aw lass, do you not see? That is why we were already drawn to each other the first time you remember seeing me. We had already shared our special smile. It had already worked on you, lass."

Emily noted that she wasn't crying or getting angry. "Dall, it's OK. I understand you didn't have any choice in it. Thank you for telling me. You didn't have to do that, and I appreciate it."

He kissed her then, and they were busy for several minutes. "Anyhow, I did think that you should know, because Eamann knows. He was there."

She put her hands on Dall's chest. "I really don't want to go see that man."

Dall raised his strong chin. "I do not, either, Drusilla. But it is not often what we want in life that we must do."

Emily didn't know about that, but she got her phone out again and checked the settings. "Ready?"

THEIR TIME and space travel went off without a hitch this time. Only Eamann was in his dungeon an hour before their original attempt. When he saw Dall and Emily enter, he simply nodded toward the stairs with his nose in an ancient scroll and his fingers examining a clay tablet of some sort.

Most of the castle was asleep, so Dall and Emily went up to their new room and busied themselves until they heard signs that others were greeting the day.

They enjoyed the morning meal with the larger red-kilted MacGregor clan, and then someone yelled out, "Colin's here."

Emily gripped Dall's hand hard under the table as Colin and his blue-kilted kin entered the hall. As he took the empty throne at the head of the table next to the ordinary chair where Alasdair MacGregor sat, she fought to keep her hatred of Cailean Liath Campbell out of her eyes. After all, the man had not yet done the deeds she hated him for. Still, she had a fleeting temptation to find something poisonous and slip it in Colin's wine.

As usual, Colin had shown up to take Dall and all the men out to do his dirty work at the Campbell borders. "Drink your fill and laugh your best this night," he said to the men, "for on the morrow we go on patrol."

The highlander men all cheered and toasted to that, but Emily noticed that among the women, only the widows joined in. The rest seemed to hate Colin almost as much as she herself did. Fortunately for the women, Colin paid them no mind. Emily was relieved to also be beneath the notice of the other Campbell men, now that she dressed in her husband's plaid and wore his mother's ring.

The men were gone a whole week, back two weeks, gone three days, and then stayed at the castle. Just as it had been the last time Emily was at the castle, some of the men didn't come home, and others came home injured. Eamann took the patients who needed limbs hacked off down into his dungeon surgery, but he left their daily care and basic wound stitching up to the women.

Emily was put to work with the rest of the women and all but the smallest children: mostly tending the sick and injured and helping prepare meals. She enjoyed being a part of the MacGregor clan, and the other women all treated her like one of them. She was, now.

Life at the castle without Dall was miserable only in that Emily missed him and worried for his safety. Day to day, it was nice. She'd never had any brothers or sisters, and these other women whose husbands were also in peril felt more like sisters than her in-laws did. Her in-laws were so isolated that they were tightly knit. Except Dall's mother. Emily felt great warmth from her mother-in-law.

These other women had left their homes to follow their men to the clan's base of operations just like Emily had. Besides, she spent more time with them, time without the men around. She and her new sisters traded advice about everything from cooking and child-rearing to the marriage bed. It was almost like being with Vange, and Emily figured in ten years, being in the castle alone with these women would feel just like being with her best friend.

One odd thing happened that helped Emily out immensely in the long run.

She didn't know if it was because she was now part of the clan and no longer a guest, or if the favor she had gained for saving Alasdair from choking had worn off, but now everyone expected Emily to learn Gaelic. They were helpful and patient but insistent with her, no longer speaking English for her benefit.

Emily cringed at the mistakes she knew she was making when she spoke their language, so much so that she was afraid to speak at all for the first day. But no one teased her. They just patiently corrected her. It helped that she was doing the tasks they were describing and holding the tools they were naming. That made her learn Gaelic much faster than she had learned French in a classroom.

She was glad to be learning Gaelic, especially if that meant she might have more power over the 'wee phone app'. She was so glad, in fact, that she volunteered for odd jobs just to learn the Gaelic names of the things involved: weeding the vegetable and herb garden, helping the others dust and straighten the cluttered rooms of the castle.

By the time she and Dall trudged back down into Eamann's cellar to go back to the 21st Century, Emily understood almost everything she heard. She was still shy about forming her own sentences and speaking them aloud, but she could do it. She was able to communicate in Gaelic.

EMILY AND DALL got back to the faire site the moment they

had left, the Monday morning two weeks after their wedding. Aiden was there alone with them once more. Seeing him brought back Emily's memory of Lews attacking her at the sparring session the Friday prior. It made her angry.

Not only was Lews trying to keep her from sparring with the others, but he was also fighting her right to be on staff at the faire. Why, she had no idea. She didn't care, either. And her anger overcame her embarrassment about speaking in her new language.

Wanting to show him that she really did fit in now, Emily spoke in Gaelic when she said to Aiden, "If I show up at the sparring match in the mornings, what are the chances you and the others will keep Lews off of me?"

But Aiden ignored her bold accusation. He looked at her as if he had been considering what she said but had decided not to address it. "I hear you accomplished your mission and everyone in Dall's time now knows he has remarried. Good. As you know, the renfest opens this coming weekend. Most of our preparations are finished, but we still need help getting the burlap wall up around the backstage area…"

Emily tuned him out after that, even though the man droned on and on about tasks the two of them would need to complete that week. He had tried to pass himself off as understanding what she had said in Gaelic, but Emily knew he hadn't. His acting would fool most laymen, but Emily had seen the way the man hesitated. Her trained eye had known he was hesitating out of fear, not out of indecision.

Aiden kept droning on in English.

She fought the smile that tried to form on her own lips. She only let it show after the tiresome man had gone through their trailer door and Dall had shut it.

Dall smiled back at her once he turned around. "Wha—"

Emily fumbled with Dall's sporran until she got the little

notebook and pen out. She wrote, "Aiden doesn't understand Gaelic."

Dall read it and then looked at her and shrugged. He wrote, "Aye, I do not think anyone here does understand the Gaelic."

Fighting the furrowing of her brows, she wrote, "Aren't any of the faire druids from your time or earlier?"

"Nay, lass, I do not think so."

Her brows furled some more, and she wrote, "You have tried speaking Gaelic with all of them?"

He wrote again this time, instead of speaking, "Aye, lass. None of them can understand the Gaelic."

Emily gave Dall her biggest, most dazzling smile and wrote, "And we're going to use that to our advantage."

Dall smiled back at her and wrote, "I did have a reason for insisting that you learn Gaelic first, you ken?"

And then they got too happy in the moment to contain themselves. He scooped her up in his arms, grabbed the little notebook, and carried it and her to their bedroom, where they remained a few hours.

§◦

HOURS LATER, when the phone was, ahem, fully charged and the two of them were able to think about anything besides each other, they used the little spiral notebook to discuss their plans.

She wrote, "We need to get out into the world and bookmark more safe locations."

He wrote, "Aye, and your Gaelic needs to get better, lass. Supposing there are other handy commands you could be giving to the wee phone app?"

They looked at each other and smiled huge smiles. Emily

was thinking of all the possibilities, and she was pretty sure Dall was doing the same.

She wrote, "I suppose we have time for more Gaelic lessons on the weekdays, but I want to get off the Faire site during the Faire weekends so we can mark more safe spots as time travel destinations."

He wrote, "More Gaelic first. It is a must."

She dug a pen out of her purse so she could write at the same time. "But we'll be leaving here in a few short weeks, and I need to be able to get to my parents cheaply while we're in Australia, so our time is best spent marking safe locations in the US right now."

Shaking his head and grinning impossibly huge, he wrote, "We have plenty of time, lass."

She wrote, "I suppose you can teach me a lot in five days."

He wrote, "We can have months if we like, you ken?"

Finally getting it, she laughed and hugged him and they were busy for another hour. They wrote to each other again over a meal.

She wrote, "If we're going to be somewhere for months, then let's go spend that time with Peadar, Peigi, and Domhnall."

They shared their special smile for a moment, and then he wrote, "We can only spend a fortnight there at a time, you ken. I must do my duty at the castle."

She wrote, "What if we skipped your time at the castle and moved ahead to the next fortnight you could be with the children?"

He shook his head and quickly wrote, "Nay, lass. I cannot skip my duty to the castle. It would not be right."

She wrote, "We could go back and fill it in later?"

His brow furrowed. He sat still for a while, obviously in thought. He had stopped eating, too. His food was getting cold on his plate. Finally, he wrote, "Aye, that will do. Howsoever, then there will be many fortnights in a row without seeing the children." He looked sad.

She caressed his face and gently shook her head, then wrote, "We can save for visiting the children the time we would normally be riding to the castle and back, if we just Time Travel all the time, using the wee phone app."

He smiled and hugged her.

So that was how they spent three months with his family. Very gradually, Emily's sisters-in-law opened up to her and let her in as part of the family. She now knew their names and the names of all their children and even the names of a few of the neighbors down the hill. She found out the family had lived in Glen Strae before being asked to take the land they now sat on from the Menzies clan.

Emily played with all the children, but she paid special attention to Peadar, Peigi, and Domhnall. She really wanted them to like her, and she was beginning to have special affection for them, along with their father. She helped mend their clothes and she took her turn watching two-year-old Domhnall every second.

Almost incidentally, this time spent with family turned Emily into a proficient speaker of Gaelic. But there wasn't any life-threatening conflict while they were there this time, and so no new Gaelic words of power came to light. Not then and there.

EMILY LAUGHED when they got back to their trailer and she saw their dirty dinner dishes on the table. The food on them was still wet, so she whisked them all into the sink and made quick business of rinsing them and loading the dishwasher, laughing all the while.

That evening, she took her phone along on their jog,

careful to show it to Dall so he wouldn't say anything they didn't want the druids to know. They had also been careful about that while they had been gone, leaving the phone in their love nest most of the time and only speaking candidly when they were out of earshot from the house. The modern druids would be foiled if they just spoke in Gaelic, but who knew what druid was on duty monitoring their phone. It was best to keep silent around it about what they knew and what they suspected.

"Let's jog up to the top of this hill this time," Emily said casually to Dall.

He nodded.

The two of them looked for a safe place to leave a book-mark that could be used when their trailer was no longer here. They had discussed this, and they could erase it once they got a better bookmark, closer to her parents. Her mom still texted her every morning, but it would be nice to be able to visit safely. And cheaply. Especially from Australia.

In her mind, Emily had gone over several possible safe destinations the past few months, and she had a few ideas. If she could just get there. She didn't dare just use the wee phone app's map and pop over. She might arrive in an area where she could be seen.

"Emily."

She came back to the present moment and followed Dall's voice through the trees and bushes until she found him. She gasped. "It's perfect."

He had wandered around to the side of a thicket away from the beaten path through the woods up the hill. There was a hole in this side of the thicket just big enough for a person to enter, and then it opened up inside to comfortably allow the two of them to lie down there, if they so desired. The young trees were evergreen, so this location would be concealed even in winter. For at least ten years, anyway.

Emily got out her phone and bookmarked this destination as Thicket Faire 2, and then they jogged back to their trailer.

Early the next morning, they showed up at sword practice. Lews was still hostile, but now they were on to him. They took turns sparring so they could watch each other's backs. That continued all week.

And then Friday night rolled around and it was time for their Scots guild members to arrive. This time, Dall and Emily were looking forward to that.

❦

DALL AND EMILY showed up arm-in-arm to the Scots guild meeting at the picnic tables in the backstage area of the faire on their own this time, without Siobhan needing to pound on their trailer door.

"Vange." Emily separated from Dall and ran to hug her friend. And then, according to their plan for how to mark more town destinations, she remarked about some strangers near Vange. "And who are your good-looking friends, here?"

Vange went with it, smiling and turning to see who Emily meant. "Oh, I don't know, but I want to."

The people behind Vange all laughed, three women and two men who looked to be college age, a few years younger than Emily and Vange.

The woman who was the most outgoing among them spoke up. "I'm Brittany, and this is Ashley and Cody, MacKenzie, and Dylan." As Brittany said their names, they bowed with funny individual flourishes. Dylan's was the best, pretending to flutter an imaginary cloak.

Emily was delighted. These were fellow drama people. She didn't know why she was so surprised, really. They were signing up to be actors at the faire. Improvisational street actors rather than stage or film, but actors nonetheless. She spoke to all of them, but she looked at their leader Brittany the most. "Well, you five are our new best friends. Come on, let's sit together for the meeting."

Looking flattered, they followed the faire's weapons professor's wife enthusiastically over to the table the farthest away from Siobhan and Ian, who looked like they were about to start the Scots guild meeting.

Dall had caught up with them, and he smoothly sat on the end of the bench next to Emily and put his arm around her. She knew he was marking his territory, but she enjoyed it.

Vange chuckled the whole way there and seated herself opposite Emily, between Brittany and Cody, who had his arm around Ashley.

Emily said in Gaelic to Dall, "Will you please listen to the meeting for both of us while I get to know our friends a bit? That way, you're the obedient one."

Dall nodded yes and smiled at her before turning his attention to Siobhan and Ian, who were addressing everyone.

"So have you all worked this faire before?" Emily asked the woman next to her.

MacKenzie said, "Yeah, this is all of our third year as ren fest people."

"Oh cool." Emily said. She turned to Brittany, but couldn't draw her attention away from Siobhan. Emily turned back to the woman beside her. "So do you know the good party spots in town?"

MacKenzie named Mr. Simmons's hotel and said that his club was about as good as it got around here.

Emily had known this, and it was part of her plan. "Oh yeah, we've been there. It is pretty good, but not like a real club in town," Emily said, catching Vange's eye and winking. She finally caught Brittany's eye, too, and she smiled at their leader.

Vange caught on to the part of Emily's plan she could guess, and joined in. "So where are you all from?"

Brittany was drawn in now. "We're from all different places, but we all go to State. We met there. Three of us are drama majors together, and Ashley and Cody wish they were." She laughed.

Ashley made a funny face at Brittany, and Cody reached behind Vange to push Brittany playfully.

Emily laughed too, but this was great. State wasn't in the town where her parents lived, but it was a lot closer than here. Close enough that a cab wouldn't be too expensive. She said, "Heh, Vange and I are graduate students at your rival school, I'm afraid, although my undergrad major was drama, too."

She had them all in the palm of her hand, she could tell. Being the wife of the guild's weapons master had its perks at the faire after all. She figured it was time to cash in on that. "So," Emily said to them all, but looking mostly at Brittany, "tomorrow after faire, you want to take us into your town and show us some real clubs?"

The other four looked to Brittany for her decision.

Emily had seen that coming. She sat back and relaxed, giving Brittany a friendly smile that she hoped said, "No big deal, but wouldn't it be funny and ironic, partying together even though we go to rival colleges?"

Brittany smiled back in a way that said, "Heck yeah, it would." Yay. Victory. Out loud, Brittany kept her cool and just said, "Sure."

Dall must have been listening in more than Emily expected, because while he kept his eyes on Siobhan, he spoke to Emily out of the corner of his mouth in Gaelic. "Arrange to hang out with them all day tomorrow so they stick with it, because Siobhan will expect us all to come party in her trailer, you ken?"

"Aye," Emily said to Dall in Gaelic, and then she addressed their new friends again, but as usual, she mostly smiled at Brittany. "This is Vange and my first time working this faire, or festival as you say here, so maybe tomorrow you can show us which shows are good here."

Brittany smiled really big and actually gasped. "Huh. Really?" Wow, she was star struck.

The others were smiling really big and looking at Brittany like they hoped she'd say yes.

Emily hugged Dall to let them know he was included in the deal, too. "Yes really." She smiled her genuine friendship smile at everyone, but mostly at Brittany.

Vange caught Emily's eye and winked. Heh. Vange knew what was up. Yep, now Vange was giving Emily their secret 'thumbs up' sign. It was an odd little chortle rather than an actual thumb up. She looked like she was shivering.

It was funny, and everyone at their table kind of laughed, enjoying it.

That must have finally been enough for Siobhan, because she marched over with her hands on her hips like a high school teacher. That made everyone laugh even more, which made Siobhan huff, she was so spun up. "Does someone want to tell me what is so funny over here?"

Brittany spoke up. "Sure. Vange just did this hilarious little wiggle thing. Show her, Vange."

Not waiting for Siobhan's permission—which Vange didn't need because she wasn't the druids' slave like Dall and this was not school but a festival, which was supposed to be fun—Vange got up on top of the table and showed the whole Scots guild her funny little wiggle.

Everyone burst out laughing, and then they all gave Vange the Scots' cheer.

Siobhan made like she was giving in and laughed, but

Emily could tell it was a forced laugh and that Siobhan was still mad. Sure enough, Siobhan gave Emily the evil eye.

Emily wasn't superstitious, but her time in the highlands among Dall's family had taught her a few things. She made the sign against the evil eye with the hand that was around Dall's shoulders.

He felt it, and he hugged her close, which made her sigh. He would protect her.

Siobhan wouldn't be talking to them anytime soon, though. After the guild meeting, everyone went to Siobhan's trailer for the usual Friday night revels. Dall and Emily beckoned their new friends to come along. No use rousing Siobhan's suspicions by asking them to Dall and Emily's trailer instead. Save their separation from the herd for tomorrow.

DALL AND EMILY LET VANGE have their trailer and enjoyed another night at Mr. Simmons' hotel. For the two of them, it had been months since they had seen this member of her parents' clan of friends, so they were a little more talkative than usual when he came over to their table at the hotel's breakfast cafe. He seemed to enjoy it, and Emily was glad.

They drove Vange's car to the festival, showed their gate passes to security, and made their way over to Murray's weapons booth for their first day of work.

They were three moves into an el duello sword fighting demonstration when Emily noticed their five new best friends in the audience. "Let's make this really fun for them." she said to Dall when she pointed them out.

Dall ended their bout with an impressive disarm, they both bowed to the audience's applause, and then he smiled and said, "We need some volunteers."

Almost everyone in the audience raised their hands.

Emily went and got their five new best friends and brought them into the arena, and then she and Dall did with them what Dall had done with Emily the first day they met: gave them self-defense lessons with the long 16th-century daggers that might as well have been short swords.

Their five new best friends had a blast. The audience bought lots of daggers and asked about lessons, which all seven of them in the Scots guild missed the Scottish stage dancing set for, and for which Dall and Emily were paid extra. They were pleased, Murray was pleased, the audience was pleased, and their new best friends loved them even more. Win, win, and win.

"Well enough," said Brittany to Emily really loudly, using her Scots accent as taught by the festival's workshop, "shall we go now to see the players on the stage, lass? It was a request you had, you ken?"

Wow, Brittany was good at that accent. Emily smiled at her and nodded.

Dall threw his arm around Emily, and they followed their new best friends to watch their first stage show at this 'ren fest', as the locals called it.

This festival site was woodsy, and to go along with that, many of the local festival workers dressed as dryads, wood sprites, fae, and fairies. It was fun to see them clasp hands and circle unsuspecting passersby. Once they had them trapped, they would chant, "You've been caught in a fairy ring. A fairy ring is a magical thing. In order to escape, you must kiss the one you're with, and kiss him well. For it will be a long, cold winter." Emily didn't get to stop and watch any of the couples kiss, but she imagined it must have been amusing.

Emily also saw the druid circle again, on the way to the stage show. At this site, the druids were in a 'sacred grove' of trees, rather than a circle of stones. They still wore their white robes and flower garland crowns, though, both the men and the women, and danced around in a circle. Emily wondered if that was just for show, or if they were really performing some sort of druid magic.

The Green Man passed by them on this fake road through the fake English village in the woods. It was getting toward autumn now here, though, and so he was portrayed as turning a bit yellow around the edges. His character was a fun person-ification of summer.

Emily also saw mongers pretending to sell all manner of 'period' things, from animals to farming implements. One particular monger gave her the willies. He pretended to be a barber surgeon selling tooth pulls. She shuddered, thinking he wouldn't have such an amused look on his face if he had been faced with the real thing back at Kilchurn Castle.

Finally, they got to the stage show. It was a good rendition of Shakespeare's 'The Taming of the Shrew,' but Emily didn't enjoy it nearly as much as she had Short Shakespeare's perfor-mances. Still, it was good, and she clapped, 'ooh'ed, 'ah'ed and 'oh'ed at appropriate times.

Dall and Emily spent the whole day with their new friends. Vange finally joined them at lunch backstage at the picnic tables, where the Scots guild meeting had been. She had a prominent part in the Scottish dance set at this site, and her shift as a boothie was during 'The Taming of the Shrew.'

Vange spoke in hushed tones, not to be overheard by any of the Scots guild leaders, whom she didn't know were real magic-wielding druids. "So how are we going to get out of here with street clothes without being noticed? Because if they notice us, you know they'll stop us. Don't ask me why, but they will."

Emily grinned and whispered just loud enough for Vange and their friends to hear, "I left extra street clothes in the car, for you too. And a change for Dall, who as you know always wears his kilt, thank goodness." Glad she had thought to leave her phone in the car as well, Emily raised her eyebrows three times quickly at her husband.

Everyone at their table laughed.

"Well that's good," Vange whispered, "but still, how are we going to get to the car without being stopped? You know Siobhan wants us all to stay on site. She's almost a lunatic about that."

Emily was thinking that her friend had no idea how true her statement was.

Dall spoke up in the sexiest hushed voice ever. "We will have to leave early, you ken. Before the staged guild meeting, and miss the ring-out parade."

"Speak of the devil, and he doth appear," Cody whispered urgently.

They all looked up to see Siobhan storming toward their table.

❧

THE LOOK in Siobhan's eye said they were all in trouble. That wasn't a surprise. After all, seven of them had missed the Scottish stage dance set.

Dall and Emily had purposely chosen to sit at the picnic tables instead of in the dining room of their trailer, thinking the more public setting would keep Siobhan from making a scene. Apparently not. Emily figured the only thing for it was to leave the backstage area. Surely the druid wouldn't make a scene in front of the festival's paying customers.

"Run." Dall said.

He must have been thinking along the same lines.

There was a split second when everyone was in shock and didn't quite believe what was happening, but when Dall abandoned his food and got up and left, they all followed suit. Dall

steered Emily toward the arena, which made sense. That was
where their next gig was.

Emily looked behind them to see if Siobhan was running
after them. Phew. She wasn't. Their five new best friends
were, though, and Vange.

Murray was also at the arena, and he seemed to understand the situation as soon as he saw the eight of them
running over. "Let's reprise our show of the morning,
shall we?"

That was a great idea. It warmed up the crowd for the
daily sword demonstration that all the performing guilds took
part in. It sold more daggers for Murray. It kept Dall and
Emily and their friends within sight and sound of the paying
customers and thus safe from Siobhan's scolding.

It also kept Dall safe from Siobhan's ordering, which was
entirely the point, for Dall and Emily. They needed to get off
the site and mark a destination closer to her parents, but Dall
would have to obey if Siobhan or any of the druids outright
ordered him to stay put. Dall and Emily couldn't give any of
the druids the opportunity to do that.

So they gave Brittany, MacKenzie, Ashley, Cody, and
Dylan another dagger lesson in self-defense, and they gathered an audience while they did so. Again this time, many
customers in the audience bought daggers and asked about
lessons for themselves. Once more, Dall and Emily offered to
stay after the sword demonstration and give those lessons—
for extra pay—and their friends stayed to watch.

Emily was relieved to not see Aiden or any of the other
druids around. Only Siobhan was on their case so far. After
all, they had only missed a dance set and now they were
missing a staged guild meeting.

They wouldn't miss anything outside the Scots guild until
they actually missed the ring-out parade at the end of the
festival day. And then Aiden would probably be upset with

them, too. Best to get destinations they needed marked as soon as possible. And hope whatever orders the druids gave Dall left a loophole that allowed them to travel and see their friends and family.

Siobhan was hopping mad, but she couldn't make a scene during the all-guild sword demonstration. During which both Dall and Emily stayed out in the arena the entire time.

Siobhan had to rush off to attend the staged guild meeting while the eight of them stayed after the demo for the paying customers' dagger lessons.

And then it was time for them to make their escape.

Dall said to Brittany, "Lass, do you know that building where they serve gas at the main highway?"

"Meet you there?" Brittany looked so excited her eyes might pop out.

Dall threw his arm around Emily and said, "Aye, we will meet you there directly."

Emily kept her eye out for any druids while they walked toward the main gate. Every few seconds, her excitement and fear tried to get Emily to run, but Dall held her back. She knew walking was the way to go. It drew less attention. But her body kept trying to run anyway. Dall steered her the long way around the circle of festival streets. She was confused until she realized they avoided the druids' sacred grove of trees that way.

"Good thinking," she said to him in Gaelic.

He smiled their contented cat smile at her, and they strolled out the main gate as if they missed the ring-out parade every festival day.

❦

CODY AND ASHLEY got in Dall and Emily's backseat when

they all met up at the gas station, and Vange got in Brittany's junker with MacKenzie and Dylan.

"I'll call you so we can coordinate where we're going, Em." Vange called out as she climbed into Brittany's front passenger seat.

"You'll be talking to Dall, 'because I'm driving." Emily shouted back.

Dall said in Gaelic, "Is it a good idea to talk about our plans where they can hear us?"

Emily answered in Gaelic, "I don't see why we shouldn't. There's nothing they can realistically do to stop us from having fun with our friends, and they need to realize sooner or later that we are going to make friends."

"Aye, that's true." Dall jumped when Emily's phone rang with the funny pop song she had set for Vange's caller ID.

Emily laughed, thinking about all the modern things her deprived 16th-Century husband was about to see for the first time.

"They ask if we might change at your home," Dall said, turning around to address Ashley, who sat in the back seat.

"Oh. Uh," she looked at Cody, who shrugged, "sure."

"Aye, she says that will do. Aye. Aye." Dall searched the phone, obviously looking for a way to disconnect the call.

Keeping her eyes on the road, Emily grabbed it from him and pushed the power button lightly, then gave it back. She turned on the radio, and three of them sang along to five-year-old pop songs while Dall watched the woods go by them at highway speeds.

An hour later, Emily's phone rang again.

Dall answered again. "Aye? Good." He must have been watching her last time, because this time he was able to disconnect the call. "They wish for you to take the next branch off the highway, lass, so that we can eat some supper."

"Good." Cody yelled over the radio from the back seat.

"Because I'm hungry. Where did they say we were going to eat?"

"At the MacDonalds'," Dall said thoughtfully. "I do not know why I am surprised to hear they have a place here." Dall seemed to be looking up the mountain as they exited the freeway.

"Heh, yeah," said Ashley with a chuckle, "I know. McDonalds is everywhere, huh."

And then they were pulling into the driveway. Dall opened his mouth to say something that would probably sound foolish.

Emily held a hand up to stop him as she followed Brittany into the drive-through. She pointed at the menu and said in Gaelic, "What looks good, Dall? We'll be eating in the car." Out loud to Cody and Ashley, she said, "Get whatever you want, our treat. We're treating for this whole night. All those extra lessons paid well, and you helped."

They all got full meals with shakes and fries and sandwiches and even apple pies for dessert.

After they ate, Dall and Emily paid to fill both cars with gas, and then they sang their way another hour over to Cody and Ashley's apartment complex. The other car stopped there to get the clothes Emily had brought for Vange, and Brittany promised to have everyone in her car back in two hours, all dressed to hit the club scene.

Emily put her arms around Dall and gave him a kiss before anyone caught him staring at the huge apartment complex as if it were a space station or something. With a tender grin on her face, she had to hold his hand and drag him along behind Cody and Ashley to keep him from going over to check out the playground equipment.

§

THEY HIT the dance club at 11pm, when things were in full swing. The women were all in short summer dresses and strappy heels. Cody and Dylan both sported the all-in-black drama guy look. Dall stood out in his clean great kilt and a black tank top, but Emily thought he cut a fine figure, indeed. She wouldn't hear of him wearing pants, not even period breaches.

Poor Dall had resembled an overexcited dog the whole evening, though, first at seeing the women so scantily dressed, and then at seeing all the city lights.

It was late enough that there wasn't a line to get in, but early enough that everyone was still sober. The perfect time to arrive. Finally, they had their drinks and had found a table where half of them could sit while half of them danced.

Emily watched Dall watching the dancers, especially during the one slow song that had come on so far. She let him watch all through the first slow dance. She had to wait through a dozen fast songs and nod and smile with everyone's conversation after that, and then finally the DJ put on another slow song.

Putting on her most practiced 'come hither' look and maintaining eye contact with her man, Emily stood, took his hand, and led him onto the dance floor.

Dall didn't disappoint her. He knew what she wanted.

Their first slow dance was every bit as great as Emily had imagined it would be. When the fast music started up again, it was as if she were waking from a dream, but her prince was right there in front of her still. She smiled and led him back to the table.

Everyone whistled and clapped for them.

"Nice slow dance."

The two of them bowed and smiled.

And then Emily took her phone out of her tiny little club

purse and held it up to Dall, gesturing toward the restroom sign.

Dall nodded and started a conversation with Dylan.

Once Emily got close to the restroom sign, she was relieved to see a dark back hallway that had more doors than just for the restrooms. Acting tipsy, she opened the first door she came to. Oh, it was an office. Too risky. No telling what hours the business end of the place might keep. The next door was the men's room, and she skipped that. Ew. Then the ladies'. Maybe. The fifth door was obviously an exit out into the back alley. Good. But she wanted to see what was behind door number 4.

Jackpot.

Door number 4 was a storage room, and she rushed inside and closed the door behind her. Using her phone as a flashlight, she worked her way around a huge fake Christmas tree into the far corner of the room. And there, she gleefully marked her first totally homemade destination in the Time Management app. She named it Brittany's Club.

She was on her way out of the closet when its door opened. Fast as she could, she ran back behind the Christmas tree, where she stood panting, praying she wouldn't be seen.

Whoever it was, they were persistent. They worked their way into the room and started parting the branches near her. And then they whispered, "Emily?" Whew. It was Dall.

Emily let out the breath she had been holding, and then she whispered, "I'm back here."

Dall made his way to her, and they kissed for a while in the dark. Then he said softly, "Well lass, do you have it?"

Emily giggled a little. "Yep. Mission accomplished. We can go back out there now and dance some more."

"Well, I was thinking we would go and visit with your parents, lass, and try to get even closer to them."

"But what about Vange and Brittany and all them? And we

have to be at festival in the morning. We can't just..." But then it dawned on Emily. She nearly spoke out loud what they could do, but then she remembered the druids could hear.

Holding her phone so that Dall could see too, she kept the location the same but set the time as 8 am on Monday. She figured people who ran a club would sleep in way past that time, so the place should be empty. She looked at his face in the light of the phone, and he nodded, so she pushed the 'go' button.

When the world stopped swirling, it was still pretty dark in the storage room. But now the faintest bit of sunlight came in under the door, so they could see without the phone. Emily put it in her purse, and they stood and listened for a minute, but didn't hear anything.

"Back door's right there," Emily whispered, pointing through the storage room door.

Dall nodded, and they tip toed to the storage room door. He put her behind him, and then he slowly opened it. The door creaked. They both winced and held still for a moment, listening for movement or voices.

9. MACGREGORS

E mily didn't hear anything. She looked at Dall to see if he did.

He shook his head no, and then cautiously opened the storage room door into the dance club's back hallway and slowly peeked out into the dim sunlight coming under the back door.

Creak. Creak creak creak creak creak.

On hearing this noise, Emily tried to pull Dall back into the storage room.

But his feet didn't budge. With grace and control, her husband slowly leaned back while also closing the door so that it fastened silently. And then he turned to her and put his finger in front of his mouth. He took control. He was in charge.

She loved it. She felt cared for, and she felt some of the weight of the world lift off of her shoulders. He was sharing that weight. She carried some responsibility for the two of them, but he carried his share. It seemed like this was how it should be, because after all, she now carried his name.

They stood there a few minutes, and then repeated the

whole scenario again, except this time he trusted her to keep quiet. They just waited, and they heard it again.

Creak. creak creak creak creak creak.

But this time, Emily realized what was making the creaking noise, and she sighed and relaxed. Then she whispered to Dall in Gaelic, "It's a child upstairs, running around, probably inside his ... home." She didn't know a Gaelic word for apartment, and she doubted there was one.

Dall listened for a moment, and then he sighed and relaxed, too, nodding yes. Whew, he agreed with her assessment. There was no danger in the creaking sound.

She whispered, "I don't hear anything down here in the club, do you?"

He listened for another moment, and then he whispered, "Nay, lass. However, let us keep quiet on account of the lack of noise being no guarantee there is no one around."

She nodded yes to show she agreed with his assessment.

He hugged her with the arm he had around her, and then he quietly opened the storage room door again. This time, they didn't jump when they heard the creaking noise. They just calmly headed for where the sunlight came streaming in under the back door to the dance club.

It was one of those doors with a push-bar across the middle of it.

"This is going to be noisy," Emily whispered.

Dall acknowledged her with a nod, and then he pushed on the bar and opened the back door into the alley behind the dance club.

The two of them rushed out and made sure the door closed behind them, hopefully before anyone who happened to be inside heard and came to investigate. When they turned around to proceed down the alley, they saw a young man coming at them with a knife.

EMILY FELT Dall shove her behind him and saw him step up to meet the young man, grabbing first the wrist of the hand that held the knife, and second the other wrist, before the other hand could grab another knife from the young man's boot.

The young man kicked at Dall then, saying amid a bunch of expletives, "You shouldn't have come into my alley. Now we're going to have to mess you up." He kept struggling viciously, but he couldn't get his wrists free of Dall's hold.

Emily looked around to see who 'we' was, but she didn't see anyone else.

All the while, the kid shouted expletives and grunted.

"Dall, I don't see anyone else but this young man," Emily reassured Dall in English, to make sure the young man understood she was on the ball and not intimidated by him.

Dall's attention was understandably 100% on the young man.

The youth kept kicking at Dall.

Dall kept dodging, which made his kilt sway all over the place.

Still using filthy language, the young man said, "What kind of man are you, huh, wearing a dress?" The young gangster laughed at that, even though Dall had a firm hold on his wrists.

"I am a MacGregor," Dall said matter-of-factly in his thick highlands accent, "And this is no dress but my plaid, which I am proud to wear."

"Whoa," said the young man, "You talk just like those Outlander people on the TV." He sounded impressed, but he didn't stop trying to kick Dall and make him let go of his wrists. Or swearing.

Dall didn't let go, and he calmly kept dodging the youth's kicks.

"Yeah," Emily said, admiring the way Dall's kilt swayed, oh, and the way he was calmly handling the situation with only the necessary amount of violence, "those Outlander people are from Scotland, like Dall is. And I'm Emily, his wife, so I'm a MacGregor too. Look, we can't stay here all day, uh, talking. We're on our way to visit my parents, and we need to get going."

Dall and the gangster were still dancing around each other.

The kid looked almost comical, the way he was caught and trying to attack.

Emily was amused, but she knew the longer they stuck around, the better the chance some of the other members of the gang would show up. Probably with guns.

With every other word a swear word, the gangster said, "Huh, you don't talk funny like your man, here. You're an American, aren't you."

It was like he used profanity as punctuation.

"Yes, I am," Emily agreed, wanting to smile and even to laugh, but starting to get anxious.

The gangster made an 'ew' face. "Why don't you get him some American clothes, then, instead of him going around dressed so weird?"

"I like his kilts," Emily said, looking up and down the alley, a little bit nervously, she had to admit. "We met at the faire when it was here. I like that sort of stuff."

It might have been Emily's imagination, but it seemed like Dall was making his kilt sway a little more now, shaking his hips as he dodged the young man's kicks.

Which was funny, because the young man was getting tired and not kicking as often or as hard. He was laughing a little now, too. "Ha ha. I should've known you were from that faire. I have a cousin who is into that [expletive]."

Dall must have realized the young man's clan would come to his aid soon, too, because Dall cut to the chase. "Lad, we mean you no harm, but we cannot stay here all the day. So give me your word you will not attack us, and I will let you go and we will be on our way."

"Dall—"

"Emily, this is between me and this man here. Stay out of it, lass."

At hearing her name, the young man seemed to perk up, but she must be seeing things. Where would he have heard of her?

The gangster relaxed, though. He quit kicking and lowered his arms. "OK, if you guys just pass right on through, I'll forget you were in my alley."

Emily jumped on that, but she wanted to make sure he meant it. Her teacher-training said that if she could get him to help them in some way, then he would be invested in letting them go without a fight. "Thanks. Which way to the closest place to eat that would be open?"

The gangster was young, but his street smarts were all there. He backed away from Dall before he jerked his thumb down one side of the alley and told them, "There's one of those espresso places across the street at the end of the alley down that way. They have rolls and [expletive]."

Keeping his eyes on the young man, Dall held out his hand for Emily.

Looking all around in case anyone was coming, she walked up to him and took it.

"I thank you, lad," Dall said, and then he turned his back on the young man and led Emily down the alley at a brisk pace, but at a dignified walk rather than a scared run.

They almost made it out of the alley without hearing any more of it.

But then behind them, the young man called out, "Hey, what were you doing in that club when it was closed, anyway?"

By silent assent, they ignored him and walked a little faster, listening in case he came running up behind them.

Emily had to hold Dall back from crossing the street without making sure a car wasn't coming.

❧

THERE WAS a line inside the espresso bar. For once, Emily was glad. She felt safer with other people around. Sure, the gang might go into a crowded place and make trouble, but it didn't seem nearly as likely as getting attacked in a dark alley. She didn't even wonder why none of these people had gone into the alley to see what all the yelling was about.

"I want to buy something," she said to Dall in Gaelic while she scanned the bakery counter, "just to pay the owner back for having this place of safety here for us."

He nodded yes and also spoke in Gaelic. "I'll watch to see if he or any of his clan show up, but I do think we are safe now, lass." Dall was taking a seat next to the door, where it looked like he could see out the window across the street to the alleyway.

Emily bought them each a latte and a cinnamon roll and put them down on Dall's table, where they were duly consumed. Shame to waste good food, right? Meanwhile, wasting no more time, Emily called a cab.

"Whew," she said to Dall, "a car will be here in ten minutes to take us to my parents' house."

"Will they be at home, lass? Remember, it is Monday now,

and you did say they both had duties outside the home during the week."

"Oh yeah, you're right. They'll be at work. I'll call my mom and ask them to meet us for a long lunch out. They'll love it."

She did just that.

Even though in her time it had only been two weeks since they last saw each other, her mom sounded elated to get the call. She enthusiastically agreed to grab Emily's dad and meet them for lunch.

But Emily's call-waiting had beeped repeatedly while she was on the phone with her mom, and now that she checked it, she saw that Vange had been the one calling. She showed Dall and then called her best friend.

"What the heck is going on, Em?" Vange asked over the phone in a huff. She sounded angry, but also like she was crying. Yep, she sniffled a little. Vange always did that when she cried.

Emily leaned in toward Dall and put the phone between them so he could hear too before she asked Vange, "What do you mean? What's wrong, Vange?"

Vange said, "My cousin Emilio just called to ask if I know you and Dall, that's what." Her friend was full-on sobbing now.

It tore at Emily's heart.

"What did you tell him?" Emily asked. She was trying to sound soothing and businesslike at the same time. She wasn't sure it was working. She had never been so upset while acting before. She hated that she had to act.

"I told him that you and I have been best friends since fourth grade, of course." Vange's voice kept getting higher and higher, until she was practically squeaking, she was so choked up. "What should I have told him, because I'm obviously not included in your plans if you just ran into him in an alley, Emily."

Oh no. This was getting dangerously close to having to discuss time travel with Vange, and Emily had promised not to discuss it with anyone except Siobhan. More importantly, so had Dall, and as Dall's wife, Emily had the feeling she could get him in trouble with his masters, if even she was the one who disobeyed them, not him.

But this was Vange. It hurt Emily, the sound of her best friend feeling left out and ignored. "We're coming into town to see my parents, Vange, and of course we want to see you too. It was a spur of the moment decision. Oh, and the cab's here to pick us up. Please hold on, OK? Don't go anywhere."

"OK." Vange still sounded hurt, but at least she hadn't ended the call. That was good, right?

"Alright,' Emily said, "we're in the cab now, headed over to see you. What do you want to do?"

Emily was glad she'd had coffee. It was starting to be a long time since she slept, and it looked like it would be a long time more.

"Nice try, Em. How could you come all that way without calling me to make plans first? I thought I was your best friend." Vange had a handle on her crying now and was getting angry instead, but Emily knew her friend was really hurt. She had a right to be.

Emily couldn't tell her best friend the truth, and it was killing her. She decided to play the married card and blame Dall. Hoping he'd understand, she said, "I wanted to, but Dall came up with the idea to see them on the spur of the moment, and then he kept me busy so I couldn't call."

Vange giggled, which was a good sign. But it sounded a little forced. And then Vange asked the question Emily was hoping wouldn't occur to her. "What were you doing back in that town where we were Saturday night, though, let alone in that alley, Em?" She sounded suspicious, but willing to hear a reasonable explanation.

And then Emily thought of one. "Dall lost his ID out in back of that club Saturday night, when he followed some of the guys out there who wanted to smoke."

"Oh no." Oh good. Vange sounded relieved and like she believed Emily's excuse. But not as warm as she usually did.

Emily knew that was because she was just finding out now, after the fact. They used to tell each other everything right away.

"Yeah, that sporran thingy isn't very secure, is it. Did he find it?" Vange said, sounding sad but trying to hide that she was.

It was on the tip of Emily's tongue to say, "No. Your cousin didn't give him a chance to look." But she realized just in time that saying that would make Vange call her cousin again. And Emilio might say something about her and Dall coming out of the club... Nope. Best to just... "Yeah. Yeah, he found it."

Dall didn't have any ID, but that was beside the point. How was he ever going to get a driver license, though? The licensing office wanted a birth certificate or a passport or some form of ID in order to give out ID...

"Oh, that's good." Vange was trying to sound like the whole thing was cleared up, but she still sounded sad.

Which hurt Emily almost as much as when her friend had been mad at her, but not quite.

"Yeah," Emily said, "so where do you want to meet us, Vange? We're meeting my parents at noon for a long lunch and then we have to head back, but we'll get into town about ten, so what'll it be?"

❧

THE THREE OF them walked around the mall. It was sort of crowded for a Monday, but then again, it was summer. All the high school girls were out of school, so of course they were shopping. The senior citizens were in the mall for the air conditioning. Middle-aged people who worked other shifts were too, but they were mostly in workout clothes, hoofing it around the walkways as fast as they could.

Dall, highlander fighter Dall who was always ready for a fight, was tripping over people, he was so busy gawking at all the glass-enclosed shops and the shiny waxed floors and the fountains and the glass ceiling and the food court and ... pretty much everything.

Vange laughed at him. "Don't they have malls in Scotland?"

"Nay, no, not in the small towns where I hail from, lass."

Emily was proud of her husband for thinking so well on his feet, and glad to see her friend's spunky side showing, but it only lasted a moment.

"Look," Vange said, "I know you guys are really into the faire and you work there and all, but not everyone appreciates that. Your parents might be embarrassed if he shows up at the restaurant in his kilt." She still sounded sad, but in a resigned, amused sort of way. That was much better.

"I know." Emily sighed and admired her man's distinctive form while he ran his fingers up and down the glass wall that enclosed a children's clothing store. "I've known all along that Dall should be wearing 'normal clothes' whenever we go see my parents, but I've been resisting because he just looks so hot in his kilt."

"I wasn't going to say so." Vange looked over at Dall and laughed. "But now that you mention it..."

The two friends hugged. Things appeared to be back to normal from the outside, but Emily could tell Vange still felt sad and left out. And Emily knew it wasn't just that she'd gotten married. The truth was, Vange was left out of the amazing fact that time travel was real. Emily didn't doubt that her friend could sense Emily was hiding something big from her.

After two hours of mall shopping, Dall wore some loose black jeans and a respectable looking T-shirt. He also had a new card wallet in his back pocket, but Vange didn't know it was empty.

In a grey nylon daypack that Vange had also insisted they buy, he carried more normal clothes, his kilt, and his sporran. He still wore his boots. He had left his sword in the trunk of Vange's car when they went into the club. Emily wondered if it would be in there if she went out to the parking lot right then and looked.

When Emily hugged her best friend goodbye until Friday, she thought she saw a tear falling from Vange's eye.

Lunch with Emily's parents was fun. They ate at Madam Wu's, Emily's favorite restaurant in town, and she grudgingly admitted to herself that Vange had been right to make Dall wear 'normal clothes' for it.

"You were right about Dall's clothes," Emily texted Vange under the table.

Vange texted back immediately. "Quit texting at the table before your mom takes your phone away."

Emily laughed, and then she passed it off as laughing at Dall.

It was funny watching his reaction to Chinese food. Emily was pretty sure her highlander had never seen chopsticks before, let alone eaten with them. But he watched her and her parents and mimicked what they did, and she was proud of him. He did OK.

While it had only been two weeks for her parents since Emily got married, it had been six months for her. She was already quite comfortable and very content in her new role as

Mrs. MacGregor. Which was why she was quite off guard
when her mother took her aside on the way back to their
table from the ladies' room.

"Emily, hon, take it easy on the alcohol from now on. I
want my grandchildren healthy."

"Uh, yeah. OK. That's... That's true, Mom. Thanks.
I will."

This put Emily into a kind of shock. She thought back on
how weird Dall's family had been treating her. It made sense
now. Dall's family expected her to be pregnant by now. And
why shouldn't she be?

And when she thought about it, she realized she hadn't
had a period since she started time traveling. And her belly
was normal size. All she could figure was that the world going
swirly prevented her from being fertile. This was huge news.

"Dall." Emily called out frantically to her husband when
she saw him, completely forgetting they were in a crowded
restaurant.

Dall was halfway out of his seat with his hand hitching up
his pants leg to get to one of his boots before he settled back
down again, presumably upon seeing she was unharmed and
unmolested. "Aye?" He looked around, probably just to make
sure no attackers were coming in through the windows.

"Sorry, later," she told him in Gaelic with what she hoped
was an apologetic look on her face. That was a look she had
not needed for any play she had done, so she wasn't sure she
was doing it right.

All was well. He threw his arm around her and hugged her
when she sat next to him.

"Wow, honey, you're learning to speak Scottish." Her mom
looked impressed. So did her dad.

"Yeah, Dall thought it would be a good idea, for when I
visit his family."

Her dad smiled and nodded. "Yes, and knowing another language is always a good thing. That's great, Em."

She smiled back at him. "Thanks." but her mind was making a mental note to definitely tell Dall the huge news later. They were going to have to change their time travel schedule, or at least hers, when they wanted to have kids, which she thought should be before she was 30...

And then she realized that with her time travel, she had already lived enough days to be 23 and 9 months, but her calendar age in her correct time stream said she was only 23 and 3 months. Yikes. Obviously, her biological clock had 23 and 9 months. Yep, she was going to have to talk this over with Dall before too long.

AFTER THEY ALL laughed over their fortune cookies, Emily realized two things. One, she had now been awake 24 hours in a row and needed to get some sleep or she was going to collapse. Two, she wanted some pictures of her parents on her new phone. They had given it to her for her birthday, just three months ago to them. In that time, she hadn't taken any pictures of them.

Emily got up and took her phone out of her tiny evening bag.

"OK, Mom, Dad, cuddle up and smile for me."

Her parents were so cute together. They cuddled up and smiled just like two teenagers would. It made Emily realize how much she would miss them if she couldn't visit whenever she wanted. Yes, marking a destination near them was worth the trouble she was in with Vange.

"I wish I could just think of my parents when I wanted to travel to them," Emily said to Dall in Gaelic while she took some more photos. "Like in some books I read. Let's drop by and mark in my room at their house before we leave town."

"Aye lass, good thinking that is."

She didn't want to leave, but it was time. She gave her parents each a big hug. "I love you."

"We love you too, sweetheart. Drive carefully back to the festival site."

Dall and Emily walked around the corner and down the street, and called a cab.

Emily still had her key to her parents' house. She took Dall into the garage as an extra precaution and got ready to mark the location.

She reassured herself that in the off chance that someone was home during work hours when she planned to travel there, they wouldn't be in the garage, and if they were, she could ask in

Gaelic for a do-over. And the garage had a back door they could leave by and then enter through the front door to make their arrival seem natural to anyone in the house.

Emily marked the location, and went through the process of labeling it "Mom and Dad Shaw's Garage."

And then her finger froze on the drop-down menu.

"Dall. Dall. Ack. You have to see this."

She saw a new destination she couldn't account for. It was labeled with today's date and a little icon she didn't recognize.

"What, lass?" He stopped examining all of her dad's guy stuff in the garage and came over to look at her phone, putting his arm around her in a gesture she knew she was beginning to take for granted.

Sinking into Dall's embrace, Emily tapped the new destination to open up the larger window with the details on it.

"Huh." Emily gasped.

There, where a destination should have come up, was one of the pictures Emily had taken of her parents.

Dall chuckled that deep sexy chuckle of his and rubbed his palm up and down Emily's arm.

"What's so funny?" Emily turned her head to look at his face, not understanding what he could possibly find to laugh about. This was weird, not funny.

"You have done it again, lass." He smiled their contented cat smile at her.

"What? What did I do?" She wanted to be able to return the smile, but she was just puzzled.

"You commanded the wee phone app, and it obeyed you."

"I did?"

"Aye."

Now she was able to return his smile, and the two of them got lost in each other for a minute, first in their eyes and then in their kiss.

Emily came up for air. "What did I say exactly, while I was taking this picture?"

There followed another hour-long lesson on Gaelic's subtleties.

Once she was certain she could duplicate the effect of marking a person as a destination, Emily realized how tired she was. She and Dall had been awake now for far too long.

"Ug, we still have to drive back to the festival from that club." she said, burying her face in Dall's chest.

"We can make some time to have a rest first, lass." Dall smiled his new knowing smile at her.

Emily laughed. "What was I thinking?" She set the Time Management app for 9 am the following morning, right here in their current location. The world went swirly, and then the two of them slept six hours in Emily's old room at her parents' house.

Her phone woke them at 3pm Tuesday afternoon, well before her parents would get home. They carefully made the bed and then took a shower in the bathroom down the hall and got back into the clothes they had been wearing when they first left the club.

Dall was putting his new clothes into his new backpack. "Lass, we will need to go and put this in Vange's car before we meet up with the others in the club, aye?"

Emily tried Dall's new knowing look on for size.

He looked at her and laughed.

Still grinning, she said, "We can just swirl over to our trailer and drop that off before we swirl back into the storage room at the club."

He grinned back. "To my way of thinking, lass, the trouble will be in knowing when we will not be there already."

Emily nodded yes, laughing, while she went through her list of destinations. And then she saw it.

"Dall. Look."

He leaned over her shoulder and hugged her tighter, peering at the phone. "What is it, Drusilla? I have only the smallest knowledge of how these wee phones work, you ken?"

"It's so cool. The Time Management app is well-named. See? This calendar is keeping track of when we've been where. These orange spaces indicate where we've been and when. Green spaces indicate times we haven't been anywhere yet, so we can go someplace."

"There is yet the time I must go to the castle and lend my own support to Alasdair. Because who of the castle men might die if I don't? Do not forget that, lass." Now Dall's brow was furrowed, but Emily didn't care if he got wrinkles.

"Yeah," she said, "if this calendar is any good, then there should be a way to mark those times on it so we don't make a mistake and go someplace else during that time. Let's see…" She fiddled with the settings and the various drop down menus until she found just what she was describing. "There. See, it marks scheduled appearances in blue. OK, now when do you need to be there…"

After they worked that out and marked the calendar accordingly, Dall said, "I do not think that I could make the wee phone app work, lass, but I trust you if you say so."

"OK with me. I'll do the phone stuff. You watch my back."

"With pleasure will I do that, lass."

They were busy for a few minutes, and then the world went swirly. They dropped Dall's new bag off at their trailer, the world went swirly, and then they were back in the storage room at the club.

Vange wolf whistled when the two of them came out of the hallway arm in arm. "Are you guys pottying together now, too, or did you just spend ten minutes in the closet?"

"Ooh." Various snickers were heard.

"Very funny, Vange, but we're married, you know." Emily flaunted Dall's mother's ring on her left ring finger. "So we can spend all the time in the closet we want."

Everyone laughed, and Emily took advantage of their smiling faces to take pictures. She especially took some of Vange, but figured what the heck and took individual pictures of all their new best friends, too. And while she took them, she said the Gaelic phrase that made them destinations.

She hoped it at least worked for Vange, but she didn't dare bring up the Time Management app while all these phone-savvy people were around.

❧

EMILY GOT a few more slow dances in with Dall, loving every movement. While they sat and watched everyone else dance in between slow songs, it was easy not to drink any alcohol because after all, she was the designated driver. Pregnancy didn't seem to be a worry now when she was popping around through time, but her friends didn't know that. And it might seem like pretty soon to them, when she did get pregnant. She rather hoped so, actually.

Everyone's faces started to droop a little come 1 am.

Dall took charge. "Och, this is fun and all, but Emily and I must be at Murray's weapons booth by nine of the clock tomorrow, and we still have a two-hour drive back to the festival, you ken."

The others at the table started to protest, but Brittany agreed. "Yep. Time to hit the road, everyone." She stood up and waited for them all to follow her lead.

"Me and Cody would like to ride with you again, Emily, if that's OK with Vange."

"If what's OK with me?" Vange came back from the dance floor just then, smiling and having a great time, still kind of dancing to the upbeat music.

Looking at her best friend standing there so happy and trusting, Emily wanted so bad to warn her about the call she would receive from her cousin Emilio Monday morning. But that would just sound crazy. Well, Vange wouldn't care if Emily sounded crazy. But they didn't need their five new best friends asking the wrong questions.

Dall kept himself in charge though, and Emily was glad to be relieved of that duty. "Vange, lass, do you wish to ride with us? Cody and Ashley say they do, but as it is now mostly your … car, you have the choice in the matter."

Ashley must have realized what was going on, though. Well, not exactly, but close enough. "Oh that's OK. We'll see you all tomorrow, and we're camping near each other anyway, so we'll ride with Brittany and them."

Yay.

They all stumbled out to the cars. Brittany looked sober, though, so Emily relaxed.

"See you tomorrow."

"We'll come to your booth again."

Emily pulled up next to Brittany's car then, so they could talk better. "Actually, I think you guys better go to the Scottish dancing from now on, or Siobhan's liable to blow a gasket. I'm already a bit worried how she's going to be tomorrow, about us missing the staged guild meeting and the ring-out parade."

Brittany laughed at the part where Siobhan might blow a gasket. "Can we at least do the pre-demo with you still, before the all-guild sword demo? That was really fun."

Emily looked to Dall.

He smiled and nodded yes.

"Fine by us," Emily said, "but really, you should ask Siobhan. She's the guild leader. Dall is the weapons advisor, but she outranks him." There. That was a diplomatic way of putting it.

"I was afraid you were going to say that." Brittany made a funny face.

"I think she'll say you can, but she'll be much happier about it if you ask her, if you know what I mean." Emily showed her teeth in a cheesy smile.

"Gotcha." Brittany winked. "OK, so we'll see you at 'Taming of the Shrew'?"

"We wouldn't miss it."

"OK, see you tomorrow."

"Bye."

Almost as soon as Emily had the window rolled up, her friend leaned forward on the front seat between her and Dall, who she now realized she was going to have to teach how to drive.

"OK, that was fun," Vange said, "but what gives? Why do we suddenly have five new besties?"

Dall surprised Emily by speaking up. "Siobhan does govern us with a strong arm. It is difficult for us, getting away from her, even for an evening like this."

Emily chimed in. "Yeah, but at the same time, she's always on us to mingle with the locals, so we just killed two birds with one stone."

Dall sighed. "She will be angry with us, however."

Emily blew her bangs out of her face. For now, they had sidestepped discussing time travel with Vange. But Emily really wished they could just tell her best friend everything. She resolved to at least think of some way to soften Vange up so she would forgive Emily after Monday.

"WE ALL MIGHT AS WELL GO to the trailer tonight," Vange said. "I always use your extra bedroom, anyway. We'll get more time to sleep if we don't stop at the hotel."

"Yeah, you're right. OK, that's what we'll do." Emily was good to go for a while, and she knew Dall was too, thanks to sleeping Tuesday away. But what else could she say that wouldn't sound crazy to Vange?

And then Emily knew how to give her friend a hint at what she and Dall were up to without 'discussing it' with her. By the letter of the command she and Dall had been given, 'discussing it' was all she was forbidden to do.

When they arrived at the renaissance festival's parking lot gate at 3 am, they got stopped at first, but when the guards saw Dall, they waved them in without asking for passes. Emily thought she heard them saying his name and Siobhan's name into their radio, but she wasn't going to worry about it.

"Done is done," Emily told herself.

Her common sense talked back. "You know Siobhan will actually blow up at you if she finds out Vange knows you time travel, no matter how Vange finds out, right?"

"Shut up," she told it. "You were all paranoid about me

getting close to Dall, too, and that has been nothing but wonderful."

Her common sense shut up.

They parked, walked across the festival grounds into the backstage area, and unlocked the trailer. And then Emily made a big show of getting out Dall's new grey nylon daypack in front of Vange. "Look at Dall's new backpack. Isn't it cool? And look, normal clothes."

Vange was so sleepy, all she said was, "Yeah, cool," but she said it with a warm smile, which was so unlike how sad she'd been on Monday morning, or would be, come Monday morning.

There. That was as much as Emily dared do. She hoped it would be enough to tickle Vange's subconscious in the same way that all of Dall's authenticity had tickled her own, making her suspect he was a time traveler. She'd thought of writing Vange a note, but she was somehow sure that would be considered 'discussing time travel' with her.

Emily put her phone in the kitchen and started the empty dishwasher, and then she and Dall found ways to keep busy in their bedroom while Vange settled down for the night.

Once Emily was sure her friend was asleep and the dishwasher was still making lots of noise, she told Dall what was on her mind. "I think we should go take pictures of Peadar, Peigi, and Domhnall, to mark them as destinations in case they ever get lost."

Dall hugged her tight. "I do love thee, lass."

Emily kissed her man's tears away, then went and got her phone, put on her long plaid skirt outfit in case anyone saw her, set their destination for Home during one of the open green slots available, and held it out where Dall could see it.

"Aye lass, this does look right to me, with the amount I know of it." He had himself under control now.

Emily didn't mind in the least seeing him cry about his

children. She found it very moving and attractive, actually, that he had a soft spot for the little ones. She knew he was a good father, and she was looking forward to having children with him.

She pushed the button, the world went swirly, and then they were in their attic love nest in the highlands, in the middle of the night. Wincing at the creaking noises, they lowered their stair-hatch. Not hearing anyone stirring, they crept down the hall to the boys' room.

Emily almost cried herself, the boys all looked so sweet sleeping. Aw, Domhnall was in with the big boys now, no longer in his grandmother's room. He had a pad on the scrubbed wooden floor, next to Peadar's bed. An older cousin bunked over Peadar, and there were two more sets of bunks in the room.

Dall kissed both of his snoring sons, and then Emily snapped their pictures. For good measure, she snapped pictures of all the boys.

They repeated this with the girls' room, kissing Peigi and snapping photos of her and all her cousins. And then they climbed back up into their attic room and pulled up the stairs.

"I'm wide awake," Emily told Dall. "How about you?"

Dall nodded.

"OK, there are a few things I need to teach you, especially how to drive. Let's go somewhere and get started on that?"

Looking nervous, but also excited, Dall nodded his head quickly.

They went to her parents' garage on Thursday, walked out, and rented a car for Dall to learn to drive in. Emily had to learn on a stick shift, but she resisted the urge to foist that on Dall on top of everything else. They also went to the library and used their computers to order ATM cards for Dall. They went ahead and used her parents' address.

And then they swirled back to their trailer to rest for what remained of Saturday night before Sunday at festival.

EMILY COULD TELL that Siobhan was livid all day Sunday, but only toward her and Dall. She kept waiting for the axe to fall, getting more and more nervous the longer it didn't. Maybe that was Siobhan's intention. If so, the druid knew what she was doing.

Emily had left her phone in their trailer as she always did, so they could speak freely with their friends with no worries about the druid who was monitoring her phone overhearing. She dressed as a 16th century Scot in her ankle-length plaid skirt and bodice with an embroidered chemise underneath, her boots that were just like Dall's, and her new leather belt with its scabbards for sword and dagger and its pouches slipped on. Dall wore his kilt, boots, billowy shift, belt, and sporran. They and all the other actors wore hats.

Murray was more than happy to see Dall and Emily Sunday morning. "Yesterday went so well, I've decided to give you a cut of all the weapons the customers buy while and right after you give lessons, kids. Like I say, it went well yesterday, but I think we can do even better."

Dall surprised Emily by taking charge again. "If a cut we are going to have in the take, then it should be a cut of the whole day's takings."

Emily admired her husband's business sense, and she scolded herself for forgetting her man was a leader and quite intelligent. She reminded herself that even though he looked foolish at times, it was because of inexperience with modern amenities. It wasn't any lack on Dall's part. She knew she would look just as silly if she'd been raised in his time and come visiting the modern world.

Murray got a twinkle in his eye. Emily knew that meant the man loved to bargain. But Murray hid his joy in the process well other than that twinkle. "How do you figure that?"

"Well," said Dall, "what sells at a faire ... or a festival, is largely because of the feeling of fun, you ken?"

Murray gave Dall an admiring smile. "And you figure you and Emily are adding to that feeling of fun."

"Aye, and that carries through to the rest of the day and even to the rest of the customers. One smiling face begets another."

"I won't argue. You're right. OK, I'll look at yesterday's take as opposed to the take last Saturday, and today's as opposed to last Sunday, and we'll work out a percentage, alright?" He held out his hand.

Dall surprised Murray by grasping the muscular man's forearm instead of his hand, but then Murray grasped Dall's forearm right back, and they shook on the deal. "Make it a good percentage, and we will keep up the lessons and mayhap even add more," Dall added into the deal during the shake.

And then Emily and Dall were sparring with rapier and dagger, her most competent sword fighting style that wasn't anachronistic in this period. They ran all over the arena, swiping and thrusting and blocking and sidestepping, and also jabbing with their daggers.

They put on an even better show than they had the day before, now that there was something to be gained from that, and they drew twice the crowd and almost twice as many lessons.

They didn't have time to notice how many weapons were selling, but when they finally said they were running off to sit with their friends at 'Taming of the Shrew', Murray had a huge grin on his face and the tables were almost empty. They knew he had boxes in his trailer to restock them from, and they figured the take had to be pretty darn big already.

Dall held out his arm, and Emily took it, and they walked alone together to the outdoor stage to meet their friends.

Now that she wasn't busy brandishing a weapon nor showing someone else how, Emily kept watching for Siobhan's angry face to pop up amid all the wonders of the festival. This was her perfect opportunity. They were alone.

This site was wooded, and many of the performers climbed up into the trees and hung down to amuse passersby. Most hung on swings, but some were on hammocks and one even hung inside a big cage. Emily was startled several times, but not by Siobhan.

"Hey." Brittany and Ashley both called out at the same time, waving them over to the straw bale where they had saved two seats.

Safe. Emily smiled, remembering the days when she and Vange would play tag with the kids in the neighborhood. And she enjoyed the stage play more than she had the day before.

"Hi Em." Vange called out from their picnic table at lunch. Her face was so happy, with none of that sadness Emily had seen ... tomorrow. Yeah, that sounded crazy, but she didn't know how else to think of it.

Emily smiled at her best friend and sat next to her.

The 8 of them were laughing and talking when Siobhan showed up.

Emily braced herself and rehearsed in her head. Siobhan, you're always telling us to do things with our guildmates. Siobhan, we're both over 21, so why's it a problem that we went to a dance club? Siobhan, renfest is supposed to be fun. Why are you trying to make it into a drudgery?

That last argument would only work where the locals would hear and wonder if Siobhan said it was Dall's duty, but they were here right now.

But Siobhan didn't give Emily a chance to use any of those arguments. She acted as if nothing was wrong, chatting and laughing along with the rest of them.

But Emily met Siobhan's eyes a few times, and inside, the older woman was seething with anger.

§♠

THE AFTERNOON ALL-GUILD SWORD DEMO, the staged Scots clan meeting, and the ring-out parade all went by in a similar manner to lunch. Siobhan didn't blow up, but she gave Emily and Dall the evil eye.

And the locals always went home Sunday evening. That particular Sunday was no exception.

"We'll walk you to your car," Emily said to Brittany with a smile, falling into step with the five of them and tugging Dall and Vange along by their hands.

Brittany laughed and then smiled sympathetically. "You're going to have to face her sometime."

Vange joined in on teasing Emily, but she looked her in the eye and did it in a friendly, questioning way. "Are you really afraid of that woman, Em? She doesn't seem at all scary to me." She wanted to be convinced, to hear what awful things Emily knew about Siobhan.

And Emily couldn't tell her. And it was hard. Until this year when she met Dall, she had always told Vange everything.

Emily acted as if it really wasn't a big deal. She made a show of fighting a smile that was forming on her face and fell into Dall's arm as he swung it around her while they walked. "She was pretty obvious at lunch with her Dall-and-me-specific anger, wasn't she?"

Her acting worked, which pleased her pride, but left her a little lonely. She clung to Dall.

Everyone snorted laughter through their noses and their pursed lips, as if they were fighting the laughter. All too soon, they reached Vange's car.

While Emily hugged her friend goodbye 'until next weekend', she whispered in her ear, "There are things I wish I could tell you, Vange."

Vange gave Emily a brief startled look as she got in her car, and then she gestured and mouthed "Call me," before she waved and drove off. As if it were that simple.

And then they were at Brittany's car, and their five new besties were driving away, calling out cheerfully.

"See you next weekend."

"If Siobhan doesn't kill you."

They were just joking. How could they know that what they had said sometimes seemed like a very real possibility?

Emily turned to Dall. They both took deep breaths and let them out. She said, "Time to face the music."

Dall laughed.

"What could possibly be funny about that?" Emily asked, dumbfounded.

"'Face the music' is what we say at the beginning of a dance, lass. It means giving respect to the players of the music. But I ken well enough the meaning you have with it, and we are in agreement, aye."

Emily expected Siobhan to be in their trailer waiting for them when they got back to it, but she wasn't. Was the feisty druid aware of how much anxiety she was causing by delaying her appearance? Best to hope not. She pretended everything was fine and this didn't bother her while she peeled potatoes for their supper.

Her phone was in her suitcase, under her bed. She wasn't sure that was enough insulation to keep the druids from spying on the two of them, but it was the best she could do.

"Are you trying to kill the wee vegetable, lass? The cause

of my asking being that you have nearly carved it down to naught." Dall put down the beef he was cubing for their stew and came up behind her and enveloped her in his embrace.

Emily took another deep breath and tried to let her tension out along with it as she relaxed into his comforting arms and answered him in Gaelic. "Ug, she's getting to me. I'm a nervous wreck. I wish she would just come chew us out, already."

Dall started rubbing her shoulders.

She groaned. His massage hurt, she was so tense, but in a good way. "It's hard to face the music when the players won't play any."

More slowly than was strictly necessary, they got back to getting the stew ingredients into the crockpot. And then they broke out a bottle of wine to enjoy while it cooked.

Feeling a little smug in their new abilities, they swirled the crockpot full of stew ingredients over to her parents' house at nine am on Wednesday and plugged it in. When they were done with their wine, they swirled back over at 4 pm on Wednesday to get their cooked stew. It smelled wonderful. It tasted good, too.

The wine was helping.

Emily didn't feel so anxious. "C'mon over, Siobhan." she said right into her phone where she knew a druid was always listening. They'd gotten it out to set the alarm for sparring the next morning. "Let's have a little talk." That was what she meant to say, but it came out a little funny. She tried to put the phone back into the pocket of her PJs, but Dall took it and walked away. She lounged on the couch. It was nice.

And then Dall was picking her up and carrying her, which made Emily feel dizzy. But he was warm and comforting, and she snuggled up next to him in their bed and the next thing she knew, it was morning.

THE ALARM on Emily's phone was loud.

She fumbled on the nightstand until she grabbed it and stopped it. At 5:01 am. "Why did we set that, again?" she said, closing her eyes and snuggling back up to Dall.

He gently sat up with her and then stood with her, holding up her mostly sleeping form. "So that we can be at the arena at sunrise, to spar with the others, lass."

"Urrg." Emily found that she could open her eyes, now that she had a reason. And Dall wasn't in the bed to snuggle with

But the sandman had liberally sprinkled her eyes, making them want to close.

Leaving her phone on the nightstand, she went into their little trailer bathroom and washed the sand out, went to their little trailer closet and got dressed, and then tucked herself under her kilted and wide awake husband's arm.

Dall already had their practice swords in his other hand, and his real claymore was strapped to his back. "This may prove to be one of our more interesting mornings, Drusilla," he said in Gaelic.

She answered him in Gaelic. "Yeah, she's bound to be there." Emily was once again nervous about facing Siobhan's anger, but she was resolved that it needed to be done.

"Aye, there is that," Dall said as if Siobhan's anger hadn't occurred to him.

His confidence tried to put Emily off, but she chose to be attracted to it and hugged him tighter to her.

He caressed her back, and then he puzzled her. "However, we also need to be back inside the trailer before it is 8 of the clock."

Emily had to think about that for a moment before his meaning dawned on her. "Oh, right. We were at the club at 8

this morning. OK, that sounded weird, but yeah. I wonder
what will happen to us here at 8?"

"I do not know, but I say we had best be in the trailer
when we find it out, lass."

They had arrived at the arena, where all of their sparring
partners were eating donuts and drinking coffee. Dall and
Emily got themselves some of each and watched a few sparring matches, and then they each sparred a few times. They
went one at a time so Lews couldn't pull a stunt like he had
that once. He still scowled at Emily whenever she looked at
him, which was less and less often.

Everyone else except Siobhan seemed OK with them,
even Eamann. It was confusing. Siobhan and Eamann talked
quietly in the corner for a few minutes, and then the
confrontation with Siobhan happened, but in a much
different way than Emily expected.

Siobhan finished her donut, put her coffee down, and
walked over to Emily in a businesslike manner, holding out
her hand. "Emily, you and I are going to practice our stage
brawling." There was no hint of anger in her eye now. She
seemed warm, but not quite friendly. More like ... motherly?

Dall squeezed Emily's shoulder, which let her know he
would be watching and would move in at the first sign of
actual fighting, should that occur.

She felt herself smiling. Siobhan might be tough in the
business sense, but surely the modern druid realized she was
no match for Dall in the arena, and that he had Emily's back.
She forgot that druids have magic.

Emily turned her smile toward Siobhan, took the offered
hand, and let the other woman help her up. "OK."

Once they were in the arena, Siobhan started their
conversation softly, so that only Emily could hear. "We're all
very interested to see that you aren't pregnant yet." She also

started their stage brawl, by putting her hands on Emily's shoulders in position for a shove.

Emily followed stage brawling protocol: she grabbed Siobhan's wrists and pushed off of them, making it look as though the other woman had pushed her. "Uh, that came out of nowhere. Who is we, and how do you know?" Emily staggered backward to make the staged push look like it had been a forceful one.

Siobhan pressed her imaginary advantage in the brawl by rushing toward Emily and positioning for another push while Emily was off balance. "We druids can sense these things that involve the life force. I can also tell you aren't on the pill and haven't had any birth-control shots. No IUD, either."

Emily grabbed the druid's wrists again, this time using them to lower herself to the ground while appearing to be pushed. "We could be using condoms."

"Those would require Dall's cooperation, and being Catholic, he wouldn't do that." Siobhan performed a stage kick at Emily's mid-section, pulling her leg back dramatically so that Emily would know the target and then kicking quickly, just short of her target.

Thanking her luck that she wouldn't have to say anything, Emily faked a painful moan about the kick, meanwhile reaching out and grabbing the leg that Siobhan was balancing on and faking a tug by bending her elbows out dramatically.

Siobhan faked a teeter, swinging her arms and her other leg around as if trying to keep her balance. "It's as if you had never started your period, which I also know isn't the case."

Everyone in the gazebo was laughing, amused by Siobhan's comical movements. Except Dall.

Emily could see Dall standing in the arena's gateway, paying rapt attention. Holding her side where she had supposedly been kicked, she got up while Siobhan was teetering. Not wanting to say anything, Emily just moaned some more about her aching side.

Siobhan kept teetering and making their audience laugh. "The only possible explanation is that you and Dall must be time traveling on your own. Your Time Management app must have gotten unlocked somehow."

SIOBHAN QUIT TEETERING, grabbed Emily's wrist with both hands, and started swinging her around in a circle.

Ug, comic fighting is the most physically strenuous kind. Emily would have preferred throwing fake punches at each other. But women don't typically fight that way, and when women do fight, people would rather it be funny. Or sexy, but the renaissance festival was a family show. Emily was just glad that at least Siobhan couldn't expect her to talk at that moment.

Siobhan let Emily go.

In keeping with the improvisational acting rule of always making the most interesting choice, Emily spun out of control on her own like a top and went stumbling across the arena, flailing her arms in the air. And not talking.

Their audience laughed again, and then started clapping.

Sure enough, Siobhan had followed another rule of improvisational acting: stop when the audience is happy. She was bowing over and over in comedic fashion.

Emily bowed, too, and then she headed back over to Dall.

But Siobhan caught her arm. "Let me near you often. So I can tell you when you are pregnant. So that you'll know when to stop time traveling and not lose your baby."

Just like that, Emily was in tears.

When they got to Dall, Siobhan breezed on by without

even talking to him. He hugged Emily tight. "Aw, lass, what did she say to you?"

"Can we just go back to the trailer now?"

"Aye, lass."

When they got there, Emily told Dall everything Siobhan had said. "I was ready for an argument. To tell Siobhan we'd just been doing as she said, making friends with the Scots guild members. Why did she... What does that... I don't understand what's going on."

Dall looked thoughtful as he sat next to her on the couch and held her close, caressing her shoulder. "Well, at least we do not have to worry about them finding out we can travel on our own."

That cheered Emily up enough to go get her phone and check the current time. It was 7:45 Monday morning. "In just fifteen minutes, we're going to meet Vange's cousin the gangster. Do you think we'll re-live it?"

Dall just smiled and shrugged, and she found that so funny that she started tickling him, and they were busy for a while. By the time Emily looked at her phone again, it was 5:25 Monday evening. She showed him, and they laughed.

"Now we know."

"Aye, and it will happen again tomorrow, lass."

"Oh yeah," Emily said, thinking about it. And then she smiled contentedly at him, cuddled up to him, and whispered in Dall's ear, "I want to take Vange along with us and time travel one more time. And then I want to stop and make more MacGregors."

10. WARRIORS

I t was weird knowing they had already spent the next five days elsewhere. They could see their time debt in orange squares on the calendar.

Dall and Emily were cuddled up together on the cheap couch in the new two-bedroom trailer the druids were letting them live in. It was backstage at the renaissance festival, where they both worked. The young married couple stared at the calendar in the Time Management app that a druid named Siobhan had put on Emily's phone.

Emily was glad Dall preferred to wear his kilt rather than the 'normal clothes' they had bought for when he visited her parents. She idly played with the wool plaid yardage he had belted at his waist while they stared at her phone. She herself wore shorts and a T-shirt.

The clock at the top of her phone said 9 pm. "I think Vange is home by now," Emily said in Gaelic, the language they always used when it was just the two of them in the conversation.

"Aye, and why do you say so?" Dall often said things that were a challenge for Emily to answer in his language, which they had discovered was the Time Management app's command language.

"I'm going to call her." Emily had to stop and think about her words for a moment.

Dall gestured for more.

"I'm worried about how mad she gets at me tomorrow about not knowing our plans." Again, Emily stopped to find the words she knew.

Dall caressed her back.

"What if I just call her now and tell her that story about how you lost your ID behind the club Saturday night? That way, I can tell her we're coming out her way tomorrow. That should fix it, right?" When Emily absolutely couldn't find a word, then she just said it in English and Dall told her the Gaelic for it.

"ID we do not have in my time, exempting a lord has a signet ring. About the matter at hand, the truth will tell, lass."

Emily dialed her best friend's cell. It rang and rang, like 15 times, and no voicemail picked up.

"That's just too weird. I'm going to try her parents' house phone."

The same thing happened. The phone rang and rang with no answer.

"What is it, lass? There cannot be that much devastation inside that wee phone." Dall was leaning in so he could hear with her.

Of course, all she was hearing was ringing.

Emily opened her contact list. "None of my calls are going through. I'm just going to push on a random phone number to see if we can reach the outside world."

"Hello, Emily?"

Emily let out a calming breath. "Hi Ashley. Uh ... "she looked at Dall for some reason even she herself didn't know.

Her 16th century highlander husband grabbed the phone

and awkwardly held it to his ear. "Hello, lass. I wish to speak with your man, Cody... Yes, I can..."

Emily finally got over her shock at seeing Dall talking on the phone and leaned in so she could hear both sides of the conversation.

Cody came on the line. "Hey, brother. What's up, my man?"

Dall laughed. "I wish to invite the five of you to a festivity in our ... trailer this Saturday night, by way of thanking you for your hospitality last Saturday evening. I will not take no for an answer, and I beg of you to tell the others."

"Oh, cool. Sure will. See ya then."

"Aye, see ya then." Dall held the phone out to Emily.

She took it. "Hello?" No one was there. She grinned.

"Well, that is better, lass, seeing you happy again, but I would be in on the reason."

Emily gave her husband a look she meant to be apologetic. "I was thinking men in different time periods aren't much different. None of you like talking on the phone, but that was the shortest phone call I ever heard."

He smiled back at her, only his smile was anything but apologetic, and he reached for her.

WHEN EMILY WOKE UP, it was 7 pm the next day. She wasn't alarmed, though. She knew she'd already spent Monday visiting Vange and her parents and Tuesday sleeping in her old room at her parents' house. She and Dall had been up 24 hours straight by then, and they had needed to stay up another five hours in order to drive back to their trailer at the festival site.

"Dall?" she called out, hoping he was inside and could hear her.

"Aye?" Oh, his voice was coming from the shower.

"Let's go see Vange." She listened for his reply over the shower noises that she now noticed down the hall in their one bathroom. Instead, those noises stopped.

And then Dall came into the room, drying his hair. "Aye, well enough. Let us go see your best lass, then." He smiled at her.

She smiled back, and things got interesting for a while.

Once they were both showered and dressed in normal clothes, Dall put his arm around Emily and she got out her phone and selected as a destination her parents' garage at their current time of 8:27 pm Monday night. The night right after Vange blew up at Emily for not sharing their plans to come into town with her and the awkwardness of having to hear about it from her cousin Emilio.

The world went swirly.

Marking in the garage had been a good plan. No one saw them appear out of nowhere, and Dall and Emily left through the back door and walked out to the street and then down to the park. Emily got on one of the swings. Dall copied her and then looked pleasantly surprised when it held him.

Emily called her best friend.

"Hi Em." Vange's voice sounded sad, rather than mad.

"Vange. We're at the park. Come on out."

The line went dead.

Vange came running over. She chuckled. "OK, if you're trying to make up after our fight today, you're doing a lousy job. You did it again. You drove all the way out here and didn't tell me you were coming." But she was smiling. Just a little.

"Glad to see you, too, Vange. Look, I really am sorry— both about this morning and about being here without telling you before now." Emily gestured for Dall to get his little notebook out of his pocket, and the pen.

He handed them to her, and while she was writing, he talked. "Aye, lass. I am truly sorry as well, for all the grief that you have suffered."

Vange started a question with "What—"

But Dall must have made a gesture that stopped Vange from asking Emily what she was writing. Good.

Emily finished and then showed it to Vange: "I can't tell you this secret; I just have to show you."

"O ... K?"

Now that she was sure Vange was paying attention, Emily wrote while she watched, "Take my hand, and don't let go."

Vange took Emily's hand while Dall had his arm around Emily.

She got her phone out and let Vange watch her set it to take them back to their trailer at the current time. And they swirled on over.

Emily put her hand in front of Vange's mouth to keep her from saying anything.

Vange nodded, wide-eyed and grinning huge and stomping her feet she was so excited—and frustrated that she couldn't say anything.

Emily nodded at their hands so that Vange would let go, and then she loaned Vange one of her long plaid skirts, a bodice that matched, a shift, and a hat. Emily dressed similarly, and Dall put his kilt on. They loaded their belts with pouches stuffed full of provisions and items to trade.

"Hold onto me, and don't let go," Emily said again, holding her finger over her lips to remind Vange not to say anything.

Vange nodded yes and latched onto Emily's arm.

"Aye lass, it was my plan ere you did say it, to hold you close and never let go." On Emily's other side, Dall squeezed her.

Emily looked Dall in the eye and then looked at her phone.

Nodding yes, Dall leaned over her phone. Yeah, it was hard to see the little screen in the glare from the cheap overhead lights in the trailer.

Emily brought up the picture they had taken of Dall's son Peadar and hovered her finger over it as a destination. She looked to Dall for his opinion on if they should try it.

"Aye, lass. We do need to find out if it can be done, finding the children, and it is a safe location where he is, all things considered. Let us go."

In Gaelic, Emily said to her husband about his son, "For when we really need to know that he is safe." And then she looked at Dall and Vange both again and pushed the 'Go' button that made the world turn swirly.

INSTEAD OF THEIR attic bedroom at Dall's mother's house on the green cloudy mountains of the Scottish highlands, Emily, Dall, and Vange found themselves in a thicket, looking out on a wide open plain. The sun was hot over their heads, and the sky was a deep clear blue. A few dozen cattle were grazing on the plain, and there was not a sign of civilization as far as the eye could see.

After Emily's eyes adjusted to the bright light, she could see men in English trews resting in a few shady spots, wearing various and sundry styles of sun hats. And when her eyes adjusted more, she could see that one of these men wore a shirt made of MacGregor plaid over his trews.

Dall's hand clenched on Emily's waist, so she figured he must have seen the MacGregor plaid, too. He started to move toward the man who wore it.

Emily clutched him tight and said in Gaelic the phrase she had at first thought meant "I want a do-over."

They swirled back into the trailer at the renfest.

"Why, lass? That was my son. That was Peadar. And that bit you said to bring us there? That meant 'Take us to him when he needs us most.' you ken? Peadar needs us, lass." He was so earnest that he was actually wringing his hands.

"Dall. Dall." Emily was desperate for him to listen to reason.

Finally, he looked at her with a question in his eyes. And he looked hurt, as if she would deny him the need to see to his son's safety. He looked betrayed, and so sad her heart nearly broke.

She had to snap him out of it. Make him see. "Those men were wearing trews, Dall. They're English. If they saw a bunch of Scots appear out of the bushes, they would enslave us. No wonder Peadar cut his kilt up and made it into shirts."

"Aye, but he needs us, lass. We must go back." He wasn't listening, he was so desperate to save Peadar.

"We will," she said, "but after we all change into trews." Emily hugged Dall. "We will go help him, love. We just need to change clothes. Just a change of clothing. We'll go back to that very same second in time." She hugged him some more.

He finally relaxed and was no longer straining to get free of her, which wasn't the way he could get to his son.

She understood he was upset and a bit irrational.

At last, despair lost its hold on Dall. He looked at her and at Vange in their long skirts and their bodices that hiked up their breasts. "Aye, some large trews and large tunics to hide your womanhood, I ken well. Come. I know who we need to see."

A few minutes later, they stood outside the large tent of Marion, the time traveler who approved the locals' handmade renaissance festival costumes for authenticity.

"Knock knock." Dall said, as was the custom at the festival site when arriving at another staffer's tent.

"Dall." came Marion's voice from inside, "come in."

Dall ducked inside the tent, pulling Emily and Vange in with him. "I would ask your assistance, lass, in making me and my wife and our friend look like English men of our time."

Marion gave the two healthy young women a look that said, "You've got to be kidding me."

Dall looked at Emily appreciatively and said, "At least, can you make them look like English men from a distance?"

Marion looked Emily and Vange up and down again, more thoughtfully. "Well enough. Do come with me. We will be needing the clothing in the costume shed for this."

An hour later, they all sported trews and tunics in varying shades of unremarkable brown. They still had their belts and pouches with provisions. They had added packs with camping items and more provisions, and they had left the items for trading behind.

Dall and Emily had their boots with their daggers sheathed in them. Vange had loaner boots that weren't the best fit but that would be far less remarkable to the people of the time they were headed for than the neon green sneakers she'd been wearing under her long skirt. Far less remarkable. Good thing her hair wasn't neon green these days.

Emily and Vange had been talking excitedly in the course of being fitted into these 16th century Englishmen's outfits. They had purposely left Emily's phone in the trailer so that this wouldn't be a problem.

"This is so much fun." Vange said, swinging her legs in her chair and glancing sideways at Dall as if she had no idea why he was so upset.

"What is?" Emily said, trying to tell Dall with her eyes she was sorry for her friend's lack of empathy for him.

"Getting all dressed up in these costumes. Where are we going, anyway?"

"Like I said before, I can't really tell you. You wouldn't believe me, anyway. I'm showing you. You'll see pretty soon, when we get there."

"The suspense is killing me."

"Call home," Emily told Vange. "Tell them you're out with me and you might stay over. We'll try to get you home this evening, but you never know."

So Vange called home, and then they went back to the trailer and hung up Dall's kilt and Emily's two Scottish outfits.

"Ready?" Emily grabbed her husband and her friend and waited for them to nod yes. "Take two." She selected her new English Thicket destination, pressed the 'Go' button, and swirled them back to Peadar.

Not even an instant had passed when the three of them arrived back in the thicket in Peadar's time. The men were all in the same positions and locations—as were all the cows, near as Emily could tell.

"Dall," she said, gently holding him back. She could tell he wanted to run to his son. Who by the way appeared to be about Dall's own age, 28. "Dall, you can't let those Englishmen hear your Scottish accent."

He was intent on his son, straining to see what peril he was in.

Emily spoke in soothing tones. "If they hear you talk, they'll know you're a Scot, and then why did we go to all the trouble to get these English clothes? And me and Vange have to keep quiet, too, or they'll know we're women. And three mutes in one group is just too far-fetched a tale for them to buy. We have to wait until Peadar is alone, and then we can go talk to him and make sure he is OK."

Dall had gradually relaxed as she talked.

"Aye lass, you have the right of it."

But neither of them had stopped to consider that Vange had never time traveled before today. The last time had been so brief, she hadn't seemed to realize that was what they had done.

Their poor friend Vange looked like she was in shock. Hardly a shy person, she stood there speechless, even trembling a bit.

❦

EMILY PUT her arm around her friend. "I guess here is as good a place to camp out as any, while we wait for them to go to sleep or something."

"Aye. Well, I shall get the camp ready then."

It wasn't a modern camping trip. Good thing it was summertime. They had rudimentary sleeping bags made of flannel, no tent, beef jerky and similar traveling food, tanned animal bladders full of water...

The only modern convenience the three had brought was a small factory-made magnifying glass for starting fires. But they dared not have a campfire with those men so near. They would smell it. So yeah, good thing it was summer and they were plenty warm enough. Emily reassured herself that the cows would draw any wolves or other predators who came. They had no need for a fire at all.

And then the waiting started.

It wasn't too dull though, once the Englishmen got on their horses and rounded up the small herd of cattle. That was actually fascinating to watch.

"I knew it. I knew you were a time traveler." Vange had finally gotten over her shock and was smiling her biggest at Dall.

They all laughed together.

And then Vange must have been back to her normal self, because she cocked her head sideways at Dall. "You look like you're unimpressed with the way these cowboys are handling the cattle, almost like you've done this before. I thought you guys raised sheep in Scotland, not cattle."

Dall's brow furrowed.

Emily laughed a little. "Yeah, I was surprised by that at first when I visited Dall in his time, in Scotland."

Vange gasped. "You've been to his time?"

Emily gave Vange a look. "How do you think I got to know him so well?"

Dall surprised both women by speaking up. "We do not have to wait for these Englishmen to fall asleep, you ken."

Vange's eyes got really big. "Can you guys make them fall asleep with magic?"

Emily giggled. "No, silly. He means we can use my phone to travel a few hours into the future, the time when it's night here and they're already asleep."

Then Vange's brow furrowed. "But... What happens if they come over here in the meantime? We won't be here. Will we?"

"We do not know, lass. If we do be here, then they will grab us in our ... sleep. If we be not here, then they will see our camp and know that we are nearby and mayhap even set someone to watch for our return. Nay, you have the right of it, Vange. We must stay and wait. Nay, we should pray that Peadar does wander over this way."

So they all bowed their heads while Dall crossed himself and prayed earnestly for his son.

And then they waited.

While they waited, Emily told Vange all about her time-traveling experiences. How Dog and his crew of biker-archers had hitched a ride to the past just like Vange had and Emily had directed them in acting Romeo and Juliet inside a castle courtyard. How she and Dall had ridden through the highlands together, stopping to eat at MacGregor houses where everyone guessed they would soon be married. About the Menzies man Emily had stabbed when he tried to kill her.

As Emily talked, she noticed something that was sweet and disturbing at the same time. Vange couldn't take her eyes off Peadar.

IN THE END, they all fell asleep on their flannel sleeping bags in broad daylight there in the thicket on the plain near some faraway English settlement in the New World. It was so calm and pastoral. The cattle stood grazing. The men on horseback moved about, but in the distance, where seeing them was more like watching a movie than being out on the range. Birds wheeled overhead, calling to each other, but the longer you heard that, the more it seemed like soothing music.

Emily's last conscious thought was "I wonder if Peadar and the Englishmen will be gone when we wake up?"

Her awakening was much ruder than that.

Fast asleep one moment, Emily felt Dall push off from her in the next moment. She sensed rather than heard a struggle. By the time she opened her eyes, Dall already had the situation well in hand.

Emily sat up and rubbed her bleary eyes. By the light of the moon, she could see that Dall was holding someone captive. He had the person hugged tight to him, face out. At the person's throat was Dall's dagger.

The person was English, she thought. He hadn't spoken, but she just thought his air seemed English...

Only then did Emily realize that person was staring at her.

Oh no.

Her mannish hat had fallen off while she slept. Her long hair obviously had given her away as a woman. Defiantly, Emily turned her gaze away from the captive. She sought out Vange in the darkness. She sighed in relief. Vange was fine, and she was sizing up the situation much the same as Emily was, her eyes bright in the moonlight now that Emily's eyes had adjusted.

Oddly, the captive held a hand to his lips, seemingly urging them to remain quiet. He pointed to the dagger at his throat and then at the two women, back and forth, with a look on his face that seemed to be trying to say, "Has either of you women a dagger with which to defend yourselves?"

That was when the cattle started moving.

It was slow at first. They had been asleep, and at first there was just a step here and there. But the steps grew faster and faster, more and more...

A look of understanding came into Dall's face. Pointing out of the thicket, he slowly released the captive. Once he had, the two men got up and headed out into the open moonlit plain.

Emily started to say something.

But Vange put a hand over Emily's mouth.

Remembering the captive's caution to remain quiet, Emily nodded to show Vange that she understood. But instead of getting her dagger out to defend them like the captive had insinuated, she got her phone out and set it to swirl the two of them back to the trailer, just in case someone besides Dall came to the thicket.

She held her phone tightly in her fist with her thumb over the 'Go' button the entire while the two best friends clung to each other in the quiet darkness, not knowing when—or Heaven forbid, if—Dall was coming back.

After what seemed like forever, the cattle stopped moving. They could see two forms approaching. Emily kept her thumb ready. Twigs broke as two men entered the thicket. Emily let out her breath, and Dall came back with the man who had been the captive.

Emily had expected Dall to come back with Peadar, but he hadn't. He'd just brought this stranger. She looked into Dall's face for any sign that he had seen his son alive since the commotion started.

Dall's face was not peaceful.

Emily got up and ran to him and embraced him with all she had.

The man whom Dall had held captive spoke then. "I do think all the indians be gone now, but begging your pardon, we should be seeing about the horses and urging the cattle closer to civilization, before more indians come."

This made Emily angry. "We don't care about your stupid cattle. We came to find ... someone, and now he's probably dead." She felt Dall's hand on her back.

He said, "I did not see Peadar's body, lass. He may yet be out there, you ken? I must go and look for him."

"We'll all go," Emily said with a small smile, wiping her tears away with the sleeve of her mannish shirt. "I don't want to stay here without you. That was torture. What happened out there?"

"I will tell you sometime when we are safe, lass, and you ask me again. But the time is now to go and find him. If you will come, then let us gather all this up."

They took a few minutes to stuff everything in their leather backpacks, and then they were on their way to where Dall and the stranger had last seen the horses.

"What's your name, anyway?" Emily said to the stranger, not even bothering to fake a 16th century English accent. Despite the training she had received by the druids who ran the renaissance festival, she knew she was terrible at that and wouldn't fool him.

"I be Johnathan, but you can call me John." He held out his hand.

Dall embraced John's forearm. "I am Dall MacGregor. This is my wife, Emily, and our friend, Evangeline."

John embraced Dall's forearm and shook it.

But Emily thought she saw John stiffen when he learned they were MacGregors.

"Yes," said John, "I am certain I did see yon Peadar mount a horse and ride toward the English settlement. That be the same direction I do wish to go. I lost all my men except for Peadar in the attack of those vicious indians. Do you know cattle driving as well as Peadar, and will you help me drive them home?"

"Aye," said Dall. And then he turned to Emily. "Let us refresh your skills on the back of a horse, lass. I do not wish for you to fall." He gave her a look that said, "I told you to practice. I sure hope you were right when you said you didn't need to, but your bottom is going to be sore, regardless."

He took an hour to make certain both of the women now knew how to ride competently, which was more individual instruction than they'd had from Lews before he went psycho on Emily.

"Very well," Dall said at last, "ride behind all the cattle. John and I will be riding around to drive the cows who wander back to the herd." He kissed her, and then rode off.

Emily and Vange used all their concentration just staying on their horses for the first few hours. But by the time the sun had come up, it had become their new normal. It was getting hot.

"Blah." Vange said to Emily, "I always thought cowboys wore bandanas because they looked cool."

"I know." Emily replied. "I so wish I had one right now. Ack. Cows raise a lot of dust."

"Oh, this is intolerable," Vange said a few minutes later. "I don't care that this is a loaner shirt from the costume shed. I'm totally ripping off part of the bottom to put over my nose."

Emily nodded. "Good idea."

A few minutes later, they both looked like Jesse James does in the movies, with rags tied over their faces.

"It was nice of Dall to agree to help drive the cattle," Vange said, "but couldn't we just use your phone to find Peadar again?"

"We could try, but there's two reasons we aren't, not yet."

"John is probably one reason."

"Yep. We can't just disappear in front of him, and really, how could we have convinced him we'd rather walk than ride, when he offered us horses?" Emily coughed. Even with the rag, some of the dust was going down her throat. Still, she knew cows stampeded sometimes, so she was more than happy to ride behind them rather than out in front.

"OK, so what's the other reason we don't just use your phone again to find Peadar?"

"Time travel is not an exact science. Well, it probably is for most of the druids, but it isn't for me. Not yet, anyway. I had no idea what year we would come to. I only knew that we would find Peadar. And I don't know if he would have to be alive in order for us to find him. We might find his grave next time we try this."

They were both silent for a while after that.

Emily checked the charge indicator on her phone one more time. Now that she was separated from Dall, their chemistry wasn't keeping it full of juice like it usually did through the magic of the druids' Time Management app. She had the phone in her solar charger brooch, and now that the sun was out it was slowly charging.

She kept the power switched off for the most part, only powering it up to check the battery level. It was only at 60%. She kept quiet about that. No sense in getting Vange worried about something her friend couldn't do anything about.

The cattle kept moving, but the noise they made gradually faded away into white noise that Emily no longer noticed.

Riding along quietly next to Vange, Emily started to imagine she heard a voice saying her name. She imagined that it came from far away very faintly, as if someone were yelling just on the edge of her hearing range. The more she thought about it, the more she thought she heard it whenever John was farthest away from her, pushing in cows from the outer edges of the herd.

Of course, she was just imagining that voice.

Emily drank from the animal bladder full of water that she carried over her shoulder like a purse. She wanted to squirt her face too, but she didn't dare waste the water. Who knew when the men would stop.

"Ug, it's so hot." Vange fanned herself with her hand.

"I know. I will never again complain about the air conditioner being too cold. In the trailer, I can just put a sweater on."

Before either of the women knew what was happening, a man had ridden in between them, grabbed the reins of both their horses, turned them around, and ridden off with them. They were already almost out of John and Dall's sight.

Emily wasn't too worried, though. The man's shirt was made of MacGregor plaid. "Peadar?" she said tentatively.

"Aye, Emily." He turned as if to look at her while he spoke to her, but it seemed to her like he was looking at Vange.

"Stop, Peadar. Your da is back there."

But Peadar didn't listen. "I ken that, lass. However, I am

certain he will come looking for you and the other lass, here." He was still riding away with them, and rather fast, too.

"But why are we leaving him behind?" Emily was beginning to feel alarmed. She wondered if she could get her phone out, set it for anywhere but here, and manage to jump off her horse and grab Vange in time to push the 'Go' button and swirl away before she hit the dirt and either broke something or died.

But Peadar spoke sense. "That Englishman, John, is not a good man. Da can take care of himself. However, I mean to give him an easier time of it by taking care of you lasses for him."

Vange was uncharacteristically quiet.

Glancing over, Emily saw that her best friend was staring at her stepson, who was now a grown man. He had called Emily 'lass'.

After sizing him up, Emily realized Peadar looked a bit older than she and Vange were... which was too weird for words. He was her stepson. She had just seen him a week ago as a seven year old. Her mind was awhirl.

§.

PEADAR KEPT hold of their horses and led them away from the cattle for about half an hour before he stopped to turn and see if anyone was following.

Emily and Vange also turned to look.

No one seemed to be following. It was easy to spot the cattle back there. With all the dust their hooves raised, they would show up for hours on this flat plain before a rider reached them.

"Aren't we closer to the indians now than we were where the cows are?" Vange asked Peadar, moving her horse a little closer to him than was strictly necessary in order to be heard.

"Aye, lass, we are." He turned his body in his saddle to look at her when he spoke to her.

The two of them stared each other in the face for a long moment before he seemed to wake up.

He went on. "However, I will take my freedom out here even with the threat of the indians, over my certain captivity in the English settlement." As if it were an afterthought, Peadar drank some water now that they were stopped.

Emily did the same. Seeing that Vange wasn't drinking, she rode over to her friend's other side and poked the woman in the ribs.

Vange startled, looked at Emily, and got her own water skin to her mouth.

"Come, lasses. We will take cover in that small forest." Not really giving them a choice, he grabbed their reins again and led their horses a few yards into the cool shade of the trees. And then he started to climb one.

Vange started to get off her horse, obviously intending to climb up after him.

He smiled, but he said, "Nay, lass. Stay on your horses. Do not go out there unless you be attacked, and if that be, then run your horses to the next group of trees and leave however it is you came, you ken?" He remained still then, halfway up the tree, waiting for them to acknowledge what he'd said.

"How about if we stay here and you go and get Dall?" Emily's unease at being separated from Dall grew more intense the farther Peadar got from her, too. It was nearly unbearable already, and it looked like he intended to go quite far up into the tree.

"That may be what I do, lass. However, I wish to see what I can from—ack."

All Emily heard after that was the sound of Peadar struggling with someone up there in the treetop. Lots of grunts and the sickening sounds of blows landing on bones.

Emily made a split-second decision. "Vange. Hitch your skirt up into your belt and climb up after him. As soon as I'm ready, I'll climb after you. All you have to do is touch him while I'm holding your ankle."

In the time it took Vange to dismount, Emily had her phone set. Sliding it into her brooch for easy-access carrying, she dismounted and climbed up after her friend ... and her stepson.

The fight above was still on. Peadar and an indian were both hanging from the tree with one hand while they kicked and slugged at each other with their legs and other hands.

Emily had a bad feeling that this was not going to end well without her intervention. Worried about arrows, she nervously searched the nearby trees. She didn't see anything, but that didn't relieve her anxiety.

"I can reach him now, Emily." Vange was a few branches above her.

"Hold on, I'm coming." Emily stretched for the next branch while the men swung and punched and kicked over her head. She stretched out and tried to grab Vange's ankle. Ug, she wasn't close enough. She stretched out to reach the next branch, slipped, caught herself, climbed up another branch, and just managed to latch onto her friend.

"OK," Vange said softly down to Emily so as not to alert the men, "are you ready for me to try and touch Peadar?" She looked down at Emily.

Emily fumbled around with her brooch, trying her best to get her phone out of it with one hand while she held on to Vange's ankle for dear life.

"Don't look down," Vange said in the nick of time to keep Emily from doing just that.

Emily's hand was shaking so bad she had to concentrate really hard not to drop her phone while she got her screen up and got her thumb over the 'Go' button. "Ready."

Vange waited until one of the men's feet came near her, and then she grabbed it. "Got it."

Emily pushed the 'Go' button.

ॐ

THE WORLD WENT SWIRLY, and then Emily, Vange, Peadar— and the indian man—were behind the Christmas tree in the storage closet at Brittany's favorite dance club. Emily had set her phone for midnight on a Saturday, so loud music came in through the walls and they could feel the beat of the bass in their bones.

The men fell down, suddenly hanging from nothing where their hands had been locked around tree branches. They landed and kept on struggling with each other, albeit in a restrained, wrestling sort of way.

Emily and Vange stayed on their feet.

Vange looked around curiously. "Wow, Emily. How did you do this? It's amazing." She caught sight of Peadar and smiled at him.

Peadar smiled back at Vange from the floor, where he was so tangled up with the indian that Emily couldn't tell who was winning.

But just then, the indian let out a loud keening yell, "Eye ee ee ee ee ee ee." It sounded like a whole pack of coyotes.

Well, that did it.

The door opened out with a bang against the wall, and two bouncers ran into the already crowded little storage room.

"What's going on in here?" said the first bouncer.

"Quit making that racket." shouted the second one.

Emily improvised. "I came in here looking for my friend." She pointed at Vange. "She was making out with this cowboy."

Vange played along, tossing her hair and smiling at Peadar.

Emily went on. "I was trying to get her to leave with me when this indian came barging in and started a fight with the cowboy. We tried to pull them apart, and he started yelling."

"I never saw any of them come in. Did you, Bud?" The bouncer was looking all of them over thoughtfully.

"Nope. Must have snuck in the back."

Both bouncers moved toward them.

With the crazed look of a cornered animal, the indian yanked away from Peadar onto his feet, lowered his head, and rammed past both bouncers and out the door, all the while screaming, "Eye ee ee ee ee ee ee."

"Get him before he hurts someone, Bud." The bouncers ran out after the indian.

Peadar made a move as if to go help them.

Emily reached out and grabbed his shirt just in time.

Peadar turned to her.

She held out her hand.

With realization dawning on his face, he took it.

"Hold on to me." Emily said to Vange.

Her best friend grabbed her arm just in time for Emily to select a different destination and push the 'Go' button again.

This time they swirled into the trailer where they stayed at the renfest.

"I have to charge my phone," Emily said, looking all over for the cord she hadn't needed for nearly a year and then plugging her phone into an outlet in the kitchen. "That'll take two hours or so. In the meantime, we might as well eat and stock up on whatever we might need if we have to rescue Dall from that John fellow."

But Vange was staring at Peadar as if she'd never seen him before. "Huh? What John fellow?" She looked around as if she expected to see Dall in the room. "Where is he?"

"Oh no. You don't remember going to Peadar's time, do you."

Vange looked worried and quickly shook her head no, then looked over at Peadar and waved.

Peadar waved back, smiling at Vange.

"Ug." Emily yelled in frustration. "How did I forget you wouldn't remember being there. OK, Vange. Peadar and I have to get ready and then go get Dall. You stay here in case he finds his way home without us, so you can tell him we've gone looking for him. He'll know what to do if that happens. OK?"

"OK, gosh. Dall's a big boy, Emily. He can take care of himself. You don't have to get snippy with me."

Emily could tell Vange wasn't really upset. Her friend was just talking big to impress Peadar. It was weird, but it worked for Emily right now. Since she was sort of afraid to watch the two of them flirt, she busied herself reheating leftovers in the trailer's tiny built-in microwave.

Every time the microwave went 'Ding.' Peadar would lower himself and freeze.

He reminded her of the cat she'd had when she was little. But the man was so preoccupied with Vange that he didn't even turn to look once he reassured himself nothing was attacking any of them.

They were all eating reheated leftover stew when Siobhan the druid burst into the trailer with a sheathed claymore and the leader of the new Chinese guild that had been started at this site of the druids' renaissance festival.

"Ju-long, this is Emily, the wife of our missing man, Dall," Siobhan said, handing Peadar the claymore and a dagger that Emily hadn't noticed before.

"So much sad." Ju-long bowed a little to Emily. He was wearing complicated brown-leather armor that had a flappy skirt with pants underneath and a brown leather helmet shaped like Darth Vader's.

But his rudimentary firearm was the most interesting part of the Chinese man's outfit.

Emily could tell that Ju-long was trying hard not to stare at her and Vange in their obvious men's wear of the 1560s. He was doing a good job. She sometimes wished she didn't know how to tell when someone was acting, but it came with her training.

"I'm not sure Peadar knows how to use that claymore," Emily said to Siobhan after she bowed back to Ju-long.

But Peadar put her uncertainty to rest by testing the heft of the claymore with a few loud swoosh sounds. Looking pleased, he re-sheathed the sword and strapped it onto his back. He tested the dagger a bit too before sheathing it in his boot.

Siobhan continued. "And this is Dall's son, Peadar, the man I explained to you."

Emily was watching for Vange's reaction, and she wasn't disappointed.

Her best friend was almost as good an actress as she was. They had been in drama together all four years of high school. Vange was fooling the men and maybe even Siobhan with her calm, cool, collected demeanor.

But Emily could tell Vange was freaking out at hearing that this grown man of Dall's age was Dall's own son. It gave Emily the tiniest bit of satisfaction, the fact that someone she'd known for a long time finally knew how weird her life was now. Emily was glad Vange had the chance to react to the big picture in relative safety, rather than just survive like they had in Peadar's time.

"So much sad." Ju-long gave Peadar his little bow.

The highlander wearing his cut-up kilt in the form of a shirt gave the Chinese man little pause at all. He bowed and then looked impatiently at everyone.

Siobhan kept talking. "And this is Vange, Emily's friend."

"So pleased." Ju-long smiled at Vange while he did his bow thing. Yes, he stared at her trews, but mostly he smiled at her pretty face.

Watching her friend meet her second time-traveler made Emily wonder for the first time how that indian was doing, back at Brittany's favorite dance club. She felt a little bad for abandoning him in her time, where he was sure to have difficulty fitting in. But just a tiny bit. After all, he had been trying to kill her stepson...

"Emily, this ... Emily? Emily."

Startled out of her thoughts, Emily looked up to see Siobhan's impatient face.

Siobhan raised an eyebrow at Emily. "I've explained the situation to Ju-long, and he's agreed to help you bring Dall back here. So long as he wears this amulet, he will remember that." She held out from around Ju-long's neck a flat green stone hung by a leather cord.

"Aren't you coming along to remind him?" Emily asked the druid.

"No. I don't ... travel well," said Siobhan. "I only go where I need to in order to help run the festivals. But I brought you each a leather backpack full of fresh provisions and a few other things that might come in handy out in the middle of nowhere."

Everyone gathered round, and Siobhan showed them what was in their packs, explaining how to use the unfamiliar items and answering their 'what if' questions matter-of-factly.

When their questions died down, Siobhan said, "I know you're all wondering about Ju-long's firearm. Yes, it is functional. He can only take one shot before he has to re-load, though, and loading takes a good ten minutes. So make his one shot count—"

And then Siobhan's phone played the catchy tune of a silly boy-band song.

"Yeah? OK, I'm coming." Siobhan looked up at Emily. "Gotta go. You bring back our Dall." She turned and hurried out of the trailer, letting the door bang on her way out.

But not before Emily caught the hint of a smile on the druid woman's serene face. What was that all about?

Peadar finally broke away from staring at Vange long enough to show concern for his da. "Well, you ken we should be going?"

Vange stepped back from Peadar, but she still drank in every word he said.

"Yeah," Emily said, "let me see if my phone is fully charged yet." She went back into the kitchen.

Peadar, Ju-long, and Vange followed her.

"Yep." Emily said, "It's at 100 percent. OK, we could go back to the last place we were, up in the tree above those three horses. How long will it take us to ride to the English settlement from there, Peadar?"

"Cannot we go directly to wherever they are holding Da? It would take a few days to ride the horses to the settlement."

"We can try," said Emily, "but I'm worried about people seeing us appear out of thin air near Dall and then not being able to get close enough to get him out of there with us."

"But—"

"I can say the 'Do over' words and we'll come back here," Emily said, "but that doesn't undo them seeing us. They might charge Dall with witchcraft for making us disappear, you see? They could burn him in the time it takes us to get back to him."

Vange gasped. "Appear out of thin air. Really?"

Emily nodded yes at her best friend. "Yep. Really. I showed you, but you don't remember."

Peadar's brow wrinkled at that, and he looked at Vange with concern. "How was it that you and Da found me, Emily? You did seem to come from nowhere, you ken, from out of the bush."

"Oh, well, we had taken your picture when you were young."

Peadar gave Emily a blank look.

"Oh yeah, you've never seen a picture." She thought for a moment and decided to just tell him the story and hope he understood it. "While you were sleeping, your da and I came into your room and captured your image with my phone."

Peadar looked more confused than ever.

"Here," Emily said, "like this." She took Peadar's picture.

He blinked and ducked when the flash went off.

Emily showed the picture to him.

Peadar grabbed her hand and brought the image close, staring at it in awe and wonder. "Do you have a likeness of Da in this wee 'phone' of yours?"

·❧·

"Yeah, here. Let go and I'll show you."

Peadar let go of Emily's wrist.

She showed him a photo of Dall in his kilt and a black tank top.

"Well, and the likeness you have of me helped you to find me?"

"Yeah. I used it as a destination. See? All these bookmarks are saved destinations where we've been. There's a map, and I think we could use it to pick destinations, but that scares me because someone might see us. We know that all these saved destinations are hidden from view."

"Aye, lass, but were you not hidden from view when you came to my destination? You were hidden by the bush, aye?"

"Well, yeah, we were, but who knows if that was just an accident? Next time, we may pop up in the middle of a street that wasn't there the last time some druid used that destination. You see what I mean?"

"Aye. However, I do think saving Da be worth a wee bit of trouble, you ken? We should be using the likeness of him to find him, before the English make him angry enough to grieve us over him."

Emily felt tears rise up in her eyes at the thought of Dall dying in a fight with his new English masters because she was afraid to use his picture to find him.

Vange's hand found Emily's, and Vange gave her a sympathetic look.

Peadar looked every bit as fierce as his father, perhaps even more so because of resentment at being a slave.

Emily's mind changed. "OK, yeah. You're right. We'll use Dall's picture as a destination. Help me with the Gaelic I'll need to say in order to go back there—but to Dall rather than to where we were when we left your time, Peadar."

So Peadar coached Emily in Gaelic pronunciation, trying to get her to say the phrase with just the right inflections in just the right places to tell the wee phone app to get the three of them to Dall in Peadar's time—and not somewhere completely different.

Vange and Ju-long were having their own conversation during this, obviously not understanding anything Emily or Peadar said. While they talked, Ju-long loaded his weapon. This was an intricate and fascinating procedure involving bottles of various powders and small metal measuring vessels.

But in the back of her mind, Emily was deeply bothered by the fact that the druids always had someone listening in on her conversations through the app that Siobhan had installed on her phone. She was a bit embarrassed in case a pre-18th century druid was listening, because they would understand every word she said in Gaelic. And from the way Peadar was reacting to her, Emily knew she sounded pretty foolish:

Peadar: Take us back to Dall near the time we left him.

Emily: I want to go 'spend time' with Dall.

Peadar (shaking his head no): Take us back to Dall near the time we left him.

Emily: Take me back to Dall's moment in time.

Peadar (with a panicked look): Take us back to Dall near the time we left him.

Emily: Take us back, we want our moments of time with Dall.

It was tough going. Sometimes Peadar laughed at her, but most of the time he looked worried, and sometimes even sick.

At long last, after an hour of practice, Peadar said she had it right.

Ju-long spoke up then. "I hear is danger when we arrive. And no one must see this small box." He gestured at Emily's phone. "So we stand in circle. Watch other backs. Yes?"

Vange ran in and hugged Emily. "You're really going away, huh. It's scary being the one staying behind. Promise you'll be careful and come back."

Emily got the feeling that even though Vange was hugging her, she was really talking to Peadar. She hugged Vange back. "We'll come back. I promise."

Vange stepped back and leaned on the kitchen counter.

"Ready?" Emily asked the men. They huddled around her phone. She looked at it and got Dall's picture ready. The two men looked over each other's shoulders, guarding their backs from any danger they might encounter upon their arrival.

"Aye."

"Yes."

"Take us back to Dall near the time we left him," Emily said in her careful Gaelic while she pressed the 'Go' button.

They swirled into a grove of trees at the top of a hill over-looking a tiny settlement by a big river. They could see where the river dumped into the ocean in the distance to their left.

The settlement consisted of four small log buildings. Singing and clapping came from one of them. It sounded a bit like a church hymn Emily had heard before, but she couldn't hear the words. The four buildings created a small dirt square.

As soon as she had her bearings, Emily saw that Vange had managed to touch her somehow so that she could come along anyway, despite agreeing to stay behind. Their eyes met briefly.

Vange made a face that said, "Sorry, but I wasn't going to be left out of this and let you take all the risks—and have all the fun." Out loud and with her biggest smile ever, Vange said to Peadar, "I remember everything now. I remember you."

The highlander-turned-cowboy was smiling at Vange like a fool.

Exasperated—and if she was honest, a little embarrassed at seeing her best friend flirt with her stepson—Emily brought Peadar back to reality. "I think our best bet is to hurry up and go get Dall while they're all singing. Come on."

"We not know where Dall is," said Ju-long.

Emily made an exaggerated gesture and spoke what she meant by it. "The druid app brought us here, so we know Dall is near. There aren't many places he could be in that teeny tiny settlement. All I have to do is touch him and then touch the 'Go' button, and we're out of here. I don't care who sees us, either. I am going to get him out. Now."

They started to answer.

Before they could, Emily was running down the hill

toward her man. She knew they would follow. She was their way home.

The flapped skirt of Ju-long's leather armor made enough noise as he ran that she could tell they weren't far behind.

Emily didn't see anyone as she ran all the way down the hill and hid in the shadow of one of the four buildings. She wasn't too worried about the people inside seeing her, because the buildings didn't have wind openings, which made sense out here in the wild frontier.

The others finally joined her in the shade, leaning against the small log cabin. Peadar took the lead now, finally back on task and looking for Dall. They crept up the side of the house toward the small dirt square.

"Do you see anyone?" Emily frantically looked every which way to make sure no people were around.

"No," said Ju-long, behind her.

"Only Da," said Peadar, ahead of her.

"Dall." Instantly mortified that she had yelled out loud, Emily kind of ducked her head, but she ran around the corner into the dirt square.

Still wearing trews, Dall was in stocks. "I did know you would come for me, lass. I did not worry one bit." Dall smiled up at Emily as best he could with his head and wrists locked between two stout pieces of wood that were tied to a stunted tree that Emily hadn't seen from the hilltop.

Peadar ran to his da and hugged him.

Emily was running in to join him when she heard Vange scream behind her.

CONFIDENT THAT PEADAR would protect Dall, Emily looked around the corner outside of the dirt square to see Vange being grabbed by two angry-looking men and Ju-long holstering his gun in order to help her.

"This is an English settlement," said one of the men.

"You indians are not welcome here," said the other.

"Grab her and pull." Emily told Ju-long. "Dall is just around this corner."

She ran after Ju-long, grabbed Vange by the middle, and started to pull against the men, who were trying to pull Vange backward, out from between their buildings.

Ju-long did Emily one better, though. Making sure she could see him so she would be ready, he raised his leather hearing protection, took out his weapon, and aimed it at the sky.

"Cover your ears, Vange." Emily let go of her friend and covered her own ears with both hands.

Vange quit struggling with the two men and raised her hands up to cover her own ears.

"What does she do?" said one of the English settlers.

"Daft if I do know," said the other. "She be a crazed indian woman. They can't be expected to act like civilized people. Look, she be wearing men's clothing."

But as soon as Vange had covered her ears, Ju-long fired his weapon into the air.

BLAM.

"Aaaaaaa." Both men dropped their hold on Vange to now hold their aching ears and cower in fear against the side of the log house.

"A cannon."

"That indian has a cannon."

"Over here." Emily yelled, motioning for Vange and Ju-long to follow her around the corner, where they all huddled up around Dall, who was still in stocks.

"Don't let go of me, anyone."

They all grabbed onto her shoulders or waist.

Emily got out her phone, dragged the destination menu down, selected the first destination that came up without even glancing at it, and pushed the 'Go' button.

The world went swirly.

Well, there wouldn't be any do-overs this time.

But Emily figured they could just pick a new destination and leave right away if they didn't like where they ended up. Except they ended up in their love nest in the attic of Dall's mother's house in the highlands.

"Oh, it's so nice to be home." Emily said to Dall, who was with them and out of the stocks and then very much all over her and kissing her for what was probably a full minute but felt like no time at all.

"I welcome in you home by you people?" said Ju-long tentatively. Poor guy, no wonder he was worried, after the way those settlers had treated him and Vange.

"Aye," said Dall.

"Hush," said Peadar, holding his hand in front of his mouth to indicate they should be quiet.

Dall moved as if to backhand Peadar for telling his own father what to do, but at the last second, Dall didn't do it. He stopped and looked in the other man's serious and worried face, then nodded once and backed off.

"What's wrong?" said Vange, who obviously remembered everything still and was squatting a bit in order to better respond to whatever threat Peadar sensed.

"Have a look inside the clothing boards, lass." Peadar was looking mostly at Vange—and with an embarrassing amount of requited longing—but he was talking to Emily.

Thinking to find a Scottish change of clothing for each of them, Emily nodded yes at Peadar and went to the free-standing closet that had been her wedding present from Dall's brothers.

What she saw inside puzzled her.

Why had Dall's mother filled it up with clothing in Campbell colors? That didn't make any sense. Emily held up one of the garments and met Dall's gaze, trying to say with her eyes, "What do you make of this? Is it a joke?"

"What year did you put in, lass, when we did swirl over here?" Dall's face was all scrunched up and worried, but still kind.

"I didn't put in any year at all," Emily said. "I just selected the first destination that came to my finger." She looked at her phone and gasped.

The year was the same one they had just left, 1560, and the destination was Dall's daughter Peigi's picture.

Peadar's face hardened with resolve, and as he spoke, everyone else's did as well. "If she be here, and the house be possessed by the Campbells, then she be here held captive, for certain."

11. LOCH

Hearing a noise in the house below, Emily quickly put her phone away inside her brooch.

When they had first arrived in the room, she hadn't noticed the blue Campbell plaid clothing in the wardrobe cabinet. Nor had she noticed the old red MacGregor kilt, torn up and made into rags which stuffed the chinks in the walls against the raging highland winds.

Vange scrambled under the bed.

Peadar scrambled under after her on the other side.

No, they had gradually come to realize this was no longer Dall's family's home. Instead, it was the home of Campbells. And Emily's history book had warned her the Campbells would almost entirely snuff out the MacGregors—but not until the MacGregors had helped the Campbells secure all the Menzies's land.

Ju-long crept into the shadows behind some trunks under the low part of the ceiling.

"Urg." Emily muffled her frustration and opened the door to the wardrobe.

Dall climbed inside with her.

She whispered to him, "Why did I put my phone away.

We could have just left."

"Hush." he whispered back, holding her close in the darkness inside the cabinet.

They heard the attic staircase open downward. Errrrack. And then they heard voices speaking Gaelic, an older man and woman.

"Oh, I really think it's best, my dear," said the man.

"But the young man wants to marry the girl."

"He will want to marry some other girl soon enough," the man said with conviction.

"It isn't our way, telling a young man who he can marry," the woman said. She sounded a little afraid.

Emily didn't blame her. One of the things she really liked about the Scots was the way they allowed young people to choose their mates. It was quite enlightened for the 16th century.

But the man didn't sound very enlightened. "She is a servant. We are doing the young man a service by channeling his interest elsewhere."

The couple got in the bed, where they argued into the night until they fell asleep, among other things.

Emily envied Vange and Peadar their spot under the bed. That sounded a lot more comfortable than standing up inside a cabinet all night. She had some sympathy for Ju-long. He didn't have much room to stretch out either, or the older couple would surely see him.

When the couple were snoring, Emily wondered out loud in a whisper to Dall, "Should we leave the cabinet and collect the others and swirl on out of here?"

"Nay, lass. Peigi is in this house somewhere, and we need to free her. I believe it was her they were speaking about just now, with the young man wanting to marry her and them not allowing it. Nay, we will not be leaving until we give her the freedom to marry whosoever she wishes to."

"It's just that Vange and Ju-long don't fit in here in Scotland any better than they did at that English settlement where Peadar was captive. No, they won't be called Indians here, but they won't be mistaken for English either. I'm worried about them."

"Vange and Ju-long are grown people, Drusilla—"

"Peigi is a grown person in 1560 too, Dall."

"... I ... Aye, well yes. But she is a grown person who is also still my daughter... Emily, you're right. You and the lass and Ju-long, you do not have to stay. There is danger here for all of you. However, I do need to stay. Peigi needs me. I would not be a father if I didn't help her."

"And I would not be a wife if I didn't help you while you help her. If you'll have me, that is."

Dall embraced her there in the cabinet, and all was well for a bit.

Emily was almost asleep when Dall whispered again.

"Emily. Emily, wake up."

"I have not gone to sleep, Dall."

"We need to get out of this cabinet before those Campbells wake up, Emily."

In her groggy mind, what Dall had said did not make any sense. Why come out of a perfectly good hiding place? But as she awakened more and more and left the pattern of sleep that she had been entering, she imagined what would happen when the couple woke up. They would need to empty their bladders, so they would go...

Oh.

Oh.

They would need to go outside to the privy, which meant they would need to get dressed—and that meant they would need to open this cabinet.

"You're right." she whispered. "Should we try to crowd under the bed with Vange and Peadar?"

"Nay, lass. And there be no room under there, we might awaken those who sleep topside of the bed. Nay, we will need to crowd into the shadows behind the chests the way Ju-long has. And probably get no sleep at all."

"Yeah, you're right." Emily looked dubiously at the cabinet door. "Do you remember if it squeaked at all, when we opened it to come in here?"

"I do not think it did, lass."

"I think it's better to open it fast. That way, if it does squeak, it won't for very long."

"Aye, you have the right of it. Here it goes." Dall pushed both cabinet doors open, but he held on to them so that they didn't bang against the sides of the cabinet.

The cabinet door hinges squeaked a little. Eeeack.

Dall and Emily winced and sat there dreading the couple awakening to see them in the cabinet. While they sat there listening to every little sound in the room, they noticed that not only were the people in the bed snoring, but they heard the budding couple under the bed snoring too.

Might as well think of them as a couple, Emily reasoned. It seemed inevitable, and she thought she was going to need time to get used to the idea—of her best friend being with her stepson, who had been seven years old when she saw him a few months before.

Dall took her hand and led her tiptoeing across the room.

She had never paid more attention to how she tiptoed in her life.

But regardless of how careful she was, one of the floor-boards creaked.

Emily's instinct told her to freeze, and if she had been alone, freeze is what she would've done. And she would have been caught by the Campbells and probably made a servant like her stepdaughter.

Good thing for Emily, Dall was with her.

He grabbed her by the waist and threw her over one of the chests lined up along the side of the room where the ceiling sloped into the floor and made a small unused space.

Emily fell into that space, and just in time too.

Dall jumped into that space behind the trunk next to hers right as the grumpy old Campbell couple woke up.

§

THE CAMPBELL WOMAN yawned loudly and spoke some more in Gaelic. "Good heavens, the grandchildren must be playing especially hard this morning. Did you hear whatever that was hit the floor a moment ago, dear?"

The Campbell man grunted as his feet squeaked over the floor toward the wardrobe cabinet. "Yes. We shall have to say something to Peigi about that. She needs to keep better control of the little ones, or why are we feeding her?"

On hearing his daughter's name, Emily and Dall exchanged looks that said:

"She is here."

"How dare he speak of her that way."

"We have to get her away from him."

They impatiently listened to some boring talk of cattle and grasslands while the Campbell couple dressed and went down to breakfast.

As soon as the stair-hatch closed behind them, Peadar, Julong, and Vange left their hiding places and came over to speak to Dall and Emily.

Keeping their voices down so as not to be heard from downstairs, Dall directed them to all sit down behind the chests in the far reaches of the attic room, where they hoped no one who came up there would notice them.

Dall spoke first. "We will take you all back home and

return for my Peigi. Emily tells me you all signed on to rescue me, and well, you have done that, aye?"

"Da," said Peadar, "I am not leaving here until Peigi is free to marry the lad she has chosen and can do whatever work she chooses without a need to worry about being fed, you ken?"

Vange and Ju-long shook their heads yes in agreement with Peadar.

"OK," said Emily, "we need to plan how we'll get Peigi out of here, then. We could grab some Campbell clothes for at least one of us and then swirl out of this house to a nearby location. Come into the village as one of them and hope to see Peigi out and about..."

"That will only work if the one of us in the Campbell clothing be you, lass," said Dall, "as you are the one with the wee phone app that can swirl Peigi out of captivity."

"Well, yeah," said Emily, making a gesture that she meant to say, "I'm the one with the acting skills, too, so I'm the obvious choice for the job."

"Nay," said Peadar, "we have gotten inside the house already, and we should stay inside. Getting inside here will be not possible from without, and I do have my doubts that Peigi does ever go out."

Dall nodded yes. "That be the way I do see things, as well. We will need to use stealth and devise a way to reach Peigi from inside, from up here in this loft, you ken."

Emily nodded.

"Right now is the only safe time to pop out and grab stuff we might need and pop back in," said Vange, chewing hard on a piece of gum she must have had in one of her pouches.

Ju-long spoke up. "May be stuff in chests that can help."

Emily's eyes popped open wide. "What would help us right now is if there were more chests to hide behind, and I wouldn't complain if there were a pile of old blankets stored behind them. Sitting on this hard floor is ... very unpleasant."

"Why go on about what we do not have, lass?" Peadar said.

"But we could have it," said Emily, getting excited. "Don't you see? I can go back to when you and your family lived here and get them to put more chests up here, and a pile of blankets behind them, and the chests can contain whatever we want them to."

"Wouldn't it be better to just warn them the Campbells are going to take over their house by 1560?" said Vange.

"We have already told them what we know of history," said Emily. "They can't really stop the big things from happening, I don't think. All we can do is make life better for those we love, despite the big things that happen."

"Well, then we shall all go back and get Ma to put more chests up here, and blankets behind the chests, Drusilla," said Dall with a smile.

"Nay, at least I will remain here," said Peadar. "I ken you mean to return. However, you might not, and then Peigi is none the better. Nay, I will stay."

"I'll stay with you," said Vange, with stars in her eyes.

Peadar didn't seem to mind that at all. In fact, he looked to be in danger of forgetting where he was and what was going on.

Emily cleared her throat.

The two of them snapped out of it. Just barely.

"I stay," said Ju-long. "I don't meet people here behind chests. Easy."

"OK," said Emily. "Stay way back here in the corner. We'll be sure to leave this space empty, and to leave open a way to crawl back here ... and out."

They all nodded yes.

Vange held out her hand. "Gimmie your phone, Em."

Very gently and carefully, Emily took their only way home out of her solar-charger brooch and handed it to her best friend.

Vange gestured for Emily to sit down next to Dall and then she took a picture of the area in the corner where they all needed to be hidden by the chests. Then she sat down next to Peadar. Really close to him. Like, way closer than she needed to. They weren't that crowded behind the chests. Ew.

Emily dealt with the disturbing sight long enough to get her phone back, and then she busied herself fiddling with it under Dall's watchful eye until she had the Time Management app set to keep them at their current location, but bring them back to one of the open green windows of time near the last time they had visited Peadar and Peigi here as children. In 1540.

"Em." Vange called out.

"Yeah?"

Vange pulled Emily's ear close to her and whispered, "Bring something we can use as a toilet."

Ooh. Good thinking. No way would they make it out to the privy anytime soon.

Giving her friend a grateful look, Emily nodded, and then she hugged her friend and her stepson.

Dall hugged Peadar, too. He said to Ju-long, "My thanks to you. I do owe you a favor, any time."

"Know what I ask, when time comes," said Ju-long, staring at the phone in Emily's hand.

Emily nodded at Ju-long. "Yep, we can figure out how to take you home to visit your family and friends." She met Dall's eyes then, and they shared their contented cat smile. Then she said to all three who were remaining here near Peigi, "We'll be right back."

❦

DALL AND EMILY swirled back in time until they were standing in the same attic room minus Vange, Ju-long, and Peadar. It was a subtle thing, but Emily knew right away she was in a time when the room was indeed theirs. It smelled different. Yes, that was it. The room once again smelled like MacGregors.

Sunshine came in through the small cracks between the boards of the walls, as they hadn't yet been stuffed with MacGregor plaid, and it was mid-day. The sounds of children playing wafted up through the floor boards.

Dall moved to lower the staircase hatch.

Emily caught his arm. "Let's make sure." She nodded at the wardrobe cabinet.

"Well enough, lass." He went over and opened the cabinet.

Emily sighed in relief.

There were all their red MacGregor plaid kilts and long skirts and bodices.

Without even saying anything, Emily stripped out of the English man-clothes she'd put on to go and rescue Peadar from the far-away English settlement, where they'd made him a 'cow boy', a Scottish slave. She put on one of the finely embroidered highlands shifts Dall's mother had sewn for her, along with a long plaid skirt and a bodice.

Smiling, Dall changed out of his English trews back into a red MacGregor kilt.

And then they lowered the staircase and went down to tell the family what was up. In Gaelic, of course.

"Da. Did you come in the middle of the night and sleep late again? It is glad I am to see you, Da."

Emily's eyes teared up. It was almost too much, seeing seven-year-old Peadar again, running into Dall's arms full of confidence that his Da would keep the world running right.

Little two-year-old Domhnall came waddling over next and put his pudgy little arms around his Da.

Dall held them both close.

And then.

"Da. I did know you were coming home soon." Little six-year-old Peigi ran into her father's arms.

He picked his daughter up and spun around, laughing and kissing her little pink cheek.

Now Emily's tears rushed down her face. Seeing Peigi free and happy really was too much for her to take. They had to save the young woman she would become, to allow her to marry and have a life.

But right at that moment, Dall just needed to love his children.

Where Dall could hear, Emily gave a significant look to the adults who had gathered to greet the two of them. "I saw something up in the attic that needs mending. Mother, will you come have a look?"

Dall's mother gave Emily a look of understanding and followed her up the lowered staircase.

Before Emily could think of a way to explain their situation, she felt Dall's mother put a hand on her arm.

"Emily, I do know that you are in distress. You came in the middle of the day. I know you need some-ought. Pray, just tell me what it is. If it is in my power, then you shall have it."

Relieved not to have to explain, Emily gestured to the spot in the far corner of the room where she and Dall had left Vange, Peadar, and Ju-long. "We need more chests up here, blocking the view of yon corner, but we also need a way to crawl into yon corner, and enough room there for five of us to sleep or sit, and some blankets to cushion our sleep."

The older woman gasped at that, but she quickly recovered. "It is tempting to ask when—"

"T—"

Dall's mother put her hand over Emily's mouth. "But truly, it is better not to know. I wish to live each day for itself, not in fear of the next day. Come, we will make this room up as you need it."

Dall's two brothers hefted ten more heavy chests up the lowered staircase. Some of the chests were flat, and there was a support beam along the low part of the ceiling. With some artful arranging, they managed to create the illusion of a solid stack of chests in the corner while creating a crawl space leading to a hidey hole big enough for five adults to lie down or sit up, and a nest of blankets for them to lie down on. And an alternate route for them to crawl out of, so that they weren't cornered back in there.

Emily was also careful to leave open the spot where she and Dall had dived over the one chest to hide behind it as the Campbell couple were waking up. And to see that a covered chamber pot was put in the corner before the chests were.

"I only wish you had some Campbell clothing to give us," Emily said with a sigh.

Dall's mother gave her a look that could only say, "I can't believe it."

"What?"

"One of the neighbors grabbed the wrong knapsack when coming home from the castle. We were all just teasing him about it this morning. He has two Campbell kilts."

Emily and the older woman stared at each other for a moment, and then they grabbed Dall and went over to the neighbor's house. They came home with the knapsack.

"Peigi." Dall gestured her to him.

"Aye?" They little girl scampered over and grabbed her Da's hands, then made him swing her back and forth by them.

It made Emily smile at a memory.

Dall spoke to his daughter as he swung her gently from

side to side by the hands. "If ever you are held captive—
which means someone is making you stay where you do not
want to—if ever that happens, I will try to come and save
you. Be on the watch for me, you ken?"

The six-year-old stared at him for a moment, and then
burst out giggling. "Good game, Da. Let's play captive now."

Well, that hadn't worked.

Emily had an idea, though. "You go on and play with your
cousins, Peigi. Da and I have an errand."

Peigi ran off to find willing playmates.

Emily took Dall up into their attic room. "We can come
back in a year and warn her again, and keep doing that, Dall,
every year until 1546. If she is warned every year at ages 6
through 12, then I really think it will stay with her until she
is 26."

So that was just what they did. Dall's face marked the
change in his daughter as she grew up, and he was careful to
adjust the way he spoke to her so that it was age-appropriate.

Emily admired that.

All the parents she knew from her time had to be coached
in things like that because they'd been so busy watching TV
and playing on their phones during their teens that they
seldom interacted with aunts and uncles and cousins. They
didn't have any parenting examples to follow.

And then Dall and Emily went back up into their attic
room, changed back into their ironically neutral English
clothing (it was neither Campbell nor MacGregor, after all),
crawled into their places in the hidden corner, and swirled
forward in time to Vange, Ju-long, and Peadar with their new
knapsack of Campbell kilts, anxious to see if their handiwork
with the chests had lasted twenty years.

"Achoo. Achoo. Achoo." Vange was sneezing out of control when Emily and Dall returned.

Looking at the blankets that were now beneath the five of them, Emily saw why. Twenty years' worth of cat hair resided thereon.

Of course. Cats would love this secluded comfy spot. At least it's still here.

Hopefully before anyone downstairs noticed the sneezing, Emily grabbed Vange and fiddled with the settings in the Time Management app while she told the men, "Move away from me and Vange." Emily pushed the 'Go' button as soon as the men moved away and only Vange was touching her.

The world went swirly.

Emily's parents' garage appeared around them. She could see the starry sky through the windows in the top of the garage door in this small town where she'd grown up.

"Vange." Emily called out as she ran to the back door. "Let's go to your parents' house and get your emergency allergy medicine."

"Achoo. Achoo. Can you get it for me? I don't want to walk across the street while I'm—Achoo.—sneezing like this. What if Tiffany saw me? Achoo. Achoo. I'd never live it down. And what was a cat doing inside your trailer, anyway? Achoo. Achoo. And where are Peadar, Dall, and Ju-long? I thought we were all going—"

Ug.

Emily had forgotten again that Vange wouldn't remember being in another time once she returned to her own.

But that wasn't the worst of it.

"What a surprise." Emily's mom came into the garage with a basketful of laundry. "Where's Dall?" She looked around.

"Achoo. Achoo. Achoo. Em, please go get my medicine.

Please?" Vange's eyes were watering, and her face was covered in snot.

Ew. Vange was right. No way could she risk Tiffany seeing her like that.

"I'll be right back." Emily called out to Vange and Mom as she dashed out the back door. It was eleven o'clock at night. What was Mom doing up?

"Oh, you poor thing," Emily heard Mom say to Vange. "What on Earth set you off like that here in our garage? And why ..."

Emily hoofed it over to Vange's parents' house as fast as she could and climbed up the tree to Vange's room. Good, the window still didn't close all the way. She hadn't been sure, because the last time she used this trick she'd been in middle school. Whew. She got Vange's medicine out of the night-stand and slipped back out through the window, careful to close it as much as she could after her.

No sense in making both sets of parents ask the kind of questions her own mom was doubtless asking Vange right now. Maybe it was just as well Vange didn't remember going back in time. The fact that Vange knew they had at least tele-ported into the garage was problematic enough.

Emily ran her fastest, hoping to get back to Mom before Vange made up a bigger cover story than Emily could catch up with. She went in the same way, through the back door into the garage.

Good, she could hear Vange and Mom talking in the kitchen.

"Achoo. Yeah, so Emily just wanted to surprise you by making that chocolate cake recipe that you like so much for your birthday—before she and Dall and the faire move to Australia in October. She was going to grab it and then I was going to take her back. I'm not sure what the plan is now that you know we're here, though."

Thank you, Vange. You're the best best-friend ever. I can
work with that. Hold on. What day is it to Mom, again? I've
lost track, I've been to so many other times lately.

Realizing she didn't need to think it through, Emily just
looked at her phone. Local day was Monday. Thinking it
through after all, she remembered it was now two days after
their night at Brittany's favorite club. It was also five days
before the party Dall had invited their five new best friends
to, in the trailer at the renaissance festival site.

"Here you go." Emily called out as she pushed through the
door into the kitchen from the garage.

"Achoo. Achoo." Vange accepted the pill bottle from
Emily and took her medicine, washing it down with some of
the tea Mom must have made for her.

"I know you like those costumes, honey," Mom said, "but
it is a little strange for you to be wearing one away from the
renaissance festival site, don't you think?"

Emily looked down at the 1560s English menswear she
and Vange had donned to go rescue Peadar. "Not any stranger
than you being up doing laundry so late at night, and on a
work night, too."

Wow. Did I just turn the tables on Mom? How is she
going to react to that? Do I have time to take it back?

But Mom was laughing. "Ha hehe ha. Touché, Emily.
Touché."

"Achoo." Vange was still sneezing. She blew her nose.

And then Mom sobered up and gave Emily a sad smile.
"Well, I guess being a married woman and all, you're old
enough to know that your father is having a tough time at
work. They're probably going out of business. But in the
meantime, they have him burning the midnight oil, trying to
get every last chance in, that they might stay afloat. And
when he isn't home, I have trouble sleeping."

Emily felt sick. "Oh Mom, you and dad shouldn't have

spent so much on me and Dall's wedding. It must have cost you your life's savings—"

"Now honey, don't you go worrying over it. Hopefully, you're only going to get married once in your life. Your father and I wouldn't do anything differently, if we had it to do all over again." Mom moved in to hug her.

Emily hugged Mom close for a long time. "I love you so much, Mom. It's going to be OK. I promise."

"I know it will, honey. I know it will," Mom said, but she only reluctantly let the hug end.

And then Emily said to Vange, "Do you mind if I just borrow the car and take myself home? I have to get going, but will you stay here with my mom until my dad gets home?"

"Achoo. Achoo. Ack. It starts right up again whenever I let go—Achoo.—with the handkerchief." Vange blew her nose again. And she nodded yes. "Yeah, good idea. Take the car. Remember to come get me for Renfest on Friday, though."

Visibly remembering the reason Vange had given for Emily's visit, Mom hugged Emily one more time and then sauntered off into the bathroom, saying, "Go ahead and go, dear. You'll already be driving late into the night. I don't want you to have an accident."

Vange pointed at Mom's recipe box on the kitchen counter, whispering, "I told her you were here—Achoo.—for her chocolate cake recipe, for her birthday."

"I heard. Thanks, Vange. You're the bestest best-friend ever."

The two best friends hugged.

Emily whispered in Vange's ear, "I'll leave the car at Shroeder's."

Vange nodded yes and gave Emily an excited look. "Promise me you'll show me the real thing soon. Achoo." She wiped her nose with the hanky. "I mean, this … traveling around is awesome, but ..." She gave Emily a face that said, "You've been holding out on me."

Emily nodded and smiled at her friend, feeling sad that time travel wasn't something they could talk about. Then she took the keys out of Vange's purse and ran off to drive the car down the street to the market before swirling back to the men in the attic in 1560.

੪

"Is ALL WELL with your best lass, Emily?" Dall whispered where they all sat in the small blanket nest space behind the trunks in the far corner of the attic room in the highlands house on Rannoch land that had once belonged to the Menzies clan.

He looked concerned.

"Huh. Where be Vange?" Peadar looked disappointed.

"Yeah, all is well with Vange, but I left her to console my mom. My dad's work is going out of business." Emily felt a tear leak out of her eye.

Dall held Emily close. "Mayhap we can help him find a new source of income, lass." He fingered the dagger in his boot.

Emily smiled in spite of herself. "You know what? I bet we can."

Ju-long grimaced and held his hands up for attention. "Emily get me outside. I fire weapon. Everyone go outside. Dall and Peadar get Peigi."

It was light outside in this time, morning, and they could hear the sounds of the family breaking their overnight fast. Everyone was awake and downstairs.

Emily looked to Dall and Peadar for criticism of Ju-long's plan. She thought it was brilliant. Simple and straightforward.

They apparently did too, because no criticisms were

raised, just questions.

Dall whispered, "Do we have the outside marked, lass?"

Emily shook her head. "No, but we do have the wee phone app's map. The surrounding area was completely free of people when we walked it together twenty years ago.

Dall started to object.

Emily rushed on. She really wanted to try the Time Management app's map. "This early in the morning, it should be fine. No one is out or about yet. Besides, when we went to Peadar, the app hid us in that thicket, and when we came here to Peigi, it hid us in this attic. I feel confident it will hide me no matter when or where I tell it to take me... within reason. It may not be able to hide me in the middle of a city."

Peadar looked convinced. "Aye, Da. It is a good plan. I say we let them try it. Shall we put on the Campbell kilts?" He waited for Dall to agree to the plan, looking at him politely. Only his hand inching toward the knapsack gave away his impatience.

Dall sighed. "Aye, well enough, let us put on the Campbell kilts." He did not look happy. "First, let us get claymores out of this chest here." He stood up in the very corner, the only place in the chest fort that would allow it, and wriggled two claymores out of the nearest chest.

Peadar smiled big when his Da handed him one of their traditional swords.

Next, the two highlander men got the blue plaid kilts out and waited for Emily and Ju-long to leave and make room for them to roll up in them.

Emily fiddled with the settings on her phone so that the time remained the same, but the destination was down the hill from the small settlement that contained her mother-in-law's old house that they were in. She selected this on the map and looked up.

Dall's eyes looked worried. "You do not have to do this,

lass. We will find another way."

Emily caressed her husband's face, and then thought better of it and kissed him soundly. "I want to help so that you can help her."

Dall nodded.

They shared their contented cat smile, and then Emily turned to Ju-long. "Is your weapon ready?"

He nodded once. He was holding the weapon out in front of him, but they were all seated on the blankets, so it looked funny.

Emily kissed Dall again. "I love you. Now stay back." She moved over away from Dall and Peadar and took Ju-long's hand. "Ready?"

Ju-long nodded again.

The world went swirly.

And Emily and Ju-long materialized right in the middle of some game a bunch of children were playing. The children were dressed in Campbell colors. The boys wore trews, but other than that, they were all dressed as mini adults.

Houses and cattle dotted the land around them. What once had been empty land now was part of the settlement, which had grown so much it should be called a town.

A ball of sorts, made out of sewn-together bits of rough leather, bounced off Ju-long's Darth-Vader-shaped brown leather helmet.

Ju-long stoically held his position, which was sitting in the dirt, because that was how he had been on the blankets in the attic. He pulled the loaded firearm closer in to his chest and sort of cradled it, looking around insecurely at the children.

Emily felt a sense of relief at that. The last thing they needed was for some child to get away with the instrument of the distraction they were trying to make. Or, OK, yeah, for a child to get hurt by the firearm. And she didn't even suggest that he fire it into the air. All of the powder would come out before he even tried, if he raised the barrel up like that. This was a primitive firearm, not yet a gun.

The children were irritated, though. In Gaelic, they called out the fact that there were strangers among them.

"Hey. Where'd you come from?"

"No fair. They weren't here a moment ago."

"Yes they were. Stop cheating."

"I'm not cheating. They weren't here."

Some grown-ups were starting to take notice of the strangers in their children's midst. They were strolling over casually so far.

But Emily had no good reason in mind to tell them, about why she was there. And Ju-long? There really was no explanation they were likely to accept for him.

She kept a firm grip on Ju-long's hand and said the Gaelic phrase she had initially thought meant, "I want a do over."

As the world went swirly, she was thinking great, now all these children are going to grow up believing in ghosts. Oh well. What can I do?

THIS TIME, Emily and Ju-long did not return the same instant they left. Emily guessed that was because on this occasion, they hadn't time traveled. They had merely teleported from one place to another (merely.).

Even though they could time travel, they still couldn't be in two different places at the same time. The upshot was that when they returned to the attic, a few minutes of time had passed since they left.

Dall and Peadar had put on the Campbell kilts and strapped their claymores to their backs. They had crawled out of the chest fort and were preparing to lower the staircase hatch.

"Dall." Emily stage whispered from where she stood in the corner.

At the sound of her saying his name, Dall turned with the precision of a fighter, a dancer, or an athlete. When he saw her standing there un-attacked and whole, he visibly relaxed. And then he smiled their contented cat smile.

"We have to pick another spot." Emily explained, again in a loud whisper.

"Well enough, lass, and you made the trip and came back whole." He smiled a different smile then, one that said, "I'm proud of you, Drusilla."

Beaming at that smile from him, Emily sat back down inside the chest fort and searched the map on her phone for another spot she thought was close enough that the house would hear Ju-long's shot, but far enough that it would be uninhabited. "Ready?"

Ju-long grunted a yes.

Emily grabbed his hand again and pushed the 'Go' button.

The world went swirly, and then they were sitting on a rug inside someone's house. A family sat breakfasting at the table, a mom, a dad, three grown children, and a little toddler in his father's lap.

They all stared at Emily and Ju-long.

Before they could start speculating aloud about ghosts, Emily said her 'do over' phrase.

The two of them swirled back to the attic.

This time, Dall was watching when Emily stood up. He had loosened his grip on the staircase hatch. He looked disappointed, but resolved. "I do not think this plan is going to work, Drusilla."

Ju-long squeezed Emily's hand and dropped it. "Too many people, cannot arrive unseen."

"We could swirl out into the mountains and then walk

closer." For some reason, Emily wanted to stick to Ju-long's plan.

Peadar shook his head no. "Nay, the Campbells will be on watch for the Menzies, the same as we were when we lived here. Mayhap they even watch for us MacGregors. They will see you coming, if you approach from outside the settlement."

Dall put his hand on his grown son's back. "Peadar does have the right of it, lass. It was a good plan when you were just to appear in hiding and sound the fire weapon, then appear back inside this house. However, the plan does fall apart now that you have the need to approach from afar. Nay. We must have a new plan."

Suddenly aware that they had left the relative safety of their chest fort for no good reason, Dall and Peadar moved back toward it with one accord.

A large tabby cat ran into the fort ahead of Dall.

Emily moved into the spot she'd been seated in earlier, and the cat made itself at home on her lap, purring. She idly pet it while she waited for the men to crawl into the fort.

Ju-long holstered his weapon, sat down beside her, and petted the cat, too.

Dall got some jerky out of his knapsack and started munching on it, and before long they all were eating from their provisions.

Emily figured they had enough for a few days, including water in their water skins, so she wasn't too discouraged. Just impatient. "So what's the new plan, Dall?"

Before Dall could answer, the attic staircase hatch went down with an Errrreak.

All four of them jumped a bit, which was difficult while sitting on blankets, but they managed.

Emily held her breath and noticed that the others held theirs as well.

The cat struggled in Emily's lap.

She let it go.

It ran out through the crawl space and started speaking to whoever had come up into the attic room. "Meow. Meow."

"Well hello, Mouser. And how are you today? Lonely up here all alone? Aye, that is me as well. We shall keep each other company, you and I..."

Once Dall and Peadar got over their shock, they both called out in quiet voices, "Peigi. Peigi."

Peigi stopped speaking to the cat, but she didn't speak to her kin.

Emily guessed that the woman—who was now older than Emily—was afraid to hope that kin had come to rescue her.

Dall and Peadar were scrambling out of the crawl spaces, calling out to their kin loudly enough that she could hear, but softly enough that hopefully no one downstairs would.

"Peigi."

"We are here to save you, Peigi."

And then Emily realized she needed to get out there too with her phone, if the rescue was going to be a success. She motioned to Ju-long to take the one crawlway out while she took the other.

Ju-long nodded and started crawling out.

Meanwhile, Dall and Peadar had gotten to Peigi and were soothing her while she cried softly, the bed half undone where she had been changing the linens. When they saw Emily and Ju-long emerging from the trunk fort, they motioned the two of them into a huddle.

"Quickly, Emily," said Dall. "Take us all back to the trailer."

Emily fiddled with her phone for half a minute, getting the settings just right and trying to make sure to take them to the trailer the minute they had left it. That wouldn't work, though. She kept getting an error message.

Oh yeah, Emily realized, she had already spent some of that time with her mom and with Vange. She patted the chocolate cake recipe in her pouch, smiling a bit.

Finally, Emily remembered the app's calendar function. Using it, the trip was simple. She just chose the trailer and then chose the next green window of time.

"Ready?" She looked around. Everyone was touching her, with Peigi in the middle against her, still crying.

Emily pushed the 'Go' button.

The world went swirly.

BACKSTAGE AT THE RENAISSANCE FESTIVAL, the trailer that the druids were letting Dall and Emily use was just as they had left it. Their stew dishes were still in the drying rack in the kitchen. Their practice swords stood in the corner. Other than that, it was difficult to tell that anyone lived here. The truth was, most of the time they didn't.

Peigi gasped, wiping her tears away with the back of her hand. "Huh. Where are we, Da?"

Dall hugged his daughter. "We are far, far away from any Campbells, and forward 500 years in time, lass. You are safe."

"Oh, but Da, I do not want to be safe. I want to be with Alan."

Everyone looked at Peigi as if she had just grown a third arm.

"Alan?" Peadar's brow was wrinkled.

Emily figured now wasn't the time to tell her stepson that would give him wrinkles.

"Yes, Alan. He's a Campbell, but he loves me, and I love him." Peigi stood there with her hands on her hips, as if she were waiting for the four of them to turn around and return her, this instant.

All this trouble to rescue her, and she wanted to go right back where she'd been.

Dall didn't resign himself to his daughter's decision to go back to a bad situation. "Lass, the Campbells who now live in our old house think of the MacGregors as servants not fit for marrying. I heard them say so with my own ears."

"Da, Alan does not think this way, and his is the opinion that matters." Peigi pushed Dall's shoulder, chiding him for his generalization.

Emily looked into her husband's face to see how he was affected by his daughter treating him as an equal, rather than with the respect due to an elder.

Dall shrugged as if to say, "After all, we are the same age, so how can I be her elder?"

Peadar didn't accept his sister's decision easily, either. "There are other men, other good men, who you could fall for here in Da's new time, Peig. Do not fash over this Alan. He cannot give you even the smallest bit of the life I have seen with Da and Emily in the few days since they did rescue me."

Emily met Dall's eyes at that, and she saw the satisfaction he had in his son's roundabout praise and gratitude.

But Peigi felt differently.

"Peadar, one day you will fall in love." She held up her hand to stop him from complaining about her line of reasoning. "Love changes you, Peadar. Love has changed me. For example, none of what you all say matters to me. I want to go back to Alan, and if you do not allow me to, then it is you who are holding me captive." She was speaking to her brother, but she looked at Dall then and raised her eyebrows as if to say, "See? I remember your warning, but you are mistaken on the situation."

Dall turned to Emily and gestured for her to get out her phone. "We asked the wee phone app that the druids do use to travel us through time to take us to your greatest hour of need, Peigi." He turned to Emily. "Show her the likeness you took of Peigi when she was a child, the one that brought us to her."

Emily searched for that picture, but she said, "Dall, we didn't say that this time, remember? I just clicked on whatever destination came up first, to get us out of—"

But Dall was fixated on the idea that they had been rescuing his daughter.

This was a new side to him that Emily was learning: stubbornness. She supposed she liked it when it applied to protecting his family. Still, she didn't think Peigi shared her admiration.

As if it would prove anything, Dall pointed to Peigi's picture on Emily's phone. "You must have a need of being rescued, because the wee phone app sent us to you—"

Peigi was smart, though.

Gently and warmly taking her young father's hand, she pleaded with him, appealing to his affection for her. "Da, I do have a need, but it is not of being rescued. It is of your prayers for me and Alan. We are running away tonight ... tonight in our time—which you must bring me back to."

Peigi got a bit frantic when she said that, looking at all of them with the beginnings of despair in her eyes.

"We will take you back," Emily said, holding out her hand for her phone, which Dall gave back slowly with a frown on his face. "We will take you back in an hour or two. But first, tell us all that you know about your grandmother and your aunts, your uncles and your cousins. Are they well? Where are they? Oh, and where are you and Alan planning on going?"

Before Peigi could answer, Siobhan opened the door without knocking and came right in.

For a moment, Emily wondered how the druid knew they were inside, but then she remembered it was their app on her phone.

"Ju-long, your assignment here is finished." Siobhan's tone was businesslike and no-nonsense. "You'll see Dall and Emily on the weekend. Go on back to your tent now and prepare for the festival."

Ju-long bowed to everyone and went out the door.

As she bowed back to him in courtesy, Emily watched the amulet he wore go out the door with him, wishing she had thought to ask him for it. He would only need it if he returned to his own time, near as she could tell. Vange could really use that thing.

Siobhan turned to Emily and took her hand. She held it for a few seconds, looking off into nowhere, and then she got a determined look on her face. "I have something to tell you in private." She looked at the bedroom door.

"Whatever you have to say, you can say it in front of my family," Emily said, gesturing to Dall and his children.

"OK, it's your privacy. Emily, you're a few hours from being fertile if you stop time traveling this minute. I think you should."

That took all the wind out of Emily's sails. There was nothing she wanted more than to have Dall's children. She looked at her husband and tried to convey with her expression the longing she felt. She longed to bear him children, ached to carry them in her womb.

Dall grabbed Emily and held her close, making all right with the world for a long moment. And then, still holding her, he turned to face Siobhan. "If Emily cannot use the wee phone app to travel, then how are Peadar and I to return Peigi to her Alan?"

SIOBHAN ROLLED her eyes and reached out for Emily's phone.

Emily handed it to the druid.

Siobhan brought up the Time Management app and held it out in front of Dall. "You've seen Emily operate this app dozens of times now. You mean to tell me you don't feel like you could do it?" She was making a face that said he was an idiot if that was what he was telling her.

Dall was trying to remain calm, and to the others he probably looked calm.

But because of her drama training, Emily noticed that her husband's breathing got heavy. And it was subtle, but he backed away ever so slightly from the phone, as if it would bite him. His hand went halfway up to his chest and then down again.

Emily thought it likely Dall had started to cross himself but thought better of it.

He swallowed a lump in his throat. "I do not understand the wee phone. It is fae work to me, what you call magic. I am fine with a sword, and I can help Emily with the language of my time. However, I am not the one who can make this ... wee thing do as I wish." He stood there calmly but warily, bent a little at the waist and with his legs apart, as if waiting for Siobhan or the phone to attack him.

Peadar perked up. "Vange does know how to operate the wee phone." He looked at everyone with such a hopeful smile that Emily couldn't help but smile, too.

Dall killed his buzz, though. "Aye, however, Vange be not here, and we cannot send Emily after her." His body was still on alert, as if a fight was inevitable.

Emily put a hand on Dall's back in an attempt to really calm him. "Peigi, certainly it won't hurt anything if you stay here for a day or two." She caressed her husband's back, feeling him respond, but not calm down.

But Peigi made a sound that was half hysteria, half rage.

Oh no. The woman thought they meant to keep her here.

Emily waved her hands in front of Peigi's eyes to get her

attention. "Vange can get you right back to the moment you left your time, Peigi. Your Alan won't even know you were gone. Please, trust us."

"Why must I—" Peigi started. She had relaxed a little and no longer looked panicked, but she was still plenty angry. Her chest heaved, and her jaw was locked.

But Emily cut her off. "We need to let Vange sleep right now. She's had an allergic reaction—"

Still angry, Peigi put her hands on her hips and gave Emily a look that said, "A what?"

"An attack of the cold?"

Relaxing a little, Peigi nodded understanding.

"And then tomorrow, Dall and I have already been someplace from 9 till 3, but Peadar can keep you company. I'll ask Vange to come here for supper tomorrow. If she can't then, she surely will the next evening."

At the news that Vange would be coming over, Peadar beamed a smile so bright, he was shining.

Yeah, he had a thing for Vange. Big time.

Ug. That still felt so weird to Emily.

Dall smiled and put his arm around Emily. "Mayhap invite your parents to come over the next night. I will do what I can to bring some-ought they can sell, to make up for his business that may be failing."

Emily tried her best to smile back, but it was sinking in: the fact that she would be staying home while everyone else went gallivanting off into the time stream. Still, she was euphoric inside. She might be able to keep Dall around long enough that she could conceive his child before he left.

Siobhan winked at Emily.

The druid was thinking the same thing.

"That suits me fine," Siobhan said. "Your friend Vange can help. But you mustn't tell anyone else, understand?"

Yay. She could finally tell Vange.

Dall was still holding Emily, and she could feel him tense up a bit. "We will be telling our children, warning them of the druid curse upon our family: that every fourth son must serve the druids. But aye, other than them, we will tell no one else."

Siobhan nodded some more on her way out.

After Siobhan left the trailer, everyone breathed easier, even Peigi.

"Aye, and now that be settled," said Dall, "do tell us all about your uncles and your aunts, your cousins and your grandmother, Peigi. Be they well?"

Peigi looked from her da to her brother. Apparently, their looks convinced her they really wondered about their kin, because she started to tell them all that had happened over the past ten years.

While she talked, slowly at first and then more and more animatedly, Emily found herself wishing she could do something useful for Dall's daughter: give her a medical exam and modern treatment for any conditions, or teach her the history of Scotland—and especially the highlands—so that she and her family could avoid heartache... But with the short amount of time they dared keep Peigi, Emily had to settle for telling her stepdaughter how to use the small magnifying glass to make fire—and giving it to her.

Peigi was delighted with the gift and hugged Emily. Other than that, she took in all the modernity of the interior of the trailer with her eyes, but she didn't move from the spot where she had landed between the trailer door and the kitchen while she filled them in on what she knew of the rest of their family.

By 2 am, Peigi was drooping on her feet. She'd been talking for almost three hours, answering the men's questions and going off on stories when she gave them answers.

Emily led her stepdaughter into the pink bedroom that Vange used on the weekends during the festival and got out one of Vange's larger sleep shirts. But she really won Peigi over when she showed her the bathroom and drew her a hot bath.

Peigi stood there stunned while Emily showed her how to turn the water on and off and explained the shampoo and conditioner, let alone showed her how to operate the wall heater.

When Emily left the bathroom, Dall had already shown Peadar to the blue bedroom, so Dall and Emily retired to their own room. They had spent many days without any time alone together. They didn't go to sleep for a long time.

§♠

EMILY'S ALARM on her phone went off early the next morning. Oh yeah. Sparring practice with the renfest staff.

Dall wasn't in bed next to her, and she got a bit worried. After ducking into the bathroom and pulling on some shorts, she went out into the kitchen.

The rest of the family were already up and seated around the tiny kitchen table, eating cold cereal and Pop-Tarts for breakfast.

Peadar and Peigi seemed to be adapting pretty well to modern food. Seemed to really relish it, actually.

Emily enjoyed watching them eat.

But then Siobhan came breezing in through the door of the trailer as if she lived there. The druid walked over to Emily and took her hand so casually that everyone else thought it was of no consequence.

Emily felt the woman squeezing her hand and looked over at her face.

Siobhan smiled and nodded, then hugged Emily.

Mystified at first, Emily slowly realized what the hug meant. She had a child growing inside her. Speechless, all she could do was cradle the place where she got cramps with her periods.

Siobhan put her arm around Emily and announced to the people eating cereal, "Emily won't be sparring with you today. She'll be taking it easy for the next nine months."

The rest of the morning was weird, but Emily was happier than she had ever been.

Dall ran over as soon as he heard Siobhan's announcement. He started to pick Emily up to whirl her around, but at a stare from Siobhan, he settled for kissing his wife deeply.

Siobhan came up with a crown of flowers to put on Emily's head, and she announced Emily's news to the renfest staff at the sparring practice, to general applause and quite a few pats on Dall's back. She stayed right by Emily's side the whole time they were there, choosing her food and drink and scaring off anyone who looked at her funny.

If Lews had any intention of attacking Emily again, he sure wasn't going to do it where Siobhan could see him.

The druids introduced Peadar and Peigi only as Dall's kin, not specifying they were his children. That made sense, and it was still truthful.

Emily sat by Siobhan in the gazebo sipping decaf coffee with milk and eating a banana while the rest of them practiced their sword fighting skills.

Peadar and Peigi took a while to warm up, but once they did, they were almost as good as Dall. After all, they'd had little other than practice swords to play with, as children and teens. Their years in captivity had kept them behind Dall in fighting ability, but Emily felt sure they would catch up, given the chance.

Which reminded her to try texting Vange.

"Can you come over for dinner?"

"Sure," Vange texted back right away. "What's up?"

"Can't say here. Bring your costume."

"Uh OK I'll see you at 4?"

"Perfect. See you at 4."

At ten minutes to 9 am, Emily's phone vibrated. She looked at it, and there was a warning message.

"6 hour time debt in 10 minutes."

Feeling a new camaraderie with the druid who was so nicely taking care of her every need and honoring her for bearing a child, Emily showed the message to Siobhan.

The woman gestured to Eamann the head druid, who blew the whistle that signaled the end of a sparring match.

"What? The match barely just started." Lews called out angrily from where he was matched up against Peigi.

"Dall." Eamann called out.

"Aye?" Dall looked around frantically, as if for a threat.

Siobhan explained, "Dall, you and your wife have time debt in ... 9 minutes. Go to your trailer so you don't disappear."

Dall came and offered his arm to Emily, the same way he had that first day at faire.

She took it.

He started walking her back to the trailer. Slowly. He kept looking back over his shoulder at his children.

Emily looked, too. Peadar and Peigi had resumed sparring and looked like they were having fun.

Dall kept looking back at his children until his view was blocked by a fake storefront. "I did not fathom they would be here with us, when we did spend this day sleeping."

"Of course not. How could you have? I'm sorry we have to leave them, Dall."

"They will be well." Dall sounded like he was trying to convince himself that.

They made it into the trailer and lay down on their bed.

Emily cuddled up close to her husband, trying to console him.

12. SCOTS

"I've been best friends with Emily since fourth grade," Vange told Brittany on speaker-phone in her car, "and she and Dall have been living in that trailer for a while now. And yeah, they let me stay there during renfest—but this is the first time they've invited me over while they're home. Isn't that just a little weird?"

Vange was bouncing in her seat to the beat of the loud music on her stereo as she drove the three hours it took her to get to the renaissance festival site.

"Aw," Brittany said, "I think it's sweet that they let you have their trailer while they stay in a hotel on the weekends."

Vange snorted. "You've seen them together, Brittany. I'm glad they 'get a room', too."

Brittany laughed.

"Don't get me wrong," Vange said, "I adore Dall. I think he's great for her. It's the renfest I don't think is so good. It's taking over Em's whole life—"

"Wait a minute," Brittany said the same way Vange's mom did, which was kind of creepy, "I seem to recall you complaining when they came over to visit you earlier this week, Vange."

"Oh no, I wasn't complaining about them coming to visit me, not at all."

But when Vange stopped to think about it, she knew deep down that she had been complaining. And even though Vange now had an explanation for that whole thing and was in on it and it all was awesomely resolved—except for the renfest still taking over Emily's life...

Vange couldn't tell Brittany that Emily was able to teleport.

What was she going to tell her?

Ug, she should never have called her on Monday, no matter how mad she'd been at Emily.

What had she been thinking?

"You weren't?" Brittany was saying, "Because it sure sounded to me like you were complaining. Admit it, you were downright whining."

Well, if Brittany already thought Vange was juvenile, why not reinforce the idea? It might make her laugh, which would distract her.

"Was not."

"Were too."

There. Brittany was laughing.

Now for a little misdirection to make Brittany buy a more logical explanation for how Dall and Emily had gotten into that club when no one else was there.

"Brittany, I'm ... worried about them, is all. The only reason I knew they came out of that club Monday morning was I got a call from my cousin Emilio. Why didn't Em call and let me know she was there? Why was she there?"

"That is weird. But there could be a logical explanation."

Bingo. OK, now what should this logical explanation be? Vange thought while she changed lanes to get around a slow dairy van.

"Em told me some story about how Dall lost his ID

outside when he followed some smokers out there, but that doesn't explain how they got inside on a Monday morning when the club was closed. My cousin doesn't hang out with the best crowd, and I'm worried that Dall and Emily are involved in all that, Brittany."

And then Brittany surprised Vange by writing the whole thing off all on her own and making this all about Vange and her insecurities. At first that was fine by Vange. She would take it.

"Are you sure it isn't just that Emily is married now, and her husband is her new best friend, and you feel lonely and left out?"

But whoa.

Where did Brittany get that idea?

She didn't know Vange and Emily well at all. They were like milk and cereal, always doing things together. They'd joined the renfest together, and Vange often wore Emily's costumes. They had sewn their pouches together, and worked at Simon's booth together ...

But Vange didn't answer out loud.

Brittany went on. "It's understandable that you feel left out and lonely, Vange, but it's not fair to Emily for you to be bitter about it. Calling me was a good idea. You need to make some other friends and let Emily and Dall spend time alone together. It's normal for her to be preoccupied with her new husband awhile."

Vange sighed.

Maybe she was a little jealous of Emily's time lately.

From out of nowhere, she heard herself say, "But getting back to my concern for Emily: she's two semesters away from being the drama teacher she always wanted to be. She worked really hard toward that, and now she's just letting it drop to work at the renfest, of all things."

"Yeah," said Brittany, "but I heard her say the program

gave her a pause, so she can go back to it whenever she wants. And she's on staff at the renfest. That's pretty cool, you have to admit. I would love to be in her shoes."

"It doesn't pay anything, Brittany."

"It doesn't?"

Aha. Brittany was finally getting the picture.

"No, it doesn't. That's why Em and Dall do those sword demos. The only money they make comes from those."

Brittany was silent.

Vange pushed to get as much info across as she could, about how disturbing it was that the renfest was taking over Emily's life.

"And that trailer they live in belongs to the renfest. It isn't theirs. And you've seen the way Siobhan treats them." Vange did an impression of Siobhan's voice, "Dall, come down here." Vange switched back to her own voice. "She orders him around like a dog."

Brittany laughed at that. "You say Siobhan's name as if she were a real druid, Vange, not just someone who plays one at renfest."

Sometimes, Vange wondered...

But there was no sense in trying to make Brittany believe Vange had been teleported. Not without showing her, anyway. She needed someone else taking this seriously, not someone who thought she herself was delusional.

Vange decided to go for the maturity angle. "Renfest is a fun place to spend weekends, but it's a crazy unstable environment to live in full time, if you ask me."

"Well, no one is saying Dall and Emily have to work at renfest forever. I bet they do it for a few years and then Emily goes back to school and Dall moves on to something else when they want to start a family."

"Idiot."

"What."

"Not you." Vange honked her horn at some guy who had just cut in front of her on the freeway. "These are other cars, not an obstacle course."

"Uh, Vange?"

"Yeah?"

"Right now I don't think you're a good judge of what is crazy or unstable."

Vange laughed. "Wait, the story gets better, Brittany. The renaissance festival moves to Australia for the winter."

"Australia."

"Yeah. That is too freaking far away. I'll never see Emily."

"But wow, Australia, Vange. Emily is so lucky. I would love to go to Australia. Come on, Emily is what, 25?"

"We're 23—Oh, now it's on."

The guy had gotten stuck behind a slow-moving truck during all his lane changes, and now he was moving to pass Vange again.

She sped up so that he couldn't. "Yes." She pumped her fist in the air when her lane opened up ahead and she was able to zoom past the guy, who was forced to slow down for the traffic in his lane and then pull back in behind Vange.

Meanwhile, Brittany was talking. "23 is young, Vange. Emily has plenty of time to be serious in life later. My advice is to just let her be a young newlywed awhile. And you should make some more friends to spend your time with. I'll be one of them, but right now I have to go."

"OK, Brittany. Thanks for putting up with me."

"See you tomorrow at the guild meeting and then at renfest this weekend."

"Bye."

"Bye."

Now that Vange was off the phone and almost to the renfest site, her thoughts turned back to Peadar.

Gorgeous Peadar.

Who kept smiling at her and putting his hand on the small of her back to lead her into rooms as if the two of them had been dating for a month.

He was some relative of Dall's, a cousin or something, who was also from Scotland. It was hard to tell exactly how they were related because the two of them spoke Gaelic most of the time to each other.

Dall and Peadar were the same age and looked a lot alike, although Dall acted like he was older. Peadar was cool about it, though. He didn't seem to mind letting Dall act that way.

It was sort of attractive.

No, it was really attractive.

Peadar was so ... yummy.

Ack.

Was he moving to Australia, too? Or did he live here somewhere? Was he a bum, or did he have a job?

Or was he just visiting and about to go home to Scotland? Ack.

The renfest guard stopped Vange's car in the dark forest at the entrance to the parking lot.

"Hey, pretty lady. You have your pass?" He smiled at her.

She recognized him from the workshops they'd all taken.

"Hey Neil, slow night? I'll make a pass at you if you want, just to keep you amused, but you should know I'm having dinner with Dall's cousin." She smiled back playfully.

Neil laughed and checked her gate pass, then waved her in.

Vange parked amid the trees and walked through the festival site, which on a weeknight, she discovered, looked eerily like a ghost town. All the fake English buildings were empty, and so were the booths where renfest people sold everything from costumes to turkey legs to juggling sticks.

Another guard checked her gate pass at the entrance to the enclosed center of the donut-shaped festival.

"Hi Tommy. Want some gum?"

"Hi sunshine." He accepted the gum with a wink.

And then Vange was inside the burlap wall that surrounded the backstage area where the staff and festival workers camped.

Dall and Emily had one of the bigger trailers there. It had three bedrooms. It was as if the festival staff expected her friend to pop out a bunch of kids, or something. And come on, renfest was not the sort of place you wanted to have kids. It was a place for partying and having fun.

Vange knocked on the trailer door.

It opened.

Vange jumped a little.

Peadar stood there in his kilt, smiling at her.

"Well come," he said in his sexy Scottish accent as he opened the door and gestured for her to come in while at the same time holding his hand out for her bag.

Usually, Vange hated the time it wasted when guys tried to carry things for her, but not with Peadar. Him she was thrilled to have carrying her bag. It wasn't even a renfest day, and he was wearing a kilt. She tried hard not to drool as she all but skipped after him down the hall—toward the bedrooms.

"Peigi did sleep in the room where you are wont to, this past night, but she has moved into the room that I was using, and now I will sleep in the common room," he said as he showed Vange into the pink bedroom where she had slept the past few weekends. He set her bag down on the bed.

She stood there just staring at him for a long moment. It wasn't awkward, though.

He was smiling back at her.

"Vange." Emily burst into the room then and hugged her.

At first, Vange thought her friend was drunk. Her smile was really goofy, and she was sort of over-reacting. They had just seen each other the night before.

But then ...

"I'm pregnant." Emily all but screamed, but in a happy way, like this was the best news she could possibly have.

Yeah, and she'd screamed right in Vange's ear.

"Um, wow. Really? Have you been to the doctor? Or did you just do one of those test kits?" Vange pulled away from the hug and looked her friend over. She wasn't showing. She looked perfectly normal. Well, normal except for the goofy smile on her face.

"I haven't been to the doctor," Emily said, "but I'm sure." She paused then like she was waiting for Vange to squeal with glee or something.

Wanting to please her friend, Vange hugged her, saying softly into her ear, "Aw, you really surprised me. But I can tell this makes you very happy, so I'm happy for you."

But Emily got that look on her face, the one that said, "I can't believe you just said that. I am so going to give you a lecture right now."

❧

FORTUNATELY, Peadar broke Vange away from Em before their disagreement turned into an argument. "Vange."

"Yeah?"

Now, while Vange did have ... concerns about Emily being pregnant, she would take any excuse to talk to Peadar. She looked into his somber and serious eyes way longer than she needed to.

He smiled at her with his eyes and looked at her a little

longer than he needed to before he said, "Vange lass, we do
need you to help us return Peigi to her home—"

Whoa.

Vange's mind moved a mile a minute. If she drove Peigi
home and Peadar came with them, then she and Peadar
would be alone in the car all the way back.

"Sure. You mean right now, or in the morning? And where
does she live?" Vange danced around a little bit. She couldn't
help it. This was great.

But Peadar's brow wrinkled, and he gestured over to
where Peigi was sitting on the couch looking nervous, uncomfortable, and angry.

"She does live in Scotland, you ken, in the Rannoch."

Vange laughed. "OK, usually I'm the one making the
jokes. You know I can't drive her to Scotland."

Vange gently pushed Peadar a little. The contact made her
hand tingle as if she had touched an electric fence. Wow, he
was hot.

Peadar sort of stumbled backward, shrugging the shoulder
she'd touched and looking deep in thought.

OK, not the reaction she'd been expecting. Most guys
flirted back. But it wasn't a disastrous reaction, either. Apparently, Peadar was shy. It was as if no woman had ever flirted
with him before. That surprised Vange, but she could adapt
to it.

As if Dall had just broken out of some sort of stupor, he
shook his head quickly and then walked over to Peigi and
spoke to her in soothing tones.

Emily came around then. Vange could tell that her friend
was no longer mad, because Emily got that excited look on
her face like when she was scheming something.

"Vange, remember how we came here to the trailer using
my phone last night?"

"Huh." Vange gasped. "You mean I'm going to use your

phone to take Peigi back to Scotland?" OK, now Vange was sure she had that excited look on her own face. In fact, she was jumping up and down.

Emily smiled at her. "Yup." She looked like she was going to say some more.

But that was plenty.

"Ooh."

Vange was finally squealing with glee. She grabbed Emily's shoulders and jumped up and down again, and then she remembered that her friend was pregnant and quit doing that.

"And I'm guessing you can't take Peigi home because of the baby, right?"

Emily smiled some more and nodded yes. "You're smarter than you look, Vange."

"Huh." Vange gasped again and turned to Peadar. "And you're going too. I know because you said 'we'."

Peadar smiled his cool manly smile at her. "Everyone will be going but for your best lass Emily. We shall sup first and have a sleep, however."

Yeah right. As if Vange would be able to sleep a wink that night. The anticipation was killing her.

She sat next to Peadar at dinner. They never quite touched, but she was keenly aware of him sitting next to her. It was as if he put out some sort of energy field and she was an absorber of it.

Up to and during dinner, Peadar, Peigi, and Dall talked about their relatives in Gaelic. It seemed like Emily joined in on their conversation, but that couldn't be. She hadn't been to Scotland to meet them yet, not to mention she hadn't had time to learn Gaelic.

Vange tried to figure out how the three Scots were all related and to follow the conversation and know who they were talking about. But it was impossible, and she just tuned out and looked at her own phone awhile, still keenly aware of Peadar sitting next to her.

"Oh, that's right." Emily exclaimed on Vange's other side. She put her hand on Vange's arm and wore her serious business face. "Vange, we need to teach you a little Gaelic, in case something goes wrong with the app you'll use to take Peigi back to Scotland."

"Huh?" Vange put her phone down and tried to let what she'd heard sink in. "Oh, I mean, OK, yeah, I guess." She'd been going to ask what Gaelic had to do with a phone app, but when you came down to it, a phone app that teleported you to different places had to be magic, so anything was possible.

Emily called across the room to her husband, who had moved back to the couch with Peigi.

"Dall. Teach Vange the 'do over' phrase."

Vange never would have thought one little phrase could take an hour to learn, but Gaelic was an inflected language, they said. Depending on her pronunciation, they said, words could have drastically different meanings. Meanings that could make the 'wee phone app' do drastically different things.

Sure enough, Vange spent a mostly sleepless night in the pink bedroom of the trailer.

And then in the morning over pancakes and coffee—with Peadar sitting beside Vange again—Dall spent another hour going over that Gaelic 'do over' phrase.

Just to be safe, they said.

Peadar watched and listened, which was distracting. It was almost too much, him sitting next to her. But neither of them moved, and Vange passed Dall's Gaelic test. He said she had the phrase down pat.

Compared to that, the app Emily showed her next was easy.

But Emily kept showing her anyway.

Vange loved her friend, but she was not herself lately. Em used to be fun. Now, she was having a baby in a place designed for fun, while at the same time, she took everything way too seriously.

"OK," Vange said, anxious to get on with it, already, "I've got it. I remember the part about how everyone in contact with me will go along." She pointed to part of the phone's screen. "This is the destination menu. I can choose any of these places, or I can choose any of these people's pictures and go wherever they are—which is really cool, by the way."

With her hands on her middle, Emily smiled in a dreamy, faraway kind of way. "Yeah, it is cool, isn't it? You were always a natural at learning new phones and new apps. I'm sure you've got it handled."

For a second, Em met Vange's eyes and was actually smiling at her.

Otherwise, Vange got the distinct impression that her friend was thinking about her baby.

Vange put her hand on Emily's arm to get her attention. "There's one thing I don't understand, though."

Emily's dreaming eyes sort of vaguely focused on Vange. "Hm?"

Vange brought Emily's phone up so that they both could see.

"It says here this app is named Time Management. Why's it called that when it's a teleportation travel app?" Vange smiled then, at how she had said 'teleportation travel app' as if that were no big deal. She tried to get Peadar in on the joke, but he looked like he was watching a science show. Just looking at him, you'd think they didn't have cell phones in Scotland.

"Oh yeah," Emily said, also like it was normal, but Vange

got the impression Emily actually thought so. "I can tell you now. It's mostly a time travel app—"

"Wait, what."

"Here, this is where you set the date you want to go to, but it's better to use this calendar..."

Vange's head was spinning by the time Emily finished, but she would not let Emily be cooler than she was. Vange continued to act like this was all normal. She smiled and lightly backhanded Emily's upper arm.

"Oh. So that's why you said to bring my costume."

"He ha ha." Emily laughed, a real laugh that kind of brought her all the way back to reality for a moment. "I can just imagine why you thought I said to bring it. Ha."

Vange rolled her eyes and went into her pink bedroom to change. But when she came out, Emily looked kind of like she wanted to say, "Oh no."

"What's wrong?" Vange asked Emily.

"I meant you should bring your English renaissance festival costume, not your Scottish one in the MacGregor plaid."

❧

PEADAR SAUNTERED OVER JUST THEN, though. Oddly, he was now wearing a kilt with a strong blue color in the plaid, rather than his usual red one.

He must have been watching and deliberately come over to stop Vange from getting into an argument with her friend. Again.

Vange smiled at Peadar gratefully.

He smiled back. "Och, lass. I do love the figure you do cut while you be wearing the plaid that does mark my family." He made no secret about openly admiring her ... figure, leaning this way and that and even bending down and looking sideways. Really closely. "Mmmmm. Aye, I do find you very appealing dressed this way."

Whoa, he was so not shy. And who cared why he'd decided to after all, so long as he was flirting with her. Vange turned this way and that, helping him admire her.

But Emily ruined it.

"Too bad, Peadar, because she's going home and changing into her English peasant costume. Probably no one will see you guys when you take Peigi home, but Vange definitely doesn't want to be seen wearing MacGregor colors inside a house where Campbells live now."

Ug.

"But I just got here." And then Vange got an idea. "Ooh, but I won't mind going home to change if you come with me, Peadar." She smiled at the highlander.

He smiled back, and she could have sworn he was about to throw his arms around her.

But Emily pushed him away.

The nerve.

Here Emily was pregnant, for goodness sake, and she wouldn't let Vange even get a hug from the guy she liked. Well, OK, Emily was married and pregnant, but still.

Vange whirled on Emily, but then she thought of the baby...

And anyway, Emily was talking. "No, silly. You don't have to drive home. Use the app. I have my parents' garage marked as a destination." She held out her hands for her phone.

But Vange wanted to do it herself. She started fiddling with the app.

Emily quit trying to get the phone out of Vange's hands and just leaned in so she could watch. "Yeah, you can find it. Go ahead. It'll be a good practice run."

Vange found the destination, and then she started looking through the calendar. "Look. You said green days were available days, right? All the days are green for me except for a few days ago." She looked at Emily for an explanation.

Only half of one came.

Emily pointed to the date and time destination settings. "Set it for after midnight next Monday, when you'll just be asleep in your room anyway."

Vange thought about that for a moment, picturing herself on Monday night, sleeping and then popping into Emily's parents' garage and going to her room again to change clothes, leaving, and then being in the bed again. She shook her head and tried not to think about it anymore, but it was confusing.

Peadar was still nearby, and he opened his mouth to say something.

But Emily put her finger in his face.

How rude.

"No. You're not going with her, Peadar." Emily paused just a little bit.

Peadar probably didn't even notice, but Vange knew Emily, and she could tell her friend was thinking of an excuse why he couldn't go with her.

"What if one of our parents sees you?" Emily said then. "My parents wouldn't think twice about Vange being in their garage. But if you were there too, they might get nervous."

OK, that was a pretty good excuse, but Peadar was older than Emily. What made her think she could tell him what to do?

The situation would have been comical if Dall hadn't backed Emily up with a stern look on his face.

Rolling her eyes, Vange showed the settings to Emily one last time. "Do I have this set up right?"

Emily acted like a teacher who was checking Vange's schoolwork, all self-important. "Mm ... mmm ... Hm mm ... Yep, that's right. Go ahead and push the 'Go' button when you're ready— Oh wait." Emily grabbed the phone before Vange could push 'Go'.

"What?" Vange was annoyed. That was how eager she was to try this.

"I need to make sure you can get back here OK."

Emily fiddled with the settings some more and made Vange change them back and forth five times before she 'passed' Em's little test and was deemed worthy of teleporting by herself.

If this was what those pregnancy hormones did to you, then Vange hoped she didn't have to be around her friend much during her pregnancy.

"Can I go now?"

Vange knew she was acting the snarky student to Emily's self-important teacher, but she didn't care. That was how she felt at the moment, just like an impatient high-school kid.

"Wait, let me have your phone, since you have mine."

Em held out her hand for Vange's phone just like the teachers did in school, too.

But Vange wanted to go already. She got her phone out of her pocket and handed it over, then jumped back a step so she wasn't touching anyone.

"OK, I'm on my way."

Vange pushed the 'Go' button before Emily could stop her again.

What happened next was like in old movies when the character falls asleep and is about to start dreaming. Everything seemed to go around and around until Vange blacked out for a second.

And then she was in Emily's parents' garage. It was midnight, so the garage was dark, but moonlight came in through the windows at the top of the garage door.

Vange went out the back door and made her way across the street and down the block to her own parents' house, let herself in with her key, crept upstairs to her room, and changed into her English peasant woman costume.

It seemed silly to go back to Emily's parents' garage again to teleport back, but she wasn't sure if she needed to or not. She found her own number in Emily's contacts and called it.

At midnight on Monday night.

Which was five days into the future for Emily.

Em answered. "Vange. Is everything OK? Where are you?"

"Uh, I'm in my room at my parents' house, where you just sent me to change into my English peasant costume. Why? What's wrong? You sound awful, Em."

"Oh. Oh... Yeah. Oh yeah. Well, OK. Uh, what can I do for you, Vange? Why are you calling?" Em was trying to be the self-important teacher again, but she wasn't fooling Vange.

Something was wrong.

ॐ

BUT AGAIN, if Emily was going to act like everything was fine, then Vange was, too. Otherwise, Vange would be breaking the cool code. You know, the unwritten rule that you must be as calm and sure of yourself as the person next to you. Or else you lose cool points.

"I just want to know if I can teleport back to you here in my room, or if I should go back to your parents' garage and travel back to the trailer from there. It's kind of tricky going down stairs in these long skirts. Heh."

Emily took a while to answer.

Vange studied the posters on her wall while she waited. They were from when she was in high school. She hadn't changed them since then. Being in this room was almost like time travel. She and Em had been roommates in college, and now Emily was married, so talking to Em on the phone was something Vange didn't do much anymore. Not like back then when they had giggled over nothing until late in the night.

Finally, Em said something.

She spoke really fast.

"It would be great if you came back from right there. That way, we'll have your room marked as a destination, and you'll be able to pop right in there next time. Maybe come back from inside your closet, so your mom won't see you pop in if she's in there vacuuming or something. OK, got to go."

And the call ended.

Super curious about what was up, Vange called again.

She got her own voicemail greeting and couldn't make herself leave a message.

Knowing she would continue to get voicemail if she kept trying to call, Vange fiddled with Emily's phone until she was sure she had it set to go back to the trailer. Then she thought of a few things she might want and put them in the pouches that hung from her belt.

Feeling sorry for Em even though she wished her friend would tell her what was wrong, Vange texted: "It will be okay."

And then she went back to the Time Management app and pressed the 'Go' button.

Round and round everything went.

"Oh good," said Em, "you made it back. Now you pretty much know how to use the phone. And good, you have your solar charger brooch, so you won't run out of charge. Just remember the Gaelic 'do over' words. I can't tell you how many times that has saved us." Emily was calm once more. Serenely pregnant.

Vange was still kind of freaked out.

"Em, while it was Monday and I was there in my room, I

called you to ask if I should go back to your parents' garage or just travel from my room."

Emily wrinkled her forehead, and then she immediately smoothed it out. "Well, sorry I didn't answer, but the phone usually doesn't work during travel."

Vange must have made a face.

"What?" Emily asked.

"You did answer, Em. That's just it. You were upset. It sounded like come Monday, you aren't going to know where we are. It sounded pretty bad."

Vange saw Emily's face contort for just a second, as if she was going to take Vange seriously and get afraid. And then the oddest thing happened.

Emily's face relaxed. She just calmed down all at once and was Ms. Cool again. "Aw, I was probably just missing you, Vange." She smiled and even gave Vange a little hug. And then she rose her voice enough so that everyone in the room would hear. "OK. Sit down here with Vange, you guys, and she'll take Peigi home."

But the trailer door opened just then.

Siobhan came barging in like she owned the place.

And now that Vange came to think of it, the festival did own the place, and Siobhan was Dall and Emily's boss.

But Siobhan spoke to Emily like the two of them were best friends. "Emily, do you want Dall to age faster than necessary?"

Emily serenely turned to Siobhan and answered as if it were the most normal thing in the world for the woman to barge in like this. "No, of course not."

Siobhan raised her chin. "Dall."

"Aye?" Dall looked confused.

"Dall, you already have six months of time debt in your own timeline, which is the time you are supposed to be at the castle. Do you intend to serve that time?"

"Aye, it is my duty to Alasdair and the clan."

Siobhan slowly made her way over to Emily. "Very well, I will send you there the usual way later, but you may not also time travel with Vange. That would age you faster than your dear wife desires to have it happen." She put her arm around Emily.

Dall probably thought Siobhan was comforting Emily.

But Vange suddenly knew that Siobhan was controlling Emily. That was the only way all this weirdness made any sense, level-headed Emily having a baby in a place like the festival most of all.

Now if only Vange knew what to do about it.

Siobhan gave Emily's shoulders a gentle squeeze and then leisurely walked to the trailer door. Just before she closed it behind herself, she told Emily, "Go on and tell the rest of them they can go now." And then she left.

If it had been just the two of them, Vange would have said something to Emily. But Dall was there, and he was intimidating, and he was just as taken in as Emily, by the idea of having kids at the renaissance festival. Which, let's face it, was not a ... wholesome environment.

Emily was smiling serenely. "OK. Now the rest of you gather around Vange. Good, now you sit here, and you sit there. Make contact with her when she sits here, and she'll take Peigi home." Emily gestured for Vange to sit on the floor in the spot she had indicated.

OK, that was ... whatever.

Vange sat down on the kitchen floor.

Peigi came over and sat next to Vange close enough that their arms were touching.

Vange figured she did need to take Peigi home before she addressed this weird hippy Bohemian commune problem that her best friend was entangled in, so she would just do that and then—

And then Peadar smiled at Vange, which was distracting enough, but he sat down in front of her, so close that his knees were touching her knees.

And fireworks went off.

They started in Vange's knees and went up her body in shivers, making goosebumps break out all over her skin.

❦

"VANGE."

Vange jumped a little. "Huh?"

"Let me see the settings, Vange."

"What? Oh." Vange swam out of the depths of Peadar's eyes. It was difficult. There was a strong undertow, pulling her in. Once she'd looked away from him, she was able to think again and to concentrate on the Time Management app and setting the destination Emily had told her to set.

She held it up for inspection. "OK. Here it is." She was still kind of feeling sparks fly out of Peadar's knees into hers, so she avoided his eyes, knowing her brain would turn to mush as soon as they met her own.

"It's set right. You guys are good to go." Emily was using her proud teacher voice again.

"Are you guys ready?" Vange asked Peigi and Peadar while looking only at Peigi.

"Aye."

"Aye."

Vange pushed the 'Go' button.

The world spun round.

The next thing Vange knew, she was staring at a cat. At the same time, she remembered being in this attic crawl space behind these trunks before. She remembered meeting Peadar when he was a cowboy out on the range—and that he was Dall's son.

But she also remembered the huge allergic reaction she'd had from this cat's hair. No way was she going through that again.

"I want a do over."

Vange figured that was what she was saying in Gaelic, anyway.

They were back in the trailer again.

"I did the do over, Em. No way am I going to be with that cat hair again." Vange said as soon as the world stopped spinning.

"Vange. You remember?" Emily asked.

"Remember what?" Vange asked. "How to do the settings to get back? You just checked my settings to get there and said they were fine." She smiled up at Em. "Don't worry. I've got this."

"OK, go ahead." Emily said. And a second later, she said it again, "Do you remember?"

"Em, if you're trying to be funny, it isn't working. Quit asking me if I remember and just let me take Peigi home, already. Gosh." Vange chuckled a little to take the edge off her anger, but she was starting to get kind of mad at Em.

"OK OK, Vange. Maybe this time you will."

"What do you mean, this time?" Vange was confused.

"Never mind, just go." Emily said. And a second later, almost sounding like her normal self, Emily said to Dall, "Wow. She remembers for just a few seconds when she first gets back, just long enough to complain about the cat, and then she forgets again."

"Aye, lass. They will be needing to arrive outside. However, we ken she knows the Gaelic well enough, for your 'do over' phrase, aye?"

Emily smiled at Dall in this way they had, and he smiled back.

Usually, Vange thought it was cute, but right now it sort of made her uneasy. It was like they'd forgotten about everyone else in the room. She cleared her throat. "Ahem. We're still sitting here, you know."

Emily didn't snap out of it, but at least she saw Vange and the other people again. "That means they will need to arrive pretty far away from the settlement, just so they aren't seen, and then they'll have to walk in."

"Aye." Dall was sizing Vange up.

She wanted to feel indignant, but the thought of arriving outside of town and having to walk a long ways didn't thrill her, until...

Peadar stood and went over to Dall and Emily's stash of 16th century weapons. He looked them all over, selected a claymore and several daggers, and stashed them in various places all over his person.

Surprising Vange, Peigi did the same.

The two of them stood over Vange as if she were their child.

"We will protect her, you ken?" Peigi said.

Nodding to Peigi as if she were a soldier and he an officer, Dall moved to Emily's side and held her close by the waist. "Aye. Very well."

Emily grabbed her phone out of Vange's hand and fiddled with it for a minute, then handed it back. "Alright, I've set the destination on the map, up and over the shortest mountain and then around a valley. If anyone is there when you appear, they'll be traveling too, not established, so you should be safe. If you see anyone when you arrive, you can take a 'do over' and change the destination for the mountain on the other side of the settlement. But hopefully that won't happen."

Vange had a thought then. "Shouldn't Peadar and Peigi wear English clothes, like me?"

Peadar plucked at the blue kilt of the Campbells and smiled at her. He liked that idea.

Encouraged, Vange went on. "I mean, it isn't like they can get away with claiming they're Campbells. Wouldn't we all be safer as English peasants?"

"Aye," said Dall.

"Sort of," said Emily at the same time. "I mean, how did three English peasants come to be wandering through the Scottish highlands?"

"Eh," Vange made a sound that said the 'why' of it was unimportant. "I doubt anyone will ask, and if they do, we'll just claim we were out hunting with some English lord or other and we got lost."

Peadar spoke up then. "Well enough, lass. However, that does leave all the speaking to you, for if Peigi or I speak up, they will know we are as highland Scottish as any."

"I may as well do the speaking," Vange said, "because you and Peigi will need to do all the swording." She snorted a laugh at her own joke.

Fortunately, the rest of them thought it funny too and laughed along.

"Ok," said Emily, "I guess it's back to the costume shed we go."

"Nah," said Vange. "Peigi can wear your English trew outfit and be a boy peasant, and Peadar can wear Dall's."

And they did. They also fixed up the leather backpacks full of 16th century camping gear and provisions. Finally, Peadar, Peigi, and Vange looked like English peasants: two men with swords and a woman with wildly colorful boots.

WHEN DALL TRIED to hand Peigi her English trews, the two of them had a long conversation in Gaelic. They even dragged Emily into it, which surprised and impressed Vange. Her friend must be good at languages.

Their talk started out nice enough, but it got more and more heated the longer it went on, until Peigi's face was red and her breathing was heavy and her voice was kind of loud.

"What was that all about?" Vange asked Emily once Peigi was finally in the pink bedroom changing.

Briefly, Emily bunched her mouth up and moved it to one side of her face, but then her face relaxed into that eerie calm again.

"Aw, that's right, you don't remember. Peigi's supposed to meet her boyfriend the night after you all arrive. The two of them are running away to get married. She doesn't want him to see her in trews. Says can't she wear her own clothes and have you bring her straight to his house. I explained we don't have his house marked as a destination, so we can't reliably get you guys there. She doesn't believe me. Oh well."

"I'll make Peadar explain it to her," Vange said with a wink meant to tell

Emily she had influence over Peadar, and wasn't that cool?

But her normally fun friend Em was all uptight suddenly.

"Vange, there's something you should know. If you have sex with Peadar there, married or not, then you will be stuck there. And the 16th century is fun to visit, but you will see what I mean when I say you do not want to be stuck there."

Vange gulped down a lump that was suddenly in her throat. "Really Em? I could get stuck there?"

Emily nodded, her face a weird combination of uptight and serene. "Yeah, so watch yourself, OK?"

Vange nodded slowly, eyes focused on nothing in particular. "Yeah, I will."

"OK you guys," Emily called out loudly but calmly, "gather back around Vange, and stand up this time and face away from each other, like the away team does in Star Trek's Next Generation."

Vange laughed at Emily's comparison, noticing it was lost

on Peadar and Peigi. It was then she realized it was true. She was really going to the 16th century.

She was excited enough about that, but then Peadar was right up close and personal, with his arm around her waist. The sparks that had flown between her knees and his were nothing compared to this. She almost couldn't breathe, it was so awesome and intense and ... exhilarating.

Peigi was there, too, but Vange barely noticed her.

"Whenever you're ready, Vange."

Vange felt a gentle push on her back and realized that Em had said something. Oh yeah. She got the phone out of its solar charger brooch where she had stowed it. Yep, she could see on the map where they were going. Great.

"Are you guys ready?"

"Aye," said Peadar with a smile and a twinkle of his eyes.

"Aye," said Peigi angrily, all but snarling the word out.

Dang. That woman was impatient.

"Hang on everybody, here we goooooooooooooooo." Vange said in her best impersonation of Peter Pan's ride at Disneyland. She could hear Emily laughing for just a second.

And then everything spun round and round.

VANGE CAME to awareness inside a thick grove of trees and stood up off the dirty ground with an "Ew."

The grove was on top of a hill overlooking a green valley. Mountains loomed majestically in the distance, and the sky was frothy with clouds. And in the green valley were cattle, scattered tiny houses, dirt roads, and some sort of farmer's market.

A bunch of birds squawked and took off from nearby, apparently startled by her and Peadar and Peigi's presence. They weren't the only ones.

"Rrraaaaaaggghhhhhhh." Peigi was screaming and wailing —and clutching to Vange's side as if she would collapse if she didn't.

"Och, Peigi, be still, aye? Och, be still." Peadar was trying to calm his sister—

"Huh." Vange gasped. "Oh my gosh." she said to Peadar, "I remember it all now. You're Dall's children." She looked at Peadar. "We rescued you from the English out on the range somewhere." She turned to Peigi. "And you were a servant in your own house. We rescued you, too."

But Peigi lunged at Vange.

Peadar held her back, and the two of them struggled while Peigi yelled at Vange.

"I did not need rescuing. And if you have made me betray the one man I do love, then forgive you I never will."

"You're welcome," Vange sang out to Peigi while she checked the map on Emily's phone. "'Dinna fash, lass,' as they say in Outlander. We'll get you to your rendezvous with your fella in time to leave with him tonight. OK, this says we need to go this way." She pointed and started to walk in that direction.

Peadar and his sister followed behind. They argued in Gaelic for another minute or so, but their struggles got less and less animated.

"Didn't Dall and Emily get this all worked out with Peigi in Emily's trailer?" Vange asked Peadar while moving to casually put a hand on his arm.

But he recoiled. Not in disgust or anything, he just moved subtly out of the way. Closer to his sister. Protectively.

Vange felt a whole lot more alone than she had a moment before.

"Nay," Peadar told her. "And where be Emily and Da?"

Realization dawned.

"Oh no. You don't remember anything that happened

while we were in Emily and my time period, do you."

Peadar and Peigi both shook their heads slightly no. But it was obvious they knew about time travel. They didn't look at her as if she were a lunatic or anything. She was curious how they knew, but ...

"We need to get moving if you're going to meet Alan," she said to Peigi.

"Aye," said Peigi, turning away from her brother to look ahead and walking faster, which wasn't easy considering there wasn't any road and they were in a thick forest. The woman clearly did not want to waste any time meeting her man.

Peadar worked his way in between Vange and his sister. "Nay, I do not have the recollection of being in any other time but now." He kept looking ahead at the branches he had to move out of the way to keep moving, but he held them out of the way for Vange, too. "Howsoever, I do not recollect how I did come to be here, though, nor why I be dressed as an Englishman, nor especially why my sister be. I am grateful, though, to be free of the English."

Vange looked around. "Do you know where we are?"

"Aye, lass. We be in Scotland." Peadar s huge smile transformed him.

Vange laughed and adjusted her leather backpack. "I knew that much. But do you know where your old house is from here? The one Peigi wants to get back to?"

Peadar shrugged. "Nay, however Peigi does say she knows the way."

"Oh, well that's good. I guess we'll just follow her then, and make sure she gets home safe." Tentatively, Vange smiled at Peadar.

"Aye." He smiled back.

But it was the smile you gave a stranger. They were starting over.

A few moments passed by in silence while they wound

their way through the woods. Peigi didn't have any trouble at all, and so Peadar was following her.

And Vange was following him. Her boots were getting much dirtier out here in the wild than they did at the renfest, but she would shine them when she got home. She got her car cup of bubblegum out of her pouch and grunted when she spilled some of it before grabbing one and popping it in her mouth. She was about to offer Peadar some, but he started talking again.

"So, now we be moving. I would that you told me where our da is. Before he came to free me of being captive, I had not seen him for nearly twenty years."

Vange stopped in the middle of blowing a bubble. "Oh yeah, well ... I'm from the future. You know that, right? And we're talking five hundred years in the future." She looked at him to make sure he believed her.

He did. "Aye."

"OK, well, your dad is there, and I'm here. We're just supposed to take Peigi home, and then your da expects both of us to go back there, to the future. You and Peigi are dressed as Englishmen because the MacGregors and the Campbells are feuding now..." Vange told him everything she knew about their situation, which now that she was talking about it, she realized was not much.

They were almost out of the woods when trouble found them.

ONE SECOND VANGE was following Peadar over logs and under branches, and the next second both of her arms were being grabbed from behind and she was lifted up off her feet.

"Eeeeaaaaahh." Vange screamed.

She kicked and struggled.

She had her dagger sheathed in her boot, but her hands weren't free to reach it. She was kind of afraid of what might happen if she did, anyway. The man who had grabbed her might grab it and use it against her.

At first, she didn't see what would stop him.

But then Peadar and Peigi had turned around and were running toward her, shouting.

Other men were with the one who had her. Blue kilted men. They passed her by and ran out to meet the disguised MacGregors.

Peadar and Peigi had drawn their claymores off their backs, and they met the Campbells fiercely.

All Vange heard for the next minute was swords ringing off each other and grunts and the odd snatch of Gaelic— which might as well have been Martian, for all she understood of it.

Dall's children put up a good fight, but Vange was surprised when they were the last ones standing among so many attackers.

Except for the man who held Vange. He growled at the brother and sister, shaking Vange in front of them.

Her heart sank. She was his human shield.

But Peigi sheathed her sword, ran right up to Vange, caught her in a hug, and started pulling her out of the man's grip.

Vange clung to Peigi for all she was worth. Tears were streaming down her face, and she let out a few sobs along with saying, "Ouch. Ouch." at the way the obstinate man held on.

Peadar must have gone around behind the man and attacked his legs then, because the man fell.

"Ahhhhh." Vange yelled, sure she was going to fall too.

Peigi held on to her though, pulling her free of the man and then steadying her until she was standing on her own.

And then the man behind her grunted and screamed. She heard him fall.

"Do you ken if any of them did get away, lass?" Peadar asked Vange as he came back around into view, looking everywhere at once.

"No, they all fell. It almost seems like someone was helping you guys, because I didn't always see one of you close by when one of them fell."

Peigi spoke up then in the tone one would use while instructing a child.

"Men do not fall from sword wounds straight away. Nay, they do bleed for a bit and then succumb to the pain and fall over."

Peadar imitated them falling over.

Peigi laughed.

Vange smiled, but she was still getting over being scared to death, so laughter was going to have to wait awhile.

Saying something that appeared to be a joke, Peigi turned around and started walking again, toward her old house, toward Alan, her man.

Chuckling and sheathing his own sword on his back, Peadar started following.

"What did she say?" Vange asked as she hurried to keep up with the Scots' long strides and get away from the ghastly scene.

"She does say the trews come in handy in a fight, and that she thinks on wearing them all the while."

That made Vange smile again. Thinking that OK, maybe Peadar's sister was alright, she climbed over roots, ducked under branches, and wove around the large trunks of some of the trees.

It seemed like Peadar was paying Vange as little attention as possible and had only grudgingly answered her question. However, he was lagging behind his sister.

Peigi noticed. She turned around and urged him on, and even if Vange couldn't understand what she said, her meaning came through loud and clear:

"Quit flirting with her and hurry up."

Yep, that was the gist of it.

Because Peadar blushed a little. And then he yelled something about their da that also had Vange's name in it.

"Ug, let's get this over with," Vange said, starting to jog. She smiled when she thought she detected the tiniest of nods from Peadar.

Just barely keeping up with the two Scots, Vange jogged along through the thinning forest as long as she could—which was about twenty minutes. And then she sat down along the bank of a stream the Scots were crossing by leaping from stone to stone.

"I need to rest." Vange managed to call out after them through the deep breaths she needed to take. While she rested, she dipped her Grayl Quest Water Filtration Cup into the stream and popped a replacement piece of bubblegum in her mouth.

Peigi said something impatiently.

Vange took a long drink of her water and called out, "You guys should come over and wash yourselves off in this stream anyway, Peigi. You don't really want to greet your fella while you're covered in blood, do you?"

She'd said that in jest, but they were getting close to that farmer's market. Did these Scots really think nothing of showing up there covered in blood?

But Peadar must have found that hilarious, because he stood there laughing with his hands on his knees, staring at all the blood on his sister's arms.

Peigi rolled her eyes and sighed, then made her way down to the bank beside Vange and washed her face and hands. Apparently deciding the weather was warm, so why not, she waded in and sat down, rinsing the blood off her trews, as well.

Laughing, Peadar waded in and was washing too.

The two of them splashed each other and laughed some more.

That was when Vange noticed.

"PEIGI, YOU'RE BLEEDING." Vange dug in her pouch and pulled out an Ace bandage. "Here, let me bind that for you. It'll slow the bleeding at least."

Peigi was moving away from Vange with a wary look in her eyes until Peadar spoke to her, and then she only hesitantly allowed Vange to apply the Ace bandage to her lower left arm, just below the elbow.

"I think that will stop the bleeding. Doesn't that hurt?"

There was a gash in the tanned part of Peigi's forearm, remarkably close to where Emily's scar was.

Both MacGregors laughed.

"OK, you guys's sense of humor escapes me. What's so funny about Peigi's arm being hurt and her maybe bleeding to death?"

That only made them laugh harder.

"Fine," Vange pouted, "I don't care why you think that's so funny, so there."

And then smiling at her, they both quickly showed off all their scars. They had so many. And most of them were nasty jagged things.

"You guys get in lots of fights, huh."

Still smiling, they both nodded and reassembled their clothing.

Vange put her stuff back in her pouches, got up, and got what she thought was a head start on walking.

But before long at all, Peigi called out, "Nay, we go this way," and pointed along the tree line, around the clearing with the market in it.

"Aw, but fruit sounds so good right now." Vange had been headed for the market. She was excited to see what one was like in this old-fashioned time, and she'd been contemplating trying to trade some bubblegum for some fresh fruit. "Can't we go see if they have any?" Vange looked ahead to the market longingly.

"Nay," said Peigi, ripping the Ace bandage off of her arm and throwing it at Vange.

Vange ducked. Who wanted a bloody Ace bandage? She'd get another one at Walmart tomorrow.

"Nay," Peigi said again more forcefully, "we must needs be going. The Campbells will find their kin soon and seek vengeance. Anyhow, we will not be stopping any more for you, Vange." She stormed off along the tree line at a quick walk.

With one nervous glance at Vange and a subtle tilt of his head to indicate he wanted her to come along but was not going to request it outright, Peadar followed his sister.

Vange hurried after him, but she had the feeling they were going the wrong way. She got out Emily's phone and brought up the map while she walked. Yep, they should be going past the farmers' market, up the mountain on the other side, and then down, and they would be there.

"Peigi. Peigi, it's over there to the right, not this way."

Peadar kept looking over his shoulder at Vange, but she had to call out ten or twelve times before his sister was persuaded to listen.

Even so, Peigi stood there with her hands on her hips and waited for Vange to come to her, rather than backtrack one step. She even stomped her foot.

Already so tired she was huffing and puffing with the exertion, Vange ran over to Peigi and tried to explain while showing her the phone map with its dot indicating their position and the line to where Peigi wanted to be.

Trying to show her, anyway.

Peigi shied away from the phone as if it were a bomb or something.

"Wow, what a difficult woman you are."

Vange held up the phone and shook it. "You know what? I can just use this to go home right now. I'm sure you two don't need me."

She waited for Peadar to tell her he wanted her to stay.

That he enjoyed her company.

That he was sorry for his sister's behavior.

The last thing Vange expected to happen was for someone to grab the phone right out of her hand.

And that was just what did happen.

"Hahahahaha." The kid who had taken it sure was amused that he had, too. He ran up the mountain into the woods laughing, in the opposite direction from where Peigi needed to go.

Vange knew that if she had been alone, she would have just stood there in shock until she collapsed in a heap and cried herself out, she was so tired and so out of shape.

But Peadar barked some Gaelic at Peigi, gently pushed his sister in the direction Vange had said she should go, grabbed Vange's hand, and started them running after the phone thief.

If they didn't catch him, the situation was dire.

But Vange was in Heaven.

Peadar had ditched his precious sister in order to help her. His hand was warm in hers. Oh, and she was pretty sure he would get Emily's phone back too, although she almost didn't care.

13. VANGE & PEADAR 1

Vange clung to Peadar's hand as they crashed uphill through the 1560 highlands forest, chasing the kid who had stolen Emily's phone and the Time Management app. She tried to hold her skirts up with her other hand, but her inner skirt kept escaping her grip. Over and over, it fell down and tripped her, so that every few steps, Peadar had to pull her upright again.

She was gasping for breath.

"I can't run anymore."

"You must, lass."

"I've already run more in the last hour than I did last year."

"Heh ha ha. You cannot mean that, lass."

Vange started to fall, she was so tired. Just before she hit the leafy ground, she felt Peadar's strong arms catching her and then hoisting her up. And then he was carrying her like a baby.

"Just set me down."

His voice was steady as ever as he ran on, even jumping over fallen branches with her in his arms.

"I cannot. I must run after the wee phone we did lose, you ken?"

Oh, she kenned that he was running, alright. Her body was being jostled in a way that was keeping her from catching her breath. The feel of his strong arms holding her was dimly stirring other thoughts, but she was so tired she couldn't even enjoy them.

"I'll rest here while you catch the little creep."

He laughed some more.

And he kept running, which was not what she had asked him to do.

"Put me down, Tarzan."

He didn't get that joke.

Of course not.

How would he?

One forest looked just like another, and Peadar was so ... distracting. She kept forgetting they were stranded there until they got Emily's phone back.

"Lass, and I put you down, you would not be there when I returned for you."

"I won't go anywhere. Please, I just want to lie down."

What she really wanted was to lie on the couch eating some of her mom's homemade lumpia rolls while she watched an episode of Outlander on demand.

But just lying down would do.

"You be lying down now."

She pounded on his arm, but it just hurt her hand.

"I want to lie down on something that isn't moving."

"And I lie you down on the grass, the first man to pass by will pick you up again. Nay, I will not."

She let that sink in for a minute and decided he was right.

"Thank you for carrying me."

"The pleasure is all mine, Vange."

At that, her other thoughts were definitely stirring. She

gazed up at the handsome face she'd been daydreaming about ever since she met him two weeks before.

But he had crowned a ridge and stopped at the top.

"Why are we stopping?"

He put her down then, and while he spoke he pointed to three different pathways down through the woods.

"I did not see which way he did go, lass."

"Let's take the path less traveled by."

Vange chuckled, proud of herself for remembering that poem they had read in 10th grade English class.

And then she remembered he wouldn't get that joke, either. Man. She needed to get some things in common with him quick, or her joking touch was going to go stale.

"Can you walk now, lass?"

"Uh, yeah, thanks."

Vange picked up the middles of her two long skirts with both hands this time and firmly hitched them over her belt. Now that her clothes dangled around her knees, she didn't trip a once. But she missed holding Peadar's hand.

They walked over to the pathway on the left, which was not even half cleared of stray branches, making it slow going unless they wanted scratches all over their faces. Both of their arms were covered with long linen sleeves. His chest was protected by a tunic and hers by a bodice. They both wore muffin caps. She wished she had on trews like he did.

No, who was she kidding? She wished he were wearing his kilt. She should never have let Emily talk the two of them into wearing English clothes. No Campbells had seen them...

"Why this pathway, lass?"

"I figure a thief doesn't want to be seen."

"Ah, aye, that be a good reckoning."

He put his hand over his mouth and spoke at barely a whisper.

She took the hint and got quiet.

The barely-a-pathway led down into a ravine, and a creek ran down the center of it from above.

They whispered some more.

"This looks like a thieves' den to me."

"Aye, lass."

He put his arm in front of her then and deftly tucked her behind him while his other hand drew his claymore from its scabbard on his back.

Without thinking about it, Vange put her hand on Peadar's back to let him know she was right behind him as they crept along the scratchy pathway.

She whispered to him.

"Do you see anything?"

"Sh."

He kept one hand on his sword and put the other behind him to shush her.

Vange felt a flicker of resentment at being treated like a child, but she got over it once she understood he was listening for any sign of their thief. Or his accomplices.

Peadar didn't have to listen for long.

Vange felt an itch in the middle of her back and moved to scratch it, only she made contact with someone else's hand.

"Huh." Vange gasped.

So fast she didn't see it happen, Peadar whirled and had his claymore at the throat of a little man.

"WHO BE YOU?" said the little man in English. He sounded incredulous, like he couldn't believe someone had gotten the drop on him. He was dressed all in green stuff that looked more like romaine lettuce than clothes.

"I be Peadar MacGregor, and you will be giving back to Evangeline the phone that was stolen, brunaidh."

Incredibly, with a sword pressed to his throat and all, the brunaidh chose to argue.

"I don't have it, and anyway what is a phone?"

Peadar had opened his mouth to speak, but Vange put a hand on his arm to stop him. She took over with the discipline methods she had learned last semester, preparing to teach second graders. After all, this guy was about that size.

She wasn't much taller, truth to tell.

"Never mind what a phone is. Just hand it over. It isn't yours."

She used the technique the teacher college had taught her. She held out her hand as if she fully expected the child to give her his phone. She'd wondered if people really bought phones for seven-year-olds, but now she was glad they might.

Meanwhile, the little man was struggling in the chokehold of Peadar, who pressed the sword up against his throat.

"I don't have it." the brunaidh whined, finally afraid.

Wow, he was a tough discipline case.

Vange crossed her arms and gave him a stern look that she hoped would brook no nonsense. She was bigger than him. A little. She stood up, straight and proud. Among her family members, she was considered tall.

She decided to try intimidating him with deduction.

That was an advanced technique. She'd gotten an A on her in-class demo of it.

"Well, you obviously know what we're talking about, so if you don't have it, then tell us where it is."

The brunaidh screamed then.

"He took it."

Peadar pressed the sword right into the little man's neck, but Vange knew it was too late. The other brunaidhs had doubtless heard that.

"Aye, that we do know, lad."

Vange tried once more, leaning into him this last time, to intimidate by proximity.

"Where did he take it? Which way did he go?"

Instinct made Vange duck down so that she was eye-to-eye with the little man when she said this, and Peadar followed her. It was a good thing, too.

Fwip. Fwip.

Two arrows raced through the area where their heads had been and juttered in a nearby tree.

"Tell them, 'Do not shoot.'"

Peadar looked angry now, which was good, because Vange was so scared she could no longer speak. Her knees gave way in fact, and she landed on her bottom, making all the leaves poof out from under her.

"Do not shoot."

As the little man yelled, his eyes definitely looked in more than one direction, which meant she and Peadar were surrounded.

Great.

Sure enough, a dozen people the size of seven-year-olds crept forward out of the trees around her, all dressed in romaine lettuce clothes.

Vange wanted to laugh, but they were all threatening her and Peadar with spears. It was still hard not to laugh. They were so cute and small, they almost seemed harmless.

Their leader was a bit taller than the rest, but not even as tall as Vange. He slowly advanced until his spear was at Peadar's throat.

"Peadar MacGregor, tell us what the phone is, and we will spare your lives."

Peadar kept his chin up, and he kept a firm grip on his claymore and on the brunaidh whose throat it was at.

"Nay, brunaidh. You must tell us where the phone is, and I will spare his life."

All of them gathered around behind their leader and whispered then. Their discussion got quite heated. They would glance at Peadar now and then, but none of them looked at Vange even once.

Hm.

Hadn't they noticed her?

This was like the part in the movie where everyone yelled at the woman, "Help him, for goodness sake. Don't just stand there."

But she was out in the woods.

There weren't any vases she could break over anyone's head.

Maybe she could sneak away and then somehow help Peadar get away? She had to do something.

Vange slowly lowered herself to the ground in preparation to crawl backward.

Oops.

That had been a bad idea.

Apparently, they had noticed her but had just dismissed her as not a threat, because now that she was moving, they stopped her.

That was all she really knew.

One moment, she'd been starting to crawl backward. The next moment she was flat on her stomach watching Peadar dance around over her with his sword extended out, batting away at the circle of spears that surrounded them.

He was pretty amazing to watch. It was as if he were in a carefully choreographed dance where all the spears came at him and he moved between some and batted some aside and jumped over others.

But it wasn't a dance.

He might die.

Vange held her breath, afraid even the small puff of air

coming from her lungs might mess up Peadar's delicate balancing act.

But the brunaidh they had captured was running around loose now, and laughing.

"Ha ha ha. That is one stupid woman you have there, Peadar MacGregor."

The others joined in on the taunting.

"Ha ha. What have you to bargain with now?"

"Naught. That be what."

Peadar put up a good fight, but in the end he was one man with a sword and they were a dozen with spears. At least they didn't kill him. Not before they knocked her on the head, anyway.

It hurt.

And then everything went black.

WHEN VANGE WOKE UP, she was staring at a spear again, but this time she was sitting on the wet and cold wooden deck of a small sailing ship, restrained against its mast by her arms and legs, which were tied around it with rough ropes at her wrists and ankles.

So far as she could tell, she still had all of her possessions —except her one dagger was missing from its sheath in her boot, and the little people still had Emily's phone.

The ship was in a vast river, or maybe a lake. Vange could see a distant shoreline on two sides.

Peadar was sitting tied to the mast as well. His claymore was missing, and he was staring at her with a stern look in his eyes.

He whispered once their eyes met and he could see she was fully awake.

"Do not say a word."

Nodding yes to him, she felt her face wrinkle up in anguish.

The small spearman didn't miss a beat, though.

"Har. Now you tell her to behave. I've half a mind to turn you loose so as you can teach her a lesson."

Fortunately, Peadar asked of the spearman the question that was on Vange's mind, because she was this close to asking it herself when he did. No one had ever told her to be quiet before. His order had already slipped from her mind.

"Where do we go?"

The spearman tipped his drinking horn all the way back and emptied the last few drops into his mouth, swallowed, and then wiped his mouth with his voluminous sleeve.

"Mull looms there even now."

He pointed.

Vange looked over at a new shore, barely visible in front of the ship.

The brunaidh leader came up from below decks then, holding two steaming cups.

"Ah, you have settled in, I see. Murl here will give you some stew to drink, if you be civil to him."

The leader patted Murl on the back and handed the small man the two steaming cups, then went back below, chuckling.

Murl smiled at them and waved the stew cups under their noses.

"Have you the will to eat? Or are you determined to fight me if I get close?"

Vange had barely started to open her mouth to answer the small man when Peadar cleared his throat.

Again she had forgotten their new agreement that he would do the talking. This was unusual, so it was hard to remember. She loved to talk, and he was usually quiet.

He spoke up.

"We will eat, and we thank you."

Vange knew it was silly to worry about stew stains down the front of her English renaissance faire costume while she was tied to the mast of a ship headed who-knew-where with little hope of getting back home to the 21st Century.

Still, she felt more anxious than hopeful as the little man approached her with the cup.

He tipped it carefully, though.

The stew tasted wonderful, mostly broth but with bits of meat, carrots, celery, and onion mixed in.

They both drank their whole cup of it, and then Murl hollered down below decks.

"Come and get the dirty cups, Fal."

Peadar was watching Murl warily, but he seemed harmless as he went about the deck pulling ropes that adjusted the sails and yelling at others to help him sometimes.

Vange whispered to Peadar.

"So what's the plan?"

He pressed his lips together into a hard line before he whispered back, never taking his eyes off Murl.

"Look about for the wee phone. Take it, and go."

She jiggled her hands in the ropes.

"But we're tied up."

His chest heaved, and his fists balled up.

"They will need to untie us, lass, in order to take us off this ship."

Vange breathed a sigh of relief.

"So as soon as they untie us, I'll run around looking for the phone while you keep them busy?"

"Aye, lass. I have only seen four of them on board. I can handle that many."

"But they've taken your sword."

"Och, they be so small. I will throw them all overboard."

Vange giggled.

And she was instantly glad that she had.

Peadar's entire face lit up with his smile.

It was marvelous to gaze at, so that was what she did for the next half hour, while he kept his eye on Murl and their other captors, visibly scheming how he would take them down so that the two of them could get Emily's phone and get back to the 21st Century.

Vange kept her eye out for the phone. He was right. It had to be on board somewhere. She didn't see it up here on deck anyplace, so it had to be down in the cabin. That was the first place she would look.

And then she realized.

"What if there's someone down in the cabin when I get down there?"

Peadar shrugged with his nose.

"My bout with those up here will be so loud, anyone below decks will run up to help. Wait just a bit before running down there, lass."

Vange nodded.

"OK."

She looked around.

"See the little nook by the door to the cabin?"

"Aye."

"I'll wait there."

"Tis a good place."

They smiled at each other.

Vange was wondering how far they had traveled away from where she'd been knocked out when the ship's gentle sway on the water got the better of her.

She became very sleepy and couldn't help leaning forward against the mast and passing into slumber.

❧

VANGE RAISED HER HAND, and her child-development professor called on her.

She was so happy.

She had studied and she knew the answer well.

"According to Piaget," Vange said with a big smile on her face, "children readily change how they already think inside to match what is going on in the outside world, but adults find this difficult."

"Correct," said the professor with his hands clasped behind his back, pacing across the front of the lecture hall to start his next point in front of a different group of students.

Grinning even bigger, Vange discreetly went to Facebook on her phone to post a brag.

But she heard rough voices that didn't fit into the college atmosphere at all.

"Get up. Get up."

"We have arrived."

"And we do not wish to carry you."

Vange tried to make the rough voices and jostling fit into what was going on there in the lecture hall, but it was difficult.

She smiled.

According to Piaget, that meant she must be an adult.

They weren't all adults there in the lecture hall, though, because someone threw a Double Big Gulp of cold water all over her. It landed mostly in her face.

Shivering from the cold and spluttering from the water in her nose, Vange looked around for the student who had done that.

"How much did you give them, Fal?"

"Twice as much as I would give you or me, is all."

"Fal."

"What were you thinking?"

"We need them, Fal."

"If they die, we'll never know what the phone is, or what it can do."

What the heck were these students behind her talking about? Who in this day and age didn't know what a phone was?

Vange turned to shush them, distracted from her search for the student who had thrown the water.

But then she stopped to write in her notebook.

Wow, this this incident had made her understand why all that emphasis was placed on laying down the rules the first few days of school. If her second-grade students were going to be anything like her classmates, then they would be a tough crowd.

"Cor, we will just need to carry them, then."

"They be heavy, Fal."

"Just put your hands under them and lift."

"Hurk."

Vange was being jostled by other students in the hallway as she headed to her next class. Funny, college hallways weren't usually this rowdy. Oh well. Maybe there was a football game or something this weekend that had everyone but her all hyped up. She didn't pay attention to such things, preferring to focus on her coursework.

"Here, put them on the wain."

☙

VANGE FINISHED her school day amazingly fast and was home in an instant. She was unusually glad to be in the small apartment that she shared with Emily, who was in the bathroom getting ready for a party...

Wait, Emily had married Dall MacGregor, and she traveled with him now, to all the various renaissance faire sites.

What was Emily doing home?

Vange's eyes opened.

She had trouble making sense out of what she saw—and what was that smell? It reminded her of when she used to babysit and the kids wet the bed.

The wall near her was painted white, but it was clearly made of hand-cut wood and stuffed with ... straw?

She was seated with her legs folded in front of her, and when she tried to get up, she found that she was tied to a post behind her. Her elbows stuck out to either side of her face, and her wrists were fastened behind her head. Her ankles were tied to the post, too, but that didn't hurt as much, because she still had her boots on.

"Aaaeeeeehhh." she screamed.

Peadar's soft voice came from behind her.

"What is it, lass? Did something bite you?"

"No. We're just stuck in this backwards time period with no TV where people don't have any manners. I want to go home."

"Quiet yourself, lass. Save your strength."

"I'm tired of doing what I'm told. I just want to leave."

She struggled against the ropes that tied her, grunting and crying.

The mature adult part of her knew she was being childish, but she didn't care. She wanted to get off this ride. It wasn't fun anymore.

His voice came as quietly as before.

"Evangeline. Get yourself together. You need your wits about you."

His calmness started to sink into her. When she stopped fighting the ropes, her mind started to come into focus and she felt less out of control, more sane. Her tears hadn't stopped flowing, though.

"You are the one who does know how to make the phone

work," Peadar said encouragingly, "I will help you get it, and then you can use it to get yourself home, lass."

Vange took a good look around. The two of them were seated back-to-back alone in a house that was not much larger than two king-sized beds.

The floor was just dirt.

There was a fireplace, a table with four chairs, and a ladder that went up to a loft, where presumably the beds were.

They couldn't reach any of it, though. The ropes that tied them to the post were just long enough that they could sit comfortably.

A thought occurred to her.

"What do you know about these little people, and what was that you called them?"

To Peadar's credit, he went with the change of subject. Perhaps he realized that dwelling on her tears would only prolong their falling.

"They are brunaidh. They do not have any territory, but rather they travel the world as they like. They speak most languages and are handy as tinkers. Very few have met them, aye? Most think they are legend."

"Will they hurt us?"

"I do hope not, lass."

His matter-of-fact steadiness helped Vange get a grip on herself. She blinked back her tears and snuffled to clear her nose. She lowered her voice to the softest whisper she could manage.

"Should I tell them what they want to know, about the phone?"

He whispered back just as quietly.

"Aye, if need be, lass. Do not hold your knowledge away from them if they do threaten to hurt you."

"But if they find out how to use the phone, then they won't need us anymore ..."

"And you ken they will turn us loose then."

"Or kill us."

He laughed.

A few minutes before, his laughter would have made her feel all the more alone. She would have cried even harder and perhaps lost all hope of ever getting home again.

But Peadar's practicality had calmed her—only now it was making her angry.

She hissed at him.

"What's so funny about the idea of us being killed?"

He whispered between chuckles.

"Och, lass, you must know."

"No, I don't."

"You cannot jest about it, Vange."

"Jest. I'm perfectly serious."

"Aye?"

"Yes, aye."

"It is nay very likely. That is all."

"Won't they want to get rid of us because they know that we know that they know about what the phone can do?"

Peadar's chuckles became more pronounced.

"Whatsoever did give you that idea, lass?"

"Every movie I ever saw about such things."

"Lass?"

"What."

"What be a movie?"

"Gggrr. It's so aggravating the way you don't know anything."

"Och, I have you to tell me, now, do I not?"

"Ug. It's not important."

They sat silently for a few minutes, and then Vange could

not stop herself from teaching him a bit of what she knew from her time.

"Movies are just ... the way we tell stories in my time."

"Ah. Well now. And it is from these stories that you know what will happen, lass?"

When he put it like that, she knew she sounded silly.

"No, I'm not at all sure anymore, but in the stories, they always kill you off after you tell them what you know."

He chuckled some more.

Vange got quite irritated with him. If her hand had been free, she would have hit his arm with the back of it. She must have tried, because he noticed.

"Be you trying to box my ear now? Here, lass, do it if you dare."

He leaned back so that she could feel his ear with her hand.

She was about to flick his ear, but she gasped.

"Huh."

His body reacted immediately. If he hadn't been tied, he would have been turned around to face whatever threat had made her gasp.

"What? What's coming, lass?"

"No, it's not that. I can touch your ropes, Peadar. Can you lean back more? I might be able to untie you."

෴

PEADAR MADE STRAINING noises while he leaned into Vange's back.

At the same time, she strained against the ropes around her wrists in order to reach those around his.

Even in their excitement at almost being loose, they remembered to whisper.

"What if they come back and see us doing this?"

"Do nay worry about it, you ken? Just take the trouble we have and do not be creating any new."

"What will we do if we manage to get untied?"

"Listen at the door and if it sounds clear, open it."

Vange rolled her eyes.

"I know that much, but if we get out of this house, then what?"

"You keep quiet and follow me."

"What will you—"

"Lass, do not ask me to explain to you all that I learned in my childhood here in the highlands, aye?"

Oh, come on. How much of that could there possibly be? Still, no reason to make him mad.

"Yeah, OK."

It took what seemed like forever, and Vange's fingers were cramping something awful toward the end, but she finally got Peadar's hands untied.

Quicker than she would have believed possible, he had both himself and her entirely free and they stood at the closed door to the house.

They had searched all over for his claymore and their daggers, not finding them. It seemed the brunaidh were familiar with the practice of sheathing a dagger in one's boot.

Vange still had all of her pouches, though. She hadn't checked the contents, but they felt like they weighed the same.

He took her hand in his.

"Do remember to keep quiet and follow me, aye?"

"Yeah."

He squeezed her hand and put his ear to the door.

Wondering if that really worked, Vange put her ear to the door as well.

"I don't hear anything."

"Sh."

He listened at the door for a long time, and then suddenly he pulled it open.

Outside, all they could see was the side of a grassy green hill going up, and parts of a wooden fence that stretched off to the right and left.

Firmly gripping her left hand, he pulled her out the door, to the left, and then quickly backed up so that their backs were against the wall of the house.

She still only saw hill, grass, and fence.

"Where is everyone?"

She remembered to whisper.

But he still shushed her.

"Quiet, lass."

He inched them along the wall until he could peek around the corner.

"Ready?" he asked her quietly.

Vange tucked her skirts up into her belt and took his hand again.

"Yeah."

They ran around the corner, down more of the hill, and into the woods. Hand in hand, they kept running, over hill and dale.

Eerily, Vange heard no sound of pursuit. No dogs barked out news of their departure.

Before half an hour had passed, her adrenaline was spent and she felt winded. Knowing they absolutely had to keep going, she tried. She really did, but it was no use.

"I've ... got a ... stitch in my side ... Peadar. Huh, huh, huh."

Before Vange knew what was happening, he had scooped her up into his arms like a baby again and was running for the both of them.

Was this going to be her life from now on, always running

from some menace and always needing Peadar to carry her
when she couldn't run long enough?

VANGE'S desirous urges returned while Peadar's arms held her
under her thighs and her shoulders. For the first ten minutes,
she was again too tired to enjoy them. After that, she started to
lapse into familiar daydreams about the two of them together.

Her studious mind scoffed at her, saying the daydreams
were silly and frivolous.

But she liked them.

Perhaps because she had mostly seen him in Emily and
Dall's trailer, all of her daydreams about Peadar involved her
routine while working at the renaissance faire in some way.

He would be wearing his kilt, of course, with his claymore
sheathed on his back and his head bare so she could admire
his hair. She would be in her Scottish plaid outfit, too, and
they would match. He would work there, too, and they would
spend all of their days together—

As partners on stage for all the folk dances...

Seated side by side through the clan meeting's mock
trials...

Peadar holding her by the waist and walking by her side in
all the parades...

Sharing their food at meals...

Watching the stage shows together and laughing...

"What brings the smile to your face, lass?"

"Oh, nothing."

"Aw, it cannot be nothing. You can tell me, you ken? I can
keep a secret."

Feeling her face turn red, Vange did her best to change
the subject.

"Are we going back tonight when they're asleep, to get Emily's phone?"

Peadar's running steps faltered a bit.

At first, Vange thought he had tripped on one of the many tree roots that jutted up out of the ground. But then he spoke.

"Lass, God has blessed us once. In His mercy, He allowed us to get away from the brunaidh—"

Vange struggled in his arms.

Out here away from everyone, they had stopped whispering long ago, but now she was outright yelling.

"I have to have that phone."

She was trying desperately to get down so that she could go back.

"Nay, lass. You do not."

"It's the only way I can get home again. Let me down."

"I cannot let you go back, lass."

"What."

In that moment, she was a little afraid of him. Would he try to keep her here in 1560 against her will? Not Peadar, surely.

"Why not?"

Vange was mortified to hear her voice come out sounding like a six-year-old's.

But Peadar sighed and even nuzzled her head a little with his cheek. He made a remarkably long speech while he continued to run with her.

"I did not tell you the truth, lass, about them not killing us once they did know all about the wee phone and how it worked. I did not want the last hours of your life to be lived in pain and fear. However ..."

Now it was Vange's turn to sigh.

At least he wasn't the controlling monster she'd been

briefly afraid of only a moment ago. That was something. She stopped yelling and spoke in a normal voice.

"I get it."

She did. Living here in 1560 was better than dying here.

But she must have gone limp with defeat, because he shook her a little, in addition to the jostling his steps gave her as he navigated the forest at a jog.

"All is not lost, lass."

"I know I know, I have my health. And you are a powerful ally. One day I may be grateful, Peadar, but right now I need some time to grieve for my old life."

Vange was not at all convinced she would live out the day here. It was brutal and primal— and she just wasn't up to it.

"Nay, do not grieve for your old way of life yet."

"I can't help it, Peadar. I mean, I know you can't carry me forever, but I'm really upset."

"The wee phone is not the only way you can return, lass."

Did she dare believe him?

"Don't lie to me again, Peadar."

"'Tis nay a lie, lass."

"I mean it, Peadar. I'll give you this one chance, but if I catch you in another lie, then I won't ever be able to trust you."

"I tell you true, lass, there is another way you can return to your time."

"And do you promise to never lie to me again, even if it means my hysterics might be the last thing you hear on this earth?"

"I give you that promise, lass, aye."

"OK. So what is this other way?"

"The druids made Emily's phone defy time, lass, and the druids do have the magic to defy time without it."

When he said that, he had just crested a hill. He stopped then.

Vange looked down.

He put her down on her feet but still held her close to him—protectively.

The sun was setting down the hill over the ocean. There was a dock, and a few boats were tied to it. A few men wearing red kilts that resembled Peadar and Dall's MacGregor kilts walked near the boats, some with nets full of fish. There were twenty or so small houses down there.

But what had brought a halt to Peadar's run and to their conversation was closer.

A two-story public house sat there on the road near the top of the hill. It was smallish, but flute music and laughter could be heard from within.

And tripping out of the doorway not ten feet from them was a well-to-do-looking older woman who was obviously drunk. She nearly fell, but she caught herself just in time on the door frame, all the while holding her voluminous long brocaded skirts up.

And she was looking at Vange and Peadar with shock in her eyes.

She had heard him.

❧

Vange smiled.

Being friendly couldn't hurt. Maybe the wealthy woman owned one of those boats and could give them a ride to the mainland. It wasn't visible here, but they couldn't have been in their drugged stupor longer than a day, so it had to be reasonably close.

Peadar took the lead.

"Have you anything in those pouches that we might give in trade for a meal, lass? I find that I hunger quite a bit, and my sporran went missing along with my claymore."

Hm, did she?

The mention of food set her mouth to watering and her stomach rumbling, and she dug through her pouches, unsure what she was looking for but convinced she would know it when she found it.

But the wealthy woman took Peadar's bait. She shouted inside authoritatively in Gaelic, and then she addressed Vange and Peadar in English, drunkenly slurring her words.

"Do come in and sup. The stew does smell good this day, and I do fancy a bit of talk with the likes of you."

"Thank you so much." Vange said, rushing to take the woman up on her offer.

But Peadar held her back.

"Tell him to include a room for us," Peadar told the woman, and then he added a bunch more in Gaelic.

Vange smiled at him. He was smarter than he looked. Now the woman had to realize he could understand what she said and would know if she lied to him about what was going on.

But Vange saw she needn't have worried.

The woman was drunk, and enthusiastic. Throwing up her arms and making a 'whoopee' sort of gesture as if she had won the lottery, she made the arrangements.

On hearing affirmative noises inside, Peadar lead Vange in through the door.

There were only four tables, and three were occupied by red-kilted fishermen and their wives, who stopped eating their stew to stare at the newcomers.

The wooden-flute player didn't miss a beat. He kept playing a merry tune.

After a few seconds, the patrons went back to their eating and talking, and after a minute they were laughing again.

The wealthy woman's party had been seated at the fourth table, but they rose when she entered. They were all men, three of them, also kilted in those confusingly familiar red kilts. They were dressed more nicely than the fishermen, but not in brocade like the wealthy woman.

Vange figured they were the woman's guards, who had probably been instructed by her son to make sure she didn't drink too much. Ha.

Serving girls were making a somewhat big production of carrying bowls of stew up the stairs.

The wealthy woman shooed Vange and Peadar up there, too.

"A good thought it was, getting a room. We shall have a talk where none can hear."

Her guards made as if to come along.

She held up her hand to stop them, saying something in Gaelic that probably meant, "No no, you stay and enjoy your ale. I'll only be gone a little while."

There were three bedrooms upstairs. A bunch of children poked their heads out of one.

The stew was set out on three tiny tables in the middle room.

"Come in, come in."

The wealthy woman gestured for them to sit with her on the one bed.

They did, and then the serving girls brought the little tables up close to them, and left.

There wasn't much else in the room besides a washstand and a nice covered chamber pot with an open curtain around it.

Vange took a long drink from the ale set before her—and immediately burped.

The woman burst into a belly laugh.

"Ha ha ha. I did have no idea you English could be earthy."

The woman took a long drink out of her own ale and also burped.

"Eeeerrrp."

Vange and Peadar smiled at her, but for the next little while they were too busy eating and drinking and pouring themselves more ale to do much else.

"Lad and lass, you have been near starved, I do see."

"Mmmhm."

"I be Saraid MacLean, aunt to the clan chief. And who might you be? Mind, lad, I ken you be not English, notwithstanding your trews."

Peadar gently squeezed Vange's elbow then.

She nodded to him and kept quiet.

"I be Peadar MacGregor, son of Dall MacGregor—"

"Ooh. A MacGregor. Well. That be a fine turn of events, indeed."

She feinted at him then, with her eating knife.

But she was drunk.

Apparently Peadar—despite having nothing to drink but ale for the past 24 hours—was sober, because so fast that Vange almost didn't see what happened, Peadar dropped his own eating knife, grabbed Saraid's wrist with one hand, and had her eating knife in his other hand.

Vange steadied their tables so that the ale wouldn't spill.

"Oh ho ho."

Saraid's laughter and obvious lack of malice must have made Peadar let go.

"You are a MacGregor."

"Aye, why did you doubt me?"

"I had to know if you had the reflexes and the experience. Good, good."

She reached out for her eating knife.

Peadar handed it to her, handle first.

"And your traveling companion, is she—"

With a fierce look on his face, Peadar cut Saraid off.

"She is the woman I will marry..."

What.

&.

VANGE DUG her fingers into Peadar's elbow. It wasn't like she didn't want to marry him, but she wanted a say in the matter.

Saraid was drinking this up almost as if it were ale.

"Ooh. And she be such an exotic woman. My money is on the tale of your meeting being a good one."

Peadar appeared reluctant to share their business.

"The story be overly long, Saraid."

The woman settled back against the wall.

"We do have the room for the entire night."

Peadar took in a deep breath.

"When I was ten and three, Caileen Liath Campbell indentured me to an Englishman keen to settle in the new world—"

"The new world. How exciting."

"Aye, it does sound so, but my days were spent herding cattle, much the same as home—"

But Saraid had turned her attention back to Vange.

"She is one of the new world natives, then, what are being called Indians?"

Vange ground her teeth and bit her tongue several times.

Peadar put his arm around her shoulders.

She wanted to push him aside and run out the door and down the stairs and outside... but where would she go? Besides, his touch calmed her, made her feel a little at home, even. It was nice.

And she reminded herself that Peadar didn't have to protect her. He could have just left her behind numerous times, but he had carried her and helped her and ... cared for her.

"Nay," he told Saraid. "She and my father and my father's wife came from another time to save me from my indenture..." He told the story Vange didn't remember, about what she had done the last time she had been in 1560: rescued him from his time as a 'cow boy'. And at the end of that story, Peadar said, "And she has my undying gratitude for that."

For a moment while Peadar told the tale, Saraid's gaze had been lucid and her eyes had been cunning.

Vange had felt Peadar's grip tighten around her shoulders.

But after he finished, Saraid spoke again, slurring her words as before.

"And how do you come to be here, on Mull?"

"Aye, it is much to fathom. We were on our way about Glen Strae when we were set upon and taken here by ship, you ken. We just got away from our captors not three hours past."

There, thought Vange.

That was a story worthy of a meal and a night's rest. Now leave us to it, Saraid. I could sleep a week, but a night will do.

What Saraid said and did next must have surprised Peadar as much as it had Vange, because he spat out a mouthful of ale.

"Well." Saraid said cheerfully, "tis a good turn I am here, then—to keep you honest till you do marry, and to see to it you can."

Saraid nodded then, and went to the door. She hollered something in Gaelic down the stairs, and her three guards came bounding up.

Vange and Peadar sat side by side on the bed hissing at each other all through the hubbub that followed—the tables and dishes being removed, a cot being brought into the room...

"Why did you have to tell her we were getting married."

"Lass, I would not have you hear her to say what she was going to say about you."

"What could be so bad."

"She was going to ask if you were a whore, lass."

"So what?"

"We cannot have people thinking that of you."

"We can if I'm back home in my own time and not here."

"But we are not."

And then one of Saraid's guards held out his hand to help Peadar up.

"Come with me to the other room, lad."

Peadar looked at Vange with near panic in his eyes.

Saraid laughed.

"I will stay with the lass."

He didn't budge.

Saraid urged her guard to bend down and grab Peadar's hand, forcing him up.

"She will be in good company."

Peadar looked from one to the next of the three highlanders in the room, with that battle look in his eyes.

Saraid stepped back and got out of their way.

Vange was afraid for him. The three looked every bit as battle worthy as Peadar, and perhaps even more so.

"There's no need for you to worry."

On hearing this from her, Peadar at last left the room peacefully with the three guards.

Vange slept on the cot, and Saraid got the bed. That was fine. Sleep was going to come very fast, with no time even to notice comfort, she somehow knew.

Vange took off her belt with all of its dangling pouches, but she kept it with her under the covers. She left her boots on, never knowing when she might have to run.

She was loosening her English bodice to make it more

comfortable to sleep in when she felt something poke her. Cursing the invention of boning, she took the bodice off, still under the covers. When she used her hands to examine the bodice a little closer, she felt a folded piece of paper that had been slipped into a new hole in the lining.

Being careful not to tear it, she eased the paper out of the hole. It was crisp and new. Overwhelmingly curious to know what it was, she painstakingly unfolded it under the blanket and then cautiously exposed the top of it to the dim moonlight that was coming in through the window.

It was the print-out of an email.

It was too dark for her to read it, but it was distinctly signed by Emily.

Vange folded the paper back up, stuffed it down into her boot, and then fell fast asleep.

᠅

"RISE AND SHINE, Evangeline. It's your wedding day."

"Huh?"

"You can wear your belt with all you have on it, but I have nice highlands clothing for you. More suitable for the wife of a highlander, aye."

Vange poked her head out from under the covers.

Saraid had laid out on the bed a beautiful women's set of red MacLean plaid clothes: two skirts whose plaid were opposites, a bodice in same plaid as the outskirt, and a lovely embroidered shift with wide sleeves. The plaid was homespun wool, and the shift was homespun linen.

"I can't take this from you, Saraid. It's too much of a gift."

"Aw, quit your fussing and get dressed, lass. The men have been ready for an hour now. I have let you sleep as long as I dared."

When Vange still hesitated, Saraid laughed.

"Och. I shall wait out in the hallway, then. But I shall open the door on the count of three hundred, so do not dawdle."

Sure enough, she went out into the hallway, and Vange could hear her slowly counting.

"One, two, three..."

Figuring she had about five minutes and desperately wanting to be clean all of a sudden, Vange tore off everything except her boots and gave herself a sponge bath at the wash-stand. She used the cleanest bits of her English clothing to dry off, and then she hurriedly put on the Scottish outfit.

She had barely laced up the bodice and was reaching for her belt when the door opened.

"Oh, good good. You will do nicely, aye."

Saraid waited while Vange put on the belt, and then she came right up to Vange.

"What are you doing, Saraid?"

"Your hair, lass. Tis a fine head you have, but tis a ratty mess."

Vange was horrified not to have her usual shampoo and conditioner, but Saraid had come prepared with a pouch full of toiletries from this time period. They smelled wonderful, like lilac.

Very deftly, Saraid washed, combed, and braided Vange's hair.

"Come on down, now. They have waited the breakfast on you."

Vange moved to bundle up the English renaissance faire costume she had spent every bit of her savings on not even three months before.

"Oh, leave it here, my dear. Carrying a bundle would ruin the lovely picture you do make in your new clothes."

Telling herself she was being silly for worrying about them, Vange left her own clothes there and went on down to breakfast. She was immensely glad that she'd found Emily's email and rescued it. Something told her she wouldn't be seeing those clothes again.

The dining room was packed with people dressed in various forms of red MacLean plaid, and they all cheered when Vange came down the stairs.

Harking back to her drama days, she gave them a bow.

They cheered all the more.

She looked all over the dining room for Peadar, but her heart sank a little when she didn't see him.

"Tsk tsk, my dear. You will not see him until we reach the kirk, but do not fash. We will go there after we break our fast."

In a daze, Vange drank hot tea and ate eggs and toast and strawberry shortcake with the people of this fishing village. Instead of topping the berries with whipped cream, they poured liquid cream into the bowl, which soaked into the cake. It was delicious.

And then Saraid was pulling her up onto her feet.

"Thank you all so much," Vange told the room at large. "It was a lovely breakfast."

They must have been the happiest people on Planet Earth, because they clapped and cheered at her tiny speech as if she were a TV celebrity or something.

And then they all followed her—not only out of the public house, but all the way up a larger hill to the kirk—ringing bells and singing.

The kirk was a tiny stone building without any windows. It wasn't big enough for half of the crowd that had bustled up the hill. The guards were at the door, and they only let in Vange and Saraid.

Vange could feel the big smile she had on her face as she stood there blind for a moment and allowed her eyes to adjust to the dim candlelight.

Once they did, she gasped.

Peadar stood there in the front of the kirk at the altar, glorious once more in a kilt. His huge smile matched the one she'd worn from all the singing and bell-ringing. He stood extra proud, and she noticed a claymore was strapped to his back once again.

"Welcome, my dear," said an old priest in robes. "Come on up here, child."

There wasn't any music playing, and Vange giggled when she caught herself humming the 'da dun da dun' of the wedding march. She was sure that music hadn't even been written yet.

Peadar took both of her hands when she got to the altar.

And that made this real.

This was her life, not some fairytale.

Vange looked up into Peadar's eyes, searching them for... She would know it when she found it. She was on the brink of thinking she had when the priest started their vows.

Peadar said his 'I do' first.

Just after he did, his eyes got really big and he was smiling even wider than he had been before. He looked positively ecstatic to be marrying her.

This was flattering, but a little disturbing.

And then it was her turn.

She was about to promise to love-honor-and-obey someone she'd only known two weeks. And in this day and age, they really meant the 'obey' part. She shouldn't have gotten herself into this situation. She should refuse to say the vows. What could they do?

Peadar would protect her anyway, she was sure of it. He was a good man. There was no reason—

But he looked so happy to be marrying her.

Was it because he loved her? Did he daydream about her,

too? Darn. She should have asked him. But how could she have even brought that up?

And it was now or never.

A deep seated instinct told Vange that if she left the man at the altar—even just to say 'not yet'—then his heart would be wounded and she would never be as close to him as she might have been.

Ulp.

IT WAS a heady moment for Vange. Knowing this would change everything in her life and looking up into Peadar's wildly happy eyes, she said the words.

"I do."

Wow.

Now she knew why Peadar's eyes had popped open.

She remembered now, all of it.

As soon as Vange said "I do" and joined her life with Peadar's, all her memories of having time traveled came flooding back to her.

They had known each other for two months rather than two weeks, and it felt more like two years, with all they had been through together.

Vange knew that the two of them were staring at one another in that same way she had found so annoying whenever Emily and Dall were together, but she didn't care. The people around them should all just go away and leave the two of them alone now anyway.

The priest put a hand on each of their shoulders.

OK, maybe not in a church.

"I now pronounce you man and wife. You may kiss the bride."

And then Peadar put his arms around her, and they were kissing. And she knew the physical part of her marriage would be … glorious. She couldn't wait to get back to their room and start it.

Peadar seemed to be thinking similar thoughts, because he all but bounded out of the kirk with her.

But the crowd was still there, waiting outside the kirk for them, and when they emerged, the crowd cheered and rang their bells some more.

The village musician was there with his flute, and the impatient couple were made to dance folk dances with the villagers while they clapped and sang and rang their bells.

Someone brought out a case of wine, and the impatient couple were made to wait while everyone's flagon was filled and then while several of the village elders proposed toasts to the newlyweds.

All the children of the village presented Vange with gifts of the flowers they had picked while she'd been inside the kirk. She politely sat for them while they wove the flowers into her braided hair.

Peadar was off with the men, getting many pats on the back.

Finally, the two of them were allowed to stand next to each other while all the other married couples gave them advice, which Vange was glad she couldn't understand.

Vange turned her puzzled face to her new husband.

"Do Scots always do this at the weddings of strangers?"

"Nay, lass," Peadar said. "'Tis as if we were family to them. 'Tis passing strange."

Shrugging, Peadar turned with his arm around her waist to walk down the larger hill to the inn.

Vange noticed Saraid falling in right behind them. And the crowd followed again, bells ringing and voices singing.

It was nothing like the wedding Vange had been planning for herself in the back of her mind since she had attended her first wedding when she was five, but it was wonderful, none the less.

W<small>HEN THEY GOT</small> to the inn, Saraid spoke up.

"Come down to the dock. I have a ship waiting for you."

Vange looked at Peadar to see if this was a surprise to him, too.

It was.

Her new husband looked disappointed at first too, which made her smile at him. He smiled back, and then he squeezed her waist and rubbed her back a bit through her bodice.

"We thank you, Saraid—for the ship, the wedding, the room, and the meals. If—"

"Do not mention it. Now come, I say. Verily, the ship has been waiting."

Vange cast one longing glance up toward their room—and not only because her costume appeared destined to remain there without her—and then she, Peadar, and Saraid led the ringing and singing parade down onto the dock.

The ship was about fifty feet long, and by the way all the villagers admired it, Vange gathered it was big for this time period. Unlike the little men's boat, this ship had those cool forward-facing sails, which were all up and flapping in the ample wind. Several port holes lined its side, which told her the ship had several rooms below deck.

The captain stepped out onto the dock to meet them.

Saraid whispered so that only Vange and Peadar could hear her.

"Do play along, or it will go ill for you. I give you a good life. Best you enjoy it."

Neither Vange nor Peadar had the chance to respond before Saraid went on from behind them in a much louder voice that at least the whole dock and perhaps the whole village could hear.

She spoke in Gaelic, but Peadar translated it for Vange.

"Captain. As the promised gallowglass in the service of Shane O'Neil, I send with you my grandson, Peadar MacLean —along with the wife he wedded this day."

The villagers all rang their bells and gave a hooting cheer which shook Vange's bones with its familiarity.

Peadar's grip on her tightened. "Sae sorry, lass."

"Let's just make a run for it."

Vange turned to jump off the dock into the water and swim away from all this. The waves here were small compared to when her parents had taken her and Emily on vacation in Hawaii one year and they'd all learned to body surf. She and Peadar could swim around the island to the side that faced the mainland and hitch a ride from there, maybe even swim across.

She almost made it, too, except that Peadar had a hold of her waist.

She teetered on the edge of the dock over the water for a moment, and then he pulled her back up so that she was standing beside him again.

All the villagers were gasping, wide eyed.

And Peadar laughed.

It was a nervous laugh, the kind of laugh that said you were embarrassed by something. Or someone.

Vange was back to being afraid she was in this all alone, that her marriage to Peadar was a sham and that he didn't really care for her. Although what his motive was, not even her fear could imagine.

And then he spoke to the captain in English, and there was no reason for him to do that unless he wanted Vange to understand, so she listened.

"I pray you, forgive my wife, Captain. Of course the lass is nay a witch who can swim. I would never marry such a person, I assure you. Howsoever, my wife does have a deathly fear of leaving the mainland. She has never been to Ireland, but I trust that we will be happy there."

Only witches could swim?

Really?

From the safety of Peadar's embrace, Vange looked at all the villagers. It seemed to be true. They shrank from the sides of the dock as if they were … deathly afraid of drowning should they fall in.

But right now, everyone seemed to be holding their breath, waiting to hear the captain's verdict.

"I forgive her," he said.

Everyone let their breath out at the same time, audibly.

The captain went on.

"And I shall do my best to make your wedding voyage a happy one. Now, come aboard."

As they walked up the gangplank, Vange whispered to Peadar.

"What's a gallowglass? And who is Shane O'Neill?"

14. VANGE & PEADAR 2

"Later, lass, I shall explain the new duties I have been assigned in Ireland," Peadar whispered.

And then, arm in arm, the two of them followed the captain down the deck and into a door. They had to go single file down a narrow wooden staircase, and then the captain stopped in front of another door below decks.

"Now, Lady MacLean," said the kilted captain matter-of-factly in English, "I did promise to do my best to make your wedding voyage a happy one, and I shall keep my word. He looked at Vange then as if she were made of glass and might shatter any second.

That was when Vange realized he meant her when he said 'Lady MacLean'. Of all the luck. It was hard enough pretending to be from this backward time period where husbands spoke for their wives and being able to swim made you a witch. She was just beginning to feel like she could handle that much. And now she had to pretend to know the first thing about being an honest-to-goodness lady?

But the captain expected a response from her.

Unsure if she should be speaking to him, she started to look up at Peadar's face for his reaction.

But using the arm he'd almost always had around her today, their wedding day, her new husband patted her back.

Hm. She knew what that pat meant somehow. This was weird and kind of cool.

He meant she should respond, but not really say anything.

She felt a slight smile forming on her face when she did respond to the captain, because it amused her that without so much as talking about it, she and Peadar had worked out this communication system of pats and waist squeezes.

"Uh, thank you?"

"Howsoever," the captain's smile was condescending as he paused.

He couldn't condescend to a lady, could he? Surely not with her lord right there to hear it?

But before Vange even tilted her head to look at him, Peadar squeezed her waist.

So she was not to comment on the captain's tone. OK.

"Please do give us your howsoever, and we shall endeavor to meet with your approval," said Peadar in a polished English she'd had no idea he possessed. It matched the captain's, which was quite good.

Trying something new, Vange patted Peadar on the back.

Her husband chuckled, but only in his throat, at so low a volume that Vange felt sure only she could hear him.

"Very well," said the captain. "Howsoever, I do know your wife be foreign, and I can tolerate a foreigner's foibles, yet there be something ... not quite right about her. See that it does nay show aboard this ship."

"Aye, Captain."

"This be your cabin here. Your trunk has already been installed within. We shall sup at sunset in my quarters, next door down. Until then, I bid you good day."

The captain said that last with a slight leer, but he

covered it up well and once again had on a professional face
as he climbed up the narrow stairs.

"Well enough," Peadar called up to the captain.

And then he whispered so only Vange could hear, lest part
of their secret be discovered, "Mrs. MacGregor."

And on that note, he simultaneously pushed the door open
and swept her off her feet so that he could carry her inside,
where the two of them spent an extremely pleasant afternoon.

🕭

PEADAR HAD TAKEN Vange's braid out, and he was combing
through her hair with his fingers as they cuddled in the tiny
bed of their honeymoon cabin, both fully relaxed.

"Aw, I am nay so bad a lover as that, am I?"

"What do you mean?"

The sea lashed up just as Vange tried to roll onto her back
so she could see his face, throwing her into him.

He laughed and cuddled her close.

"Heh ha ha. This be more to my liking."

Vange tried to tickle him, but it didn't work. Drat. He had
to have some weakness she could tease him about.

"More to your liking than the past four hours? I find that
hard to believe."

She finally succeeded at looking into his face.

He smiled at her.

"Nay, naught could be so satisfying as that, lass. Howsoever, you were laughing a few moments gone by."

"Oh."

Vange hugged Peadar tight. It was wonderful to be here
alone with him. For a few hours, she'd been able to forget the
panic that had started to seep into her the moment that thief
had grabbed Emily's phone.

Now that panic was coming back.

She put on a funny face and forced a giggle for his benefit. No sense in being weepy. She might lose him, and his was the only real company she had.

"Hehehe. I was laughing because this cabin is about the size of my bathroom."

"Ha ha. If yours is anything like the one Da and Emily have, then aye, tis true."

They lay there caressing each other, looking up at the shelves built into the one straight wall and at the curved wooden hull with its one porthole near the top, fitted with a metal cover.

Vaguely, Vange remembered the captain yelling at them to close that during one particularly rough point in the voyage. She also dimly remembered Peadar pulling the bed down over the trunk that had been the only thing inside the cabin when they had arrived.

Knock knock knock.

There came a loud banging on their door, followed by the captain's voice.

"On with your supper clothes, loveys, and meet me in my quarters."

Softly so that only her husband could hear, Vange joked about this.

"Do we have to?"

But of course he was unfamiliar with that joke. He put on a grave face.

"Aye, lass. The captain has great powers out here at sea. Do not anger him."

"I won't."

"Oh, but 'tis very likely you will, lass."

He sighed, finished combing her hair, got them up of the bed, and folded it up and away.

"Now my love, you are a married woman who can wear the am breid on your head."

From the trunk, he took out a perfectly triangular piece of finely handwoven white linen, embroidered around the edges in vines and flowers, a gorgeous garment.

"Breid?"

"In English, they say kertch."

"I like breid better."

He smiled at her.

Vange took it and stood there not knowing what to do.

He partly closed the metal door over the porthole so that she could see her reflection in the shiny metal.

Vange stared at herself there in his arms.

It was like staring at another woman from a different age, and her mate.

They were dressed in fresh matching embroidered leine shirts. He wore a fine plaid kilt made of many colors and she had a fine skirt of the same cloth plus an overdress that worked as both bodice and outer skirt.

And then Peadar spoke to Vange, and the reflection solidified in Vange's mind as yes indeed herself and her new husband.

"The breid is the highland islands version of your wedding ring. It says you be married, and fully an adult person who does have a say at clan meetings, and who can go to court on her own behalf. Wear it proudly, Vange."

As he spoke, he tied the breid around her head like a scarf, twisting the long ends at the top of her head and then tucking them under the twist so that three points stuck out in back. He touched them one after another and then crossed himself.

Peadar was being so thoughtful.

She knew she was favored not to be stuck here with some lunk who treated her poorly.

The captain's leers came to mind.

She shook them off.

No sense in dwelling on unpleasant things.

Even so, Vange looked up into Peadar's eyes to see if that would calm the mounting panic she felt.

She had already changed cultures once, when her parents moved to America with her from the Phillippeans when she was 9. Emily's fast friendship had helped a lot, but that move had been the hardest thing Vange had ever done.

But moving to 1560 permanently?

This made moving to America look easy.

But Peadar's look was kind. Loving. Compassionate.

"I will wear it proudly," she said to him with a simple smile.

If he noticed how she trembled in his embrace, he didn't mention it.

As Vange strapped her belt on in preparation to go to the captain's cabin for supper, she felt Emily's email printout poke her through one of the many pouches which dangled from it.

"Oh. I found this in my old bodice last night, Peadar. It's a letter from Emily."

"Och, we scarcely have the time--"

"When will we ever?"

"Very well, but read it fast, you ken?"

"Huh?"

"We cannot keep the captain waiting."

Vange resisted the urge to roll her eyes.

Just barely.

This email was so much more important than what some stranger thought.

With trembling fingers, she untied the drawstring, opened the pouch, and took out the crumpled paper, thanking Heaven that she'd found it before she'd had to ditch her English clothes.

Peadar read it over her shoulder.

----To: Felix and Ana Andrade

----From: Emily MacGregor

I don't quite know how to tell you this, so I'll just come right out and say it: Vange has traveled to Scotland, and she is stuck there. We may have a chance to get a message to her and help her come home if you print out this email and put it in her English renaissance faire costume.

I can't tell you how this will help.

I am sworn to secrecy.

Besides, you can't interfere.

Our chance to communicate with her may be lost if you interfere.

So please print this out as soon as you read it and stow it in her costume. Then call her phone because I have it, and tell me it's done, OK?

Vange,

I love you almost as much as I love Dall and my parents and Dall's children. Please keep yourself safe.

I live under a shadow now, as you are most likely aware. Most of the time, I myself am unaware of it, through means I dare not mention.

But even when I wake up in the middle of the night fully conscious of what I'm missing, such as now, I cannot say or do much that goes unnoticed, and I cannot discuss the cause of it with anyone.

So I hope you get the meaning of what I'm about to write. By necessity, it's vague.

Vange, they have my phone.

It's bugged, so they've known where it was all along.

They've recovered it, and you won't get it.

But don't panic.

Even without a phone, they have the ability to get you home. Go to them. You can find one of their healers in any castle in Scotland, at least in the highlands. Maybe in the lowlands as well.

Until you can get to a castle, stay with Peigi. She can still get into her grandmother's old house, and Dall and I hid many useful things in trunks up in that attic.

I'm sure Peigi has told you this by now, but I want to re-enforce it:

Peadar had best not tell anyone he's a MacGregor. In a few years, things will get really nasty for anyone who claims the MacGregor name.

And whatever you do Vange, don't go to Ireland. Everyone who might have helped you come home has been driven out of there.

EIGHT HOURS into their voyage to Ireland, Vange and Peadar knocked on the door to the captain's cabin.

Knock knock knock.

"Do come in and seat yourselves. There be wine on the table. Will you pour for us, Evangeline?"

Feeling a pat on her back, Vange obliged.

Instead of wine glasses, the captain had small pottery cups without handles, and they fit into holes in the table. It was a good thing too, because the ship kept bobbing on the waves.

As she poured, Vange snuck glances at the fourth person at the table.

She figured he must be Irish. He wore a leine shirt similar to hers and Peadar's and the captain's, but unlike the other two men, he didn't wear a kilt over it. He still had plenty of clothing on by modern standards, but to someone used to seeing men in kilts, the 1560 Irishman looked like he was in his underwear.

Once everyone had their wine, Vange sat down next to Peadar with hers and tried to understand what the three men said to each other in Gaelic.

She wasn't very successful.

She caught a word here and there, but that was all.

All four of them ate a good meal of stew and bannocks, on metal plates with metal spoons. Vange was asked to dish their food onto the plates from the serving dishes the cook brought in, and she did so graciously, for her.

After the meal, the men continued to talk.

The Irishman kept looking at Vange with curiosity.

She felt her anger rising up at his stares. Most of the crew on this ship were Polynesian, so surely he had seen a woman like her before. There was no need to stare.

But then she realized that the three men looked very similar in appearance to her, the two Scots and the Irishman. Perhaps she was the first Polynesian wife anyone they knew had taken?

Seeing Peadar so raptly involved in conversation with them and seeming to get along with them, Vange decided to give the Irishman the benefit of the doubt. For now.

Several hours later, Peadar helped Vange to her feet, said their goodbyes until the morning, and escorted her back to their own cabin.

They were busy awhile, and then as they lay in each other's arms with the boat rocking them to sleep, they got to talking.

"So who was that Irish man?"

"One of Shane O'Neil's top men, come to inspect me, lass."

"Oh. Well, he seemed to approve of you."

"Aye, thus far."

"Thus far?"

"Aye, on the morrow they'll have a sword trial."

Vange clung to him tightly.

"Could you die?"

"Heh ha ha. Nay."

"Really?"

"Aye ... well ..."

"Well, what?"

"Well, I could always die, you ken?"

"But probably not tomorrow?"

"Aye, we will be using practice swords, lass."

"And those are ... what?"

"Wooden swords with nay edges nor points."

"Yeah, there's no point, alright."

Peadar rewarded her with a rich deep laugh that shook both of them in the bed every few minutes until they were both fast asleep.

As she drifted off, Vange kept thinking *yay. I finally cracked a joke that Peadar got.*

VANGE WOKE UP ALONE. For a brief moment, she had no idea where she was. When it hit her, the panic that she'd barely been keeping at bay set in full force.

Where had Peadar gone?

Was he fighting right now?

Could she stop it?

Was she too late?

The more questions she asked herself, the more she shook with worry.

An odd thing also happened, though. She got curious to know the answers.

Vange grabbed her plaids from the night before off the shelf where they'd been shoved in a fit of passion, washed her face with part of her sleeve and the water from the wash-stand, fixed her breid hat the best she could in the reflection of the metal porthole cover, pulled on her handmade boots made of purple and orange leather, used the chamber pot in the corner of the tiny cabin, and...

She found the cabin door had been locked from the outside.

"No no no no no. I am not some shrinking violet you men can lock away in a closet." she screamed, not at all sure anyone could hear her.

And then the metal porthole cover caught her eye.

No, I'm small enough to crawl out through a porthole.

Vange got up on the bed, opened the porthole cover, and was halfway through when she realized her skirts weren't going to fit.

"No problem at all, guys." she called out to no one in particular. "I'd rather wear pants anyway."

Vange tore off first her outskirt and then her inner skirt and threw the fold-down bed back up so she could rummage through the trunk.

"There has to be a pair of pants in here somewhere."

She tore through the contents, not even mildly impressed with all the finery she found neatly folded inside.

"Aha. I knew there would be a pair of pants."

She shimmied into the one pair of pants she found.

They would probably have been knee-length on Peadar. On her they were mid-calf. They probably would have fit Peadar's waist exactly. On her they were so loose that she had to take all the pouches off her belt and use it to keep the pants from sagging down to her knees.

These leine sleeves are a problem, too. They're big enough to carry all the clothes from the trunk. Not the kind of thing a gymnast wears.

Vange's experience as a gymnast had been in the first, second, and third grades back home in the Phillippeans. Hardly professional level, but it did give her confidence. Perhaps too much.

Heck with these sleeves. There are plenty more shirts in the trunk. I'll just cut the sleeves right off this one.

And that's just what she did, only her dagger had been stolen by the little people, so she had to tear the sleeves off.

Riiiiiiiiiiip. Riiiiiiiiiiip.

That had been fun.

What else could she cut? What would make the men quit staring at her inappropriately?

"Ug. And this hair is next."

Vange looked around for something to hack her hair off with, but not finding anything, she re-tied her breid scarf so that all her hair was trapped inside it.

Only pausing briefly to look at her reflection for a change, Vange threw open the porthole cover and climbed out.

THE EARLY MORNING sun was in Vange's eyes, and the ship was heading straight into the waves, bouncing over each one, but that didn't deter her.

She was angry.

They would lock her up in a cabin, would they?

Men.

They were all alike when you got right down to it: inconsiderate pigs.

From her perch on the porthole, she could reach the lip of the ship's deck. She turned so she was facing the side of the ship, grabbed the deck, and climbed up onto it.

She was up top.

From here, she could see that the ship was in the middle

of the sea, with land visible in the distance in most directions, but a little closer in front. That must be Ireland.

She also saw several of the ship's crew members messing with the ropes attached to the sails. Yep, most of them were Polynesian, like her. And they all wore mid-calf trousers much like the ones she had on.

She also saw Peadar fighting with the Irishman, all over the deck. Sure enough, they were both using wooden swords. Making quite a lot of noise with them, too...

But.

Oh.

Wow.

Their fight was good.

Way better than watching a martial arts movie.

Vange hadn't really paid much attention to the sword demonstrations at the renaissance faire. Those had seemed ... fake and irrelevant to her. But this?

This was art. Poetry in motion. OK, that was trite, but wow, it was true.

Peadar and the Irishman moved so fast she could barely keep up, but every time one of them attacked, the other counter-attacked, and this happened in such fluid motion that it looked like a choreographed dance.

Vange didn't know how long she'd been sitting there on the deck gawping at the sword fight when she heard a male voice five or so years younger than hers speaking next to her in the 1560 version of some Polynesian language.

"You'd better get to work before they see you slacking."

"I don't know how to do any of the work," Vange answered in Tagalog.

"I can show you."

"Oh, good."

"I'm Toj."

"Hi. I'm Mika."

She wasn't lying, per se. Mika was the nickname all her relatives had used for her when she was little.

Vange was still watching the sword fight out of the corner of her eye. She was reassured that it was indeed just a test and not to the death, because every once in a while the two men would stop to mop the sweat off their brows and drink lots of ale, which Vange hoped had a weak alcohol content.

Meanwhile, Toj showed Vange how to trim the sails—and he talked her ear off.

"Don't you hate this Irish food? Oatmeal, bleck."

"Last night's dinner was good."

"Are you joking?"

"I like to joke, but no, I'm not right now."

"That soup was so thin the sea water would have been more filling."

Oh. The crew didn't eat the same food as the captain and his fine guests. She'd had no idea. Best to change the subject.

"How long have you been on this ship?"

"We just took on in London, me and my dad and my brothers."

"London? I thought this ship was going to Ireland?"

"It is, but many ships go back and forth from London to there."

"Really?"

"Yeah."

"Huh. That's interesting."

"It is?"

"Yeah. I thought Ireland had more in common with Scotland."

"Well, yeah, but England is taking over Ireland."

"Oh?"

"Yeah. They already have a large piece of it that they call The Pale."

"Is that where this ship is headed?"

"Oh no. The Scots always land around the backside of Ireland, beyond The Pale, where their Irish brothers seek their aid in keeping the English at bay. That's why they've recruited this one."

Toj nodded toward Peadar.

"So he'll be fighting the English?"

"Yep."

"Have you seen much sword fighting?"

"Yeah, almost all of them practice on the deck like this. Why?"

"Does this one look up to the task?"

Toj watched Peadar for a few minutes while he and Vange worked.

"Hm. This one is odd. He doesn't fight the same way as the rest of them."

"In a bad way?"

"No no, in a good way."

Vange and Toj both watched while Peadar kept the Irish man running after him, never quite letting him get a hit in. Every once in a while though, Peadar would stop unexpectedly. The Irish man would all but run into his practice sword. If it had been a real sword...

The kilted man and the skirted man came near Vange and Toj then.

And Peadar looked up.

Her husband's eyes got huge when he saw her.

Huge with terror.

"I'VE GOT TO GO," Vange told Toj.

"Where could you need to go? We all need to share the work."

But as soon as she'd seen Peadar's reaction to her outfit,

Vange had understood what Peadar was so horrified about. She was supposed to be a lady, and look at her. She could not let the captain see her like this—and nor could she allow the captain to open their cabin door and find her missing.

"Maybe I'll see you again, Toj, but probably not."

She was running for the edge of the ship where her port-hole was.

It probably looked like she meant to dive into the sea.

Poor Toj.

"Wait."

Before he could get to her, Vange slipped over the side and in through the porthole, then slammed it shut and secured it with its bar.

Before anyone else saw her in the Mika get-up, she had all those clothes off and was frantically putting on first an intact leine shirt and then an underskirt and overdress.

She was lacing her boots when she heard a key in the lock and glanced up at her reflection in the porthole cover.

Her hair was still entirely tucked up into her breid scarf, but from what she'd heard at the faire workshops, that was more proper, rather than less.

Peadar's worried voice came through the cabin wall.

And then the captain's assertive one.

"Come on in." Vange called out. "I'm dressed."

"See?" the captain said in that old-fashioned English they spoke, "your wife is much more accommodating than you were led to believe. I daresay if she had a kitchen, she might even serve us tea."

Vange gritted her teeth. Yeah, she might, but she would probably spit in the captain's when he wasn't looking, male chauvinist pig that he was.

And then the door was open and the two kilted men were looking her over—the captain as if she were meat for sale in the market, and Peadar as if he would find her looking like what she was: a Polynesian woman, rather than some Scottish lady.

But now Peadar wasn't her only friend in this backward world. She could go join the other Polynesians. She could ...

But who was she kidding?

Emily's email had been clear: the only known way for Vange to get home to her own time period was to get back to the Scottish highlands somehow and find a druid who would send her home. From conversations she'd had with Emily, Vange knew that the "They" in Emily's email were the druids.

No, Peadar wasn't her only friend, but he was her best bet at getting home.

She smiled at her husband and then addressed the captain.

"Tea would be nice, but breakfast sounds even better."

"Aye, and so we shall have some."

The captain gestured for her to follow.

But Peadar came and offered her his arm.

She took it, but less happily than she would have before their wedding. Was this how marriage was for everyone?

Company aside, it was hard to enjoy the omelets, scones, jam, tea, and fresh apples knowing that the Polynesian crew were having oatmeal and not liking it.

And then there was the problem of the fork tines being excessively long and handmade, meaning sharp.

Vange ate mostly with her tablespoon.

No one mentioned her error, but she didn't kid herself into thinking they hadn't noticed.

Oh well.

They already thought she was a savage who needed to be locked up in a cabin, so...

"The eggs are lovely. Do you keep chickens on board?"

The captain seemed flattered.

"Aye, we keep four. Just enough for three guests and myself."

"Of course." Vange smiled at him sweetly and then turned to the Irish man. "And how did Peadar do at your trial by sword this morning?"

Vange felt a gentle squeeze at her waist from where Peadar sat next to her. Yeah. Well, trusting him had gotten her locked into a cabin, so...

"He will do, that he will. I am Tam, by the by, and it is pleased I am to make your acquaintance, Lady MacLean."

"Please call me Evangeline."

Because there's no way I'll remember to answer when called Lady MacLean.

Again Peadar gently squeezed her waist.

This time he kept right on squeezing.

Almost like he was in a panic, himself.

Good. He deserves to be upset after allowing the captain to lock me in our cabin.

But her traitorous body was trying to be calmed by Peadar's touch. Worse, it was still drawn to him, still wanted to scoot closer to him on the bench at the table.

"Oh, and with your lord's permission, I will call you Evangeline, then."

Tam smiled pleasantly at Peadar, waiting for his assent.

"Aye now, being that you and I will be working close together, you may call my wife by her given name..."

And here, Vange felt a still gentle but very firm squeeze on her waist.

Oho. A warning, then. This ought to be good.

"Howsoever, you may only do so in my presence."

Well, yeah. When else is Tam going to see me?

But Peadar continued.

"When I am away on the duties you assign to me, she will be Lady MacLean."

Vange dropped her teacup.

It didn't break, heavy pottery that it was, but it did land on her plate and spill tea all over what remained of her food.

From the way the captain winced at that, she took it tea was very expensive in 1560.

"Oh poor dear," said the captain, "I see your meal is ruined."

From the way he was smiling at her, she surmised the captain knew exactly how badly her meal had just been ruined. He knew she had been taken by surprise about being left behind while Tam sent Peadar off to do his bidding.

She must have shrunk in closer to her husband, because she felt his arm go around her.

It felt nice. Safe.

What have I done?

Vange made a big show of turning to Peadar and smiling at him, the doting wife. "Oh, on second thought, Tam should always call me Lady MacLean."

Peadar smiled back at her, just as showy.

"Well enough," said the kilted captain, "let us send the love birds back to their nest. I do not want to see them croon at each other any longer."

"Sure and be gone, love birds." Tam waved them away.

Vange didn't have to be told twice.

Neither did Peadar.

꙰

THE TWO OF them got up and skedaddled out of there before the captain could change his mind and stop them.

Peadar kept his arm around her the whole time.

Vange breathed a little easier once they were in their cabin with the door shut, but only a little.

Vange grabbed Peadar and held him close.

"That man is going to send you away from me?"

Peadar's arms went around her.

"Aye, lass, and for that did I tell you I was sorry, as soon as I heard Saraid say I was to be a gallowglass in her grandson's place."

"So a gallowglass is a soldier?"

"Aye, a foreign soldier in Ireland, whose loyalty is only to his leader, nay a part of local politics."

"And Tam is your leader?"

"Aye well, Shane O'Neill will be my leader, but Tam is my handler, you ken?"

"Yeah. People have handlers in my time, too. So is Shane O'Neill Ireland's king or something?"

"His clan think him so, howsoever, the English and the other Irish clans favor others for that honor."

"We're going to be in the thick of it, aren't we?"

"So sorry, lass."

She clung to him as her life line for a long while after that, and they soothed each other tenderly—and yet.

Lying there in his arms, Vange felt resentment building up inside her. Yes, this was a different time in the history of mankind, when men were in charge and women just went with that. But she'd grown up with women's liberation. She just couldn't submit to being locked in her cabin. It had made her feel such rage.

Rather than explode at her husband when the last straw landed on her back, Vange knew she had to vent her anger now, while both of them were calm, relaxed, and feeling affectionate.

"Peadar?"

"Aye, lass?"

"I have something to say, and it will be difficult for me, so I need you to hear me out without interrupting, OK?"

Peadar continued caressing Vange's back.

"Aye."

In a rush and barely stopping for breath, Vange said what was on her mind.

"I understand why you locked me in the cabin. You wanted to make sure I was safe and that I didn't try and stop your swordfight and get hurt in the process. I know you care what happens to me and that you were only looking out for me, doing what you thought was best for me, and all the stuff my parents used to say when they prevented me from doing something they thought was dangerous for me."

Vange couldn't quite believe it.

Peadar was still gently caressing her back.

She shrugged and pushed to get the rest of what was on her mind out, before he stopped her.

"But I'm an adult, Peadar, not a child. Let me decide what is best for me. I know it will be difficult in this backward time in history for you to do so, but I need you to treat me like an equal, at least in private."

Vange was amazed she'd gotten this much out without him butting in.

He was quietly listening, eyes intent on her when she looked back at him.

And he was making her back feel wonderful.

Hm. Not the reaction she'd been expecting.

Vange made herself keep talking until she got it all off her mind.

"You can be the spokesman for us in public, and I want you to be the managing partner in our enterprise, but give me a say. Listen to my advice. Tell me what's going on. That's what is normal in my day and age. Husbands and wives work things out between them and come up with solutions together, even if his name is still the only one that appears on some documents because of antiquated ideas that still pervade our society even in the 21st Century."

She knew he wasn't asleep, because now he was massaging her back.

It felt great.

"In short, if you ever lock me up again, as soon as I get away you will never see me again. OK, thanks for listening. Please answer me. Do you understand?"

"Aye."

"Good."

"And just so you know, I did not know anyone had tried to lock you into this cabin until I found the captain there at the door, unlocking it."

"Really?"

"Aye."

"Then why were you so horrified when you saw me on deck?"

"I thought you had left me to join the crew."

Vange laughed then, a deep hearty laugh that reached the bottom of her lungs.

"That was my plan, actually, for about two seconds."

He turned his massage into something more.

"Oh really? And what made you change it?"

She sighed.

"Honestly? The fact that all the druids who can get me home are back in the highlands, and you are my best ticket back there."

Peadar laughed then, a deep laugh that matched the one she'd had.

She kissed him with a tender passion she hadn't known existed before now.

"But I'm very glad I didn't join the crew."

They clung to each other for the rest of the voyage, taking their meals in their cabin and comforting one another.

A week after the ship set sail, Vange and Peadar watched

through their porthole as land approached, and then it was time to face other people again.

Knock knock knock.

The captain's voice boomed through their cabin door.

"Wake up, love birds. Time to fly away to your new home."

A second later, the door flew inward and he was there, smiling in delight at what he apparently thought he was going to see.

"We're ready," Vange said, fully dressed, sober, tearless, and holding her chin up.

CLINGING TO PEADAR'S ARM, Vange followed as her new husband was led off the ship and into one of a series of small boats that sat at the mouth of a river inside a huge bay.

The ship had docked in a fishing village much like the one they had left on Mull. There were no signs, so she really had no clue where she was, but Vange wished she could leave these overexcited people they were with and take her chances in the village.

But they had a firm hold on Peadar.

Perhaps they realized what she was thinking.

People were speaking excitedly in Gaelic all around her, and to Peadar.

As some workmen in leine and little else rowed them upstream on the river, Peadar explained to her what he had learned.

"We be headed to the town of Newry."

Peadar's brow was wrinkled up, and he held her close.

"I'm sorry, that doesn't mean anything to me."

"It be dangerously near the fighting, you ken?"

"Yes. Toj told me the English were at war with Ireland. Already."

Peadar gave her a haunted look.

"Already? Do you mean to tell me this war is some-ought you do know about, even in your time?"

She put a hand that she hoped was calming on his shoulder.

"Yeah, in my time the English control a large portion of Ireland—and all of Scotland."

Peadar was quiet for a long time after that.

They watched the land glide by their small boat.

Finally, curiosity got the better of Vange, and she simply had to ask him questions.

"So we'll be staying in Newry?"

"Ah, nay. We journey a day farther by horse then, to a castle the O'Neill keeps stocked against his enemies."

Rather than ride sidesaddle on her own and stretch her horsemanship skills to the breaking point, Vange elected to ride in the saddle with Peadar, which was fun and thrilling. The ride took all day, with several stops to rest and water the horses.

Ireland was marvelous and scenic. Even in late August, everything was so green, and the journey went by way too quickly.

All too soon, they approached what looked much more like a fort than a castle. There were no windows on the bottom floor. It was large and made of stone and looked quite insurmountable, but it was not surrounded by a moat, which greatly disappointed Vange.

They rode their horses right inside, where they got off and handed the reigns to attendants, who took them inside a barn built right into the castle courtyard.

She and Peadar were shown up to a room that was only slightly bigger than their cabin on the ship had been. They had one tall narrow window angled down and fit only for shooting arrows into anyone trying to storm the castle. Their bed stayed down all the time, and it was about the size of the twin bed in Vange's room at her parents' house. The trunk that had been in their cabin already sat beside their bed.

And that was all they had, beside what was in his sporran and her pouches.

"We are to make ourselves fresh for the evening meal, lass."

Being considered a lady had its privileges. Vange had not been asked to do one bit of work on the voyage, only to enjoy her new status as a married woman. Her clothes had been mysteriously taken away and returned clean. They had even returned smelling of sweet lilac and herbs.

It seemed this would continue here at Shane O'Neill's fortress.

They went down to a hall on the ground floor and dined with the O'Neill himself, along with his wife and Tam – and no one else.

Peadar, Tam, and Shane talked well into the evening while Shane's wife Mary pointedly ignored Vange's attempts at conversation.

Peadar showed his sympathy through pats on Vange's back.

Even though she understood that he really couldn't say anything bad about his boss's wife, Vange was upset throughout the meal and the long chat over wine afterward.

She pointedly ignored Tam's smiles.

Later on, after she and Peadar had been tenderly affectionate with each other, they talked.

"What was Shane going on and on about?"

"You will be cared for here, lass, when I do go off with the O'Neill as part of his protection."

"That doesn't sound too bad, so long as he mostly stays at home."

"Nay, but we shall be leaving on the morrow."

Vange clung to him then, and they stayed up quite late reassuring each other, but eventually she fell asleep.

VANGE'S DREAMS were often of Peadar. She knew that meant she was really gone over him, but she could live with that now. But when she didn't dream about her husband, she dreamed about what she thought of as her 'real life' back in the modern world.

Watching her favorite TV shows.

Driving her car.

Being able to find whatever she felt like eating.

Feeling like her strongest worry was not being able to find the shoes that were on sale.

Knowing all human knowledge was a click away on the Internet.

Calling or texting her parents and Emily.

And Vange never knew it was a dream when she had one of those. It always seemed like she was really back there in that easier, safer age.

This age was interesting, but so tiring. And waking up was always so ... disappointing.

This first morning in the Irish castle, she was having one of those 'real life' dreams.

And when she woke up she was not only in 1560, but also there alone.

Peadar was gone.

Vange used the chamber pot and then crawled back into bed, but she couldn't make herself fall back asleep. Finally she gave up trying, got up, and dressed in one of the many fine

Scottish plaid skirted outfits in the trunk, complete with the am breid on her head.

Holding the door lest it open too far and allow people to see her, she peeked out into the dark hallway.

And she was instantly sorry she hadn't flung the door open. Tam was there.

With a huge leer on his face.

And he immediately tried to push his way into her room.

She slammed the door as hard as she could and got ready to lean against it.

But the door didn't quite shut.

Tam was stronger than her, and slowly he was opening the door again.

With her heart pounding the adrenaline through her veins until she wished she had a clear path to run down, Vange screamed as loud as she could.

"Eeeeaaaaaa."

Over and over she kept on screaming, praying that some-one, anyone, would come see what the commotion was about.

"Eeeaaaaa."

"Eeeaaaaa."

That had obviously not been the reaction Tam was expecting.

He pushed his way into her room and stood there staring at her with his mouth just about watering, but wincing at her screams.

His face looked annoyed rather than concerned, though. He rubbed his nose and looked out into the hallway, visibly calculating whether he should proceed as planned or abort his mission so as not to be discovered in a compromising posi-tion with a married woman.

After what seemed like forever, a workman hurried into Vange's room and asked Tam something in Gaelic.

"A mouse. A mouse." Vange squeaked.

And then she took the opportunity to leave the room and rush down the stairs.

Vange was hungry, and she figured everyone else was too. And she knew there was safety in numbers—so long as the company was mixed with men and women. So she decided to try and find the dining hall.

Instead, a grey-haired old woman popped out of a door at the bottom of the stairs. She looked up when Tam's voice came down.

"Evangeline, lass." he said. "Hold a seat for me. We shall break our fast together."

The old woman beckoned to Vange.

"Quickly, lass. Come in."

Vange didn't hesitate.

She rushed through the door and discovered she had found the kitchen.

A huge fireplace covered one wall, with wood piled up nearby. It was big enough to roast a deer, but at the moment kettles and pots hung from hooks over the fire, and pans sat on a grate that stood right in the fireplace, over coals set off to the side. An iron oven stood in the fire as well. It was empty, but the room smelled of freshly baked bread, along with all the smoke.

There was a chair at the fireplace, where the old woman had probably been stirring the pots and shaking the pans.

The room had three doors, and the rest of it was filled by a huge butcher block table with three young women around it, cutting and kneading and mixing. They wore kerchiefs similar to Vange's, but she didn't know if that meant they were married, or if they just wisely covered their hair while they did kitchen work.

The old woman quietly shut the door.

"Thank you so much," Vange told her in a small shaky voice.

"Call me Aideen, and it is well come you are, lass."

"Call me Vange please."

Aideen looked uncertain.

"It's short for Evangeline, but only my mother ever uses that, and only when she's angry."

Everyone laughed.

"Where is she lass, your mother?"

Vange fought tears. "Far, far away."

"Your man took you far from her, then?"

"Something like that, yes."

"IT IS in good company you are. Nora and Isleen and Cara also allowed men to lure them away from all they knew and to cause them to make this their home."

"Hello Nora, Isleen, Cara. I'm Vange."

The three smiled at her as they worked.

Aideen thrust a plate into Vange's hand.

"To that table with you and eat, Vange. It is needing your strength you are."

The food was strange but good, and Vange surprised herself by asking for seconds and finishing the second plate.

"Where do I put my dirty dishes?"

"Show her, Cara."

Cara put down her paring knife and the carrot she was working on, brushed her hands off on her apron, and walked to the door opposite where Vange had entered the kitchen.

"It is in here."

Cara spoke halting English with such a thick Gaelic accent that Vange was glad she basically knew what the woman was saying as she followed her.

"Thank you."

About a dozen children aged six to ten were working in the next room: heating water over a small fire, pouring it into the wash basins, taking dirty wash basins outside to empty them, bringing water up from a well, washing dishes, drying them, putting the dishes away on shelves they climbed up to on a ladder...

Vange could see the dining hall through one of the room's three doors when a boy about nine brought in more dirty dishes. It was full of what she figured must be Irish soldiers, clothed in leine with no kilts over them. She didn't see Tam, so she counted her blessings that he didn't see her as she ducked out of view behind a drying rack for towels.

A girl unceremoniously took Vange's plate and plunged it into one of six wash basins.

And then Cara took Vange's hand and led her back into the kitchen, where she approached Aideen at the fireplace.

"Thank you for letting me eat in here, away from Tam. Do you know where I'm expected to spend my time while my husband, Peadar, is away?"

Aideen stood up from her chair at the kitchen fireplace and put a hand on Vange's shoulder.

"Oh dearie, he will be away more of the time than not, your man."

Vange took a deep breath and fought tears again.

Aideen patted her shoulder.

"I say it in kindness, lass. Best you be knowing this, it is."

Vange nodded and sobbed as the tears came.

"I ... just don't know what ... to do with myself ... while he's gone."

Aideen gave her a handkerchief.

"Do what the other young wives do, my dear. Help me here in the kitchen, where the likes of Tam will never think to find you."

Vange looked at Cara, who nodded.

And then Vange looked down at her Scottish finery.

Aideen laughed and opened the third door in the kitchen.

"Come, lass. You can wear one of my shifts in here, then change back to your fancy clothes whenever they summon you out there."

Vange followed Aideen into her room, which was quite crowded.

Hooks and nails covered one wall. There hung not only half a dozen worn and faded leine like those Cara, Aideen, and the other two wore in the kitchen, but also three sets of Irish finery, in colors that would look good on the other three young wives.

The room also had a washstand, a small bed—and three sleeping pallets made up on the floor.

"I will be making up a pallet for you as well, if you so desire, Vange."

"I do. I hate to think what would have happened if Tam had entered my room while I still slept. Thank you so much."

Aideen crossed herself and nodded. "Choose a shift and change, dearie."

So Vange helped out in the kitchen—chopping, mixing, measuring, stirring, and generally doing work she'd been doing to help her mother in the kitchen since she was six and tall enough to reach the counter. Barely.

Vange also helped in the vegetable and herb gardens— weeding, watering, and picking.

She went out to the hen house and collected eggs.

All in all, she was happy to be busy and hidden away from Tam and men of his ilk, which Aideen said all the men who stayed behind pretty much were.

The hidden women let the children serve the meals and bus the tables.

Out there with the remaining men some of the stranded wives chose to remain, and Vange didn't judge them.

VANGE HAD BEEN HELPING in the kitchen for a week, and eating very healthily. She only left the kitchen to go into the garden in the courtyard. She and the other women kept each other company telling funny stories from their childhoods and avoiding all talk of their deployed husbands.

Cara told of getting into her grandmother's blackberry patch and then lying and saying she hadn't—all the while covered head to toe in blackberry juice.

Isleen had come home with blood all over her face. Her mother had screamed and cried about her murdered daughter —only to find a small cut on her forehead that had been the source of all that blood.

Nora had run away from home—only to come back as soon as her food pouch was empty an hour later.

Of course, Vange had to edit her stories quite a bit. For example, instead of her long dress getting caught in her bicycle chain and ripping clean off her body, she said it got caught in a tree branch, which knowing her, it might as well have.

On the surface, Vange was content, but deep down she was getting depressed. Not only was she stranded in this backward time away from her parents and Emily, but also she'd been abandoned by Peadar. Not by his choice, but she still felt abandoned. With no hope of escape in sight.

Aideen laughed while she stirred the soup.

"Heh heh heh."

Vange flicked the last of the onion skins off her cutting board.

"What?"

"Tam keeps asking for you, but the other women want him to themselves, so they make excuses for you. They say you're sleeping in the children's room ... that you're embroidering with another of them .... or—closest to the truth— that you have taken ill and are recovering here in the kitchen where I can tend to you."

"Huh."

Vange threw down her knife and twirled to face Aideen.

"What if he comes in here looking for me."

"Soft, soft. It is not that he will be doing."

"How can you know for sure?"

"He will not brave sickness. Surely you know that?"

"I suppose."

"No need."

"But why would you put a sick person in the kitchen?"

"Because warm it is, of course."

"But what about getting germs in the food?"

"I have never heard it called 'germs', lassie, but that sounds like old superstition to me. There be no such thing as germs, lass. That be the sort of thing we old folks tell children in order to get them to obey us, that be all it is."

Vange had to bite her tongue to keep from arguing with that.

"Dust on the road." Nora yelled as she poked her head in the door and then disappeared.

"Dust on the road?" Vange asked Aideen.

"Lassie, wonder where you come from, I do, and you have not heard of dust on the road."

"There are no roads where I come from. It's an island, and we get around on boats."

"Oh. Well, dust on the road means some of the men are returning, lass."

Maybe Peadar is one of them.

"I have to change clothes."

"Go, go."

Aideen's shooing motions were not the least bit necessary.

Vange was changed and ready in under five minutes, and out the door she went, into the courtyard to join the pack of women waiting to see their husbands.

They jostled for places where they could see the greatest distance along the road, out to where the dust came up. They all smoothed their dresses and neatened their kerchiefs.

The men who remained at the castle went out to meet the men who were returning.

It was all Vange could do to keep from running out the castle's courtyard gate to join them, but she did restrain herself.

She replayed over and over again in her mind Aideen's comments on Vange's need of restraint.

"Lassie, sorry I am that you ever left your island. It does seem everyone was equal there, and that we women could comment on what the men did or said."

"I don't—"

"You do comment on the men's behavior, child."

"But I—"

"With your very body if not with your words."

"No I—"

Aideen stopped shaking the pans to turn and face Vange with her hands on her hips.

"I have seen it, and so have Cara, Nora, and Isleen."

"Like when?"

How could she give credence to anything said by a kooky old woman who thought germs were superstition? These people were like children. They were full of the funniest ideas and beliefs.

"Many times, lassie."

Aideen was shaking her finger at Vange.

"I see the rolling of your eyes, lass, whenever you hear

Tam's bragging. I hear the snort of air from your nose when-ever someone says his name."

Vange was listening now. She hadn't been aware she was doing those things, but they sounded just like her.

"What can I say? I like making jokes."

"They'll whip you for joking like that, lass. Or worse."

"What. Of all the male chauvinist crap I ever heard, this takes the cake."

Aideen met Vange's eyes and looked at her dead seriously.

"Get angry now about it, lass, but then put that behind you. Quit those contemptuous thoughts if you cannot keep them from showing in your actions."

"But how?"

"How?"

"How do I quit having contemptuous thoughts about men who behave contemptuously?"

"I do not know, child, for most of us fear them enough to keep from having those thoughts ever at all."

Vange took a deep breath and let it out.

Aideen hugged her.

"You should have never left your island if women were equal with men there."

VANGE JOSTLED some more with the other wives, hoping for a glimpse of their returning husbands.

And then all the women cheered when the marching men came into view.

"Oooooooooooh."

Vange stood there smiling as all the men came filing in, grabbing their wives for rare public kisses and then running off to their bedrooms.

She still stood there smiling after the last one had come

in, standing on her tip toes and looking out at the road, daring to hope that Peadar was just a little behind the rest of them, and at the same time dreading that he had been killed in action.

"He is not with this group," said Tam, who was suddenly right next to Vange.

She turned her questioning tear-filled eyes to him.

"Your husband is with the O'Neill, and we shall see the O'Neill's banner flying ahead of the group when he returns."

All Vange could do was nod absently. This was good news. Peadar's absence from this group didn't mean he'd been killed, as she had feared.

Tam offered his arm.

In Vange's disappointed stupor, she was on the verge of taking it.

And then Cara breezed up in her Irish finery and grabbed Vange.

"Come to my room for wine and commiseration. My husband didn't return with this group either."

Vange woke up from her stupor and smiled at Cara. She didn't even give Tam a parting glance.

Three more groups returned and three months passed before Peadar finally did come back to the castle, hale and hearty.

Vange threw herself into his arms.

"Peadar. I've never been so happy to see anyone in all my life."

He picked her up and spun her around, laughing.

"Aye, lass. Neither have I."

Hand in hand, they ran to their bedroom, where they hugged and kissed and hugged some more.

Words came pouring out of Vange's mouth amid her tears and sobbing.

"Peadar, we have to get away from here. Tam is after me

so bad that I have to hide in the kitchen, and three other women are hiding in there with me. Aideen the cook is nice to us and helps us hide, but Peadar, it's no way to live. Please, you have to take me and run. We can get a ship to take us to Scotland once we get to Newry. I remember the way. Please, let's go first thing tomorrow."

"Aye, well enough, lass. We cannot take any of the horses, as that is thievery payable with death. We will have to walk, and we will have to pray that the folk here in the castle do not find retrieving us worth the trouble."

"Thank you, Peadar. I'm sure Aideen will give us food for the journey. Oh Peadar. I've missed you so much."

"And I have missed you, Vange, more than words can say."

"So don't use words."

They got up at first light, put on the most travel-worthy clothes they could find in the trunk, and snuck down to the kitchen without running into anyone on the stairs.

"Aideen, pack us as much food as you can, please. We're running away. Thank you for all your company and everything you have done for me."

Vange hugged the old woman.

Aideen stroked her hair.

"Peadar, if you wish to leave, I cannot stop you. But please, consider the child your wife carries in her womb. A journey on foot in the winter would almost surely make her lose it."

15. VANGE & PEADAR 3

V ange fought the news at first. No, she couldn't be pregnant. She was stranded in 1560, for goodness sake. She wanted children, yes, but she wanted to have her babies in a modern hospital where the doctor gave you an injection and you didn't feel the pain. She wanted her children to be vaccinated. She wanted them to get an education, not spend all day drawing water from a well so they could wash dishes.

She wanted her mother.

She tried denial. Didn't a doctor have to diagnose pregnancy?

"Oh, how do you know I'm pregnant, Aideen? Are you trained in such things?"

But as soon as Vange said that, she realized that Aideen had probably seen hundreds of pregnancies. Her official job was cook, but really she was the matron caretaker of the warriors' wives at this isolated Irish castle fortress.

The old woman just shook her head and put her hand on Vange's belly, which Vange had to admit showed a distinctive bump.

"Be it really a mystery to you?" Aideen said.

"Yes."

Aideen cocked an eyebrow.

"Well, no, not really. How long have you known?"

It was months later when Vange realized Aideen hadn't answered this question. She had replied, to be sure, but she had skirted around the question rather than answering it directly.

"Surely you have noticed the child growing out under your leine? I have seen it nigh on a month, now."

"No, but I noticed that my period hadn't come."

"Mm, a strange way you be saying it that is, but yes. That be a true sign of motherhood."

There it was.

She was pregnant.

Stunned, all Vange could do was watch Peadar's face, waiting for his reaction.

He grabbed her and held her tightly to him. Wait, was he weeping?

"A child, lass. We are to have a child. I cannot count a child as a misfortune. Nay, a child be a blessing."

Vange had been trying to convince herself she'd been ravenously hungry and missing periods only because of stress. As she had far too often lately, she succumbed to tears, started sobbing, and got all choked up.

"Yes, a child is a blessing, but I want to go home."

Peadar looked ... frustrated with her.

Aideen started lecturing, but she stroked Vange's hair while she did, which kind of prevented Vange from getting mad at the old woman. Not too mad, anyway.

"Hushhhhh. Hushhhhh. Surely your island home is too far for you to go. That is the younger Vange speaking, it is. But now you are a mother, and you must grow up and be strong, for the sake of the life that grows within you."

What the old cook said was true, of course, but Vange

wasn't ready to grow up. Not here. Not if it meant having a baby under these conditions. But she couldn't say that to anyone but Peadar, and being from this time himself, he wouldn't understand. A mix of terror and frustration made her sobbing all the worse and her tears flow all the more.

"Is there no way at all we can leave?"

Aideen turned Vange around and looked into her face, plainly willing her to come back to reality and see how silly she was being.

Well, I can't tell her my main reason for wanting to leave, but she can help me tell Peadar my second reason.

"I hate it here. Tell him how awful Tam is, Aideen."

Peadar stiffened.

Aha. That's working. Please, Peadar, rescue me.

But Aideen calmed him.

"Sure and Tam is a womanizer. But Vange, soon your pregnant belly will put him off, it will. Your belly will help you be rid of his advances, mark my words."

Vange was glad the other three young wives hadn't made it down to the kitchen yet. It was bad enough having this breakdown in front of Aideen and Peadar. But what Aideen said made sense, and it calmed her just enough that she could breathe again and stop sobbing.

Aideen gave Vange a handkerchief.

"Anyhow, the winter will stop the fighting for now, and Lord willing, Peadar will remain here with us for a time."

Vange wiped her eyes and blew her nose, and then she hugged Peadar tight again. Yes, he was frustrated with her, and yes, she was getting frustrated with him. But she was pretty sure his ten-year stint as a Scottish slave on a faraway English settlement made him empathize with how stranded she felt in his time.

"Is it so, Peadar? Are you here to stay for the winter?"

Peadar held her tenderly and kissed her tears away.

"It does sound likely, aye. Howsoever, the O'Neill does not confide in me his plans, lass."

Aideen scooted them to seats at the tiny kitchen table.

"Yes, yes, now eat you should, and relax your cares away," she said as she dished up food and set the plates in front of them.

As Vange tore into the stew and fresh bread, she actually smiled.

"Well now, that smile be pretty lass. Do tell a man what brought it."

Vange swallowed, and for once she cleared her mouth between bites.

"At least now my huge new appetite makes sense."

They all had a good laugh.

As Vange sat eating next to her husband, his soothing presence, the food, the laughter, and the warmth of the kitchen all worked together to calm her tears away.

IN THE MONTHS she'd been there while Peadar was off fighting, Vange had learned that five hundred men were stationed at this large Irish castle stronghold. Most of them slept in barracks, but about thirty slept in private rooms with their wives and children. Over the three months of winter, all five hundred men were home.

Peadar seemed to be doing his best to keep Vange's tears away.

She was grateful enough that she tried to be cheerful and pleasant.

He was attentive.

Vange adored how he rubbed her aching back and feet, helped her down the stairs in the morning, and just about carried her up the stairs at night. He even helped her get out of bed when she needed the chamber pot, which was often. And he was an enthusiastic but tender lover—even though she was already getting big with his child.

Even though she denied it, Peadar must have sensed that she loved all the fancy clothes in the trunk. The man made sure the two of them were magnificent at supper and at court and for Christmas in their fine MacLean plaids—he in his great kilt and she in her underskirt and overdress. He brushed and braided her hair for her and tied her am breid over it.

He also helped with getting her boots on below the huge belly that made it so she couldn't see her feet.

It was easy to adapt this 16th century clothing to pregnancy. The skirts were already long and voluminous. All Vange had to do was change the way she laced her bodice. She even found a bodice insert in the trunk that covered the gap where her huge belly peeked out under the lacings.

Vange had to admit:

Peadar really was trying to make her time in the castle splendid.

And most of the time, it was. Most of the time, Tam was ensconced in the study with the O'Neill.

Peadar walked Vange through the magnificent rooms of the castle on his arm, he in his kilt and she in her matching plaid. All the other nobles—for as MacLeans, Vange and Peadar were nobles—greeted them cheerfully in passing. Some even asked them to stop into their rooms to share some delicacy the man had hoarded: tea usually, but sometimes candy or even fruit, right after the men came home.

There were dances on some evenings, with soldiers playing their pipes and drums. Peadar was a grand dance partner who made it easy for the hugely pregnant Vange to follow him through all the intricacies of set dances. At first she was nervous to participate, but Aideen told her it was good for her so long as she walked and didn't skip or run. Vange was glad she had learned the basic folkdance steps and figures at the renaissance faires and festivals she'd attended.

She didn't have much time to become upset that the set dances reminded her of Emily and her real life. With everyone shut in for the winter, the castle was booming with things to do or watch.

When there weren't dances there were sword-fighting tournaments—which Peadar did well in, and plays, games, or sing-alongs. It was everything Vange had dreamed of when she imagined what living in a castle might be like.

But Tam took the fun out of being in a castle whenever Vange encountered him.

Vange thought Tam looked surprised to see her on Peadar's arm the first time they met in the large formal dining hall. She smiled to herself.

Good. He thought I wasn't even here. My hiding place in the kitchen is effective. Aideen is so smart.

But Tam quickly recovered from his surprise, and then he looked determined.

Vange squeezed Peadar's arm to alert him.

When he glanced at her face, she nodded toward where Tam was approaching the two of them.

The ten long tables and five short tables were all set for supper. The common soldiers all sat at the long tables, while the noble officers and their wives sat at the short tables. Beyond that, they didn't have assigned seats.

Everyone was in the process of choosing places, except for the wives of the common soldiers, whose duty it was to serve everyone. They and the children ate earlier.

Tam asserted his way next to the seat Vange was about to take, and he gave her that snide grin that said he was going to get what he wanted some day—that it was only a matter of time because after all, he would see to it her husband remained stationed here. She wasn't going anywhere. That was all just in his grin, though. Out loud, he was civil in a way that only she and Peadar understood how insinuating he was.

"It is pleased I am to see you—Evangeline. You must tell me where you've been hiding yourself."

Vange narrowed her eyes at Tam. It was all she could do not to tell him 'In your dreams.' That was what she would have said to a creeper her age in her time, but somehow she knew that would only encourage Tam, so she tried just being cold. She looked the other way.

"Must I?"

Tam started to move in, but thwarted, he raised his chin defiantly.

Peadar had moved in closer to Vange. He gave her waist a gentle squeeze.

Vange decided it would be prudent to obey her husband's subtle and wordless request that she let him handle this.

Peadar had apparently chosen to diffuse the situation. He made a show of suddenly noticing some noble Irish officer and his wife and addressing them.

"Nay, please, I would be honored if you would sit here. My wife and I will just move down a bit. Tis no worry."

And so, leaving Tam to sit with that other couple, they moved down and had a nice supper.

That night in the privacy of their room—once their affections were slowing down—Vange spoke of Tam.

"Good job getting Tam out of our hair at dinner tonight."

Peadar rolled over to face her, smiling.

"Aye lass. I thought I had better. You looked about to spit in his eye."

"Yeah, I really wanted to."

They both laughed.

"He puzzles me though, Peadar."

"In what way, lass?"

Slowly, because of her bulging belly, Vange turned her back to him and moved into a spooning position to avoid looking in his eyes for a reaction as she explained. It was also the best way to get close to him in her condition.

"Well, what does he think he's going to get from talking to me with you right there? He can't think you're going to allow him to get close to me, but that didn't seem to put him off in the slightest."

Instead of the laughter she'd hoped for, this brought out the fiercely protective clench she had come to expect as his normal reaction to her mishaps here in his time period. She glanced back at him.

Pain showed in Peadar's eyes.

Vange grabbed his hands and squeezed them.

"What's wrong?"

Peadar squeezed her hands back so tightly she had to shake them to get him to stop.

He stopped immediately and then rubbed up and down her arm in a way that made him seem agitated. When he spoke, she had no doubt he was.

"He does not really want you so much as he wants to take some-ought away from me, lass."

That didn't make any sense to her at all.

"What?"

"He makes time for you as a way to be cruel to me, you ken?"

Suddenly, she did understand. Now she stiffened.

"Wow, you mean he's a sadist?"

"What be that, lass?"

She took a deep breath and let it out slowly, relaxing as she did so.

"Someone who takes pleasure in other people's pain."

"Aye, yes, that exactly."

"Makes me all the more grateful for Aideen's kitchen refuge while you're away."

Peadar's voice took on a quality that didn't suit the fierce highlander at all. It was a haunted, helpless tone.

"Aye, me as well, lass. Do take care not to leave there, aye?"

"Don't worry. I have no intention of seeing Tam while you're away."

It was a long time before either of them fell asleep that night. They slept late into the morning, only waking when there was a knock at their door.

Knock knock.

"Just a minute." Vange called out as she pulled the covers up over them both.

"What is it?" Peadar called out at the same time.

With a wink at Vange, Aideen brought them their break-fast to eat in bed.

"Just a bit of porridge, it is. We must feed expecting mothers, you know."

She set a board in front of them on the bed, and on it she placed not only porridge, but also berries from the small courtyard garden, as well as expensive tea from ... China, Vange could only guess. And then the old cook left again, but not before she got a good look at Peadar.

Vange was giggling so much about that, she almost couldn't eat her oatmeal.

ॐ

VANGE DID ENJOY HAVING Peadar home. Unlike how she hid in the kitchen with Aideen while he was deployed, when he was home the two of them spent most of their time in pleas-antries: tutoring Vange in Gaelic while reading one of the dozen handwritten books the O'Neill had in his library, looking at all the old weaponry, the tapestries, and even some paintings that were on display at the castle fortress, hearing the soldiers sing carols at Christmas and plain old drinking songs other times, and watching the children play in the courtyard with their toy swords.

Peadar had to keep his weapons skills up of course, as did all the men. They practiced every afternoon in the courtyard, shooting arrows at targets and skirmishing with their swords while Vange and all the other wives and children watched from the castle parapets. She never tired of watching her man demonstrate his physical prowess. His bouts still struck her as better entertainment than any martial arts movie.

Curiously and thankfully, Tam didn't appear at most events, but Vange was always looking over her shoulder for him. Always on her guard. That alone made castle life less splendid than it should have been.

She next saw Tam one curious winter day when the sun came out and everyone either watched or played in the stool-ball game the O'Neill had called just outside the fortress walls. A stool had been set up near the castle wall, and in a rough pattern that resembled a baseball diamond, four posts had been driven into the ground. Most of the people sat on the side of a nearby hill to watch and to see if they got chosen to play.

Some people—mostly nobles but some pregnant non-noble wives—sat on top of the castle wall, including Vange and Peadar.

Vange was surprised when the team captains called on both women and men to play. And she was a little disappointed when Peadar was chosen to be on one of the teams.

"Aw, you're all the way up here. Just tell them you don't want to play."

He gallantly kissed her hand and then stood up and waved his assent to be on one of the teams.

"Nay, playing is an honor."

Vange sighed. *Sometimes, chivalry is inconvenient.* But his playful mood reminded her of something she'd been meaning to ask him.

"Why do they call you a gallowglass? What does that mean?"

He pronounced it a bit differently, now that she was listening.

"It is Gaelic, lass, gallóglaigh. Can you hear how it means 'foreign young warrior'?"

"Oh. Now that you say it that way, yes I can."

"Peadar." called the O'Neill, and then he added in Gaelic, "are you coming or not?"

Vange gasped after her husband gave her a quick kiss and then disappeared over the side of the castle wall. With much difficulty, she stood up and went over to look.

Peadar was climbing down a ladder someone had placed there.

Whew.

And then she was called on in Gaelic herself to play.

"Vange. How about it?"

But she patted her huge pregnant belly and shook her head. Laughing, she slowly lowered herself back into the chair that Peadar had moved up there on top of the castle wall for her.

And of course while Peadar was busy playing, Tam found his way over to Vange and sat beside her in the chair Peadar had brought up there for himself.

She slouched in her seat, making her pregnant belly stick up even higher than it normally did.

Peadar was at bat.

CRACK.

Her husband whacked the ball off the stool so hard that it went over the hill where people were sitting, and everyone cheered as all his teammates ran to the fourth post.

Tam tried to use the excitement to cover his advances. He started to take her hand.

"Well hello, my dear Evangeline."

But he was too slow. Peadar was by Vange's side that instant, taking her other hand and helping her get up.

"Aye, and we were just leaving. My wife does not feel well, you ken."

Tam gave Peadar a look which said, 'That line would never work if it was just the three of us, but since other people are listening, I'll let it slide.'

Vange glued herself to her husband's side and called out to some people who were standing up there as she and Peadar left.

"You can use those two chairs."

While Tam the creeper wasn't at most of the events, he was at enough of them that Vange was tempted to ask Peadar to just stay with her in their room whenever he wasn't practicing his weaponry, and to let her hide in the kitchen when he was practicing.

Over and over this happened. Despite Vange's huge belly, Tam kept trying to move in on her, right under her husband's nose.

He even tried it in the chapel.

"Eh," Tam said on the one day a priest made it to the castle, "I find you at mass—"

Peadar and Vange bent their heads devotedly.

"Shhhh."

Tam wouldn't be dismissed.

"Oh, what's a greeting among friends at mass, eh?"

Other people nearby joined in this time with Vange and Peadar.

"Shhhh."

They all abruptly stopped shushing him, though, and their eyes got big.

Tam gave them the evil eye.

"I really must insist that you have a word—"

Vange gasped as the priest himself put his hand on Tam's shoulder.

"This is not the place to be talking, my son. Now go and talk elsewhere, or stay and be silent."

For a second, Vange thought Tam was going to hit the priest.

But Tam unruffled his feathers and left.

Vange held Peadar's arm tightly on these stressful occasions, extremely grateful that she had his company and trying hard to see her pregnancy as a blessing, the way he clearly continued to.

He frequently caressed her baby belly and talked to his son—he was sure it was a boy in there.

One good thing was that despite what she and Peadar had told Tam at the stoolball game, Vange was flourishing in her pregnancy. She never once got sick, and she felt more alive and healthy than ever before in her life.

She was just always hungry.

Very hungry.

And when the men were home, the meals were so much more elaborate. They had brought livestock and other supplies home with them, and Aideen roasted the meat in her huge kitchen fireplace.

Vange hadn't ever thought about it before, but of course barbeque was one of the oldest ways of cooking.

Peadar cut her meat for her and hand fed her at the table so she wouldn't get her dainty hands greasy. He cleaned his own hands in a bowl of water that sat in front of him on the table.

Vange felt like a lady in the castle while her husband was

there, and the other women treated her well when they saw
her in the finery she didn't dare wear around Tam when
Peadar wasn't home.

But winter passed.

On the first sunny early morning, the men left to restart
the fighting.

Wearing the saffron leine that the O'Neill had given all his
foreign young warriors as a sort of uniform, Peadar went out
there with them.

Vange made sure he walked her down the stairs to the
kitchen first, and closed the door.

DURING THE LAST month of Vange's pregnancy, Peadar
returned to the castle for a few days now and then, but
Aideen had been right. Vange's husband was away fighting
much more than he was with her.

The first day after his winter break, Vange sat at the huge
kitchen fireplace once more, stirring the soup while Aideen
cut up veggies, Isleen kneaded the bread dough, and Nora
made pudding. Cara's husband was still home right then,
lucky lady. As usual, they talked and laughed while they
worked, doing their best to make it a merry old time.

Unable to turn in her seat anymore, Vange just spoke to
the fireplace and let it echo back to her friends.

"I hope you were right about my baby belly."

Aideen leaned over Vange's shoulder and smiled a
knowing smile.

"Know I am right about that I do, lassie."

"What was it you did say about her baby belly?"
asked Nora.

"Only that it would put Tam off her tail."

"It didn't seem to while Peadar was here. Let's hope and pray it works now," said Vange.

And then the baby was kicking, and they all gathered around to feel it. Aideen seemed to stay and feel it more than the others, but Vange figured it was just that she was past childbearing and wanted to live vicariously a bit.

"But even if I didn't have Tam to worry about, I'm glad I can stay down here with you now anyway. The company is nice, and those stairs are pretty scary without Peadar around to help me. I haven't seen my feet since Christmas."

Aideen rubbed Vange's shoulders.

"It is letting you have the bed now, I am."

Vange dropped the spoon in the soup as she tried to turn in her chair to face the old cook.

"Oh no, Aideen. I can't take your bed."

Aideen held Vange firmly in the chair, not letting her try anymore to turn.

"You can and you will, Vange. And it is hurting yourself you will be, if you try anymore to turn in your seat."

"But—"

Aideen put her hands on her hips and leaned over to smile at Vange.

"It is helping you get up off the floor we will not be doing."

Uh, yeah. Now that she thought about it, how on Earth did she think she would get down there onto her pallet on the floor, let alone get up from it?

Vange smiled back at Aideen.

"Thank you. Thank you for everything."

Aideen hugged her, and then Nora and Isleen joined in.

So Vange stayed in the kitchen night and day, only going out in the courtyard in the mornings to empty her chamber pot. Whenever she wanted to wash herself, she had one of the children bring a bucket of water and a rag into Aideen's room.

THE WIVES of the non-noble soldiers, relieved of their winter meal-serving duties, were now washing all the soiled bed linens that had been piled up in storerooms over the winter. They also washed clothing: the children's, the noble women's, their own, and that of Tam and the few other men still about the castle. They did the wash in the castle courtyard during the warmest part of the day, employing several large washtubs in these efforts, big enough that four women could gather around them and scrub clothing clean on washboards.

While Vange watched them through the half-open courtyard door from the kitchen one day, she considered her situation. Right now, she was hugely pregnant, and so she and Peadar couldn't travel even though spring was in full bloom. But soon she would have a baby, and so they wouldn't be able to travel for another year, at least.

And if she wasn't careful, there would be another baby.

And another.

So that's what Emily meant when she said I would be stuck here if I married Peadar here.

Vange had studied birth control in school, of course. At the time, it had been unbearably embarrassing. She and Emily had a male health teacher.

But now Vange was glad for the knowledge.

Once she got over being angry at herself for being impulsive and getting pregnant this first time, knowledge of birth control gave her the feeling she was now in charge of her situation, in this one little very important matter.

She felt sorry for all the other women in the castle, but she didn't quite dare tell all of them what she knew. For one thing, that would expose her to Tam. No, she only felt OK about telling Isleen, Cara, and Nora. Something told her Aideen already knew.

Vange made plans for herself.

She would breastfeed of course—for as long as possible, as she knew her breast milk would give the baby her immunities —and that should work as birth control so long as the baby was only drinking her milk and not eating any food. Here in this backward time of no vaccinations, she planned to stretch that out to a year.

But her schooling told her she needed to use at least two birth-control methods.

She'd heard some of her middle-school classmates snickering that 'back in the olden days, they used animal guts for condoms.' And right now, animal guts were something Vange had a ready source of, unlike in her real life.

But how did one broach the subject of using animal guts as contraceptives?

In the privacy of the kitchen with only women around, that was how.

Vange was always the one seated now, stirring the pots and shaking the pans.

"Aideen?"

Today, the cook was the one kneading the bread dough.

"Hm?"

"I find I'm quite happy now with the baby coming, but I want to wait awhile before the next one, you know?"

"Oh, yes and I do."

"So ... I was thinking ..."

"Hm heh heh."

"What's so funny?"

Nora poked Vange in the side, causing her to giggle.

"Tis thinking you often are, Vange."

Isleen came over and mopped Vange's hot face with a damp towel.

"You will bring all the monks down on us from all the monasteries you will, with all that thinking you do."

"Uh, huh?"

As she often did, Aideen came over and rubbed the sore spot right at the base of Vange's back. How did she find it every time, anyway?

"Pay them no mind, lassie. Pray tell us what it was you were thinking."

Vange decided the only way to ask this was bluntly, so she just blurted it out.

"After I have the baby, I want all the big animal guts you get."

"Ah, fancy some tripe, do you?"

"Ew. No. I want them raw and cleaned, to use as a marital aid."

The other young wives stood and blinked at Vange.

But when Aideen answered her, Vange could tell that the old cook knew exactly what she had in mind.

"Very well, you shall have them, Vange."

§🐍

A FEW WEEKS LATER, Vange's water broke right there in her chair by the huge kitchen fireplace. It was a while after supper, so she was only piling the glowing coals up into the far corner for the night so that they didn't go out while she and the other kitchen workers slept.

Aideen served as Vange's midwife, of course. The old Irish woman had all kinds of weird but effective ideas about how to manage Vange's pain.

When Vange's water broke, Aideen gestured, and Isleen

and Nora came over and supported Vange by the arms while
she got up.

"Walk her slowly around the room. Do keep her moving."

The women obliged.

For a while, Vange was glad just to have company and
something to do.

"Is it really necessary for them to hold me up, Aideen? I
learned to walk a long time ago, you know."

The other young wives laughed at this and several other
jokes Vange cracked for a while as they walked around and
around the kitchen.

And then ...

"Vange, your breathing has grown weak," said Aideen.
"That be the sign your babes are nigh on ready to appear.
Breathe shallowly but often, such as this: *Huh. Huh. Huh.*"

Vange tried that. *Huh. Huh. Huh.* Wouldn't you know it
helped, but it kept her from telling any more jokes.

Her friends seemed too tense to lead any conversation.
Their tenseness was rubbing off on her. They really needed to
lighten up.

To pass the time now, Vange silently counted how many
circles they walked her around the kitchen. She got up to 468
before she got bored with that.

*Huh. Come on, people. Huh. Say something. Huh. Entertain
me. Huh.*

Seeming to understand Vange's state of mind, Aideen
started humming a strange song.

Vange found it was soothing, but at the same time seemed
to make her more alert. In the back of her mind she found
that odd, but the soothing sensation was so pleasant and
helpful that in the moment, she welcomed Aideen's song.

After the contractions sped up a certain amount, Aideen
spoke some Gaelic words into the washroom and some non-

noble wives brought one of their large washtubs into the kitchen and filled it with heated water.

"Get in and be comfortable, lassie. Isleen and Nora will help you."

Puffing for breath by now, Vange eyed the water doubtfully.

"*Huh.* Won't the baby drown? *Huh.*"

Aideen laughed merrily.

"It is water that broke out of you earlier, and to water they be accustomed."

(Huh. Huh. Huh.) Of all her weird ideas, this has to be the weirdest—wait a minute.

"They?"

"There be two inside you, lassie."

"Twins."

Vange's shock soon gave way to outright anger. Between puffy breaths, she gave the old cook a piece of her mind.

"*Huh.* How long *Huh.* have you known *Huh.* I was having twins *Huh.* Aideen, and why *Huh.* didn't you tell me? *Huh.*"

"I have always known—"

"What do you *Huh.* mean, *Huh.* always?"

But Aideen seemed not to have heard that question. At least she answered Vange's other question in her sing-song Irish lilt.

"And I could not be telling you, Vange, the reason being you could not do a thing to change it. Only worry could you, and that is not good for the wee ones."

Puffing her breaths even faster, Vange waited for an apology, but when she got none, she slowly realized the truth in what the old cook had just said. Their mother's worry probably would have a bad effect on her babies. After a bit, Vange surrendered to the relaxing warmth of the tub water.

The two women didn't talk for a while.

Every minute or so, Aideen wiped the sweat off Vange's

forehead with a damp cloth and smoothed the stray strands of Vange's hair out of her eyes.

Huh. Huh. Huh.

From her health classes, Vange intellectually knew terrible pain lurked just a moment away, but the warm water seemed to be helping. She felt the odd sensation of her pelvic bones and her cervix opening, and of her womb contracting. While all that inner activity did make it impossible for her to breathe deeply, it didn't hurt, exactly.

Every time the tub water cooled below a relaxing warmth, Aideen would rap on the door to the washroom.

A girl would come in with a pan of hot water and slowly pour it into the tub far enough away from Vange that it didn't hurt her.

Vange marveled that the girls didn't stare.

"How *Huh.* often do you do this, Aideen? *Huh.*"

"A few dozen babes enter the world in this castle every year."

"*Huh.* Where are they, *Huh.* all the other babes?"

"It is in their mothers' rooms with them they be."

Oh. Of course. Not all the wives stayed in the kitchen with Aideen...

"Oh. *Huh.* I think mine are *Huh.* here, Aideen."

Sure enough, they popped right out into the warm water, and Aideen had time to lift each one up out of the water before he tried to breathe air.

Peadar had been right, only doubly so. Two boys.

Vange named them Michael and Gabriel, because they seemed like two little angels to her.

Aideen pulled some strings and set Vange and her family up in a larger room on the bottom floor of the castle, right across the staircase from the kitchen. She produced from storage a large cradle where they both could sleep, though they seldom slept at the same time. That was fine. There were always at least two women in the kitchen who would hold them and rock them and sing to them. Often they had three women doting on them, and sometimes four.

Aideen also produced from storage everything else the new family required: baby clothes, cloth diapers, gourd rattles, hand-carved wooden toy swords, and baby blankets.

Vange was content to watch her boys grow into toddlerhood there, but she was determined to get them back to her time before they got so big they would be expected to work. She wanted them to go to school and have much brighter futures and easier lives than they ever could in the 16th century.

VANGE SMILED at how obviously delighted Peadar was to meet his sons. They were three months old, and she held one in each arm inside their private room across the stairs from the kitchen.

"This is Michael, and this is Gabriel."

Having just arrived home, Peadar still wore his battle-bloodied saffron leine. He unloaded all his weapons on the floor, first the claymore and then the large bow and quiver of arrows. The fierce appearance all of this paraphernalia gave him contrasted with the soft loving look on his face as he stepped up to her to coo at his sons.

"Heh ha ha ha ha. Och lad, that does tickle, it does."

Michael and Gabriel were putting everything in their mouths these days, including all ten of Peadar's fingers. Between that, they wrinkled their little brows and stared up at this man whose hands were tough but whose voice and manner were gentle with them.

Peadar reached out his arms for them.

"Give them to me, lass. I wish to hold my sons."

She did. Ever so slowly, she moved in close to Peadar and passed both babies to him, helping him cradle both of them in his arms.

"Do you need help holding them?" she asked.

But she could already see that he didn't.

He only had eyes for his sons when he spoke to confirm this.

"Nay. I was taken by the English young, but not too young to have been holding babes for five years already."

Not having anything she needed to run off and do—her kitchen duties were voluntary and unneeded with her husband home to keep Tam at bay—Vange found herself just watching her sons and her husband get acquainted. It was the kind of thing she would have taken a picture of in her 'real life': the first time something happened in her children's lives.

Peadar looked content simply to hold them and coo at them and let them gum his fingers.

And Vange sighed with contentment at watching all three of them.

Until Michael was hungry...

For the most part, Vange was elated to be done with her pregnancy. Everything from walking to climbing stairs to using the chamber pot to getting up from her seat was much easier.

Nursing the babies was a vacation by comparison. And it was a time for her to bond with them. Truly, with so many women anxious to hold them and coo over them, she rarely got that chance.

But she was glad to see their father relishing the chance to hold his sons. That did her a world of good. It was nice having Peadar home.

And it was wonderful being able to leave the babies with Isleen and a now-pregnant Cara for a few hours that night and play castle with Peadar. Even after being here a year, the greater castle outside of the kitchen felt like a playhouse to Vange: never quite real.

But now that she had lost the baby weight, and with Peadar around, Tam took an interest in her again. And Peadar appeared to be right: Tam was only showing interest in his wife in order to make Peadar angry.

Gradually, Tam was succeeding. Each time he had to defend Vange, Peadar showed a tiny bit less restraint and patience with his superior officer.

And this was always when they were all dressed in their finery.

With breakable things nearby.

Tam would move in whenever Vange left Peadar's side for even a moment, such as that night, when she stopped to admire a vase in the great hall.

Daring to put his hand on the small of her back, Tam also put his mouth near her ear and whispered.

"Very fine work I see you know it is."

Vange tensed to run away and retorted as loudly as she could, hoping to attract attention from some of the other people milling about in the great hall.

"Leave me alone."

But the other people must have feared Tam. They must have heard her, but they all made a show of pretending not to have.

Tam grabbed her by the waist. He squeezed her hard, unlike when her husband squeezed her waist, and Tam continued whispering in her ear.

"Oh, but there is much too much amusement to be had of you, my dear."

Wow, he knows what he's doing. He does this often, and he gets away with it.

Fortunately for Vange, she had read articles in *Cosmopolitan* magazine about what to do when some creeper tried to make it look like you were just being crabby and he was your husband or father.

She yelled for help at the top of her lungs.

"Peadar. Help me."

"Ha. He's gone down into the courtyard by now and can't hear you, pretty thing. You'll have plenty to tell him about just as soon as I get you into that room over there. Won't that ruin him. Ha ha."

Vange was moving to push the vase off its pedestal to draw a crowd when she heard Tam grunt.

"Ulp."

Tam's hand came loose from Vange's waist instantly.

Vange ran from the room straight into the kitchen without stopping to see what transpired. Only half an hour later did she hear it from Nora, who came running in through the kitchen door with her face red and her breath huffing as if she'd just run there from the farthest corner of the fortress.

"Vange. Your man is the talk of the castle, he is."

Vange dropped the knife she'd been trying to use for cutting up veggies, but which she'd merely been playing with while Aideen burped Michael and Isleen burped Gabriel after the hasty feeding Aideen had insisted Vange give them.

"Where is he? I expected him to come get me by now."

Nora looked surprised.

"Do you not know?"

"Know what?"

Nora shook her head quickly in apparent agitation.

"There was a fight, Vange. Peadar struck the O'Neill's man Tam in the face. In the O'Neill's study they both are, telling the tale."

Vange was halfway to the door when she was grabbed from behind. She struggled, but she couldn't get free.

"Let me go. I'm going up there as a witness. Peadar was just protecting me. Tam started it."

Aideen's voice came out as strong as her arms felt.

"It is staying here you will be, near your babes. Need you they do, Vange. A mother must put her children first, even before her husband."

Vange tried to shrug Aideen off, but to no effect.

"I'm not going to fight and die, just to testify. Let me go."

Aideen held her even tighter.

"Vange, I do not know how these matters be settled on your home island, and hearing how fair it seems to be, I truly do wish betimes that we all lived there. But here—"

Vange's adrenaline was all used up.

How in the world did an old woman overpower a young one in the middle of an adrenaline rush? Aideen's strong hold on her was beginning to calm her anger so that doubt and fear could set in. But she wasn't quite done struggling. Not yet.

"Here, what? Get to the point."

Aideen was hugging Vange now, as much as restraining her.

"Here in Ireland, women do not interfere in the affairs of men. No, we do not."

Again Vange tried to shrug Aideen off, and again she failed.

"Affairs of men? You've got it all wrong."

Aideen must have been getting frustrated, because she shook Vange a little.

"It is you who have it all wrong, Vange. It is not your place to go and tell the O'Neill a thing, lassie. You must stay here with your children and not make a spectacle of yourself, for their sakes, if not for your own."

"But I was there. I know what started their fight. Tam was

behaving horribly to me, with his hand on me even. If I just go tell the O'Neill—"

Aideen shook Vange even more.

"Woman. You are not listening to me. They can kill you for overstepping your bounds."

All the struggle went out of Vange at these words. She slumped against Aideen, who held her tenderly now. But it was as if only Vange's body knew Aideen spoke the truth. Slowly, weakly, her mouth kept right on denying it.

"They're not really going to kill me for going to talk to them. They can't be that backward and barbaric."

Aideen calmly and gently held her.

"Then can and they will here, lassie. Shane O'Neill is all but king in these lands. He has but to say it, and it will happen. There is no one to say otherwise. The sooner you understand that, the safer you will be."

Vange's mind tried to hold on to optimism, to deny what her body had already resigned to being the truth. Her mind told her to search the faces of the other women for signs that they didn't believe what they heard. In desperation she did. She searched Nora's face, and Isleen's.

Without a doubt, both faces looked worried for her.

Vange took a deep breath and let it out slowly, the way her gym teacher had taught her to let go of tension and relax. It worked, a little.

"Well, if I have to stay here and wonder what's going on, then at least tell me everything you've heard, Nora. What happened in the fight."

Nora looked to Aideen

The old cook nodded that she should go ahead and tell.

So in her heavily accented English, Nora said more words in the next few minutes than Vange had ever heard her say yet.

"They say there were words between Lord MacLean and

the O'Neill's top man. They say the words got louder and louder until Lady MacLean became distressed and ran from the room. And then they say that Lord MacLean struck the other across the face, they do, and that once the other recovered, he tried to strike Lord MacLean, but he was not able to, because you see, his arm had broken when he fell from being struck all the way across the room and banging against the wall."

VANGE AND PEADAR'S bed and room were bigger than Aideen's, and Vange didn't want to sleep alone. Aideen and Isleen climbed with her into the big bed that seemed so empty without Peadar in it, now that he was home but not with her. Michael and Gabriel were both asleep in their cradle, for once. Nora's husband was home too, so she was in her own bed.

They stayed up for quite a while, talking about what really had happened and why everyone made it out to be more Peadar's fault than it actually was.

Vange hadn't dared ask what might happen to her husband if the O'Neill believed those accounts. She'd learned long ago not to ask the question if she didn't want to hear the answer. So she rolled over on her side with her knees bent halfway, like she always did just before drifting off to sleep. Wow, this was so comfortable compared to her pallet on the floor in Aideen's room.

At long last, Vange felt herself getting sleepy.

"Why haven't we been sleeping in here this whole time?" Aideen sounded wide awake still.

"Safe enough now, it is, but my room does have that extra layer of protection, the entrance being through the kitchen."

Now that she heard this, Vange was wide awake again.

And her anger was back on the rise. She sat up in the bed, facing the door and looking for something to block it with.

"There are three of us, though, and sometimes five, plus two babies. We really should be safe in our own home."

Aideen was sitting similarly.

"Go to sleep, Vange. Keep watch I shall."

Vange kept looking for something to block the door, but there was only the cradle. She wouldn't place her children between herself and danger. She looked at Aideen again.

The old woman nodded her assurance that she was on watch.

Vange woke to a noise and jumped up out of bed, willing her eyes to see in the dim early morning light. She looked over at Aideen.

The old woman was sound asleep.

The noise was footsteps coming down the stairs.

Remembering the pile of weapons, Vange scrambled over to it, leaning across the other gear to grab for the claymore. She felt more confident with the bow and would have chosen it normally, but there was no time to nock an arrow. There was barely time to get ahold of the claymore, but she managed it, glad that it stuck out above the rest of the gear.

The footsteps stopped at her door.

Vange hefted the heavy two-handed sword like she would a bat, and she took her best batter's stance, staring at the door and almost daring it to open.

The door did open.

Vange started to swing at the man who was coming in, but it was difficult with the early morning sun shining in her eyes from the open courtyard door behind him, making him a silhouette.

She felt him grab the sword from her even as she swung it at him

"I do not think you are going to need that, lass. Howso-ever, I do wish to know who you have with you in our bed."

"Peadar."

He put the sword down and took her in his arms.

"Aye, none other."

Vange clung to him.

By now, Isleen was awake too.

Aideen urged the young Irish wife out of the bed and toward the door.

"Leaving now we will be. Good night to you, Peadar."

He nodded at them.

"Have a good night. Sorry to disturb your rest, and I do thank you for keeping my wife safe while I was away, and while I be away yet again, many times to come."

Aideen sort of bowed and sort of nodded to him, and then she and Isleen were out and shutting the door.

Reluctantly, Vange let go of Peadar's embrace and went over to nurse Michael and Gabriel, who had woken up from all the activity and were crying for their food. Feeling able to use her joking tone now that her husband was here in the room with her, safe and sound, she laid it on thick, complete with exaggerated tones and funny faces, sticking her tongue out at the end to imitate a dead animal she'd seen once, on the road.

"So what happened in Shane's office? How did you get out of there alive? Aideen warned me to stay away or I'd be killed."

Peadar laughed heartily and came over to sit next to her on the bed, with his arm around her and his other hand caressing the angelic faces of his sons.

"Aye, it looked to me as if the incident would mean my death for a bit as well, lass." He caressed her back. "And I cursed myself for a fool."

"Why? I loved how you stood up for me."

"Aye, but who would stand up for you with me dead, lass, eh? And you would have our sons to fend for." He choked up a bit. "Nay, what I did last evening was foolish, not brave."

With a baby in each arm, she couldn't do much but turn her head and kiss him, so that was what she did.

"Well what would bravery have looked like last night then, if not the way you acted, hm?"

She had meant it as a rhetorical question.

But he took it seriously.

"Bravery last night would have looked like me taking his insults on myself while I got you safely away and was able to stay away with you, lass."

Vange thought that over for a moment.

"OK, you have a point."

He rested his chin on top of her head and hugged her warmly.

"I did lose my temper, lass. I cannot say it will not happen again, but I can and will pray it does not endanger you or our sons when it does."

Vange enjoyed his sincerity, but only for a moment. After that, it began to remind her how very alone the four of them were. She wanted some comic relief. Or at least entertainment.

"OK, the mood in here is getting way too serious, so tell me how you convinced Shane you weren't to blame. That must be a good story worth telling."

But Peadar's deep sigh warned her this would be anything but comic.

"Tam ranted and raved for a long while, lass, saying how I had insulted him and I was nay a man of honor. He ranted loudly. To be sure, that entire side of the fortress heard him. And then at long last, they took him away for doctoring."

"And then?"

"And then Shane told me privately that he did not mind if I had insulted the man."

"What?"

"Aye. Shane O'Neill is desperate to defeat the English. He explained it at length to me, what they are doing to set up an Englishman to rule in Shane's stead, despite Shane having the support of his clan and other supporting clans."

"So he thinks you did all those terrible things Tam accused you of doing?"

"That does not bother me, lass."

"Oh. Well what part of it bothers you then?"

"The part that bothers me is that it will take a lot of doing to fend off these English from the Irish lands. I do not believe that it can be done in fewer than fifty years."

"Why do you care?"

"Och, I do care because we are here in the service of the O'Neill until it be done, lass."

THOSE TINY TOY wooden swords got a lot of use now that Peadar was home again. Even though he had fashioned armor and helmets for their sons, complete with face guards, Vange could not stand to watch her six-month-old babies whacking at each other with sticks in their cradle, so she listened from the kitchen while Peadar narrated their play in the bedroom.

"Och, there you have it, Michael, get him."

"Ah, good block, Gabriel. That's it, counter attack."

"Nay, you do not want to eat the sword. That would leave you defenseless, you ken."

"Aye, that be the way of it, Michael."

He played with his sons until they fell asleep, and then he came into the kitchen and brought her into the bedroom.

The two of them gazed at their sleeping sons for a

moment.

Vange gently removed their protective headgear and covered them with a blanket.

Peadar had other ideas.

Vange knew she couldn't wait any longer to start using another form of birth control. She thought she was pretty safe from being fertile again so long as they nursed twelve times a day between them. Her milk was still coming strong, and the twins could easily take all of it.

But the boys had started teething at four months, and Gabriel had a top and a bottom tooth that met each other now. She didn't know how much longer she could take the wear and tear.

So when the time came, Vange tried to hand her husband one of the condoms she and Aideen had made from animal intestines.

"Here, put a condom on first."

Peadar shied away from the thing.

"Och, none of your joking now, lass."

Oh yeah. He's probably never heard of a condom. She took a deep breath. *OK, here goes the big talk.* She took his hand gently to try and let him know this was important to her, while at the same time smiling at him to bring out one of his lighter moods.

"It isn't a joke."

He looked at her dubiously.

"What is the thing then?"

Wow, he was a little on guard. She couldn't let that continue. *If he shuts me out, it's over. Best to use someone else's familiarity with it in order to reassure him.*

"It's something I got from Aideen."

There, that put him a bit at ease. He took hold of it.

"What for, lass?"

It was a moot point right now. The moment had passed.

But Vange needed Peadar to be on board with the plan to get her back to her real life. She didn't know how much longer she could take it here in this backward society, and now they also had their sons to consider.

The boys would be so much safer in her time—from disease especially, but also from violence, and poor prospects at any future away from violence.

Vange looked into her husband's eyes, trying her hardest to communicate the gravity of their situation, to tell him just with her look how important this was—to her and to all of them.

"Condoms provide a way for us to be intimate without me getting pregnant again right away."

She could see in his eyes that he understood now, but her relief was short-lived. Calmly and with love, he jumped right to the heart of the matter, onto a subject she hadn't planned to discuss right away.

"Oh lass, you cannot mean to travel with two babes."

Don't panic. Don't panic. You can bring him around. He'll understand if you explain it right.

"No, not with babies, but they can travel once they can walk—if we don't have another baby right away, they can."

He took both of her hands in his.

"Do you ken how dangerous travel is for young ones?

"I do, but—"

"It would be murder lass, to travel all the way back to Scotland with children before they were old enough to defend themselves—eight years old, at least. Nay, I will not do it."

The tears came then, unbidden.

"Peadar, I have to get back to my time."

He tried to hold her close.

But she turned away and withdrew her hands, feeling betrayed by him.

He gently put his hand on her back.

She waited for him to order her to see reason.

But he didn't. He just remained there silently with his warm hand on her back, gentle, loving.

Finally, she turned back to face him.

He looked at her softly, lovingly, soothingly.

"I will get you back to your time somehow and someday, Vange. I do promise that. Howsoever, I will not put our sons in danger while doing so. It would not be right. You do ken that, aye?"

A tiny kernel of hope—and of trust in Peadar—peered into the dark place Vange had retreated to inside her mind. Ignoring her fear that this was a false hope, she grabbed onto it.

"You promise?"

Keeping his eyes on hers, he slowly solemnly nodded his head once.

"Aye. I will get you back to your old life sometime. I do promise you that. Just ... I will not put our sons in danger for it, and I do not believe you would either, Vange. I do not believe you see just how much danger lurks out there."

Finally able to breathe now, she could see that the father of her sons was right. Their children wouldn't be safe traveling out in the wilds until they could fight off animals, at least. *So what* if the boys had to work in the castle drawing up water and washing dishes for a few years before they went to school?

At least Michael and Gabriel would make it to school.

She supposed that had to be enough comfort for her. She chose to rest on that.

So she let Peadar hold her close now, and soon the question of the condom came up again.

This time, he agreed to use it.

At least there was that.

16. VANGE & PEADAR 4

This feast topped all the others over the past two years at the castle. The two of them were decked out in their plaid finery, sharing a tender cut of beef from the roast, and there were also pies, puddings, chestnuts, and figs. Because she hadn't quite stopped nursing Michael and Gabriel, Vange didn't dare try the wine, but Peadar said it was excellent.

The twins were a year old now, and running. Vange had spent most of the summer out in the courtyard playing with them, and she had plans to entertain them and the other toddlers in the dining hall this winter, between meals.

The past six months had been good. She and Peadar were getting along well, and Tam had stayed away from her. Vange thanked God and her lucky stars every day for Aideen. Without the old cook's help, Vange knew she would never have survived the 16th century a day, let alone two years.

Peadar was laughing.

Vange came out of her thoughts and asked him a question in Gaelic, which she spoke fluently now, although Peadar was amused that she had an Irish accent, rather than his Scottish one. He teased her about it often, saying it clashed with their Scottish highlands clothing and last name.

"What's so funny? Did I miss something?"

"Nay, lass. I was just thinking."

Vange giggled.

"You don't often admit to doing that."

Peadar tickled her, which she hated because it made her squirm. He cut a big bite of beef off for her while he swallowed what he'd been chewing, then leaned in close to her and lowered his voice.

"Now then, I was thinking you would never know my family was cursed, to see me living the good life in a castle like this, dressed in this finery and seated at a noble's table."

That was interesting, and Vange went into learning mode right away, asking questions. Her favorite days in her 'real life' back home had been at college, and she would have taken notes on what her husband had to say if she had anything to write on, or with.

As it was, she grabbed a small pie off the tray that one of the non-noble soldiers' wives appeared with at her side. Ooh. It looked good. Mincemeat. She prepared a bite as she spoke, lowering her own voice to match his.

"Cursed? What do you mean?"

Peadar's brow wrinkled at her, and he grabbed her other hand, leaned in to put his mouth to her ear, and whispered.

"I did think you knew about the family curse, lass."

While she chewed her pie, Vange lowered one eyebrow in a face she'd practiced in the mirror, back in her old life at graduate school, training to be a teacher. The look was supposed to say, "You haven't given me enough information." Just for good measure, she said that out loud too, once she swallowed her pie.

"Uh, I don't think I do, but tell me and I'll let you know."

Wow, Peadar was really upset by this. He got an intense look on his face.

Vange shook his hands a little and smiled at him.

"Careful, Peadar. Let's not make a scene."

He nodded then and leaned back in his seat, pulling her chair close to him and putting his arm around her so that her head rested on his shoulder and they were both watching the room. And so he could whisper in her ear without making a scene.

"So so so sorry, lass. I thought Emily had told you. I should have made sure that you knew. I vowed to tell my wife before we married. I have failed you."

"I accept your apology, Peadar. Now please just tell me already."

He whispered.

"Our family's branch of MacGregors are cursed, Vange." She whispered back.

"I gathered that. What kind of curse?"

He held her close.

"Every fourth son of ours must serve the druids if he lives to be twenty and five. My father Dall was the fourth son of his father, and so he has the birthmark and must serve them the rest of his life."

"OK. That doesn't bother me, Peadar. That's why Dall met Emily, and why I met you."

He turned and kissed her cheek.

"Aye, that is true, and for that I am grateful. But ..."

Vange turned her head to look at him.

"But?"

He smiled at her nervously.

"But Vange, if you and I have a fourth son, the druids are going to call him into their service when he's five and twenty."

"Oh ... well, let's stop with the two we have, then."

He seemed to think that over, which she guessed wasn't surprising for a guy who'd only found out about condoms six months ago.

"Aye, it is a good idea, and with us being away here in Ireland at this castle with no lands nor cattle to tend, well, we do not need a large family anyhow."

"For now."

"For now?"

You've forgotten. Barely remembering the need for secrecy in her anger at his inconsideration, Vange hissed at her husband instead of yelling at him.

"Yes, for now. Peadar, you promised you would get me *home*."

He sat up in his seat and looked at her, crossing his arms.

"Aye, and I will. But Vange, I did say someday, you ken? I did not say soon."

The first either of them was aware of Tam was when they heard his voice right next to them. The man had a sugary smile on his face, and his head was tilted to the side, slowly shaking no.

"Aw, Evangeline. If it is going home you dream of, then your dreams will all be sad, I'm afraid."

Vange spoke before she really thought about what she was saying.

"What's it to you?"

Peadar's arm was around her, and he was gently squeezing her waist. He was probably right in telling her to keep quiet, but oh well. She'd already spoken, and she actually was interested in how Tam would answer the question.

Tam cut Peadar off before her husband could speak in her defense.

"Oho. You've gotten brave in your speech, Evangeline. And I suppose this indicates that you feel able to fend for yourself over the long journey your husband will soon embark on?"

Peadar's squeeze was insistent, though not at all painful.

"She is correct nonetheless, Tam. She is my wife and no concern at all of yours."

Tam affected to have had his nonexistent feelings hurt.

"Aw, you insult me. I am merely looking out for the family of one of the warriors in my lord's charge. It is my duty, you see, to provide for the widows and the orphans."

Vange was getting a bit scared now, and she was glad when Peadar got up, pulled her up, and stormed off with her without even saying another word to Tam.

ॐ

BOTH OF THEIR emotions were in such a frenzied state when they got back to their room that they got their sons fed, got in bed, and made love passionately without saying a word. In the brief time after that and before they went to sleep, they did manage to talk, a little.

She started.

"All of this is normal to you, isn't it."

"All of what, lass?"

"Only being home with me and the children a tenth of the time. Being gone fighting the rest of the time, unless it's winter."

"Ah, aye, that it is."

"Well it is the farthest thing from normal that I could ever have imagined for my life."

"Surely men fight in your time, aye?"

"We have professional armies, made of only one man in a thousand, I think. The rest of our men stay home with their families all the time. My father does. He and my mom run a business together."

"So ... you did not expect to be without your husband so much, is that it?"

"Yeah, that's a big part of it. But there's more reasons I want to go home. You've seen it there, and you remember, right?"

"Aye, it is grand, that is true."

"It isn't the grandness that I miss."

"Nay?"

"No."

"Then what is it?"

"Peadar, I don't feel safe here. Not even here in our room with you here, not really. You've made me see that yeah, we have to wait until the children can fight a little before we leave, but ... I almost think they would have a better shot at good lives if we left with them right now."

"How can that be true, Vange? You know how defenseless they are."

"Yes, and that will only get worse the longer they stay here without being vaccinated against all the diseases that can kill them."

"What does that mean?"

"In my time, doctors can prevent many diseases, Peadar, like smallpox and measles and mumps. Almost no one dies of contagious diseases. Most people die when they're over sixty, of heart failure and cancer. I want our children to have the protection the doctors can provide them. That wasn't why I wanted to go home at first, but it is the number one reason I want to get home now."

He held her close and caressed her back.

"Our children come from strong stock, lass. We MacGregors are tough. Do not fash."

"I know you're tough, Peadar, and I am very glad. But—"

"Hushhhh. Hush, now. None of your worries can change anything, lass. Facts are facts. We are here in Ireland, and the children cannot travel for half a dozen years yet, anyhow. Do your best to enjoy these years at the castle, eh?"

The more he said, the deeper her depression became. But she resigned herself to the situation and all but gave up on trying to convince him to leave with her and their children.

"I'll try."

He combed her long hair with his fingers.

"At least we are away from the druids and their meddling, lass."

PEADAR WAS AWAY FIGHTING for the O'Neill when Vange finally got her preschool arranged in the castle's dining hall. Why no one else had thought to put all the little ones together so that they could learn from and entertain each other, Vange couldn't imagine. There were four other toddlers in the castle besides Michael and Gabriel—big enough to run around and play, but not quite responsible enough to put to work washing dishes.

In the afternoons the men and older children took the toddlers out into the courtyard for sword practice. Yes, children in this society not only played with toy swords in the cradle, but also practiced right alongside the men. The girls kept at sword practice until they got married and pregnant, but they moved on from dishes to laundry duty when they turned twelve or so.

Vange had finally convinced the other moms to bring their toddlers to her preschool in the mornings, rather than spend that time cooped up in their rooms. It had taken some doing, because Cara was the only other mom she really knew.

There they all were with the toddlers inside a circle of dining chairs in a large open corner of the dining hall. They had gotten a few of the men to move two of the small tables, which never got used except when everyone was home for the winter. The moms had scrubbed the floors and put down some carpets they had washed.

As she taught Michael and Gabriel how to play with their new friends, Vange shared a smile with Cara, whose little daughter Emma was barely nine months old but already walking.

The toddlers weren't playing with swords, either, but with other toys that Vange had either made Aideen dig out of storage or created from scratch herself: a pair of ragdolls and a smallish cradle, three leather balls, and dozens of small stuffed animals.

Vange figured her sons had four years of playtime before they would be expected to work, and she meant to make the best of that time. She had made up games to teach them their colors, their numbers, their directions—and how to read. Yes, she could and would do all that with just her two in the privacy of their room, but she also wanted them to socialize with other children sometimes. There was enough room out here in the dining hall that the children could play games like 'Duck, Duck, Goose.'

At the moment, Vange had all the toddlers seated in an inner circle on one of the carpets, rolling the ball to each other and learning each other's names. The other moms were seated along the outer circle of dining chairs, watching. That was part of it, too.

Vange was teaching the other moms how to teach the toddlers.

It was very satisfying.

Vange herself made up part of the circle of toddlers on the floor.

"That's it, Michael, roll it over to Emma now."

"Good catch, Emma. Roll it to Sasha."

Sasha missed the ball.

Michael was up in an instant, running after it.

"I get it."

"Thank you, Michael. Please sit down and roll it to Sean."

Vange was honest with herself, too. She acknowledged that she was anxious to use what she had learned about the art of teaching. Sure, she had trained to teach second graders, but she had studied child development, and many of the teaching techniques worked across both ages. And the more students, the better. Well, more were better to a certain point, anyway, but she was in no danger of having too many toddlers to teach here—

"Evangeline. I'm so pleased to have unearthed your hiding place. And to think, if I had but stayed late after the morning meal, I might have discovered you here long ago."

What was Tam up to now?

Now that he knows Peadar can and will pulverize him, that is.

The pompous man had left her alone for so long that Vange had all but forgotten about him.

"Hello, Tam."

"Hello, Evangeline. Might I have a word with you in the O'Neill's study?"

He can't think I'll go for that.

She gestured around the circle of toddlers as if to say, 'I'm busy here.'

"That hardly seems necessary," she said out loud, "go ahead and speak here."

But the other moms gasped.

Vange took a fresh look at Tam.

His chin was raised in that arrogant way of command that he had, and his foot was tapping impatiently.

He thinks that just because I'm out here in the common area where he can see me, I'm fair game.

Looking at his air of confident command, Vange realized

Tam had fully expected her to follow him up to that private study—like a lamb to the slaughter.

There was a hard tone in his voice when he spoke next. All pretense at friendliness was gone.

"I don't think I made myself clear. You are to come with me. Now."

Vange very pointedly did not look at the man. She was starting to feel afraid, and she wouldn't give him the satisfaction of seeing it in her eyes.

She would not leave this public room with him, either.

She kept her own voice neutral, but she spoke as loudly as she could, hoping someone would hear and come to investigate, like that first morning at the castle in her old room at the top of the stairs.

"You're frightening the children, Tam."

It was true. The children had stopped rolling the ball and were in various stages of becoming upset. Little Emma had her thumb in her mouth.

If he comes anywhere near the children, then I'm going to have to go with him in order to keep them safe.

Vange didn't see any other adults in the hall besides Tam and the moms. She kept her ears open for the first sound of wooden chairs scuffing across the stone floor to indicate Tam was approaching her while she held her arms out for Gabriel and Michael to come to her.

She nodded when she saw the other moms doing the same thing.

But Tam surprised her.

"Well, if I can't get the answers I want from you, Evangeline, then I'll just have to get them from one of these other women you've dragged out of their rooms to pass the time with you here in the dining hall. Let me see ... which one looks the most likely to tell me ..."

All in a rush, Vange stood up and went to Tam.

"All right, you win. I'll go with you."

But Tam gave Vange a hard look and continued leering at the other moms.

And then his gaze landed on Cara.

"You. Come with me."

Cara handed Emma to Roisin and obediently got up.

But her face was stricken with terror.

Vange moved between Cara and Tam.

She kept her voice as loud as she dared, still in the hope that someone would hear what was going on—and care enough to interfere.

"You don't need her, Tam. Please leave her be. I'll go. I'm sorry I didn't go with you right away."

Tam smiled cruelly at Vange.

"Very well," he told Cara, "It turns out I won't be needing to see you in private after all. You may sit down and resume your silly baby games, if that's how you wish to squander your time."

Cara let out a breath, took Emma into her arms, gave Vange a frightened look, and fled the room.

Tam addressed the other mothers.

"If the rest of you wish to go back to your rooms, I think that would be wise."

They all started getting up and gathering their children.

"You." Tam pointed to Roisin.

Vange was horrified at the look Roisin gave Tam. It was all fear with not one bit of defiance.

But that wasn't what disturbed her most. No, it was Roisin's resignation that unsettled Vange. Roisin had grown up with the idea that men were better than her and had the right to just take her if she looked at all available—and Roisin accepted that.

And that wasn't all.

Vange had insisted that Roisin would be fine in the dining

hall with her children.

"Please," Vange said, "Please, Tam, let me be enough. Let the rest of them alone."

Tam smiled that cruel smile at her again.

And then he turned to Roisin.

"Be a dear and take Evangeline's boys up to your room with you."

To Vange's horror, Tam then addressed Michael and Gabriel directly, though to his credit, he put a nice face on while he did so.

"She'll be busy for an hour or so, but she'll come get you after that, eh?"

He knows where my children will be.

Vange meekly followed Tam to the O'Neill's study and stepped inside.

TAM SHUT the door behind the two of them and leaned against it.

"Disappointed you might be at the news, Evangeline, but I truly do wish to speak with you here, nothing more."

Vange had backed away from him and was cursing herself for getting trapped there so close to him, leaning back against the O'Neill's huge desk.

"What?"

"Out with the men I went, and only now just returned am I. While I was out, a curious bit of news I did hear."

"Tam, please get to the point."

This made him laugh, a deep boisterous gut-laugh.

"Ha ha ha ha ha ha. Oh Evangeline, such a study in contradiction you are. Even when you beg do you order men about."

Vange tried to swallow the lump that was forming in her

throat.

Why won't he just spit it out?

Tam moved closer to her.

She shrank away from him until she realized if she kept it up, then she'd be lying down on the desk. She froze in an awkward half-reclined position. It was uncomfortable.

Tam smiled cruelly at her discomfort. He didn't give her even an inch to rise back up into a standing position, either, just stood there crowding her.

"I know your secret, Vange."

No way. How on Earth would he know I was from the future? Huh. Did Saraid send him word? Why would she do that?

Vange felt herself start to sweat profusely. Her heartbeat accelerated, and her mouth went dry.

Tam continued to gloat over her.

"Imagine Peadar's face when I tell everyone at supper. Imagine his shame and his fear. What will they do to him back in Scotland if they find out he lives, hm?"

Huh? What is he talking about?

Tam's chin went up haughtily.

"I knew you were no lady, Evangeline. Why would any lord stoop so low? Only a MacGregor would marry a brown island savage."

Just then, the door opened abruptly.

Tam turned to see who was there.

Vange used the distraction to get out from between Tam and the desk. In fact, she moved as close to the open doorway as she could.

Aideen came bustling in with a tray full of food. Humming an odd tune, she placed the tray on the desk, took Vange's arm, and started to leave with her.

The older woman just about jumped out of her shoes when Tam spoke to Vange, but she kept her composure. And she kept humming.

Tam had sat down at the desk and started picking at the food.

"You may go, Evangeline. But think on what I told you. I can be patient. Decide which way things should go. Decide which course of events would upset Peadar less."

Aideen stopped in the open doorway and shooed Vange out, still humming.

Vange didn't need to be told twice. If she hadn't been wearing two long skirts, she would have run to Roisin's room to get her children. She walked as fast as she could.

Once Vange, Michael, and Gabriel were all safe in the kitchen, Aideen returned. She looked at Vange and spoke matter-of-factly.

"Yes, a great risk I did take in getting you out of that study, Vange, but do it I did. What be the cause you say, Vange? It is pregnant you are again."

NEEDLESS TO SAY, no one wanted to do preschool anymore.

Vange and Cara brought their three kids into Aideen's kitchen instead.

Vange threw herself into teaching the little ones, and the kitchen turned out to be a good place for that. They were all starting to eat solid food. They liked it, and they would listen carefully to all the words associated with food.

She arranged the veggie bits she chopped up for the stews into letters on the butcher block, and all three children knew all their letters the first week. And then she started in on the sounds the letters made.

Cara, Isleen, and Nora held Emma, Michael, and Gabriel so that they could see the cutting board while Vange arranged her veggies on it.

"Which vegetable is this, Emma?"

"Celery."

Vange gave Emma a bite of celery.

"Good. What color is celery, Gabriel?"

"Green."

Gabriel got a bite of celery, too.

"Good. Which two letters are these, Michael?"

"S and H."

Michael got his bite.

"Good. And now listen. Here's something new. SH makes the sound 'shhhh'. Everybody say, 'shhhhhh'."

"Sshhbbhhbbhh," said the children, invariably spitting a bit and bubbling up through their lips.

"Shhhhh," said the women, grinning at each other over how cute the children sounded.

Vange knew Aideen had a heart of gold, and she truly owed the woman her life twice over now for how she'd been saved from Tam, but the old cook made Vange a bit uncomfortable with her comments about Vange's teaching.

"A bit surprised I am, to find you learned reading on your island."

Vange frowned at her.

"Would it surprise you to know we have houses there too, and don't live in mud huts?"

Although Aideen rolled her eyes, Vange could tell she really had believed the island was that primitive.

Maybe here in 1562 it really was? Oh well.

But inside her mind, Vange was anything but calm, cool, or collected.

She was pregnant again.

She knew she should feel joy about having a new child to love, but she didn't. All it meant to her was being stuck here away from her real life for another two years.

So then I feel guilty, too, for not being joyful and feeling love for you, baby.

Tam knew she and Peadar were really MacGregors.

Miraculously, he still hadn't found her secret kitchen hangout. But she lived in even deeper dread of him than before.

Peadar would come home.

This was normally what sustained Vange through the long boring times hiding in the kitchen, but now she dreaded her husband's return. Emily's email had warned about the MacGregors being persecuted soon. Would that go on here in Ireland too, or only in the highlands?

As if all that weren't enough, Vange had another source of guilt.

Her deepest hope was that on finding out they were MacGregors, the O'Neill would ship her and Peadar and their children back to the highlands—so that Vange could find a druid castle healer who would send her back to the 21st century.

So Vange passed the time in this stressful state until Peadar did come home. That day, she was waiting with the other wives of men assigned to the O'Neill's personal guard. By now, she knew to look for the O'Neill's flag flying over the hill when the dust started.

There he was.

Vange was three months pregnant. Aideen had been keeping her pretty sedate, advising her it was best she didn't jar her body. And yet Vange was so full of dread about how Tam was planning to reveal Peadar was a MacGregor that as soon as she saw Peadar coming, she took off running out to meet him.

"Peadar. Peadar."

The other men laughed as Vange ran by them.

Vange ran headlong into Peadar and nearly tackled him. As it was, she had managed to move Peadar a good ten feet away from the other men. She made a show of grabbing her

man and kissing him, but under her breath, she
warned him.

"Tam knows you're a MacGregor, Peadar."

But it had obviously been too long since Peadar enjoyed
one of her kisses. He was really into it—or perhaps into
showing her off in front of the other men.

He deepened their kiss until he started drawing wolf whis-
tles from the other men.

Vange ended the kiss and hissed at her husband.

"Peadar. Tam knows you're a MacGregor."

Peadar glanced over at the O'Neill.

Vange did too, and she saw the O'Neill nod at Peadar.

Her husband at last focused on Vange as he grabbed her
by the waist and started them walking at a distance from the
other men.

"Sorry I am, lass. I do not understand this jest."

Vange was furious with him, and her hissing was hurting
her throat it became so vicious.

"It's not a jest. Tam tried to get me to sleep with him,
Peadar, in order to stop him from telling. I've been avoiding
him, but now that you're home, he'll tell, and—"

Peadar put his hand over Vange's mouth to stop her.

She looked at him to see if he was feverish or something,
which was the only way she could explain to herself why he
wasn't as freaked out as she was.

But of all things, Peadar looked … guilty.

"Aye, lass. He has known for a time now, as I did tell the
O'Neill in Tam's presence."

Vange beat her fist on her husband's chest. It was purely
symbolic. She knew she was nowhere near strong enough to
actually hurt him.

"You should have told me that you'd told them, Peadar."

He didn't stop her from beating on his chest. It couldn't
have made him look any too tough in front of the other men.

"Aye lass, I should have."

Vange continued her feeble attempt at getting her anger out.

"All these months I've lived in dread of him blabbing it."

Peadar continued walking with his arm around her waist, enduring the humiliation of his wife striking him without stopping her.

"Aye, I can see that now."

She was no longer hissing, but worse. Vange was crying. Still, she gave him a piece of her mind.

"We have to tell each other when we decide something, if we're ever going to have a good marriage, Peadar."

At that he stopped and took her in his arms.

Anger spent, needing him, and all-out sobbing now, she let him hold her close as the sun set behind them over the castle stronghold and the men marched by them with their rattling weapons.

"There's more, Peadar."

"Aye, lass?"

"I'm pregnant again."

VANGE HAD Michael and Gabriel show their father all that they had learned—their colors, the names of different foods, their letters, and the sounds the letters made—and then she put the boys to bed in Aideen's room off the kitchen so that she and Peadar could spend a good night together. The two of them awoke once more to breakfast in bed courtesy of Aideen and the boys, who enjoyed it with them.

"Aideen, can you watch the boys while—"

Aideen held out her hands, and the boys climbed down off the bed to take them. They stood there smiling.

"Shoo. It is watching them I will be while Peadar is home.

I will bring the boys to you now and then to visit, but enjoy your time together. Now go on."

Vange waved goodbye to their sons as they left.

The boys waved back, but they looked perfectly happy to go to the kitchen with Aideen.

Peadar offered Vange a hand up from the bed.

"Let us dress, lass, and then I am going to give Tam another lesson in how to treat my wife."

Vange was of a mixed mind as she dressed.

Yay. That's my man.

Wait, is this a good idea?

Are you kidding? It's a great idea.

Looking very much the highlands lord and his lady in their matching red plaid finery, the two of them went down to the great hall of the castle fortress. The O'Neill sat in a throne, in judgement of disputes. Tam was seated in the throne beside him instead of the O'Neill's wife, which Vange found amusing.

A long line of petitioners awaited the O'Neill's attention.

Peadar led Vange to the end of the line and stood with her there.

Vange caught Tam looking at them.

Tam looked curious at first.

And then Vange saw Peadar glaring at Tam.

The arrogant Irishman looked away.

Peadar and Vange moved up in the line a spot.

Tam started to fidget.

Another case done, another move up in line.

The man behind Peadar and Vange laughed a little.

"Sure and you have Tam on edge."

Peadar turned to nod at the man.

"Aye Diarmuid, and if Tam does know what is good for him, then he will come down here and apologize before I do get up to the front of the line and tell the entire company what he has done."

Murmurs of Peadar's intentions spread out from him through the crowd, and everyone watched Tam with interest.

Especially when Tam got up and started slinking toward the door.

Peadar pointed at Tam and shouted.

"Stop that man who does slink away like a common thief. My dispute is with him, and he will hear the O'Neill's judgement."

Grinning, some of the men casually moved in front of the door to block Tam's path.

Vange looked at Shane O'Neill to see his reaction to all this.

Oh no.

The O'Neill looked annoyed, but Vange's anxiety decreased when he spoke.

"Tam, stay you will, and hear Peadar's complaint."

With a hard stare at Peadar, Tam strode back to his throne and sat with his arms crossed.

The O'Neill looked to the next petitioners in line and took care of their complaints while Tam and Peadar glared at each other and the others in the room laid bets on who would win the confrontation.

And then Peadar was before the enthroned O'Neill.

Everyone fell silent.

Peadar nodded a sort of bow, and Shane gestured for Peadar to rise. And then Peadar spoke.

"Shane O'Neill, there lies a dispute between your best man Tam and myself. I do take the blame for my part."

The men and women in the room made questioning noises.

Peadar turned to face the crowd, and he took off the fine jacket he was wearing and threw it on the floor.

"I did come here under false pretenses. I am not a MacNeal, nay, nor any lord. I am but a simple highlands warrior, from clan MacGregor."

The men looked confused. Some looked shocked.

Seeing a few who looked angry, Vange inched the two of them closer to Shane, who she felt reasonably sure would protect her and Peadar with a decree.

She also saw Tam gloating there on his throne, with a cruel look on his face.

Shane O'Neill held up his hand for silence. When it didn't come, he stood.

That worked.

The room quickly fell silent, with all eyes on Shane when he spoke to Peadar.

"On that I have already judged thee, and found thee free from guilt."

Shane then raised his eyes to the people.

"He is not a MacNeal nor a lord, but Peadar does have more honor than they, for he is here in their place, by their treachery. I will hear nothing against Peadar for it, for even though treachery brought him, he does serve me well, and I am grateful."

Vange heard the people murmuring to each other, clarifying what Shane had said, and what that meant. At first, some of them seemed alarmed, but gradually they calmed down.

"So he is not a lord?"

"No, the lords did make him take their place in the fighting."

"And Shane says he fights well."

"Sure, and he is a MacGregor, the best fighters of all are they."

"Tis true. Much of the Norse stock have they."

Shane let the murmurings die down before he continued.

"If that is all of the dispute on your side, Peadar, then I would hear what you have to say against Tam."

Peadar did that nodding bow thing again to Shane.

"Well enough."

And then Peadar faced Tam.

"If I hear one more time of you mistreating my wife or restricting her activities or those of any of the other wives under this roof, so help me God I will kill you."

SHANE MADE enquiries and got the whole story. He then proclaimed Tam unfit for the position of best man at court and removed him from that duty, demoting him to a common soldier. This meant of course that Tam would go out with all the men to the fighting and not remain behind to oversee the castle fortress as he had been doing.

This made Vange sigh with relief.

It seemed to Vange that the rest of the men looked up to Peadar even more than they had before, after he stood up to Tam so publicly. And her impression turned out to be shared by Shane. The men went out to the fighting, and Tam went with them.

And Shane left Peadar behind to keep an eye on the castle while he was gone.

Vange and Peadar and the boys enjoyed a wonderful two months at home without Tam and with fairly little to actually do besides making sure the boys learned as much as they could from their father, and that the boys got as much love from their father as they wanted.

Shane gathered everyone in the castle courtyard for the afternoon sword practice when his troop of men came home for a break from the fighting, and Shane made a big announcement.

"As a foreign young warrior, Peadar cannot be filling the place of best man at court that Tam left behind. However, you all look up to him. So I have decided to allow him to lead the sword practices here. So Peadar, go on and start them."

Vange had always enjoyed watching sword practice, and her chest swelled with pride at watching her man lead it. She thought it went exceptionally well under his leadership, too.

A bit anxious, Vange looked around for Tam at the practice, but she didn't see him.

"He is out with another company of men."

Vange looked for the owner of the voice she'd just heard, and there was Diarmuid. She smiled at him.

"You mean Tam is out fighting still?"

Diarmuid nodded yes.

"Yay, that he is."

"Was it obvious I was looking for Tam?"

Diarmuid made a staying gesture and settled in beside her to watch the sword practices until his turn.

"Blaming you I will not be, lassie."

That evening, Vange and Peadar dressed in the least fine clothing in the trunk and went down to supper in the great hall, taking a place with the common soldiers now that everyone knew they weren't nobility.

But a page showed up and addressed them.

"The O'Neill insists that you join him at the head table. Follow me."

Everyone smiled at the two of them as they passed by, and some even toasted them with their tankards.

Vange smiled back nervously. She didn't want all this attention. Tam was bound to come home sooner or later, and he would be furious. And Peadar couldn't be by her side every moment...

It kept getting worse until it was ridiculous.

Peadar was invited to stand by while Shane and his new

wife held court and heard petitioners. Peadar was shown the study and asked to do the paperwork. In fact, over the next six months, Peadar was given every honor that Tam previously had, short only of the name of best man at court.

And Tam still hadn't come home, but he had to eventually.

Vange commented on that one night as they spooned in their room alone, his hands on her gigantic belly and the children as usual happily tucked in bed in Aideen's room.

"I never expected Shane to give you Tam's position."

"Nay, nor did I."

Vange sighed.

"He'll be furious when he comes home and sees you in all his old places, but I do like that you're home all the time now."

Peadar fidgeted with the tie on Vange's night dress.

"I do feel cooped up here in the castle, lass."

As if I don't. I love my children, but they are keeping me hostage here. You lucky men can have it both ways.

Vange groaned. She knew better than to argue with him. He would just shut down, like her father always did when her mother argued. Ug. It figured that once he had a job he could do right there at home with her, he wished it away so that he could leave again.

She tried the tactic of understanding his reasoning.

"Yeah, that's why you've started taking one of the men with you, huh, so that someone else can do the job and you can go back out with the men?"

Peadar laughed.

"Heh ha ha. Aye, lass. There is naught that does get past you."

Vange smiled at the compliment at the same time as she inwardly seethed at him for not telling her this plan before he set it in motion. When was he going to learn to treat her like a partner and not just someone who depended on him for protection and a roof over her head? Did he even listen when she talked of that?

Her mind whirled with those thoughts as she tried to think of a new way to make him understand.

And then her water broke.

"Uh, Peadar, the baby is coming. Will you go wake Aideen for me please?"

He did.

And then he was in the great hall being toasted as the father of three. She could hear the laughing and carousing all the way from the kitchen.

No matter, though. She was with her friends. Vange had missed talking with Cara, Isleen, and Nora the past six months, and they caught each other up on their lives these past six months as they walked Vange round and round the kitchen again.

And again, once the contractions got close together, Aideen had one of the huge washtubs brought in and filled with warm water so that Vange could give birth in it.

Also again, Aideen hummed an odd tune the while.

And once again, even though Vange knew she should be feeling pain, she didn't. It was like when the dentist numbed her mouth up and filled a cavity. She felt her womb contracting, but she didn't feel the pain. She was fine with that.

And then she suddenly wasn't.

The baby came. She felt it come out of her into the world. She was filled with joy when they told her she had another son. She named him Jeffrey, and she smiled while they washed him.

But then she felt more contractions.

She was having twins again.

Which is statistically so unlikely as to be impossible.

Vange looked at Aideen.

The woman was still humming, but it seemed she had a knowing glint in her eye.

She's responsible for this.

She poked holes in the condoms.

Why did I trust her?

She has magic, or how would her humming take my pain away?

She's a druid.

She's part of the curse on the MacGregors.

And right as Vange realized that, she had Johnathan, Peadar MacGregor's fourth son.

VANGE THOUGHT Aideen must have realized she would figure all this out as soon as her fourth son was born, because the two of them were alone with the babies in the kitchen now. Aideen must have excused Cara, Isleen, and Nora during the birth this time.

Vange had opened her mouth to berate the old woman for trapping her there in the castle in Ireland.

How dare she. I want to throttle her.

But then she realized something else.

If Aideen was a druid...

Then Aideen could send Vange home.

The elation of realizing that overpowered all else for a moment, and Vange felt herself beaming a smile at the old cook.

Aideen gave Vange a knowing smile in return. It was a friendly smile, almost a hopeful smile, but at the same time, it was reserved and almost fearful.

She can send me home.

But how do I make sure she will?

Gazing into the old woman's hopeful yet fearful eyes, Vange thought it over and realized that she herself held a

powerful card in this situation. The Irish believed that Saint
Patrick had driven all the druids off their island. This was a
Catholic place now, and the priests had some power.

'All roads lead to Rome,' indeed.

The priests would not take kindly to the idea that a druid
had been living among them for fifty years. They would ... get
rid of any druid they uncovered.

And now that Peadar sat at his right hand, Shane would
believe Vange if she told him about Aideen. He would report
the druid presence to the priests. She knew he would.

Vange came back to the moment at hand.

Aideen was still smiling her hopeful yet fearful smile.

*She has magic, and there's no telling what she might prefer to do,
rather than send me home. She might run. She might reveal my
greater secret to the people here, and who knows what they would do
to me and my children.*

Could Aideen use her magic to pop herself right out of here?

Vange knew she had to play her card just right. She
couldn't rush into what she said to the old cook. She had to
think it through. Be deliberate. Negotiate. While she mulled
this over, Vange lowered her eyes from Aideen to examine her
fourth son the way any new mother would: ten fingers,
ten toes.

Yep, he's whole and healthy.

And there around Johnathan's ankle was the same birthmark that his grandfather Dall had, the one that looked like a
ring of standing stones.

When Vange looked up from the birthmark to find
Aideen, the two women's eyes met again. If she didn't say
something soon, the silence was going to get awkward.

Vange decided to be direct and simple as she sat in the
tub nursing Jeffrey and Johnathan, but at the same time, she
kept her voice as quiet as she could while still allowing the
other woman to hear her. If anyone else heard that Aideen

was a druid, it would ruin all of Vange's leverage—and very likely kill her one chance at getting home.

"Send me and Peadar and all four of our boys home to my parents now."

Winking at Vange, Aideen kept her voice just as low.

"It is clever you are, Evangeline."

Vange smirked.

"I try."

"In such a place as yours, most women would threaten an old cook, try to make her fear their newly made alliance with the O'Neill. But not you, eh?"

Vange felt her lips pursing.

"Aideen, you've done so much for me and my family. I know you saved me from terrible grief at Tam's hands."

The old cook reached out, perhaps to caress Vange's face.

Arms busy holding both of her newborn sons so they could nurse, Vange flinched away.

"I choose to believe you were going to send us home anyway, eventually."

The two looked at each other some more, and Vange wondered if the other woman was wishing, as she was, that they truly were just friends, and that all this druid stuff was just a fairy tale.

Vange continued.

"Look, you've acknowledged my leverage with Shane. Let it compel you to send us back now. Today."

Aideen withdrew her hand and gave Vange a sad look.

"Shane and the men will wonder where you have gone—"

Vange interrupted, staring pointedly at the older woman.

"Yeah, they will—unless you work some of your humming magic on them."

Now Aideen grimaced.

"Clever, indeed."

Vange relaxed a little. She'd expected the old cook to deny

what she was. Maybe this was going to be easy.

"I'm confident in your abilities, Aideen."

But maybe it wasn't going to be easy.

Oh no.

Vange knew that look.

Aideen was looking at her the same way her mother had looked at her when she went off to college. And just as Vange had then, she felt an urgent need to be gone, to start the next chapter of her life. To be out on her own. Out from under an older person's wing.

The old woman is fond of me, is she? Hm.

How can I use that to my advantage without sending her over the edge into crazy clingy-ville?

She looks about ready to go there.

Thinking of everything the old cook had done for her, Vange followed her instincts and allowed a genuine and tender smile to show on her face.

"My children deserve to know their grandparents, Aideen."

The cook nodded yes, but then she looked concerned.

"Tis true, tis true. You know, Vange, when Johnathan is five and twenty, he will be called to serve ... us, eh?"

Vange nodded and felt her face grow serious. She lowered her voice even more, and she kicked the water in the tub to make some cover-up noise, for good measure.

"Yeah. Peadar explained the curse to me. That's why you ... people wanted me to come here to the 16th century, isn't it. You knew that here, you could force me to have four sons in quick succession, whereas at home in the 21st century ..."

A haunted look crossed Aideen's face.

"I did not make the curse, Vange. And I do not agree with it. However, I serve under some compulsion as well. It is sorry I am, to see your son saddled with service, but glad I am that he lives, that he was not killed in the womb."

That's not a fair thing to say.

❧

VANGE GROUND her teeth at the older woman's presumption to know what was right for her—especially in light of the fact that the old druid had been keeping Vange's babies away from the modern medical world of vaccinations.

Ooh, I ought to tell her just how wrong she is.

But just in time, Vange remembered to keep the peace. Remembered that she still needed Aideen to get her and her family home.

And anyway, she had another burning question, with no one better to answer it.

"But Aideen, why did you … people allow Peadar to come to the … place where he met me, then? Wouldn't it have been easier for you to just keep him here and marry him off to a woman from his own … place and give him four sons through her?"

Aideen gave Vange a friendly and sad frown.

"Easy is not the way, lassie. No, profit is the way. Too much money they make, and too easily, impressing the folk of your time with the lore of our time."

What? No way. That's just silly.

"Huh. The renaissance faire? All this is just so they can run that? You can't be serious."

But Aideen was shaking her head yes.

"Oh, but I am, dead serious. The money they make from that funds … everything."

Vange struggled to understand.

"But why don't you … people just travel back and forth in time yourselves and put the faires on? Why have slaves do it?"

Aideen winced at the word 'slaves'.

Vange lowered her chin and raised her eyebrows at
the woman.

Aideen gave a little sideways nod, and then she lowered
her voice to the barest of whispers so that Vange had to lean
way forward in her tub over her babies, to make out what the
druid said.

"We cannot travel through time ourselves, lassie. It does
not work that way. We can only travel to other places, and
only by sending each other. Nay, we must have ... help."

Vange felt kind of awestruck at the implications for a
moment.

The druids need us.

That gave her more cards to play in the future, on Emily
and Dall's behalf. Vange smiled gratefully at her friend.

Aideen's return smile was finally full of hope and lacking
the fear.

But she still hasn't said she'll send us home.

Appealing to the older woman's humanity with her eyes,
Vange gave out her unspoken ultimatum again.

"Figure out some cover story and get all six of us to my
parents today." *Or else I'll tell Shane you're a druid, and the priests
will come burn you. I will, too. None of this new information means a
thing to me here in 1563. I am so done being here.*

Vange held her breath and prayed that the woman would
do the right thing.

Aideen nodded yes, reached for the babies, and put them
in a cradle just inside her bedroom.

Vange was astonished to see Michael and Gabriel in there
too, on Aideen's bed, sound asleep.

Aideen came back to the tub and held out her hand.

"You must be dry to travel home, eh?"

"Oh. Yeah."

Once Vange had dried off, dressed in her least fine Scottish clothing, and had seated herself on the bed between

Michael and Gabriel, Aideen went and opened the door to the room where the children washed dishes.

"Maebh."

Vange next heard the voice of a girl of twelve or so.

"Yes?"

"Go and discreetly tell Peadar that he has two more sons. Ask will he come alone to the kitchen and see them."

"Yes, 'm."

Vange was snuggled between Michael and Gabriel on the bed and rocking the cradle with her foot when Peadar came into Aideen's room off the kitchen. The door closed gently behind him, leaving their growing family alone in private. All the boys were still asleep, miraculously—or more likely due to Aideen's humming.

"Is it so, lass? Do we have two more sons?"

Vange stopped the cradle with her foot so that it was rocked toward Peadar and he could see inside.

"Yes. That's Jeffrey on the left, and Johnathan on the right —your fourth son."

Peadar calmly knelt by the cradle and examined both babies pretty much the same way Vange had: ten fingers, ten toes ... and oh yeah, Johnathan's birthmark that declared the druids' curse on him.

Peadar held Johnathan to his chest and cried for a minute before he could speak.

"I did not mean for the druids to get another MacGregor servant. You were right, Vange. We should have left that first night when I returned here. You were pregnant, but we had a chance at getting back home. Now, with four children and who knows how many more to come, I do not know how—"

While Peadar spoke, Vange leaned over and took Johnathan from Peadar's stiff arm and put him in the cradle. Then she put what she hoped was a soothing hand on her husband's shoulder and spoke to him quietly.

"It's OK, Peadar. We have a way home. We're going as soon as you're ready."

She lowered her voice to a whisper.

"And the trip will be over in an instant."

Peadar looked up at Vange with a question in his eyes, and also with hope there.

Vange pointed into the kitchen, put her mouth to her husband's ear, and whispered her lowest, barely audible whisper.

"Aideen is a druid."

VANGE SAW the anger on Peadar's face, saw his fists balling up. She understood his urge to punish the one druid who was present and accessible, to punish her for the curse that the druids of old had put on their whole family generations ago. She even shared a bit of that urge.

But the druids were her one ticket home. Without their cooperation, she and her children would for sure be stuck here in this backward time for the rest of their lives.

Vange was sure Aideen could hear the two of them talking right now. She had to keep her husband from killing their ticket home without cluing her in to just how dependent they were on her, and without alerting anyone else.

So she whispered to him yet again, pleading with her eyes and caressing his shoulder with her hand in as calming a way as she could manage.

"Please, Peadar. She's been good to me. She saved me from Tam, remember. She isn't the one who put the curse on us."

She felt Peadar slowly relax under her hand.

He took a deep breath and let it out, swallowed, and then nodded yes.

"Aye, very well, lass. You have the right of it."

As if she had already been in the room and heard what they were saying, Aideen breezed up to them just then.

"Gather all that you would take home with you. I do recommend you take some artifacts that will make you a good profit. Like as not you will need it to fend for your family, eh?"

Peadar nodded yes and went to their room, returning with all of his weapons: the bow and dozens of arrows, his claymore, four daggers, and a shield. He also had a pouch that Vange had seen on him before whenever he'd left for battle, and a large canvas sack, which he opened to show her most of the clothing from the trunk. He handed Vange her own belt of pouches, which she put on.

And then Peadar loaded all of his weapons on his body, tied the sack to his belt, and sat next to Vange on the bed.

"Now we are ready, mistress. Send us on our way."

Remembering she had to be touching everyone who time traveled with her before, Vange reached out to pick up Jeffrey and Johnathan from their cradle.

Aideen put her hands on Vange and Peadar's shoulders.

"Good that you are ready, and go we shall, when the hour is right. For now, sleep. Hmmmm hm hmm hm hmmm..."

Vange's arms grew heavy on their way down to pick up her newborn babies, and she slumped down on the bed against Peadar and fell fast asleep.

SHE AWOKE what seemed like the next instant, but when she looked around, she noticed it was dark. No light came under Aideen's bedroom door.

Jeffrey and Johnathan started crying to be fed the same instant.

Vange reached for them, and noisily with all the weapons on his person, Peadar helped her.

Their babies were wrapped in soft quilted blankets, and Vange smiled tenderly as she started them nursing.

The door opened, and Vange saw Michael and Gabriel sitting on high stools at the butcher block in the kitchen, gobbling down a meal of their own. They were dressed for outside, even with tiny leather shoes on.

She also got a good look out the window into the court-yard and saw that it was indeed pitch black outside. Thousands of stars dazzled the sky.

We must have slept eight hours at least, because even after giving birth yesterday, I feel well rested.

Aideen breezed into her room and handed Vange and Peadar their own late supper. She also put all of their cloaks on the bed. When everyone was done eating and Aideen had washed both the toddlers' faces, she put her own cloak on and watched while all of them put on their cloaks. And then she lit a torch in the fireplace and called them all into the dishwashing room, of all places.

Vange cradled Johnathan and held Michael's hand.

Peadar did similar with Jeffrey and Gabriel.

Aideen pushed aside a cupboard in the dishwashing room to reveal a hidden tunnel in the floor. She held her torch over the entrance.

Vange saw that the tunnel went down toward the outside of the castle, on the side where there was a large forest. The walls of the tunnel were roughly hewn stone, which meant the tunnel had been chipped out of the rock foundation of the castle stronghold. She had no idea how this had been done in such a primitive time period, and she marveled at it.

Aideen entered the tunnel and stood aside, waiting for them to enter.

"Tis not far, the sacred grove where we need to be in

order to send you on your way."

Vange looked at Peadar, who gave her a tentative smile and then entered the tunnel. She followed.

Behind her, she heard a bunch of noises that scared her and made her start running until she realized what was going on. Aideen was pulling the cupboard back over the entrance. The druid passed by them in the narrow stone passageway and then led them through the tunnel with her torch.

It wasn't far, just a hundred feet or so. The tunnel went down enough to get them under the castle, then straight, and finally up. There were tiny holes in the floor, and Vange guessed they were drains for any water that got in. The tunnel was very well-built.

It seemed to come to a dead end, but then Aideen pushed forward on the stone to the right of the end, and it swung open like a door.

Holding the torch in the doorway, the old druid spoke to them calmly and quietly.

"My brothers and sisters have come to help send you on your way. We have not the time for you to make conversation with them, nor even for introductions. Just walk to the center of the circle and sit down so that all six of you are touching each other."

Vange followed Peadar out of the tunnel and into the sacred grove of trees.

A dozen other people were there, standing in a circle holding torches up to the starry sky.

Peadar had Vange hold both babies while he sat down, and then he arranged both toddlers in his lap, had her put the babies in his arms, and asked her to sit down facing them and move close so that they were all touching each other.

And then all the druids around them hummed until at long last the world started to go round and round—and she was on her way home.

17. VANGE & PEADAR 5

T he world swirled. Vange was on the verge of feeling too dizzy from it when it stopped abruptly—and she, Peadar, and their four tiny sons were sitting on the floor in her room at her parents' house.

Whew. They were back in the 21ˢᵗ century.

Her clothes still hung in the open closet, so she felt reassured that her parents hadn't given up on her. It was dead winter outside—daytime, but snowy, dark, and dreary.

While she clung to her husband and waited for the dizziness to subside, Vange remembered her hurried conversation with Aideen back in 1563, just before the druids all hummed in their circle and the world started swirling.

"BUT MY PARENTS will be so worried then. Why can't you just send me home five minutes after I left?"

Aideen looked significantly at Vange's four tiny sons.

"There would be no way to explain how they came to be, lassie. Though I suppose if returning the same day you left is important to you, then you could leave all your children here with me?"

Vange gazed down on her children. Her heart ached for them. She loved them despite the druid's use of them to manipulate her into staying. She wouldn't even think of leaving her precious babies behind.

Cringing away from Aideen in fear, Vange kissed them all and huddled in closer to them and Peadar.

Was that her plan all along?

Get me to have these beautiful babies and then leave them with her, to do her bidding.

But Aideen smiled kindly at Vange, put a calming hand on her shoulder, and then retreated into the circle of druids, who started humming.

VANGE SNAPPED back to the present moment.

Mom ran into her room through the open door, calling out to her in Tagalog.

"Vangie. Vangie. Oh my baby. I thought I'd never see you again. How dare you go and not tell me. Never do that again, you hear me? Felix. Felix. Felix."

Vange got up and ran to Mom, and the two of them were clamped together in a bear hug when Dad's voice came up from downstairs.

"On my way up there. What is it, Ana? You know I don't like it when you yell through the house like that. Next time, use the intercom on the phone like I—Mika. Vangie. Oh, my little girl is home."

Vange felt warm and safe in her parents' embrace. She let their love pour into her and calm her and pacify her racing heart.

But eventually they noticed the man in her room.

She realized it was probably confusing and then shocking for them. Seeing him sitting there holding two toddlers and two newborn babies—who all looked like their daughter.

Her parents looked from the babies to Vange and back again, a wide range of emotions on their faces. They trembled a little.

Vange checked to see how well her children were handling all this.

The newborns were sound asleep, but the toddlers sat there with their thumbs in their mouths, staring at their grandparents as if they were strangers. Which unfortunately, they were.

Vange spoke up.

"Mom, Dad, this is my husband, Peadar MacGregor. He's a relative of Emily's husband Dall. And these are our children: Michael, Gabriel, Jeffrey, and Johnathan. Boys, this is Grandma and Grandpa."

Grandpa came over and squatted near where Michael sat nestled in Daddy's lap. Grandpa then made funny noises until both Michael and Gabriel were laughing and clapping.

Vange encouraged all this.

Meanwhile, Grandma made a nest for the newborns out of the covers on Vange's bed. She then turned to Peadar and held out her arms for first Jeffrey and then Johnathan. She tucked them in securely and kissed them both.

And then Mom turned around and gave Vange that 'Mom knows best' look.

"Vangie honey, will you come down and help me in the kitchen while the men play with the boys?"

Vange turned to see how Peadar was doing with Dad, to see if he would be OK for a little while.

He seemed to be doing fine, enjoying the playtime with his sons. He grinned at her and nodded, as if to say, "Good luck. Glad I don't have to hear the lecture."

Trying not to laugh, she smiled at her husband, reacting to his joke with her eyes.

Gosh, it's so good to be home. All I have to worry about is a lecture. And Dad has experience watching babies, even if Peadar doesn't. They'll be fine.

"Holler for me if Jeff or John wakes up, OK?"

Peadar nodded yes and then resumed making sure that Michael and Gabriel felt safe and secure while they got to know their grandpa.

Vange followed Mom down the stairs and into the kitchen.

Sure enough, once Mom had closed the door behind them, she took Vange by the upper arms, searched her face, and lectured her in Tagalog.

"Vange. Where have you been? Emily said she could only tell us you were traveling—and how in the world is it that both of you have twin boys?"

What.

Whoa, I was right. Allowing us modern girls to time travel is all about the druids getting us to have babies with their cursed MacGregors so that they have more fourth sons to boss around.

Mom was still talking.

"You know fertility drugs are dangerous. What were you thinking? And you appear out of nowhere and you're married? I don't know where to start. Well, I am so so so so glad you're OK and that you came home, but Evangeline, you can't just disappear like that."

Mom, I am *a grown-up, you know.*

Have been for seven years now.

You got to make the rules while you were paying my college tuition, and I realize now that I haven't always been the most responsible person.

But I'm a mom now, a good one.

And I've been living independent of you for two years. I'm sorry you didn't get to see that. Peadar and I will get our own place to live somewhere in town. He'll get some sort of job, and we'll take care of ourselves.

Vange kept waiting for a chance to tell Mom what she was thinking, but Mom had not stopped talking. Vange knew from experience that once Mom started lecturing, it was best just to wait until she was finished before saying anything.

She was winding down.

It won't be long now.

"Emily told us you would get in some kind of trouble if we called the police or anything, but Vange. You were just gone one day. We didn't know where you were, and ... ah oh oh..."

Vange caught Mom when she collapsed into tears and sobbing. She held Mom while she cried, slowly admitting to herself just how messed up the situation had been for her parents.

How would I feel if one of my boys disappeared for two years?

Vange burst into tears herself.

That's it. I'm telling her everything.

Hugging her and holding her tight, Vange did tell Mom everything.

The whole unbelievable story.

Time travel.

Little phone thieves.

Saraid's surprise wedding and how she shipped Peadar off to Ireland in place of her grandson.

Tam.

Shane.

The curse.

Aideen and the other humming druids.

Mom was still sniffling when she opened her eyes wide and really inspected the Scottish island finery Vange wore. Homespun wool plaid underskirt and overdress. Homespun and hand-embroidered linen am breid hat and leine shirt.

Mom smelled Vange's clothes then, and her hair, and finally her skin. Staring at Vange's clothing, Mom wiped her own tears with an industrially made linen dishtowel.

And then just like Vange would do in the same situation, Mom said something funny.

"OK, now I understand how Emily's parents were able to quit their jobs and start that antiques store."

⁂

NOW THAT MOM was done hyperventilating and had gone to the bathroom to freshen up, Vange picked up the house phone and dialed her old cell number.

Her old voicemail picked up.

I may as well just get this all over with as fast as possible, like tearing off a bandage.

"Hi Em, it's Vange. We're back and we're married and we have four sons, two sets of twins. I hear you had twin boys, too. Isn't that amazing? We had two sets of twin boys. Born right after each other. Even though we used protection after the first two were born. Call me."

But Mom's voice rang out from the bathroom.

"Emily doesn't have your phone anymore, Vangie. Here, you can have it."

Vange's heart sank as Mom gave her phone back to her.

"When did she give it back to you?"

"Oh, she didn't. That lady from the fair she works at brought it by just before they all went off to Australia the first time. I kept paying the bill, thinking you'd be home any day …"

"The first time?"

"Oh yeah, Emily's in Australia right now with that fair."

That made Vange hold her phone gingerly. If some lady from the fair had given it back instead of Emily, then it had been a druid—probably Siobhan. Not that it mattered which druid. Some of them were nice, but none of them could be trusted.

Vange made a worried face at Mom and pointed to the phone.

Mom made writing motions.

Vange nodded and grabbed the pen and paper from near the house phone. She wrote Mom a note:

"The druids can probably hear us through this phone. I'm sorry, but have to get rid of it."

Her mom got a pained expression on her face.

Vange hugged her some more.

My poor mom. She's probably thinking of all the money she poured into this phone for nothing.

But to her credit, Mom nodded yes for Vange to go ahead and get rid of her phone.

Not wanting to talk at all until the phone was safely gone, Vange silently took her sim card out and then threw the phone on the floor and stomped on it. Not confident that that would defeat the druids' spy magic, she filled a pot with hot tap water and threw the phone into it. Still unsatisfied, she then took it out in the back yard and buried it, using the hot water to soften the frozen dirt.

Once that was done, Vange went upstairs to check on her boys.

Peadar smiled at her from where he appeared to be getting along just fine with Dad, who was keeping their toddlers busy with blocks on the floor.

"Mama, I build a castle."

"I build one too."

After she had marveled at what Michael and Gabriel were building enough to satisfy their need to impress her, Vange excused Dad from the room and nursed her newborns while Peadar continued playing with the toddlers. Then she

called Dad back into the room to help Peadar watch
the kids.

Vange went down to the kitchen table and sat with Mom.

"I need to go to Australia to help her."

Mom's face grew determined.

"You mean with the curse that affects my grandsons?"

"Yes."

"Your dad and I will watch the kids."

"Take them to see the doctor and get their immunizations
while you're at it, OK?"

Now, Mom's face looked resigned, but still determined.

"Yes, we definitely will."

Vange ran upstairs and came back down with Peadar's
sack of loot from the Irish castle. She opened it and poured
the contents out on the table.

"We brought all this stuff home from 1563, Mom. We're
going to ask Emily's parents to sell it for us. So we'll pay for
the doctor. You aren't going to have to support us. I know
you're worried about that."

Mom looked at the stuff in wonder for a minute, and then
she turned her crafty eyes back onto her daughter's.

"You'll pay for that phone you destroyed, too."

Vange laughed.

"Deal. So I hope Emily's parents know where she is? Does
she have a new phone? I have to talk to her."

"Of course they do. Here, let's call them and work out
a plan."

And that was just what they did.

They called, and Emily's parents closed their store and
came right over.

Before they even got to the front door, Vange ran out and
hugged them almost as hard as she'd hugged her own parents.

"What's Emily's number? I have to talk to her."

Vange's mom called out from inside the house.

"Bring them inside before you all freeze, Vangie."

So impatiently, Vange did.

Once they were all inside and had been helped off with their coats and been seated comfortably in the living room, Emily's mom took out a piece of scratch paper and wrote on it, talking as she did.

"I'll give you Em's number, but just so you know, Siobhan answers it most of the time."

"What."

"Yeah, I know. She tries to get you to think she's like a secretary to Em, but it's obvious the woman's a control freak. Otherwise, Emily would bring our grandchildren home to visit during the week."

Vange nodded yes.

"They all are control freaks." Vange looked at Mom. "Will you go send Dad down? I think he should hear about the druids and the curse from me. And then please stay with the kids. Peadar's never watched them by himself."

Mom nodded and ran upstairs.

But Dad, Peadar, and all the boys came down. Vange told him and Emily's parents everything, and they all stayed up late into the night, talking and taking turns holding the babies.

WITH THE MODERN conveniences of baby formula and being in business for themselves, Vange's parents were able to look after their grandchildren while she and Peadar went to Australia. A week was all the time her parents could afford to close their insurance agency, but Vange was resolved to make it be enough.

She and Peadar were on a plane the very next morning.

They hadn't spoken much the night before, being exhausted after staying up so late talking with everyone.

Peadar seemed much less awkward on the plane than Vange had imagined he would. Instead of asking what to do or where to go, he had a way of hanging back and observing and then copying those around him, much like his father, she now realized.

Peadar did brace himself with his hands on the armrests right as they took off, but after that he was back to his regular calm and relaxed preparedness.

"So lass." He looked into her eyes with ... curiosity, and then he said softly, "We go to this Australia to find Da and Emily and then persuade the druids there to let up on the curse, aye?"

"Heh heh heh." Vange laughed. "You make it sound so easy. Yeah, that's the plan."

"Well enough. And when we are done with that, then we shall return to Shane in Ireland—"

"What."

"Hush, lass. Other passengers can hear, you ken?"

Vange took a deep breath to keep herself from screaming, and then she hissed in her husband's ear.

"Why in the world would we go back?"

He calmly whispered back to her.

"I must, lass, and I do want you with me."

How can he be so calm as he talks about putting us all in danger again?

"No, you mustn't. We barely got away by threatening to expose the druids there. They won't feel like sending us back home again. And the children are much safer here. What could possibly make you want to go back?"

Peadar got a ... patient look on his face.

"I did give my word to Shane, that I would serve him. Only he can release me from that service, lass. Howsoever, I do agree that the children are safer here in your time, with your clan. Your da gave me some hope we can make that a more permanent arrangement."

Of all the backwards applications of honor, this has got to be the stupidest one I ever heard. He's so stubborn about it, too. Why didn't I know he was so foolishly old fashioned before I married him?

But suddenly the solution was so obvious to Vange that she shook her head 'no' rapidly while she told it to him.

"But you took that oath under duress."

Peadar tilted his head to the side and gave her an incredulous look.

"Aye, howsoever, Shane O'Neill is innocent of that injury."

What the heck is he talking about?

"Huh?"

Peadar's incredulity started to outweigh the patience in his face.

"Saraid put us into duress, not Shane. He did nay wrong."

Is he serious?

"But ... but an oath taken under duress is not binding."

The incredulity on Peadar's face was definitely winning now. That, and ...

Oh no.

Resolve.

"I do not owe my service to the one who wronged us, lass. Theretofore, I still owe the service I gave my word that I would provide. And that makes the end of my need to discuss it."

Peadar crossed his arms.

Vange felt all alone once more. She kept going over and over in her mind what she might say to talk him out of this insanity, but she came up with nothing.

Together physically but not mentally, the two of them changed planes three times, ate six meals in airports, and slept fitfully in an airport motel before they set foot on Australian soil.

Throughout this time, Peadar still put his hand on Vange's back to guide her when they walked.

She shrank away from his touch.

He still opened doors for her.

She rushed ahead and opened her own door whenever she could.

He carried their bulky carry-on luggage and wheeled two rolling bags while she only rolled one.

She let him do that.

Another thing was bothering Vange, too. Emily's parents had given them a check as an advance on the antiques they would sell in their store. Her dad had cashed it for them while she and Peadar spent as much time as possible with the boys before they left.

And Dad had handed the cash VISA card to Peadar.

So it was Peadar who paid whenever they ate and for the motel.

Why did Dad do that? I'm perfectly capable of handling money. It's just one more thing that makes me feel like I'm all alone with no one to trust.

Well, I can trust Mom.

And Emily. I think.

Throughout their journey though, Peadar was loving, kind, considerate, and respectful.

So why does he have to be so pig-headed?

Once they arrived in Australia, they took first a cab and then a bus, rented a big SUV, checked into another motel for a week, slept one night there, donned their 16th century clothes again, left most of their luggage at the motel, and drove half an hour to a lovely spot out in the wilderness.

At last, they had arrived at the renaissance faire.

THERE IT WAS, a reconstructed English village surrounded first by a burlap wall and then by parking lots on all but one side, which was a thick forest. It was made from a different set of props than Emily's troupe of druids used in the US, but very similar.

It was summer here, on the Friday of a four-day weekend. They had to leave Monday right after the faire closed, in order to make their flight home. Vange's parents could only afford to watch the kids for a week.

Vange was glad to let Peadar be the one seen buying their tickets. It felt weird, paying to get in. The last fifty times she'd been to renfaire, she'd had a gate pass and been one of the insiders.

But as soon as the two of them entered in through the gate, she felt at home. She found that she was smiling in spite of the curse and all her frustration with Peadar and his silly word.

And then she heard a chorus of strangers' voices.

"Nice garb."

"Wow, yeah, you look great."

"Did you buy that here or did you make it yourselves?"

"Aren't you hot, though?"

Vange turned around to find a clump of fake Scots.

They were trying to look authentic. A little. Their kilts were pure wool and their leine shirts were pure linen, even if it was all machine made rather than homespun. But one wore plastic glasses, another was smoking a cigarette, all the women wore makeup, and of course most of them had on impossibly colorful boots from Simon's booth—like Vange's own.

She smiled for a second, thinking she might run into Simon while she was there.

Well, there was one authentic-looking Scot there, but he ruined the effect when he jokingly joined in on the compliments, saying things they had all heard a thousand times from the customers at the faire.

"Yeah, aren't you hot? Did you make that yourself? Are you the queen?"

Vange ran to the man and gave him a big hug.

"Ian."

He hugged her back.

"Vange. OK, before this gets awkward, is that Peadar? And I see you're wearing matching plaid. Congratulations, Mrs. MacGregor."

Vange felt herself smiling big. It was the first time she'd been called by her true married name, and despite things being frosty right now between her and her husband, she found that she liked the way it sounded.

Ian broke away from her and reached out to clasp forearms with Peadar.

Her husband met her eyes over Ian's shoulder and gave her a look that said, "Do you trust Ian?"

Abruptly, Vange grew sad and realized that no, she didn't trust Ian. They didn't dare share their plans with him. For all they knew, he was a druid himself by now.

She shook her head ever so slightly 'no'.

Still looking at her over Ian's shoulder, Peadar made a grim expression of acknowledgement.

That whole exchange had lasted barely a few seconds, and then Ian released Peadar's arm.

"It's great to see you both. Are you here for the whole long weekend? Come on over to Celt Camp and hang out with us. If money's tight, I can see about getting your tickets refunded and getting you gate passes."

Vange noted with amusement that the fake Scots who had

admired her garb were with Ian, and they were now looking at her and Peadar with even more admiration.

How far I've come up in the world of the faire folk in two years. But at what cost?

Out loud, she kept the conversation light and superficial. "Celt Camp?"

"Heh heh." Ian laughed. "That's right, this started after your time. Yeah, that's what we call the permanent setting the Scots guild has now at faire. It's really cool. You have to come see it."

While he was talking, Vange moved close to Peadar.

He put his arm around her waist.

It was comforting, and she felt safe.

She was still mad at him for being so stubborn, but his query about Ian had made her remember that she was far from home again. And that until she found Emily, her husband was the only person she could trust—on this whole unfamiliar continent.

Peadar lightly patted her on the back once Ian finished his spiel, so Vange knew he wanted her to accept the man's invitation.

She agreed they should accept.

It may be our only hope of getting close enough to Emily to talk to her. They probably have her and her children caged up in this Celt Camp.

Vange smiled at Ian and put on her faire accent, which she wasn't surprised to hear come out sounding more Irish than Scottish.

"Aye, pray do show the way. Tis eager we are to see the new Celt Camp."

Ian raised his eyebrows at her Irish lilt.

She just smiled sweetly and shrugged.

So Ian led the way.

They all formed a procession behind him in twos to

trudge through the mongers shouting out they had fresh fish for sale and to tiptoe past the fire eaters and the sword swallowers. To stop and share a kiss on the kissing bridge—which Vange found she enjoyed even through her anger at Peadar. And to pass the booths of all the vendors, including Simon, who saw Vange and waved.

All along the way, Vange was planning how to get Emily alone to talk. She was sure she could. Casually so as to not raise suspicion, she asked Ian questions that she hoped would help her plan.

"So is this a castle setting, like we had for the old clan meetings in front of the public?"

Ian seemed like he was still a nice guy and not a druid. He turned his head and showed her a friendly expression as he answered each of her questions.

"Nay, it is a traveling clan village, much like the whole faire is an English village."

That was amusing.

But Vange kept her mind on her goal. She was proud of herself. A dozen jokes came to mind at every one of Ian's answers. It was tempting to try and entertain all their followers and make herself popular with them.

But rather than do that and satisfy her mischievous curiosity by asking why a whole highlands clan would be traveling through an English village, she stuck to questions about the cage she had to get Emily out of.

"But there's something going on, right? Something like the clan chief judging disputes like it was on the castle set?"

Ian nodded.

"Oh, aye. The clan chief and his wife sit in state in our camp. They hear disputes and are the main focus of entertainments. We do all those inside our area now by the way, the Scottish dancing, the weapons demonstrations and such, and we even cook period food for our clan there now."

"Cool."

That should work out well for her plan. If there was a lot going on, then she should be able to grab Emily's hand and excuse the two of them to the privies for a few minutes, at least. And then she and Emily would make plans to be alone later.

The four of them would figure out how to get their kids and Dall out of the worst parts of the druid-MacGregor curse:

-The uncertainty of never knowing when they would be asked to do what

-That bit about not remembering travel to another time unless they were married.

Those poor working conditions had to go. They were unacceptable.

The procession of kilted Scots went along the dirt road through the faire to the edge of the English village.

And there lay Celt Camp.

A dozen large undyed canvas tents stood amid a hundred clan banners that flapped satisfactorily in the wind. The tents were in a half circle, and fifty Scots were gathered in the center. Most were dancing to the bagpipe music.

Vange was surprised how big the camp was. It was set up with its long side against the outer edge of the circular faire road, between it and the forest.

As Vange walked arm in arm with kilted Peadar down the hill to the camp looking for Emily, she saw there was a black-smith shop in one tent, a leatherworking one in the next, a tent full of looms where women wove the clan plaid...

Where is Emily?

First she looked among the dancers.

Surprisingly, her friend wasn't there.

Next, she scoured the people sitting off to the side.

Nope.

Out of curiosity, she looked in the clan chief's chair to see who the unfortunate soul was who had to be the center of attention all the time. And she gasped. The kilted clan chief was Dall. And his dutiful wife Emily sat by his side.

❦

"SURPRISE," said Ian, presumably having heard her gasp.

Vange was at a loss for words, and she felt wary somehow of entering the camp, so she kept quiet and stood there holding Peadar in the road while the others all entered the camp and sat down on the handmade wooden furniture.

Ian stayed back with them. He was talking to her.

"Yeah, it's amazing how fast Dall and Emily rose up in the ranks, but not really since they're on staff and all. Still, at every site the locals are a bit put off at first, with such new people getting to be in charge..."

But instead of reacting to Ian, Vange caught Emily's eye and waved.

Emily smiled at her.

Vange waited for her best friend to gesture her over for a hug—or really, to get up and squeal about how glad she was to see her.

But it didn't happen.

That's it?

I disappear for two years and all you can give me is a smile, Em?

OK, this is not the real you. You're magically sedated or something. Arrrgg. This is going to be even harder than I thought.

The clan watched the dancers and clapped.

Vange clapped, but she only had eyes for Emily, except to notice that Peadar was staring at Dall in equal frustration.

In fact, Peadar moved to charge on up there.

Vange almost didn't stop him. She kind of liked the idea of him going savage on Siobhan. It would serve her right.

Almost. At the last second, she squeezed his waist and whispered in his ear.

"If we make a scene, the druids will just kick us out of here and never let us near your da or Emily again. We have to fight them ... politely."

Peadar clenched his fists, but he nodded and stayed with her.

She whispered to him some more.

"Besides, I feel ... uneasy about entering this camp. Something about it isn't right. Look at your da and Emily. They should be running over to see us. Druid magic is at work here, altering their moods."

Ian seemed oblivious to Peadar's urge to run up to his father and to Vange whispering in Peadar's ear. The fact was, the man wasn't very quick on the uptake.

Was I really interested in Ian, back when we first met? He's so immature. So clueless to what other people are going through.

Please tell me I wasn't that bad myself.

Was I?

The handsome young Ian stood by them the while, clapping and watching the dancers—and yammering on about Dall and Emily's new place in the Scottish acting troupe at the faire.

"...Most of the locals have been in the guild longer than Dall, and some of them were in it before he was born, let alone before Emily was. Heh. But the two of them have this way about them, and everyone has come around to seeing them as the good leaders they are. Yeah, they make really good clan leaders. There was this one time..."

While he talked, Vange looked around for Siobhan.

She hadn't seen her in any of the places she'd looked for Emily, but Vange knew a druid must be nearby. That was the only way to explain Emily's lack of enthusiasm at seeing her best friend after two years of no contact. And Dall's lack of the same at seeing his son.

Aha.

After all of Aideen's humming, I should have known to look for Siobhan among the musicians. These druids think they're so slick.

And I guess they are.

But we need to be slicker. We need to stand up for ourselves.

Vange nudged Peadar.

When he looked at her, she tilted her head toward the musicians and gestured like she was playing Siobhan's wooden flute.

Good, Peadar recognizes the druid woman.

Vange whispered to him.

"As soon as the music stops, I'm going to run over and distract Siobhan. Go greet Dall as a relative and invite him and his wife out with us this evening, loud enough that people hear you."

Peadar pulled her in for a kiss.

She kissed him back and felt herself reacting to him more than she'd planned to.

Whoa. What was that? Why am I so eager to kiss him even when I'm mad at the man?

But in her ear, he breathily supplied the answer for her.

"We make a good team, my love."

Their eyes met, and Vange knew he was right. He had hit on exactly the reason she was responding to him as she was. She really enjoyed being on an adventure with him. Solving problems together. She went to kiss him again.

But just then, the music stopped.

Vange squeezed Peadar's hand, let go, and went running into the camp waving both arms over her head and flapping her droopy leine sleeves like wings.

"Siobhan. Siobhan."

The druid turned and caught Vange's eye. She recovered

quickly, but Vange could tell the woman was angry she had been interrupted. Vange could briefly see it in her eyes.

Good. Let's hope Dall comes to his senses enough to make dinner plans with his own son. But I don't dare look over there to see. Siobhan would notice that for sure.

I know what I'll do.

Vange ran up and hugged the druid like the long lost friend she should have been.

Siobhan froze at first, but then she hugged Vange back.

"Vange. What a surprise to see you here."

I'll bet it is. You thought I would be in Ireland for another ten or even twenty years, huh? Raising a dozen children?

But Vange smiled sweetly at the druid.

"Siobhan. Peadar and I are just here for the long weekend, but Ian says we can get gate passes. Can we?"

Siobhan cocked her head sideways in a sort of disapproval, as if she were older and wiser.

"Well this was a long trip for you, just for the long weekend."

Heck yeah we made the long trip home to the 21st Century. No thanks to you.

That was what Vange wanted to say, but she noticed that the local clan members were watching the conversation with interest. No way did she want the locals to know time travel was real. They would worship the druids. So Vange said what she needed to say in a way that only Siobhan would understand.

"Yeah, it was a long trip, but we just had to see all of our old friends from two years ago."

Siobhan got the message. She looked over to see Peadar and Dall arm in arm and Emily running toward Vange.

"Ian." the druid called out.

Ian started running over.

He's so under their spell, and he doesn't even know it. At least Emily knows she is.

Siobhan looked like she wanted to interfere before Emily got to Vange, but she looked over at the straw bales where the clan's audience sat, on a hillside across the dirt road.

Vange looked over there too.

Good. Siobhan knows she needs to do something or the clan will lose their audience because of all of this down time. Heh. So what? But she's a control freak. She won't be able to stop herself from taking charge, now that Dall and Emily are distracted.

Ian arrived before Emily did.

Siobhan ordered him.

"Go ahead and get Vange and Peadar gate passes. They only need them for this weekend."

"OK."

Ian ran off.

But Siobhan wasn't stupid. She raised her voice to project out to the clan and across the road to the dwindling audience.

"Let us have a weapons demonstration."

Smart. The clan probably can't do a weapons demo without Dall there to supervise them. Heh, but also not so smart. It doesn't require Emily to be here, and she and I are the schemers in this family.

EMILY SLAMMED into Vange at full speed and hugged her so tight her bodice seemed loose. And Vange didn't care. She hugged back just as hard.

Finally. Oh, I finally have my best friend back.

Emily was crying.

"Vange. Oh, I'm so sorry, Vange."

Vange looked around at what was going on.

Thank you, Dall.

Her father-in-law was matching half the clan up into sparring pairs and encouraging the other half to all move over to one side of the area to give them some room.

In this chaos, Emily and I can escape for a few minutes. What's Siobhan going to say, 'No, you can't go catch up for a few minutes with the best friend you haven't seen in two years?' She'd have no credible reason to say that. And we need to get out of here before she starts playing music again or humming or whatever, so that at least two of us are always free of that magic they have that lulls you into complacence.

Vange smiled at her best friend and nodded up the road.

"You're forgiven. But *they* aren't. Let's go for a walk."

For the audience of local clan members nearby, Vange made a show of unfastening Emily's solar charger brooch and putting it in Dall's special clan-chief chair. She commented on only one percent of the reason she had done so.

"And leave your phone here, Emily. I want your complete attention."

A few locals laughed at Vange's joke.

But Emily looked around with panic on her face for a moment, clearly fearing that Siobhan was going to stop them.

Vange firmly planted her feet, grabbed her best friend's arm, and all but dragged Emily out of Celt Camp.

This made more locals laugh, because of how small Vange was compared to Emily.

Encouraged by their laughter, Vange used her urgings at Emily to further make her case with these witnesses: Siobhan had no cause at all to stop the two of them from going for a walk.

"Come on, Emily. I haven't seen you in two years. Dall can run this just fine without you, see? He's got it all under control, and Peadar's helping. Come on. And tell me all about your kids. Where are they, anyway? Mine are with my parents, back in the states."

Emily stopped resisting. She started walking fast along with Vange, high-tailing it out of that scene.

"I hope you have a car here."

"Yeah, Peadar and I rented one, but we can't just leave the guys behind."

"No no, we'll just go there to talk. It's the only place we can be sure no one is listening."

Vange looked her friend over as the two of them rushed through the faire toward her car.

"Are you sure they haven't put anything in your clothes or pouches that lets them spy on you? Any anyway, I don't have my gate pass yet."

"I'm on staff. I can get you back in. And no I'm not sure, but I have a pad and a pen, so we can pass notes like in fourth grade."

"Wow Em, you made a joke."

"Yes I did."

"OK, we'll pass notes in the car, but in the meantime let's chit chat. So where are your kids? Mom tells me you have twin boys. We have two sets, by the way."

Emily gave Vange a look that was happy and sad and pained, all at the same time. Then she took a deep breath and let it out.

"Congratulations on yours, although I see you know they're cursed. Dall will be as happy as I am to hear your news."

"Thanks. Emily, where are your children?"

"They're in childcare here at the faire. I wanted to stay home in the trailer with them during faire and take them to see my parents during the week, but Siobhan can be very persuasive."

"If you think they're in any danger whatsoever, then let's go get them right now."

Emily tripped over a loose rock in the dirt road

and swore.

"No, not danger per se, but they might be getting brainwashed."

"My youngest are only three days old, Em. If this curse didn't involve them, I never would have left them, not even with my parents."

"Like I said, Siobhan can be very persuasive."

"Yeah, I noticed. You barely acknowledged me when I showed up. After two years. I knew something was wrong, and then I saw her playing that flute..."

Vange gave Emily the short version of what had happened to her and Peadar after Emily's phone had been stolen.

Emily gave Vange a frightened look again, and whispered in Vange's ear.

"Is your rental car big enough for all six of us?"

"Yeah, here it is."

They got in, started it, and turned on the air so they could leave the windows rolled up tight. They still didn't dare talk, but they felt more private that way.

Emily got out a pen and a small spiral-bound notepad, and they passed these back and forth.

Emily wrote first.

"I know you want me to escape them. I don't think I can. But let's sneak away like this as much as we can while you're here. I missed you soooo much."

Vange hugged her oldest friend and then took up the pen and the pad of paper.

"No, driving away in this rental car and even flying you back to the States doesn't address the curse. They have magic, Emily. They can find us wherever we go."

Emily nodded. A few tears landed on the pad as she wrote.

"Yes, exactly. That's why I don't think we can escape them. I've used their magic, and I may have even made it easier for them to find us, by applying their magic to pictures of us all, and of Peadar's brothers and sisters and cousins. :("

Vange was curling her fingers for the pen. She wrote back.

"I don't want to escape the druids. I want to make them loosen up on the curse."

Emily gave Vange a look of hope and wrote furiously fast.

"That sounds so good, but how?"

"The way I got Aideen to send me back here: threaten them."

Emily looked sad again.

"But hardly anyone in this time period would believe you if you told them there were druids, and if they did believe, they would think it was cool, not burn them at the stake."

Even as Emily was writing that, Vange was shaking her head no and gesturing for Emily to hand the pen over.

"Emily, the druids need us. They can't time travel themselves. They need women like us to bring their ... servants back and forth."

Emily stared at that for a long time, deep in thought. Finally, she started writing again.

"I don't know why I never saw that. What's not so obvious is how to use that to our advantage. A million possibilities are going through my mind. I'll need to think about it."

"I'll give you until Sunday to think, Em. I hope you come up with something good, but no matter what, before faire is over on Monday we are going to do something about these druids and their curse."

Emily was sobbing along with her tears now, but she nodded vigorously as she wiped her eyes with her leine sleeve.

"And it starts right now with Siobhan. I hate myself for letting that woman have such control over my family. Just when I gained financial independence from my parents, I went and let some bad boss gain control of my whole family."

Vange agreed out loud.

"It happened to me, too. I know exactly how you feel."

They hugged some more and cried together.

꧁꧂

VANGE AND EMILY were getting out of the rental car to walk back to the men they loved when Emily reached over and grabbed Vange's arm and spoke out loud.

"Wait, Vange."

"What is it?"

Emily started writing again.

"We need a united plan now. Siobhan has some powerful magic. If we just go wandering back into her circle of influence, we'll probably succumb."

Vange took the pad and wrote her own note.

"How big an area do we have to avoid?"

Emily wrote heavily, tearing the paper in places she was so emphatic.

"I don't want to avoid her. I want to neutralize her—like you did by making a scene and yelling her name as you ran up to her. That was great, by the way."

"Thanks," Vange said out loud.

"Thanks for doing it." Emily said back with a smile. And then she wrote, "Yeah, distractions neutralize her effect. I've been watching her for two years, and I've been lucid during times of upheaval..." Emily passed into thought.

"Upheaval? What happened?" Vange said.

"Huh?" Emily snapped out of her reverie and said, "Oh, you know, drunk customers getting too 'friendly' with clan women, parties getting too loud near older staff's trailers, the usual."

"Ha heh heh. I miss faire." Vange laughed.

Emily smiled and nodded while she wrote some more to the story.

"We had a real fight break out between two staffers once though, during morning sparring. That Lews guy had attacked me before, but only Dall believed me. They sent him home to his time and haven't brought him back."

Vange held out her hand for the pen and pad and started writing fast as soon as she got them.

"So we just keep making scenes around Siobhan so she can't send us all into la la land and make us forget that Peadar and I came here to bring you and Dall to your senses?"

Emily shook her head no, apparently remembered she had another pen in one of her pouches, dug it out, and scribbled another set of quick lines.

"We can't make big scenes, or other druids will get involved and it will get away from us."

Emily looked at her intently.

Vange nodded yes to show that she understood and agreed.

Emily wrote some more.

"But yes, we make small scenes—either to distract Siobhan, or to distract those under her magically calming influence. And that gives me an idea on how we can beat them at their own game, Vange."

"How?"

"By becoming more popular with the local faire actors than the druids are. As soon as we can get to town and use the Internet, we'll set up a website with a forum..."

They wrote back and forth for another two pages and then decided they really did need to get back to Celt Camp and check to make sure their husbands were OK.

Vange was still apprehensive about getting back into the faire without a gate pass. Peadar had her ticket stub.

But when they got to the front gate, Emily just vouched

for her with the guards and the ticket takers.

"Good morning. She's with me."

"OK, Emily."

"Have a great faire day."

"Say hi to Dall for us."

Vange was impressed, but she elbowed her friend and teased her.

"Wow, there was no resistance at all. You really are on staff here, you bigshot."

Emily seemed to be coming back to her senses, because she sort of joked back.

"Heh. I might as well enjoy the perks."

Vange hugged her sideways as they walked.

"That's the spirit."

They were almost to the top of the hill above Celt Camp when Emily started walking even faster.

"I know what we'll do right now."

"What?"

"Ready for the second iteration of 'Operation Five New Best Friends'?"

"Ha. Sure."

"Good. First we make sure the guys are OK, and then we launch into it."

"Sounds like a plan."

"Very funny."

"I thought so."

"You would."

Gosh it's great to have you back, Em.

As they had planned, the two friends went around to the woodsy back of Celt Camp, rather than approach on the road where Siobhan could see them. No bagpipes were playing, so they knew something other than dancing was afoot.

Vange whispered when the two of them were a hundred feet away.

"All I can see is the tents from back here. I can't see where anyone is or if they're OK or what they're doing. Are you sure this is a good idea?"

"Yes." Emily whispered back. "Look."

"Cool."

One of the white canvas tents had a back door.

As they crept forward through the trees, Vange looked for the reason for this and discovered an area where food waste had been dumped.

"Heh, let me guess. This is the kitchen tent."

"Yep. Just smile at the kitchen workers while I find out what's going on."

"No problem."

❧

VANGE AND EMILY CREPT on into the kitchen tent at Celt Camp. Inside were three young women with aprons on. They weren't doing much of anything. There were also a dozen coolers, three large folding tables, a large camp stove, and standing shelves full of food and packaged drinks.

Emily put her finger over her lips.

Apparently oblivious to Siobhan's manipulations, the other women giggled while they all had a whispered conversation.

"Hehe. Why are you sneaking around, Emily?"

"I wanted to know what Dall was really doing while I was gone," Emily joked.

The three women reassured her.

"Pfft, you don't have anything to worry about."

"No."

"Not at all. He was running a long weapons demonstration until just a few minutes ago, and now he is sitting in state and hearing petitioners."

Emily rolled her eyes.

"Oh, petitioners."

They all laughed.

Emily turned to explain to Vange.

"We all hate playing petitioners. It's really hard coming up with stuff we haven't said before. But you guys, it's even worse when you're up there hearing the petitions."

"Ha hehehe. I'll bet."

Vange spoke up.

"So Emily, now we know how your man's doing. What about mine?"

Emily looked to the others.

"Jessamin, where is Peadar?"

Jessamin peeked out through the tent flap.

"Sitting off to the side, watching and pretty much being ignored."

"Go grab him," Emily ordered, "and be discreet."

Nodding, Jessamin slunk out of the tent. Less than a minute later, she came back with Peadar in tow.

With a wink, Emily playfully shoved him into Vange.

"Here he is. You two can cuddle out back."

Catching on to Emily's intent right away, Vange grabbed her man, took him out back, and made a show of making out with him while she quietly filled him in on her and Emily's plans.

Peadar upped the ante, and for a while they weren't putting on a show at all.

I guess I've forgiven him...

When Vange and Peadar got back into the kitchen tent, Dall was there in Emily's place.

Vange nodded at Peadar, then Dall, and then back to the tent's back door.

"Go on and catch up with your kinsman. Emily and I can watch over things here."

Dall and Peadar clasped arms solidly, and then Peadar led his da outside.

"Aye, kinsman. Do let us walk and talk together, such as the womenfolk did, aye?"

Vange watched them go, and then she was surprised for a moment to find herself alone with Jessamin and the other two young women. She gave them a dramatic pose to get their attention and to break the ice.

"I'm Vange, by the way, Emily's best friend since we were nine."

They smiled at her dramatics.

"Hi. I'm Aga."

"Bethany."

"Jessamin."

"Hi, great to meet you all. So Peadar and I are only in Australia for this one weekend, and we hoped that after faire tonight you all might show us how you have a good time in these parts, you know, out on the town."

The three looked dubious.

"There's a big night-show here on the faire site every night this weekend."

"Yeah, the long weekend is when everyone from faraway comes, so it's the biggest audience we have for the whole run of the faire."

"People have been talking up these night shows for weeks."

Of course they have. Score a point for those clever druids. Keeping everyone on the site works in their favor. This is going to be harder than I thought.

Oh hey, I know how to get Dall and Emily's faire clan to come out with us.

"Oh well. We'll just go out the four of us, then. Just thought I'd ask you, though. You all seem so nice and everything."

A few seconds passed by, and then Jessamin piped up.

"By the four of you, do you mean you'll be out with Dall and Emily?"

"Of course. Peadar is Dall's kinsman in real life. Can't you tell?"

All three woman nodded that yes, they could tell.

"They look like they could be twins."

"Yeah, they're at least cousins, right?"

Vange nodded.

"Yeah, at least."

She could see the picture she had planted in their imaginations taking shape. A night out with their chiefs, Dall and Emily, would seem like a night out with celebrities to their faire clan.

Just as Vange had been counting on, the three of them came around, one by one.

Jessamin was the first one to cave in and tell the other two she had changed her mind.

"You know what, I think I'd rather go out with Dall and Emily."

The other two instantly agreed.

"Yeah, I was thinking that too."

"The night shows are pretty much the same old thing, anyway. Let's go have a break from the faire."

I'm so smart. Hey, maybe being a mom does make you wiser.

"Great. So you three decide where we'll go. Plan it all out, and come tell Dall and Emily at the end of the faire day. Peadar and I have an SUV big enough for the four of us plus you three."

Jessamin, Aga, and Bethany all squealed in glee at that last part.

Vange crossed her arms and smiled as she watched the three of them eagerly start planning their night out.

Your excitement over that ought to be enough to distract Dall and

Emily from anything Siobhan throws at them in an attempt to keep them here under her thumb tonight.

With Vange and Peadar's help, Emily and Dall skillfully switched places in the kitchen tent all day long. When Emily was out there under Siobhan's spell, then Dall was free to visit with his son, and if Dall was bewitched, then Emily was free to visit with Vange.

It worked like this through the clan's midday meal and through one more hour each of petitions, Scottish dancing, and weapons demonstrations.

But then Siobhan must have figured out what was going on.

"Let us begin a new tradition." the druid woman called out to the clan in a voice that was charged with undeniable charm.

Various clan members answered her.

"What shall that be?"

"Aye, and what would you have?"

Vange felt the urge to peek outside through the tent flap. She saw that Siobhan held the clan enthralled. They eagerly listened for the details of whatever scheme Siobhan had to keep them all there that night.

Even Emily was listening.

Darn.

Vange looked back inside the tent. Oh no. Even the three kitchen ladies were enthralled.

Good thing Dall and Peadar are out back where they can't hear the druid witch.

Vange looked back outside.

Siobhan was on a roll.

"Let us have the clan chief and his wife preside over our lead place in the procession, where we shall always partake in ring-out. Emily."

Vange looked around for her best friend.

Oh, there's Emily.

"Aye?"

"Come up here and head the procession."

The clan leader had a smile on her face as she skipped forward to stand where the new tradition called for her presence.

Aw, she's having so much fun.

"Clan. Fall in."

Hearing the call to fall in, Vange obeyed. She lined up behind Jessamin and Aga, who had headed outside just in front of her. They all smiled at each other.

Something's missing, but I don't know what. Oh well.

And then Peadar was at Vange's side, and all was right with the world. He offered her his arm.

"Ready to process, lass?"

"Aye." Vange hooked her arm through his and felt the little rush she'd forgotten he gave her whenever they touched. Now she was having real fun.

Dall took his place at the beginning of the procession next to Emily, and they all started walking. As they walked, they sang and had great fun.

EMILY WAS HAVING the time of her life. She was on the arm of her sexy highlander husband, the envy of every woman on the faire site, and the two of them were leading ring-out. They marched sometimes, and everyone behind them marched too. They danced sometimes, and everyone else danced as well.

They started the clan's kilted men on the non-period but so delicious Can-can dance, kicking up their kilted legs and showing off the neon shorts all wore underneath, and the crowd went wild, whistling and cheering and applauding. It was a heady feeling, entertaining so many people and being loved by all of them.

Emily bowed graciously at the customers who waved at them, and Dall bowed with her.

All the merchants in their booths waved at her and Dall, smiling. She waved back like a queen. She saw Simon out there at his booth with his family, and Murray at his weapons booth. She smiled so big at them, they ran up and gave her hugs.

Dall wasn't jealous or threatened. He just laughed.

All the way around the village the two of them led the procession, singing one of the faire's many songs that gently told the customers the faire was closed and it was time for them to go home—*so that our parties can start.*

Farwell friends from in our shire
To our homes we now retire,
Let our voices e'er sing higher
When we're met together.

LET union be in all our hearts.
Let union join our hearts as one.
We'll end the day as it begun.
We'll end it all in pleasure.

TOO SOON, the ring-out parade was over. Down the road, Emily saw that Siobhan was coming up the ranks to escort her and Dall to their trailer to change for the evening, and then Emily would have a blast watching the night show.

But then Jessamin, Aga, and Bethany were right behind Emily and Dall, squealing and laughing and practically talking right on top of each other. It took three rounds of their conversation before Emily understood it.

"Ooh, are we going to show you all a great time."

"Yeah, we've made reservations at the best restaurant."

"Uh huh. And then we're all off to the hottest dance club."

"Oh, and Vange said to remind you we'll change in their hotel room instead of in your trailer, because she brought presents of new clothes for the both of you."

"We brought a change of clothes with us."

"Yeah, see? So we're all ready to go."

"Oh yeah, and Peadar said we should all go and grab him and Vange."

"How did he put it?"

"'Because you know how Vange likes to talk. You'd best drag her away or we'll never get out of here.'"

"Ha ha ha. Those two are so funny."

Like waking up from a dream, coming out of the druid's complacence spell happened gradually. As it did, fear overtook Emily.

We can't fall back under that spell. This was our one chance. Yay that it worked, but ...

Emily put on her best actor's face though, so as not to make her three new best friends afraid of Emily herself instead of the real enemy.

As she frantically looked around for Vange and Peadar, she saw Siobhan's determined face coming at her from closer up the road. But Vange and Peadar were closer, chatting with some of the clan as if they meant to stay at the faire site overnight.

They will *stay overnight if we don't get over there and snap them out of it.*

Grabbing Dall's hand and Jessamin's hand, Emily pushed through the crowd toward Vange and Peadar.

E mily was both panicked and annoyed.

I am so sorry, all of you who had to put up with me when I was young and clueless.

Jessamin thought their mad dash through the crowd toward Vange and Peadar was a game.

Come on, Emily, be patient. How could she know otherwise? Just rein her in.

Made playful by the giddiness of being invited out with her clan chiefs—such a momentous outing—Jessamin poked her friends as she pushed by with Bethany and Aga in tow, and she laughed when people turned around to see who had done it.

Jessamin talked to the people, too, but Emily was too worried about actually leaving the faire site to pay attention to what it was she said.

"Vange." Emily called out.

Her friend and Dall's son were happily chatting with some of the faire Scots.

"Come on, Vange."

Vange looked up at Emily and smiled, but then she went

right back to laughing and joking with people who were strangers to her.

Yep, Vange is under the druids' spell, alright.

Emily was getting desperate, but she didn't dare let Jessamin, Aga, or Bethany see that.

They have to be having fun, or they'll fall under the spell, too.

Using her actor training and experience, Emily kept her voice upbeat and excited, rather than afraid and panicky. Now she was right next to her friend.

Dall kept hold of Emily's hand and helped out by making their chain of people a circle behind his son Peadar, if only he and Vange would turn around.

Emily did the talking.

"Turn around, Vange, Peadar. Dall and I want to talk to you."

Thankfully, the two complied with out Vange making a wisecrack.

My hold on reality is so tenuous, even that might throw me under the spell.

Dall clasped wrists with Peadar.

Emily talked a mile a minute, apprehensively glancing over her shoulder to see that Siobhan would be on them any second.

"Vange, Peadar. We're taking Jessamin and her friends out on the town tonight. *We have to start running for the SUV now.* They have a great restaurant and a hot club picked out for us to see. Besides, I hear you have presents of clothes for me and Dall back at your hotel."

Thank God. They're waking up. Come on. Wake up faster. Shake the spell off and help me with the situation again.

They did, and Emily breathed easier.

"OK."

"Aye, lead the way."

In the nick of time, the group was on the run toward the

main gate out of the renaissance faire and into the parking lot.

Emily smiled now that she did hear Bethany and Aga and Jessamin talking.

Their cluelessness snapped you out of the spell, Emily. Be thankful. You may yet need them to wake you up. Two years was long enough to be under the spell. No more.

"Yeah, our reservation is for eight."

"OK, so that gives us half an hour to drive to Vange and Peadar's hotel and 75 minutes for us all to shower and change."

"It's a tight schedule, but it's doable..."

That talk ought to keep them out from under the spell all the way out to the SUV, and I'm pretty sure we're safe once we get through the gate and out into the parking lot.

But there were strangers manning the main gate. And in her waking state, it was obvious to Emily that they had been ordered not to let faire people leave easily. She could only imagine how that conversation had gone, but plainly they had been told to detain whoever was leaving as long as they could.

Yeah, so that one of the druids can come work their magic and turn us back into zombies.

One gate guard held out his hand at them, beckoning them over.

"Gate passes, please."

Emily showed her 'Faire Staff' badge and gave the guard a look.

"They're with me."

The guard shrugged.

"They may not be when they want to come back in." He smiled at the customers who were leaving and told them to have a nice night before he turned back to Vange and the others, who he was claiming to be concerned about. "Just trying to help you out."

But the pause had been enough.

Here comes Siobhan.

Emily wanted to put her hands over her ears, but in her growing panic she couldn't think of any theatrics that would explain why she would do such a thing.

Jessamin, Bethany, and Aga had shown their gate passes and were still talking excitedly about the evening ahead.

Good. Keep that up. Ack, she's almost here.

The guard was on Vange and Peadar now.

Peadar was trying to reason with him.

"Nay, we do not have passes yet, lad, but we will be with my kin all the evening and return with them beside."

The guard rolled his eyes.

"The beer's in the pickup, buddy. OK, if you don't have passes, you will need to be with a staff member."

Vange gave him a look and put her other arm around Emily.

"We *are* with a staff member. That's what we keep telling you."

Siobhan had arrived, and of course she tried to bring everyone back into the faire site.

"Short Shakespeare are here as a special treat for everyone tonight. Maybe you heard about it? They're going to do Romeo and Juliet backwards. Come on. I'll get you all seats up front where you'll be chosen as volunteers to go on stage."

But Emily's guildmates surprised and overjoyed her. She hadn't noticed before, but all the people Jessamin had poked had been following along behind them. They had quite a crowd gathered. Probably a third of the guild of 60 people.

Jessamin spoke.

"That's OK, Siobhan. Bethany and Aga and I are going out on the town with Dall and Emily, right?" She turned and smiled proudly at the chiefs of the Scottish clan they were all re-enacting on the faire site.

Emily nodded yes, and so did Dall.

The guild cheered and called out encouragement.

"That's so cool."

"Maybe we can all go out tomorrow, eh Dall?"

"Yeah. We would love to show you our favorite hangouts, too."

Wow, I had no idea we were so popular. What else have I been missing?

Dall held up his hand, and the clan grew quiet, visibly anxious to see what their leader had to say to them.

"We would be honored if the entire Scots guild of actors would meet us at the Hastings Hotel tomorrow at eight in the evening for a clan gathering in casual modern dress. Please go and tell the others, and while you do, please come up with some games we can play and some modern music we can dance to."

They all cheered some more.

"That's my man, Dall."

"Awesome."

"Way to go."

Dall pulled Emily close to him so that she shared in this moment, which she appreciated. The guild was on fire with excitement about Dall's invitation to them. Someone started chanting, and before she knew what was going on, they all had joined in.

"The Hastings Saturday at Eight."

"The Hastings Saturday at Eight. Huzzah."

"The Hastings Saturday at Eight. Huzzah."

The saying was repeated all up and down 'the shire', as they called this faire site.

Emily turned to Dall, laughing.

"We had better get to the Hastings and make some kind of arrangements. Ha heh heh."

With his arm around her, he led the seven of them out the

gate past the guards while Siobhan just stood there with her arms crossed, trying to hide the fact that she was frustrated.

"Aye, and we shall, lass."

❦

EMILY HAD BEEN RIDING in the back seat of the SUV next to Dall for twenty minutes when Jessamin got a phone call. Which reminded her. She tapped on the driver's shoulder.

"Vange, let me use your phone."

"I ... I don't have it anymore, Em. I'm between phones at the moment."

"Ooooh K. You'll have to tell me that story sometime. Bethany, can I borrow your phone? I left ours in Celt Camp."

Bethany handed it to her.

"Sure, if you're calling inside Australia."

Emily handed her a large cash bill.

"I'm calling the US. Please let me know if this doesn't cover it, and I'll pay you back. Promise?"

Bethany took the large bill with a look of pleasure.

"Oh, this will cover it. Thanks."

Emily called her parents for the first time this trip to Australia.

"Hi Mom, it's Em."

"Is everything alright, Sweetheart? Did Vange get there OK?"

"It's going well so far, Mom. Will you get Dad on the other phone? I would really like to hear both of your voices for a little while."

"Oh. Sure, I'll take you with me and go get him."

Her dad's voice came on the line then, and Emily felt guilty for not calling more often, even though she had only neglected her family under the druids' magic influence.

"Hiya Em. How is the plan going? Are you going to be able to break the c—"

Emily didn't think anyone could hear her dad, but just in case, she cut him off.

"I can't talk long. I'm borrowing Bethany's phone. Here, on the count of three, both of you say, 'Thank you, Bethany.' One, two three."

Here's hoping they take the hint and keep quiet about the curse.

Bethany giggled when they thanked her.

"I called just to hear your voices and to let you hear mine. To connect. I'm so sorry for not doing that often enough. I promise it will be a more regular habit from now on."

Tears flowed on both ends of the phone line.

"We love you, Em. Give our love to Tomas and Tavish."

"I will. Love you too, bye."

"Bye Em."

Emily wiped her tears and handed back the phone.

"Thanks, Bethany."

"No problem. It's gotta be tough, being so far away from family."

"It is, but I didn't expect it to be. I was foolish."

It was a fabulous night out. Just as they had promised, Bethany, Jessamin, and Aga had picked out a marvelous restaurant and a fun hot spot to hang out in afterward. Everyone had a great time.

Dall and Emily had rented the hotel room adjoining Vange and Peadar's and got some rollaway beds so they could all get ready faster and crash there for the night. They got up early to make arrangements for that night's party before they drove back to the faire.

The hotel desk people didn't say a word about his kilt or her matching long plaid dress. Or when everyone else came down in similar outfits. They raised their eyebrows when Dall asked to see the manager, but they said they would let him know they wanted to speak with him.

Emily used the hotel's business center to send out a bunch of emails while they waited, inviting people to start that clan website and forum she and Vange had dreamed up and promising to be on it as soon as she could.

At last, the hotel manager came down from his room to see them. Even though it was seven in the morning, he was clean shaven and wore an impeccable business suit. He spoke to Dall as he came down the hallway toward them, holding his hand out.

"Hello, I am Mr. Perry. You wished to see me? I trust all is well?"

Dall clasped forearms with him.

"My gratitude stretches to you for arising at such an early hour."

Mr. Perry smiled, clearly a bit charmed by Dall's accent and amused by their traditional Scottish clothing.

"Well, now I'm intrigued. What brings you down to see me?"

Dall released the man's forearm.

"We have sixty guests coming this evening for a time of festivity. We wish to engage a hall here in your hotel."

"Ah, I'm sorry. We have but one such hall, and it is already engaged. You might try Hintel House, across town."

Emily's heart sank.

Well, that's just our luck. Darn it. I suppose one of us will have to stay here and redirect people to the other hotel. Maybe Vange will stay here with me...

Emily and Vange shared a sad 'oh well' look.

But Dall was not giving up.

"We have secured accommodations here at your inn. Mayhap we could invite our guests up into our two rooms to pass some time with us?"

But Mr. Perry was shaking his head no.

"A party of sixty in two regular rooms would disturb our other guests too much, I'm afraid. Parties of that size are only allowed in our hall or in our suite rooms, up on the top floor. Renting the hall is less expensive, but alas, it is engaged. Your best bet is Hintel House. If you like, I can call them for you."

Hope bloomed in Emily's heart. She turned and looked at Dall.

He was smiling.

We have this. Wow, what a change from Mr. Simmons taking care of us. And hahaha. I could almost thank Siobhan for keeping us so complacent we didn't spend any of the money we earned because of Murray insisting we demo his weapons for him. We owe him. Big time. There must be twenty thousand in that Australian account, and that's not even touching the US account we have for our antiques business.

Dall held up a hand to stay the manager from leaving, and then he handed the man their debit card.

"Please use this to verify that we can pay, and then do show us the largest of these suite rooms you have, and let us discuss your food and drink service. We also will require music."

Mr. Perry dubiously looked them over, these seven twenty-something foreigners in homespun wool and linen with weird hats and archaic weapons.

Emily imagined what he saw:

A bunch of kooky ragamuffins who couldn't afford to eat in the lobby café, much less rent a party suite.

She fought the urge to giggle.

No sense in sounding like the kooks he fears we are.

Apparently remembering his manners, the hotel manager pulled himself together and addressed them civilly, if dismissively.

"Ah ... yes. Will you excuse me for a moment?"

Wow, cool, a top floor suite. This party is going to be fun.

ﻬ

THEY BOOKED the largest suite that night for their guild party, bought four phones in the hotel's gift shop, ran out to the SUV, let Bethany drive, and called home again to check in while there were cell towers around.

Emily's parents were surprised but pleased to hear from her again so soon.

After Vange hung up, she said all four of her boys were doing fine, and that sent a pang of guilt through Emily about leaving her two boys in childcare.

Before long, the seven of them were walking up to the faire's main gate.

What do you know, the usual faire employee guards are back on duty this morning.

Emily smiled and held an arm out toward her friends.

"All of them are with us."

"OK Emily. Have a great faire day."

"You too."

Emily turned to Vange and Peadar.

"OK, let's go right on up to the shack and get you two gate passes this instant." She turned and waved to Aga, Bethany, and Jessamin. "Bye, ladies. Thanks again for a wonderful evening, and we'll see you back at Celt Camp."

Surprising Emily, all three of them hugged her.

"Thank you so much for inviting us out with you and Dall."

"Yeah, it was really fun showing you two around."

"You're fun to hang out with."

Emily didn't know quite what to do with all this admiration, so she just let her pleasure in their company show on her face.

"Aw, thanks."

They waved then and took off toward the guild site, calling back to her over their shoulders.

"And we can't wait for the party tonight."

"Yeah. It's going to be so nice."

"Whoa yeah. The party suite."

Vange and Peadar did gate passes. It was no problem with Dall and Emily right there: two staff people who were the leaders of one of the biggest guilds at the faire talking to another staff member—who wasn't a druid.

Vange hugged Emily.

"Thanks, Em. So I guess you have to go run the guild now, huh. No more free time for you."

Emily hugged her best friend back and then she squeezed Dall's waist.

"Yeah, we do have to go run the guild. But there's hot breakfast waiting for us there. And Dall and I have some ideas on how to run it much better today."

The four grinned at each other as they left the little ID shack.

As soon as they were outside and relatively alone, they had a little private meeting. Dall softly confirmed the plans Emily and Vange had come up with. Peadar gave some of his own suggestions. And then Dall made Vange cry.

He hugged her and Peadar together while he spoke.

"Lass, it is time we were properly welcoming you into the family. You're a MacGregor now, part of a royal family, so be proud and fight to the last."

When the four of them got to the guild encampment, everyone cheered them.

"Tonight at Hastings at eight."

"Yeah, can't wait."

Dall shouted from the road as they walked down.

"Aye. Be sure to come, as I have ordered much ale and wine."

Emily and Vange ran ahead and entered the guild area first.

Everyone was hugging Emily and saying good morning to her and thanking her and Dall for inviting them to the party and saying how much they were looking forward to it.

Siobhan got up to make a speech.

But no one paid attention to her.

All eyes were on Emily, and right in the middle of it all she spoke up to everyone, then rushed over to the other side of the encampment.

"Once you have your breakfast, everyone who wants to work on dances, crafts, and games this morning, come over to this side of camp with me."

As she rushed off with half the guild, Emily glanced at Siobhan's face.

The druid was pissed.

But what can she do, say I'm not really a clan leader? Nope. She just has to suck it up.

Emily gestured for her group to sit down while she watched Dall and Peadar enter Celt Camp and organize their half of the guild.

Dall didn't stand in front of Siobhan. He was too much of a gentleman for that, but he did speak up in his strong and gorgeous voice before the druid had a chance to interfere.

"Aye, and everyone who wants to work on weapons skills this morning, stay over here with me. Midday, we shall switch the groups, so nary a one of you need fear missing out on anything."

The clan loved it. They cheered.

Keeping an eye on Dall's side of the camp where Siobhan was, Emily got her people moving with looms a weaving and dances a reeling and the children running about playing tag all the while.

Stepping around Siobhan without seeming to disrespect her, Dall got his team into pairs that sparred in formation for a time and then he paired them off one by one for practice duels for an alternate time.

In this way, the leaders effectively created twice as much activity and interest in their stage area.

The audiences were twice as large as they normally would be, and they grew larger by the hour as word spread around the faire and customers brought others over to see this awesome 'new' show.

Emily noticed that this person was good at getting the dances going and that person was a natural at keeping the children occupied, while this other woman had a knack for keeping all the looms moving. As planned, she took note of who was good at what so that she could eventually delegate leadership in each smaller area.

Dall did the same with the weapons drills and skills.

Peadar and Vange cheerfully helped.

Vange is really in her element here, making everyone laugh and have a good time. Oh, how I've missed her.

Everyone but the four of them switched sides at the midday meal, just as Dall had said.

All their faire clan were complimenting them on a job well done.

"I really hope the guild runs this way from now on."

"Yeah, for some reason clan life feels more real today."

"Aye. And look how much the audience is enjoying it."

But Emily and her kin were uneasy. It seemed as if they had taken over real control of the guild. It was the first step on their path to getting the druids to ease their control over the MacGregors.

Perhaps they should have been ecstatic.

But most of their reason for splitting into two groups had really been to make it impossible for Siobhan to put all of them under her spell.

And Siobhan hadn't tried to do that today. She hadn't said anything.

And there was no way the druid had given up.

In fact, where is *Siobhan?*

The answer to that question froze Emily in her tracks.

There was Siobhan coming down the road, bringing Aiden with her.

❦

"Vange." Emily said as softly as she could and still be heard.

Vange came over with a big smile on her face.

"Aye?"

Vange's smile faded when Emily spoke next.

"Quickly but discretely, go get Peadar and leave Celt Camp so you can wake us up later."

Vange moved to say something.

But Emily just nodded sideways toward the road and waited anxiously.

There. Vange saw for herself what was happening and went and grabbed Peadar. And then she turned toward Emily and made a circling motion.

Emily didn't understand, but it didn't matter. Frantically, Emily made shooing motions and mouthed at her friend.

"Get the heck out of here."

Vange gave her a quick nod, and the two of them ran off down the road toward the fence.

Why did she go that way? Oh well, at least she's out of range.

And then Emily just stood there, frozen, while Siobhan and Aiden approached.

What to do? Two druids and two of us left. No more avoiding the

*daze. And I was really starting to like having a clear mind. I guess
we just let the druids have their fun and then hope they go away
before faire is out so Vange and Peadar can wake us all up in time to
go to the party. At least everyone's so spread out that they won't all fall
under the spell. We got that part right.*

Emily sought Dall's gaze and caught it, then nodded to
where Siobhan and Aiden approached. And then Aga and
Bethany's voices brought her attention back to her immediate
area.

"Should we start another game?"

"There's a lull over in the game area."

Emily did her best to smile at them and not show her
unease. Again, no sense in frightening them. They might
make a scene and cause a panic...

*What am I thinking? The only thing that really makes sense is to
scare them all clean away from the faire site so they never come back.
But ... they would just be scared of me. I don't have enough of their
trust yet to make them believe what I know about the druids. They
would run to them from me.*

Out loud, Emily kept her comments practical, supportive,
and about fun.

"Aye, do go ahead and start another game. One of your
choice. Mayhap you will be put in charge of the games, if this
goes well."

They curtsied.

"Thank you, Emily."

"Aye, we do thank you."

Emily looked back at Dall. He was talking to Aiden.

She surveyed her side of the guild area. The fact that
everyone was having fun entertaining the customers and their
whole setting was being used to advantage made her smile in
spite of the impending loss of her wits.

And just like that, Siobhan was at Emily's side.

Think of the devil and she will appear.

Siobhan's voice was haughty.

"How convenient. You've made the guild run without you. Come on over and see Aiden. He has some things to say to you and Dall."

Unable to think of any plausible reason to refuse, Emily followed Siobhan over to where Aiden and Dall were standing on the other side of the blacksmith's booth, which was so noisy that no one on this side could hear what they were saying.

Am I under their spell now? Why do I care so much what they have to say? Why do I care so much about working here at the faire? Wouldn't I be smarter to stay away and keep the children away, even if it meant being away from Dall too?

But as she settled against her husband and he rested his arm around her shoulders, Emily knew the answer to that.

She didn't want to be away from him.

It was bad enough when they went to his time and he had to go off to battle. They could see about leaving the boys with her parents, but she was not going to let the druids scare her into cowering away somewhere while Dall was here in her time and not even fighting.

No. The cowering and the complacency have to end. Now.

Aiden addressed her.

"I was just telling Dall that while we admire your leadership and your initiative, you are to bow out and let Siobhan handle things as before. You are leaders here in name only."

Emily looked over where she and Dall had the guild pleasing the audience better than Siobhan ever had on a good day.

"Oh? And what was Dall telling you?"

This ought to be good.

Dall held her close for reassurance, but hers or his? She wasn't sure.

Emily held him too, squeezing to let him know she was one hundred percent with him.

He spoke solidly in that tough matter-of-fact highlands way she had so admired in the women in his family, among whom it was especially striking.

"I would know the time and the place of the service I owe beforehand, and I now declare it has a limit."

Aiden laughed.

"It's well and fine for you to declare such a thing, Dall, but you are oath-bound by your forebear to serve us. You know this, and your bride knows this, and Peadar knows it, and his bride, and one day your other children will know, and theirs, and so on. This is old news. Why bring it up now?"

Dall stood tall and patient—and resolved.

"The cause be the ending now of the open-ended nature of our service."

Aiden started to speak, but Dall cut him off.

"My line of MacGregors are oath-bound to you, aye, but I cannot believe we were ever meant to be your outright slaves in the manner you use us. Hence, looking forward, we serve you in the way we serve a liege laird, keeping our own lives and our own homes, and coming to do your bidding not always, but only some of the time we are here in the twenty-first century."

Aiden and Siobhan both had their mouths open to speak the whole time.

But Dall continued on forcefully.

"And we will know ahead of the time when we are to serve, and you will allow us to remember it afterward. And nay more of your having a hand in selecting our brides for us, either. As I say, we are as tenants, not as chattel to you, I so declare. Nay more spelling us or the local volunteer actors with your complacency, either."

Dall paused then, finally giving Aiden a patch of quiet to fill with his own words.

Aiden's eyes narrowed on Dall.

"So those are your demands, are they?"

"Aye, they are."

"Yes." Emily added to show her solidarity with Dall.

The faire's owner smiled at him and Emily for the crowds, but just where the two of them could see, he held up a toy sword that belonged to their sons.

Emily gasped.

Dall moaned.

"Yes Dall, Emily. We have your children in our custody. Had you forgotten? I would not want to see any harm come to the wee ones, but we only need to ensure the survival of your fourth son, not your third."

❧

EMILY SAW RED, she was so angry at Tea Dye Aiden.

This man needs to be put away somewhere. He's threatening my children.

And he thinks he'll get away with it.

Will he?

In the time it took Emily to have these thoughts, her husband had released his hold on her and moved into Aiden's space.

Quicker than her reaction time to look in his direction, Dall had a dagger at Aiden's throat.

Before she got used to that idea, Dall was dragging the man up the dirt road toward the children's dell.

And yelling.

Making a scene.

"Make way."

Drag drag drag.

"For a man who is desperate to be sure his children are safe."

Drag drag drag.

"From this man who did threaten them with bodily harm."

Drag drag drag.

The customers made way, but they lined the sides of the dirt road ahead too, craning their necks to get a good look at the 'criminal' passing by them. They thought it was all part of the show—that Dall and Aiden were just acting—but the customers were effectively clearing a path for Dall nonetheless.

The entire Scots guild had run after Dall in support of him. They were just acting, but the guild were effectively buffering the audience from real and genuine violence nonetheless.

And then it got really showy, and Emily found herself caught up in the spectacle.

Several guild men grabbed Aiden's feet and legs—gently.

Aiden didn't struggle much.

Dall plainly meant business and wasn't giving the old druid much chance to struggle.

More guild men grabbed Aiden's middle.

Abruptly, they were bearing the druid aloft above them.

Dall still held the dagger at the dangerous man's throat.

And then Emily's attention was drawn to the back of the moving crowd, where Siobhan was trying to get her boss loose.

"Leave him be."

But she was having no effect at all.

"He's hurting him."

Looking the part of the loyal wife defending her criminal husband—and getting pointed at and tsk'ed over by laughing customers—Siobhan kept trying.

"He didn't mean it like that, Dall."

Emily shook her head no in disappointment and anger.

Sure he didn't. I once thought you and I were friends, Hailey. Now I see your true colors.

The frantic woman looked determined to get the head druid loose and dispel the atmosphere of hatred that was thick around him now.

Emily wanted to chase after them. Desperately. She yearned to go make sure her children were safe.

But only she could do what else needed to be done. She turned and ran to Dall's throne chair. She had pushed her phone into a hole in the upholstery.

While she ran over there, Vange and Peadar came out of hiding behind the woodwork of the blacksmith's booth.

Vange spoke first.

"I can't believe he threatened the kids."

Peadar spoke too.

"Do you wish for us to stay and keep you safe, or to go along with Da and see to your wee ones?"

So that's *what Vange meant with her circular gesture. They went around to the back of the setting.*

Emily hugged both of them.

"You heard him threaten them? You're witnesses?"

"Aye, loud and clear we did. Just me at first, but I did call her over when I knew I still had my wits and I was hearing Da make our case."

Emily fumbled with the chair until she had her phone in her hot little hands. On impulse, she switched it on and snapped a photo of Siobhan and the retreating crowd just before they crested the hill and went out of sight.

"Awesome. Go with Dall, you two. Peadar, you stay with him as his witness."

Peadar nodded once firmly yes.

Emily put a hand on her stepson's arm to thank him, and

then she hugged her best friend again and quickly continued, glad that this woman she trusted was legally family now—her step daughter.

Being family should make it easier for Vange to get the children to safety should anything happen to me and Dall and Peadar…

"Vange, will you please take my boys to the hotel right away? We'll get someone else to take us there as soon as we can."

Vange hugged Emily back, and then she stared at Emily's phone.

"OK. Are you … leaving?"

Emily shook her head no even as she navigated to the Time Management app.

"No, they've disabled actual travel on this thing. I can't leave anymore, but I know how to report Aiden to 'druid central' for threatening my children."

❧

"Good," said Vange. "Come on, Peadar. Let's go rescue our kin."

The two of them hugged Emily again and ran off to follow Dall. It wouldn't be difficult. Emily could hear the commotion from fifty yards and see the crowds rushing toward it. Not to mention all the dust they were raising.

Emily stepped into the empty kitchen tent.

After fiddling with the settings in the Time Management app, she finally brought up a reporting screen and tapped in what amounted to a long text message.

And waited what seemed like forever.

She got a message back.

She tapped in a series of replies.

"Yes, Aiden really threatened my children."

"Yes, I demand justice."

"Yes, he is being detained nearby."

"Yes, there are witnesses."

"In fact, I bet if you check, the whole thing is logged right here on my phone. Just listen for Aiden's voice as you go backward from now. It hasn't been very long since he uttered the threat."

The druids replied in a businesslike manner.

"Stand by while we retrieve and review that log."

Emily spent the longest fifteen minutes of her life waiting for them to do just that. She wanted to go check on Vange and Tomas and Tavish, but she didn't dare leave the privacy of the tent, in case—

A visual whirlwind appeared in front of her.

And then Eamann was there in the cooking tent.

A woman who was a stranger to Emily stood there with him.

Eamann visually reeled for a moment, and then he set his jaw and looked stern.

Emily gawked.

"Vange says druids can't time travel, yet here you are."

Eamann opened his mouth to answer.

But at the mention of Vange's name, the woman stranger grabbed Emily's hand.

"So worried I am about our Evangeline. Pray tell me she is safe."

Emily did her best to reassure the stranger, half looking at Eamann for his answer.

"Vange is safe. Who are you?"

"Aideen. Evangeline's friend I hope I am."

Eamann spoke briefly.

"Aye, we can travel through time, but we only do in dire circumstance, as it does shorten our lifetimes." And then he grilled her on what had happened and why she had called him and what she planned to do next.

She explained she wasn't going to do anything. She had done all she'd planned on doing by calling him.

And I'm starting to wonder if that was enough. Come on. Dall can only hold the man for so long.

Finally, Eamann seemed satisfied.

"Do take me to where he is being detained. Take me to Aiden."

Emily ran up the road with the elder druids.

They were an unusual sight, but the few faire customers who lagged behind barely glanced at Eamann and Aideen after the show Dall and Aiden and the whole Scots guild had put on.

As soon as she could see the children's dell, Emily started running to it, turning briefly aside to hail Bethany, point out her guests, and then shoo them over to her.

Dall and Peadar and Aiden were nowhere to be seen, but the clan were whooping and drumming and bagpiping such a clamor that Emily felt confident no one but the clan knew where they had gone.

I need to know Tomas and Tavish are safe with Vange.

Emily composed herself and slowed to a brisk walk before she got to the dell.

No need to run up in a panic.

The childcare worker, a nice woman named Jade, smiled in greeting.

"Hi Emily. Dall checked your boys out a few minutes ago and sent them home with your sister-in-law."

"Oh, good. That's ... that's so good. Thank you. I was just checking to make sure. Did you see where Dall went?"

Before the childcare worker could answer, Bethany and Aga came running up.

"Uh, hi Jade. Emily. Come quick."

"Bye Jade. Thank you."

Emily followed after the two, who ran right past where

the clan were now dancing to bagpipes before a clapping and stomping crowd. The two women ran up over a hill, stopped to lift the burlap wall, and ran off into the woods shouting.

"Are you coming Emily?"

She shouted back.

"Yeah, I'm right behind you."

At last they came to a clearing. Dall stood behind Aiden and held him by his elbows, while Peadar guarded the front of him. Eamann and Aideen had just stopped talking to them all and turned around, probably to see what the interruption was. Their faces relaxed when they saw Emily.

Eamann pointed back toward the clan.

"I thank you, lasses. Do go and rejoin your fellow actors. You shall see Dall and Emily at this evening's festivities."

Bethany and Aga nodded uncertainly, waving at Aiden.

"Bye Dall, everyone."

"Bye." they all said cheerfully.

Even Aiden said it that way.

Wow, the habit of keeping the secret goes deep. I might be pleading with Aga and Bethany to go get the police, in similar circumstances. But then again, I would never threaten a child...

Apparently satisfied that this was some secret ritual or another non-worrisome affair, the young women turned and trotted away.

Emily watched to make sure Aga and Bethany went under the burlap wall, and then she went to stand by her husband and listen to Eamann.

I hope Eamann doesn't still wish I weren't with Dall. We're married now, so he'll just have to accept me.

"Dall and Peadar have completely satisfied our questioning on the matter, Emily. Aideen and I will be taking Aiden in for justice. Lend us a hand and use your phone, if it please you."

Emily sighed.

"I can't travel with my phone anymore, Eamann."

He reached for it.

She handed it over.

Eamann swiped the screen a few times, tapped in a password, and handed the phone back to her.

"Now you shall be able." He looked over at Dall. "She will be back to get you. I ask that you all come and speak to me further after your festivities conclude this evening."

They all nodded in affirmation.

But Dall's brow wrinkled.

"For what reason do you wish to see us all later?"

Eamann looked back toward the faire.

"For to work out how you will take over the running of this traveling enterprise for us in this timeline, you ken?"

§&

EMILY HADN'T SWIRLED in two years, but she went right to the correct place inside the Time Management app and set it for Kilchurn Castle in 1543. Eamann had to help her with the date, and he suggested a time, but she did the rest.

Eamann took out some rope and tied Aiden's hands behind his back in much the same way as today's police officers handcuff someone they have apprehended.

"Here, Emily lass, hold him by the arm so that he travels with us."

Emily didn't want to touch the creepy old druid, but it was far better than him touching her. She looked the other way while she grabbed his arm.

She gave Dall an air kiss, hit the button, and then the three of them were swirling.

--Swirl--

They arrived behind that same curtain in Eamann's dungeon healer hole.

Emily hadn't been to the Highlands in two years. Dall had gone back to his time without her ever since children came into their lives.

When Eamann pulled back the curtain, her Kilchurn Castle arrival point looked much the same: a basement carved out of stone with a large wooden examination table in the center and several counters and cupboards filled with herbs, large iron saws and razors, leech jars, rolls of cloth for bandaging, and other medieval barber surgeon implements.

This was also a dungeon, complete with iron chains attached to the walls. Eamann chained Aiden to the far wall with his back to them.

Emily didn't want to dwell on that. She looked longingly at the stairs.

Eamann smiled with the corner of his mouth.

"Go on, lass. Have a quick look up the stairs. I chose this day and time as there is much activity, what with the fair on inside the castle courtyard, aye? You will just be one more person in the clamor."

Emily beamed a smile and held up her long plaid skirts as she rushed up the stairs into the large castle kitchen.

She hadn't noticed before, but there was a lot of activity. She didn't know any of the people she saw.

But then someone was hugging her.

Emily's heart soared at the sight of her, and she addressed the woman in her now fluent Gaelic, thankful that she and Dall still used his language at home.

"Hello, Mairi."

"Emily. How long are you staying?"

Emily hugged Mairi back.

What am I going to tell her?

As much of the truth as possible, of course, said her common sense.

OK, good idea, she told it.

"Nay, I am but passing through. Eamann has a man downstairs who has threatened my children. I came as a witness, but I must go back to them."

Mairi tsked at that.

"Have you time for a wee walk and talk? It has been so long."

You couldn't keep me from walking out there to behold the Highlands again.

"Aye, a wee walk I do have the time for."

Arm in arm, the two friends walked out into the courtyard.

Mairi moved as if to take Emily around the fair, which looked more like a farmer's market than the renaissance fairs she helped run in modern times.

Emily instead tugged Mairi past the cistern and out through the gateway cut into the rock of the castle wall. The two friends talked and got caught up about how their children were doing.

But Emily was drinking in the view of Loch Awe all the while she walked and chatted.

All manner of wagons were parked outside, and the horses were grazing along with the castle's cattle and sheep. They made a pretty foreground for the water of the loch, which surrounded the castle on three sides.

Today the sky was full of puffy clouds with rays of sunlight cutting down onto the loch in jagged patterns that made dazzling light shows on the waves blown by the cold wind from the snowy mountain peaks all around.

Mairi stopped once they had reached the shore of the loch and were alone. They knelt and scooped up water in their cups, which were fastened to their belts along with their pouches. Emily didn't drink out of hers.

Mairi drank hers down and refilled it again, then gave Emily a sad smile.

"Aye, you are vexed I can see, about your children."

Emily nodded.

"I am. I must leave now to return to them. Eamann has arranged transport for me, and—"

Mairi hugged Emily again.

"No need for stories, Emily. I do know thy mode of travel."

EMILY BLINKED AT MAIRI. "Does everyone know my mode of travel?"

"Ha heh. No. No, but Alistair does, and I do."

Emily had a moment of panic for her friend.

"Mairi. Listen. In 1547, the Campbells are going to kick the MacGregors out of Kilchurn Castle—"

But the tough highlander woman put a hand over Emily's mouth.

"Nay, do not tell me the future. Today has enough trouble of its own. I would learn to find the joy in life and not dwell on what I cannot change, you ken?"

Emily hugged her.

"Aye. Aye, I do ken. Take care of yourself and yours, Mairi. I hope to see you again soon, more often, and under happier conditions."

"You take care too, Emily. I would that you fared well."

Emily walked Mairi back to the kitchen, went back down the stairs, waved goodbye to Eamann, ignored Aiden, ducked behind the curtain, and used her bookmark of Vange's photo to go check on her boys.

--Swirl--

Emily found Vange slumped between two cars in the parking lot of the faire. The boys were nowhere to be seen. Vange's face was bruised, she was crying.

"Vange. What happened? Vange."

Emily shook her friend to get her to stop wailing and answer her.

Vange sobbed out a response and then collapsed into crying so intense it was crippling.

"Siobhan surprised me, Emily. She took the boys. She's got them in her trailer by now. I'm so sorry, Emily."

Now I know why I had the urge to take that picture of Siobhan.

Emily pulled up that photograph, set it as a bookmark in the app, and put her phone in front of Vange's face.

"Look, Vange. We can go right to her this instant. We're going to get them back."

Vange's eyes filled with resolve and she was up on her feet in two seconds, wiping her tears away and no longer sobbing.

"She took me by surprise last time, but that won't happen again. I'm ready. Let's do this."

Emily gave her friend a hug and a sharp nod.

"If she has other people with her, then I'll say the 'do over' phrase and we'll go get Dall, Peadar, and more of the guild if we have to. But if she's alone with the boys, then I want to take care of it right here and now, before she has a chance to do them any harm."

They spent a few minutes planning and preparing, and then Emily pressed the 'Go' button to take them wherever Siobhan was with Tomas and Tavish.

--Swirl--

Yep, they were in the living room of Siobhan's trailer. The rays of the setting sun came in through the trees, making weird shadows all over. It wasn't the same trailer they had stayed in back in the states. This one was all blue and green, but the layout was the same.

The druid had the boys tucked into makeshift beds on the couch. They were under her spell, because although it was early yet and they were fidgeting a bit, they were falling asleep.

Emily looked into Vange's eyes to make sure her friend was ready.

Vange's eyes showed a fierceness when she nodded back.

As soon as Siobhan's hands were free of her sons, Emily ran and tackled the druid woman, pushing her across the room and onto the floor.

Siobhan was saying something.

Emily paid no attention. She didn't care at all what the druid might be saying.

She did spare a second to glance over and see how Vange was doing as she passed by in the middle of her tackle.

Her friend met her eyes with panic.

Emily glanced down to her boys.

They were still fast asleep and showed no sign of waking up.

Vange was picking Tomas up and she nodded to indicate she would take him outside and come back for Tavish.

Emily had to trust that her oldest friend would accomplish her part of the plan, because Siobhan was fighting her for real this time. If Emily didn't defend herself...

The druid landed on her side with Emily on top of her and was turning toward her, trying to get her arms beneath her so she could get up. At first, her face was concentrating on whatever she was saying or singing, but as soon as she realized her magic was having no effect, her face turned mean.

Cruel.

Crazed.

There was nothing left visible of Hailey at all, just a druid who had stolen Emily's children and beaten up Emily's friend.

That makes it easier to do whatever I need to do.

Emily got her foot in front of her and kicked the druid in the stomach as hard as she could.

Twice.

Three times.

Four times.

The druid finally quit struggling and doubled over.

Looking up to see Vange getting Tavish out of bed, Emily stood up and got her phone out of her pouch.

Siobhan lunged up from the floor at Emily.

Emily kicked her back down, sat on her enemy, found the setting, and pushed the 'Go' button.

--Swirl--

"I have another one for you, Eamann. Will you please help me get Vange's bubble gum out of my ears?"

19. 10 YEARS LATER

Emily smiled proudly as she stood on main stage facing the local volunteer actors who had shown up for the first day of workshops. There were a record number of them this year, as there had been every year since she and Vange had started the website and forum—the same year that the four of them had taken over running the faire. She turned and smiled at Vange.

Her best friend and closest confidante grinned back at her and crossed her eyes. Even at 35, Vange was full of silliness, and Emily hoped she always would be.

Peadar turned toward them briefly to see if he was missing anything, but he just chuckled and shook his head when he saw it was only his wife's normal kidding around.

Dall was finishing his excellent motivational speech.

Their old friends in the audience of volunteers heckled him whenever he paused, making everyone laugh.

"Aren't you hot?"

"Did you make that yourself?"

"Are you the queen?"

But this was all pre-arranged.

Part of the reason the faire had grown so much was that

the four of them made everything genuinely fun now, without relying on druid magic to subdue everyone and just make them think they were having fun.

And then they all four went backstage together—a special backstage only for them, where they could truly be 'off' for a few minutes every once in a while.

This faire site was in a hard-packed desert.

Their private area was a huge yard on the outside of the donut, away from the parking lot and walled off with burlap. Inside it, they had several nice trailers, an outdoor seating area under a canopy, and some play equipment for the kids.

Emily told everyone what was on her mind.

"I wish we had more time to ourselves."

Everyone laughed.

"You have time to yourselves during the week," said her dad.

"This is the cushiest job ever, only working weekends," said Vange's dad.

"You know that's not true," said Emily.

"We do? Where could you possibly go during the week? We never see your car leave," said her mom.

This was the teasing game they played about not being able to discuss time travel.

But…

The antiques business was still in full swing because Dall always showed up to help his clan out and Peadar never missed a chance to help Shane. But they knew ahead of time when that would be now.

We spend plenty of time together, but it's all adventuring and socializing and …

And she was happy.

Emily went and hugged all four of their parents and tickled her own until they laughed.

She looked over where all six boys were playing basketball nearby.

The boys liked the faire alright, but by now they didn't need the workshops. This was about the hundredth opening day of workshops they remembered. Four of them were twelve and the other two were ten.

Emily watched them have fun awhile before she tried another way to say what was bothering her.

"We hardly ever spend time as a family. Dall and I have to zip off to ... away, and so do Vange and Peadar..."

Her dad put an arm around her. "Don't feel bad about that. We love being with Tomas and Tavish. Be glad they're with family."

Emily hugged him. "Oh, I absolutely am glad they're with family. Never doubt that."

Her dad chuckled. "And I'm absolutely glad you're the ones supporting this family. Retiring was the best thing I did in too long."

Her mom brought their brunch over to the outdoor seating area, and while they all sat down and dug in, she made her own observations on the subject.

"I agree. Our lives are better and fuller than ever, Emily. We're all doing something we love."

Emily looked over again at where Tomas and Tavish were playing.

"This is hardly a good life for them, though, being home-schooled by their grandparents and moving around so much. They should have a steady group of friends besides each other. They should be in school."

Dall surprised her by speaking up then.

"I did not go away from home to be schooled, and you have never had nary a worry about my education, lass."

Emily smirked at him.

"That's different, Dall."

"Aye? How is it different?"

Emily looked her husband in the eye to make sure he wasn't teasing her. But no, Dall was being serious. She lowered her chin at him in a way meant to show him she couldn't believe he was in earnest.

"You were homeschooled in another time."

Calm as ever, her husband was unaffected by her exasperation.

"Aye, but how else? I do not see it."

"Dall, the whole clan passed on the knowledge you got."

"Aye, and your whole clan does the same with our lads, you ken?"

What is he talking about? There aren't clans anymore. And in modern times we have a whole extended system of civilization that our kids are missing out on. We're depriving them. How can I make him see that? And do my parents really not see it?

"Gggrr. But all we can pass on to them is how to run a renaissance faire. They need the skills and knowledge to do whatever is in their hearts to do."

Surprisingly, her dad felt otherwise.

"Emily, you and Dall and Vange and Peadar ought to be training the boys to take over running the faire for you one day."

Emily gave her dad her best incredulous look.

"Dad. They're just kids."

He gave her a knowing look and shook his head no.

"That's how it seems, but the time goes by really fast from here on out, Em. They'll be dating before you know it."

Her mom was nodding and smiling. When Emily noticed, her mom made a joke that hit Emily right in the gut, though her mom was smiling and innocently laughing as she said it.

"And that's six new women you'll be dealing with. Best the boys get to know them at the faire so that you meet them early."

AFTERWORD

The story continues!

Dall and Emily watch grown-up Tavish and Tomas adventure with the women who were their faire girlfriends in **Druid Magic**.

Johnathan is a woad warrior in the time of Hadrian's Wall in **Celtic Druids**, and his adventures continue in the early 1700's in **Meehall** (which is also about Michael) and **Ciaran**.

Jeffrey sends the woman who was his faire girlfriend away on time travel adventures in **Druid Dagger**.

Gabriel goes by the more Scottish name **Conall**, and his books will be out in 2019.

Sign up for new book alerts at
www.janestain.com

Jane Stain

Made in the USA
Middletown, DE
16 April 2021